PARENTS AND CHILDREN

£1-50

Ivy Compton-Burnett once wrote: 'I have had such an uneventful life that there is little information to give. I was educated with my brothers in the country as a child, and later went to Holloway College, and took a degree in Classics. I lived with my family when I was quite young, but for most of my life have had my own flat in London. I see a good deal of a good many friends, not all of them writing people. And there is really no more to say.'

Ivy Compton-Burnett died in 1969 and in her obituary *The Times* wrote: 'Her work, from the first appreciated by a few discerning admirers, was for many years dismissed by the critics and by the general public as the object of a modish cult. The bare, stylized dialogue needs a closer attention than most novel-readers are prepared to give. But the fine comedy and the deep humanity of her books in later years achieved a wider recognition', and Pamela Hansford-Johnson said of her: 'Writing of a dying age she stands apart from the mainstream of English fiction. She is not an easy writer nor a consoling one. Her work is an arras of embroidered concealments beneath which the cat's sharp claws flash out and are withdrawn, behind which the bitter quarrels of the soul are conducted "tiffishly", as if cruelty and revenge and desire, the very heart itself, were all trivial compared with the great going clock of society, ticking on implacably for ever behind the clotted veilings.'

In 1925 she published *Pastors and Masters*, which began the series of novels in which she created a chilling world of late Victorian upper-class people; the other titles are: *Brothers and Sisters, Men and Wives, More Women than Men, A House and its Head, Daughters and Sons, A Family and a Fortune, Parents and Children, Elders and Betters, Manservant and Maidservant, Two Worlds and their Ways, Darkness and Day, The Present and the Past, Mother and Son* (which won the James Tait Black Memorial Prize), *A Father and his Fate, A Heritage and its History, The Mighty and their Fall, A God and his Gifts* and *The Last and the First*. Several of these are published by Penguin.

IVY COMPTON-BURNETT

PARENTS AND CHILDREN

PENGUIN BOOKS

Penguin Books Ltd, Harmondsworth, Middlesex, England
Penguin Books, 40 West 23rd Street, New York, New York 10010, U.S.A.
Penguin Books Australia Ltd, Ringwood, Victoria, Australia
Penguin Books Canada Ltd, 2801 John Street, Markham, Ontario, Canada L3R 1B4
Penguin Books (N.Z.) Ltd, 182–190 Wairau Road, Auckland 10, New Zealand

First published by Victor Gollancz 1941
Published in Penguin Books 1970
Reprinted 1984

Printed and bound in Great Britain by
Cox & Wyman Ltd, Reading
Set in Plantin

CHAPTER ONE

'I SUPPOSE my thoughts are nothing to be proud of,' said Eleanor Sullivan.

'Then they are different from the rest of you, I am sure, dear.'

'I always mean what I say, Fulbert.'

Mr Sullivan did not make the protest of himself.

'If you reveal the thoughts, I will give them my attention,' he said, leaning back and folding his arms with this purpose.

'It is the old grievance of spending my best years in your parents' home.'

'It would be worse not to spend them in a home of any kind.'

'You must turn everything into a joke, of course.'

'I should be hard put to it to manage it with that. You would have a right to your long face.'

'We should do better in a cottage of our own, than as guests in this great house.'

'No chance of it with nine children. The cottage would not contain them. And I am not a guest: I am a son of the house.'

Fulbert uttered the words with an expression of his own, as if the position were a rather surprising one. He had a tendency to unction in speaking of himself, and the death of an elder brother had given him a place to which he had not been born.

'And what am I?' said Eleanor.

'The son's wife and the mother of his children,' said her husband, completing his picture.

'That is what I am. And it is not so very little. But if you are to go abroad, I shall have to be a good deal more.'

'That will be enough. The family can get along on it.'

'Is it necessary that you should go?'

'The old man insists upon it.'

'Is that the same thing?'

'Under this roof, my dear, as you give signs of knowing.'

'Your father believes in his divine right.'

'Well, there is a certain reason in it. His position will pass to others in their turn.'

'I don't see how it can go beyond you. The money will come to an end. This place is not part of the essential order of things. And though it is your old home, it is not mine.'

'Where your treasure is, there must your heart be also,' said Fulbert, in his deliberate, strident tones.

'That is true. No woman is more fundamentally satisfied.'

'Well, the deepest experience is known to be hidden, my dear.'

'I may be a murmuring woman. But I shall not feel the house is my home while your parents are alive. And that is not a generous thought.'

'It has no claim to be,' said Fulbert, throwing up his voice.

'I must try to conquer myself,' said his wife, with the sigh natural to this purpose.

'As you only have your own power to do it with, it sounds as if it would be an equal struggle.'

'Heaven helps those who help themselves.'

'It sounds grudging of Heaven to stipulate for its work to be done for it.'

It would have been clear to an observer at this point that Eleanor held the accepted religious beliefs, and that her husband held none.

'I wish you would not take that tone, Fulbert. It shows me how poor my example is.'

'Well, you have not been recommending it, my dear.'

'I know you do not like me to talk of my religion.'

'People are not at their best, doing that, and it is wise to accept that as the truth.'

'I suppose actions speak louder than words.'

'I find no fault with silence.'

Eleanor followed the hint and changed her tone.

'This is an odd little room to give us for ourselves.'

'Not according to your preference for a cottage.'

'If we live in this house, we may as well have the benefit of it.'

'The dozen rooms allotted to us upstairs constitute our advantage,' said Fulbert, spacing his words as if they had a certain merit.

'I still think we might be happier, living on our own small income.'

'A family as large as ours is nothing under such conditions.'

'After all, our children are your parents' grandchildren.'

'That is their claim upon them, which is fortunately recognized.'

'You think you have a clever tongue, Fulbert.'

'You have hinted at advantages of your own, my dear.'

'I do not dispute it. I only meant you were conscious of it.'

'I have yet to meet the man unaware of his endowments. I have met many a one sensible of some that are not his.'

'And to which class do you belong?'

Fulbert rested his eyes in quizzical acceptance on his wife. His reasons for not mentioning women in connexion with endowments was not that he thought they would not have them, but that he saw little connexion between such things and their lives. He had a full respect for the woman's sphere, but was glad it was not his own. It seemed to him that his peculiar attributes would have little exercise in it.

'I must not make claims if I do not live up to them,' said Eleanor.

'Not if you want them recognized.'

'I wish there were a little more sympathy and warmth about you, Fulbert.'

'I wish you had a husband after your own heart, my dear.'

Fulbert Sullivan was a spare, muscular man of fifty, with a sort of springy quality going through his frame, which gave him a suggestion of controlling superfluous force. As he was a man of considerable vigour and no less leisure, this may have been the case. The suggestion of pent-up energy appeared in his narrow, near-set eyes, in his long, unmodelled lips, and even in his solid brow and nose and chin. His strong, metallic voice had a sudden rise and fall, and his manner might have been self-conscious, if its deliberate confidence had been less real. There was a suggestion about him of being prepared to be criticized at sight, and of meeting the attitude with unprejudiced and rallying goodwill.

His wife was a tall, angular woman of forty-eight, with large, pale grey eyes, a narrow, shapely head, a serious, honest, somewhat equine face, and a nervous, uneasy, controlled expression. Her long, gentle hands and long, easy stride and deep, unaffected voice seemed less essential to her, than such attributes to other people. To those who knew her, all her physical qualities seemed to be accidental. To a stranger she gave the impression of being indefinite in colour, but very definite in everything else.

'Mother,' said a voice at the door, 'can you bear with Graham for a moment? I am allowing him a break from work and there is no service that I require of him.'

A youth led another into the room, deposited him in a chair and remained with his hands on his collar. Eleanor surveyed the pair as if the situation were familiar, and Fulbert watched with lively vigilance.

The occupant of the seat leaned back with an almost obliging air. He was a tall, bony youth of twenty-one, with head and hands and feet too heavy for his yielding frame, prominent, pale, absent eyes, and features that were between the fine and the ungainly. He had a deep, jerky voice and a laugh that was without mirth, as was perhaps natural, as he was continually called upon to exercise it at his own expense. His brother, who was older by a year, resembled Eleanor except for his weight and breadth, and for a widening and shortening of the face, which resulted in a look of greater power. He had a ready smile and an air of having the wisdom to find content in his lot. Eleanor surveyed her sons with affection, sympathy and interest, but with singularly little pride.

'What ought you both to be doing? Are you not wasting your time?'

'It is one of his worse days, Mother,' said the elder son. 'But a mother's words may succeed when all else fails. And I can only say that it has failed.'

Graham turned his eyes to Eleanor in automatic response.

'Do you never take a holiday?' said Fulbert, his eyes seeming to be riveted to his sons.

'Their grandfather likes them to work in the morning, when they are not at Cambridge,' said his wife.

'Graham, how do you fulfil that trust?' said Daniel. 'Think of that old man's faith in you.'

'I believe it has not struck me,' said Fulbert, with a laugh. 'I wonder what will be the end of all this poring over books.'

'Some sort of self-support,' said Daniel. 'Or that is accepted.'

'You can't both be ushers in a school.'

'It is good to know that,' said Graham.

'There are good posts in the scholastic world,' said Eleanor.

'Many more poor ones, my dear,' said her husband.

'I can imagine myself that accepted butt, a poor schoolmaster,' said Graham.

> "When land is gone and money spent,
> Then learning is most excellent,"

said Fulbert, as if the quotation put the matter on its final basis.

'I wish we could follow in your steps, Father,' said Daniel.

'In what way, my boy?' said Fulbert, with his eyes alight.

'You toil not, neither do you spin.'

'Your father worked hard as a young man,' said Eleanor.

'I did the work I could get, my dear. That was not often the word.'

'Success at the Bar is always some time in coming.'

'And in your servant's case it delayed too long.'

'You lost your patience too soon.'

'I kept it for a good many years, though patience is not my point,' said Fulbert, speaking as though he would hardly feel more self-esteem, if it were.

'It may have been the wisest thing to give up hope.'

'It was the only thing. My income did not meet my expenses, and my family was increasing them.'

'I do not mind a little pinching and scraping to keep out of debt.'

'It did not secure the end. And it has little advantage in itself.'

'Father,' said a new voice at Fulbert's elbow, where his daughter had been standing in silence for a time, 'we should remember that Mother's income went on our needs in those days. It is not fair to forget the source of so much of what we had.'

'And who is going to do so?' said Fulbert, turning with amused and tolerant eyes.

'No one while I am here, Father. And it seemed to me that a reminder was needed.'

Fulbert jumped to his feet, took his daughter's face in both his hands and implanted a kiss upon it, and then threw himself back in his chair as if he had disposed of the matter.

Lucia Sullivan was two years older than her brother Daniel. She was in appearance a cross between her parents, but was shorter and rounder in build, with more colour in her eyes and skin and a more lightly chiselled face. There was something solemn and almost wondering in her large, steady, hazel eyes, as if the world struck her as an arresting and impressive place. Her voice was full and deliberate; her lips moved more than other people's; and her eyes seldom left the face of the person she addressed.

'Father,' she said, with these attributes in evidence, 'Grandpa is by himself in the library. Grandma is doing the housekeeping. Ought he to be alone?'

'He can join us at his pleasure.'

'He never comes into this room, Father. He leaves it to you and Mother. He always waits to be asked.'

'If I reward his delicacy by joining him, I do not see what I gain.'

'I hardly agree with you there, Father. I can't feel it would be the same thing, if he came in and out at will. It is the intangibility of the distinction that gives it its point.'

'Well, perhaps that is why it escapes me,' said Fulbert, remaining in his chair, and then suddenly springing to his feet and running to the door.

Lucia looked after him and quietly turned to her mother.

'Mother, I don't think Father much liked my saying that about your money. But it did seem a fair point to make. I should not have been at ease with myself, if I had not said it.'

'It was a case for Father's being sacrificed,' said Daniel.

'No, boys,' said Luce, turning calm, full eyes on her brothers. 'Dealt with as a normal, intelligent being. It is how I should wish to be treated myself.'

'I should like all allowance to be made for me,' said Graham, with his eyes on the window.

'It is a good thing the boy is not embarrassed by the necessity,' said Daniel.

Luce threw a swift look at Graham and turned again to Eleanor.

'Mother, there is another little doubt. Was it a welcome reminder about Grandpa? Or quite well received? But I do not feel it right for him to be too much alone.'

'Your father agreed with you, my dear. He has gone to be with him.'

Eleanor spoke with natural simplicity. She had the power of esteeming people for their qualities, and as Lucia had honesty and kindliness, she valued her for these. Moreover her daughter had the gift of appreciation, and used it especially upon herself. Many people were put out of countenance by her dramatization of daily things, but Eleanor was affected in this way by few things that were innocent.

'Luce, you might make an effort with Graham,' said Daniel. 'A sister's influence may do much.'

'Mother is here, Daniel,' said Luce, with quiet emphasis.

Graham's face did not change.

'Will you be able to look at your grandfather and say you have done a morning's work?' said Eleanor to her sons, in an almost sardonic manner.

'I acquired the accomplishment years ago,' said Graham, absently.

'Was there a hesitation in the lad, in spite of those hardened words?' said Daniel. 'Where there is any sign of feeling, there is hope.'

'I shall not support you in what is not true,' said Eleanor.

'So our mother will fail us,' said Graham, in the same absent tone.

'Both of you away to your books,' said Luce, making a driving movement. 'I want to have a talk with Mother.'

Daniel led his brother from the room, while his sister looked on with gentle, dubious eyes.

'Mother, do you think it is good for Graham to be teased and made a butt? Because I really do not feel it is.'

'I don't suppose it does him much harm. He could stop it if he liked. He gives no sign of minding.'

'But, Mother, could he stop it? And don't you think that things may hurt all the more, that they are allowed no outlet?'

'I hardly think he seems to need any sympathy.'

'Mother, do you think you are right?' said Luce, sitting on the arm of Eleanor's chair. 'Don't you think there are feelings that shrink and shiver away from the touch, just because they are so alive and deep?'

'There may be, but those of boys would not often be among them.'

'Mother, I believe a boy is a very sensitive thing. Almost more so in some ways than a girl.'

'The sensitiveness of both is generally a form of self-consciousness. It does not relate to other people.'

'But may not a thing that relates to oneself be very real and tormenting? The more so for that?'

'No doubt, but that is not a reason for fostering it.'

'Don't you think that withholding sympathy may cause it to crystallize into something very hard and deep?'

'They seem to prefer it to be withheld.'

Luce went into slow laughter, with her eyes on her mother in rueful appreciation.

'Mother, you and I are very near to each other,' she said in a moment. 'I always feel it a tragic thing when a mother and daughter are separate. And yet I suppose it is common.'

'I wonder if I shall get on as well with my other daughters.'

'You know, I think you will, Mother,' said Luce, swinging to and fro on her chair, with her eyes turned upwards. 'I think there is nothing in you that would repel the young, or send them shuddering into themselves.'

'This youthful sensitiveness seems a problem,' said Eleanor, rising. 'I cannot say how far I am equipped to cope with it.'

'I think you are qualified, Mother,' said Luce, looking dreamily after her. 'I should think there is that in you, that will carry you through.'

'Your grandmother has gone into the drawing-room,' said Eleanor, leaving the subject. 'Perhaps we had better follow her.'

'Do you know, Mother, you have quicker ears than I have?' said Luce, remaining where she was. 'I had not heard Grandma.

As far as I am concerned, she might still be at her duties.'

'She never takes more than an hour.'

'I had not noticed that either, Mother,' said Luce, slipping off the chair. 'I had no idea of the time she needed. You are a sharper person than I am, more alert to our little, everyday attributes. And yet I do not think I am indifferent to people, or blunt to their demands.'

'Your grandmother would not say so.'

'I think she depends on me, Mother,' said Luce, taking Eleanor's arm. 'And as long as she does, I hold myself at her service. It makes me dependent on her in a way. Well, Grandma dear, so you have finished your duties for the day.'

Lady Sullivan appeared unconcerned by this limit placed to her usefulness. She was sitting in the chair on the hearth, where she sat throughout the year, as though her comfort depended alternately on a full grate and an empty one. She was a portly, almost cumbrous woman of seventy-six, with a broad, exposed brow, features resembling her son's under their covering of flesh, pale, protruding eyes that recalled her second grandson's, large, heavy, sensitive hands, and an expression that varied from fond benevolence to a sort of fierce emotion. Her name of Regan had been chosen by her father, a man of country tastes, and, as it must appear, of no others, who had learned from an article on Shakespeare that his women were people of significance, and decided that his daughter should bear the name of one of them, in accordance with his hopes. When Regan came to a knowledge of her namesake, she observed that the name must have been in use before Shakespeare chose it, or it would not have been a name; and did not reveal the truth to her father, who was not in danger of discovering it. When people said that the name suited her, she accepted the compliment from those who intended one, and smiled on the others, or smiled to herself with regard to them in a manner that preserved them from further risk. So the name brought her no ill result, and a good one at the time of Sir Jesse Sullivan's approach, when the name in itself and the manner of her support of it determined his desired advance. Regan was a woman who only loved her family. She loved her husband deeply, her children fiercely, her grandchildren fondly, and loved no one

15

else, resenting other people's lack of the qualities and endearing failings of these. And it meant that she had loved thirteen people, which may be above the average number.

She looked at Eleanor with a guarded, neutral expression. She could not see her with affection, as they were not bound by blood; and the motives of her son's choice of her were as obscure to her as such motives to other mothers; but she respected her for her hold on him, and was grateful to her for her children. And she had a strong appreciation of her living beneath her roof. If Eleanor saw it as a hard choice, her husband's mother saw it as an heroic one, and bowed to her as able for things above herself. The two women lived in a formal accord, which had never come to dependence; and while each saw the other as a fellow and an equal, neither would have grieved at the other's death.

Luce sat down on the floor and laid her head on her grandmother's lap. Regan put a hand on her head. Eleanor took her usual seat and her skilled needlework. She was a woman who did not make or mend for her family. Her daughter broke the silence by throwing her arms across Regan's knees and giving a sigh.

'Grandma,' she said, putting back her head to regard the latter's knitting, 'your needles flying in and out remind me of the things that work in and out of our lives. Each stitch a little happening, a little step forward or back. I daresay there are as many backward steps as forward. But that is not like your knitting, is it?'

She continued to survey the needles with a steadiness that was natural, in view of what she derived from them; and Regan smiled and continued to knit, as if she did not take so much account of the employment.

'We have not much chance of going back,' said Eleanor.

'Not in your sense, Mother,' said Luce, not moving her eyes. 'But there is a certain progression in our lives, which we do not always maintain. It so often comes to a swinging to and fro.'

'You mean in ourselves, don't you?'

'Yes, Mother, I do mean that,' said Luce, looking at her mother as if struck by the acuteness of her thought.

'My days for progress are past,' said Regan.

'I wonder why people say that in such a contented tone,' said Eleanor.

'They may as well put a good face on it.'

'No, Grandma, I do not think it is that,' said Luce, tilting back her head to look into Regan's face. 'I think it is just that many things still stretch in front of them, though some may be behind. I think we all go on advancing in ways of our own, until some sort of climax comes, that we all look towards as a goal.' She said the last words lightly, as if not quite sure if she had made or avoided a reference to her grandmother's death, and settled herself in a better position on the floor to indicate that her thoughts were on trivial, material things.

Regan kept her eyes on her needles, which she seldom did if her thoughts were on them. She was thinking for a moment of her own end. It engaged her mind no oftener as it drew nearer, and it did this so lightly at the moment that it failed to keep its hold.

'Where is Grandpa, dear?' she said to Luce, in a tone that offered the tenderness due to a child, and the respect due to a woman.

'I don't know, Grandma; I hope he is not by himself.'

'Your father is with him,' said Eleanor. 'You reminded him to go to him.'

'So I did, Mother,' said Luce, putting frank eyes on her mother's face.

'Fulbert will find it a change to have regular work, if it has to come,' said Regan, with the thrust in her tone that seemed to be an outlet for emotion.

'And it seems that it must,' said Eleanor.

Luce glanced from one face to another, as if she would not seek information where it was not given.

'I think Father sometimes does more for Grandpa than appears at a glance, Mother. His desk is often littered with accounts.'

Eleanor did not dispute this.

'It all appears at a glance perhaps,' said Regan, with a smile of pure indulgence.

'Grandma, you are not at heart a critical parent. Your children must always have found you a refuge from the censorious world.'

Regan's face worked at mention of her children, two of whom were dead.

'You would not say the same of your mother,' said Eleanor.

'No, Mother, no,' said Luce in a deliberate tone, lifting her eyes in sincere thought. 'But we can say other things.'

A sound of singing came from the hall, and the performer entered and proceeded to the hearth, where he ended his song with his eyes on his hearers and an expression of absent goodwill. Regan looked at him with automatic fondness; Luce gave him a smile; and Eleanor did not move her eyes.

'Grandpa,' said Luce, moving hers so much that they almost rolled, 'did you feel the impulse to come to us about three minutes ago?'

'Just about, just about, my dear,' said Sir Jesse, adapting his measure to the words.

'Then it is a case of telepathy,' said Luce, looking round. 'I have noticed that Grandpa is sensitive in such ways. His response is almost consistent.'

'Well, how are all of you?' said Sir Jesse, surveying the women as if they belonged to a different sphere, as he felt they did.

'We are well and happy, Grandpa,' said Luce, in a personally satisfied tone.

Regan's face showed her support for this view, and Eleanor's face told nothing.

'How has this young woman been behaving?' said Sir Jesse, displacing his wife's cap and causing her to simulate a pleased amusement.

'She has been behaving well, Grandpa,' said Luce, turning up her eyes to Regan's face.

'And this younger woman?' said Sir Jesse, indicating Eleanor, but disturbing nothing about her.

'She has been behaving well too, Grandpa,' said Luce, in a demure tone.

'And this youngest woman of all?'

'Well too, Grandpa,' said Luce, hardly uttering the words.

'Three good women,' began Sir Jesse to the tune of a song, but broke off as his grandsons entered, and spoke with a change of tone. 'Well, I suppose it is time to eat, as you appear amongst us. What meal do we expect?'

'Luncheon, Grandpa,' said Luce, in the same tone.

'It is a pity we cannot break Graham of this way of eating,' said Daniel. 'It is such a primitive habit.'

'Do not talk nonsense,' said Eleanor, in a low tone.

Sir Jesse Sullivan was a large, strong man of seventy-nine, whose movements were surprisingly supple for his build and age, perhaps the result of his frequent mild exercise, and perhaps the cause of it. His small, dark, deep-set eyes looked out under a jutting, almost jagged brow, and his blunt, bony features seemed to mould themselves to his mood in a manner inconsistent with themselves. This element of inconsistence seemed to go through him. His solid, old hands had a simple flexibility, and his hard, husky voice had vibrations that suggested another being. His eyes were familiar and fond on his wife, less familiar and faintly admiring on Eleanor, comradely and somehow unrelenting on his son, indulgent on Luce, and sharp and piercing on his grandsons, who as males dependent on their education, and dependent on him for its cost, struck him as suitably occupied only at their books. The expense of the training that produced schoolmasters and curates and such dependent men, was so startling to Sir Jesse, who had himself had little education and no thought that he required more, that he put it from his sight; and it seemed inconsiderate and almost insubordinate in his grandsons to act as a reminder.

'Is Father ready for luncheon, Grandpa?' said Luce.

'He is, my dear,' said Fulbert, running into the room, 'and he hopes it bears the same relation to him.'

'It will be ready at the right time, Father,' said Luce, folding her arms round her knees in preparation for waiting.

'I suppose Graham must come to meals,' said Daniel. 'There ought to be some other way of managing about him.'

'We must eat to live,' said Fulbert.

'But is that necessary for Graham, Father?'

Luce gave a quick look at her second brother.

'The gong gets a little later every day,' said Fulbert consulting his watch.

'It is the someone behind the gong, Father,' said Luce, and in a tone so light and even that it might have escaped notice. 'And then the someone behind that.'

'You would think it would help the household to have things on time.'

'Such a household would be above help,' said Daniel.

'It is a tribute to Grandma's management that you can talk like that, Father,' said Luce.

'Well, I may be allowed to pay her the compliment.'

Regan looked touched beyond the demand of the occasion.

'The gong must soon sound with so much behind it,' said Graham, in his toneless voice.

'It will sound when luncheon is ready,' said Eleanor.

'It will be our last luncheon without the babies at the end,' said Luce. 'Their holiday ends today. I cannot get used to being without them.'

'Luce has not forgotten her brothers and sister in three weeks,' said Daniel. 'It must be the depth of her nature.'

'You did not remember them enough to speak of them,' said Sir Jesse.

As the gong sounded through the house, Fulbert walked swiftly to the door and held it open for the women, sending his eyes to different objects in the room, as if he felt no inclination to hurry this part of the proceedings. He rather enjoyed any duty that had a touch of the formal or official. At the table he did the carving, a duty deputed by his father, and performed it with attention, swiftness and skill, supplying his own plate at the end with equal but not extra care. Daniel and Graham were talking under their breath, and their mother threw them a glance.

'You need not concern yourself with them,' said Sir Jesse. 'They are about to address themselves to their business.'

'Isn't it a repellent trait in my brother?' said Daniel.

'So is Grandpa,' murmured Graham. 'He and I are of the same old stock.'

'Any word you have to say of me, you can say to my face,' said Sir Jesse.

Graham was about to reply, but his mother's eyes prevented him. He was dependent on Sir Jesse for most of what he had, and this was not a forfeiture it was wise to incur. Daniel took his grandfather in an easier spirit and reckoned with him in so far as he served his purposes. Sir Jesse thought him better behaved, a not uncommon result of this attitude of youth.

'Well, my boy, we must break our news,' said Sir Jesse to his son.

'Of the prospect that takes me from the bosom of my family,' said Fulbert, looking with mingled apprehension and resolution at the faces round him.

'Mother, Grandpa,' said Luce, turning steady eyes upon them, 'we should be glad to have this thing cleared up, whatever it is. We have been living for days under the sword of Damocles, and it will be a relief to have it fall. What is this threat of losing Father for some reason unexplained? We should be grateful for the truth, and we feel we have a right to it.'

'Your father has to go to South America to look into the estate,' said Eleanor. 'Your grandfather had the final letters today.'

'Thank you, Mother. That is at once a shock and a satisfaction. We had no idea what the dark hints might portend, and imagination was outstripping the truth. Now we may hope that the exile will not be long.'

'A matter of six months,' said Fulbert, with courage and ease.

'Thank you, Father. That would have been a blow not so many days ago. As it is, we chiefly experience relief.'

'You could have asked before,' said Eleanor.

'No, Mother, we could not,' said Luce, meeting her eyes. 'There was that about you, that precluded approach of the subject.'

'What led our elders to conceal the simple matter?' said Daniel, in a low tone.

'The instinct to keep all things from the young,' said Graham. 'Even a temporary concealment was better than nothing.'

'Six months is a moderate sentence,' said Daniel. 'We can hardly expect Graham to show a new son to Father on his return.'

Graham glanced at Regan in imagination of her feeling.

'I shall not live six months many more times,' she said.

'Yes, you will, Grandma,' said Luce, in an even tone. 'Probably a good many more.'

'What about me in exile?' said Fulbert.

'Poor Father! You did not expect to have to ask that question.'

'I would go myself if I were younger by a few years,' said Sir Jesse, with an undernote of inflexibility that revealed his true relation with his son. 'And it is not only for that reason that I wish I were.'

'I cannot imagine you in a stage more becoming, Grandpa,' said Luce.

'I have liked others better, my dear,' said Sir Jesse, smiling to himself as he recalled these.

'Perhaps I ought to pay Grandpa an occasional compliment,' murmured Graham.

Regan made an emotional sound, and Luce came and stood behind her, stroking her shoulders as she continued to talk.

'A great part of Father's duty must devolve on Mother.'

'And she will be equal to it,' said Fulbert, in a tone of paying the fullest tribute.

'She will have but little support in one of her sons,' said Daniel.

'I wish the time were behind us,' said Eleanor. 'And I may make other people wish it more.'

'A mother's life is not all sacrifice,' said Fulbert.

'It is not indeed,' said Regan, in allusion to her own lot.

Luce gave Regan's shoulder a final caress, and left her as if her attendance had done its work, as it appeared it had.

'Father, perhaps a word from you would touch Graham at this time,' said Daniel.

'Nothing is asked of either of you, but that you shall consider your future,' said Sir Jesse.

'Grandpa, that is rather hard,' said Luce. 'More than that must be expected of everyone. And long months spent over books may not strike young men in that light.'

'Then they are not what you call them.'

'Well, they scarcely are as yet,' said Eleanor.

'Mother, that is even harder,' said Luce, with a laugh.

'The mot abandoned youth is a child to his mother,' murmured Graham.

'Mother, you are setting a gallant example,' said Luce. 'Father has not a wife who will make things harder for him.'

'We are none of us taking the line of showing him how much we are affected.'

'No, we are not engaging in that competition, Mother. But we might not follow the other course with so much success.'

'Those who show the least, feel the most,' stated Fulbert.

'That is not the line to take with me,' said Regan, with smiling reference to her swift emotions.

'You are a self-satisfied old woman,' said her son.

'Grandma has no need to wear a disguise,' said Luce.

'And have the rest of us?' said Eleanor.

'Well, Mother, many people do wear one. That is all I meant.'

> '"This above all, to thine own self be true;
> And it must follow, as the night the day,
> Thou canst not then be false to any man,"'

quoted Fulbert, in conclusion of the matter.

'Why is that so?' said Graham. 'It might be true to ourselves to do all manner of wrong to other people.'

'The only thing is to conquer that self, Graham,' said Daniel.

'It depends on the sense of the word, true,' said Eleanor. 'It means it would be dealing falsely with our own natures to do what degrades them.'

'I expect it does mean that, Mother,' said Luce, in a tone of receiving light and giving her mother the credit. 'No doubt it should be taken so.'

Sir Jesse broke into a song of his youth, a habit he had when he was not attentive to the talk, and sang in muffled reminiscent tones, which seemed at once to croon with sentiment and throb with experience. He glanced at the portraits of his dead son and daughter, as if his emotion prepared the way for recalling them; and sang on, as though the possession of life overcame all else.

His wife followed his look and his thought, though her eyes were not on him. She would have given her life for her children's,

23

and knew he would have done this for nothing at all, and accepted and supported his feeling. The pair lived with their son and his family, feeling amongst and not apart from them. They saw themselves as so young for their age, that they shared the common future. They were neither of them quite ordinary people, but they were ordinary in this.

'Well, don't I deserve a word to myself on the eve of my banishment?' said Fulbert.

'You do, Father,' said Luce, 'and you would have had it, if you had not contrived to forfeit it. I cannot see how we are to live the next six months. We shall have to take each day as it comes.'

'Why is that a help?' said Graham. 'It seems to spin things out. It would be better if we could compress the days.'

'Graham, are you going to let these months be different?' said Daniel.

'I have not heard either of you say a reasonable word for days,' said Eleanor.

'Mother, let them veil the occasion in their own way,' said Luce.

'Our boyish folly covers real feeling,' said Graham, stating the truth of himself.

'Would you like to be going with your father, Daniel?' said Eleanor.

'Mother, don't speak in that cold voice,' said Luce, laughing. 'It is not Daniel's fault that Father has to leave us.'

'He can answer my question nevertheless. Your father is going partly for his sake.'

'It is a good thing that everything is easier when it is shared,' said Daniel. 'If there were enough of us, I suppose it would disappear.'

'You would think there were enough,' said Graham, dreamily.

'I am tired of hearing nothing but nonsense,' said Eleanor, with a break in her voice.

'Graham, how many young men have heard their mothers use that tone!'

'I daresay the larger number,' said Eleanor, sighing.

Sir Jesse broke again into song, and sang very low, as if unsure of the fitness of the words for the audience. Regan smiled with an indulgence that was more apposite than she knew, or betrayed that she knew; and Fulbert took up the song in a strong, metallic voice and with a certain gusto. Graham kept his eyes down, as if he could only meet the manifestation with discomfiture, and Sir Jesse flashed his eyes into his son's and turned to his luncheon.

Luce had sat with her eyes on the men, and now addressed her father, as if quietly putting behind her what she saw.

'Father, is there any writing to be done? I had better undertake it, as my hand is clear.'

'This is an awkward moment for Graham,' said Daniel.

'After my advantages,' said Graham, in his absent tone.

'I had a reminder of those only this morning,' said Sir Jesse. 'An account came with my breakfast. You had nothing at yours but what you could swallow.'

'It is impossible of Graham,' aid Daniel. 'Simply eating at the table! He seems to live by bread alone.'

'Be silent,' said Sir Jesse, with sudden harshness. 'I blush to think you have been brought up in my house.'

'We have always had to blush for that,' muttered Daniel. 'But I did not think Grandpa would ever do so.'

'Will neither of you speak again until you have something to say?' said Eleanor.

'Would you have the lads dumb?' said her husband.

'It might strike many people as an improvement.'

'Mother, you don't mind what you say,' said Luce, laughing under her breath.

'You must grow up, my sons,' said Fulbert. 'I am leaving burdens upon you.'

'I need not become a baby again to comfort Mother,' said Graham.

'It does not seem to have that result,' said Fulbert. 'Well, do any of you give a thought to my exile?'

'Many thoughts, Father,' said Luce, 'but we are not to help it. We are sad to our hearts, but we do not feel guilty.'

'That must be wonderful,' said Graham.

'We ought to feel grateful,' said Eleanor.

'That involves guilt,' said Daniel. 'It seems grasping to have so much done for you.'

'I suppose that is what it is about gratitude,' mused Luce. 'I have wondered what it is, that takes from it what it ought to have.'

'I should always be glad of a chance of feeling it,' said Fulbert.

'That is a sign of a generous nature,' said Regan, who was direct in tribute to her family.

'Father does not say he has had the chance,' said Daniel.

'He is a proud man,' said Graham.

'Do you wish you were old enough to help your father, Daniel?' said Sir Jesse.

'I should like to be considered to be so, if it would mean my going with him.'

'What is your reason for desiring it?'

'It would make a change,' said Daniel, keeping his face grave.

'That shows you are not old enough,' said his mother at once. 'That is not your father's reason for leaving us.'

'No, but it will be one of the results.'

Regan gave a laugh and Eleanor looked at her.

'You are too kind to them, Lady Sullivan. Their life in this house will hardly prepare them for the world outside.'

'I never feel that that sphere is as bad as it is painted,' said Daniel.

'You can talk of it when you are qualified,' said Sir Jesse.

'Grandpa does not set us the example,' murmured Graham.

'Your experience of it at Cambridge has not taken you far,' said Eleanor.

'No, Mother dear, but farther than you think,' said Luce. 'Cambridge would be a miniature world.'

'I am to have a good, long glimpse of a far corner of the real one,' said Fulbert.

'I shall have to be father as well as mother here,' said Eleanor.

'There goes the attention from Father again,' said Daniel, while Graham gave a glance at Fulbert.

'Hatton will be both to the little ones,' said Luce.

'Don't you know more about it than that?' said her mother. 'But that is how it would be, I suppose. The nurse who does it for a living is the one preferred. Mothers must learn that they come second.'

'My dear, do not talk without sense,' said Fulbert. 'You do not make the affairs of childhood your province. You cannot shine in a sphere where you have not chosen to function.'

'Do you want a nurse for your children, or a mother?'

'I want both, and my children have them. And I hope they also have a father. But we must not claim other people's credit.'

'I suppose I may have my own. I can expect a little recognition in the family that takes my life.'

Regan looked on without a change of expression, as though having no feeling that would cause one. She had neither pity nor blame for a woman who gave way under the demand of her family. She had never done so herself, but to her the family was the only thing that did not produce such a result.

'We know what you give us, my dear,' said Sir Jesse to Eleanor. 'You do not think we do not?'

'If feelings are always covered we may not remember them.'

'They are no less safe like that, Mother,' said Luce.

'I know they are there, my dear. I ought not to need to be reminded.'

'Father,' said Luce, turning her eyes on Fulbert's face, 'what did you mean by saying that Mother did not make the affairs of childhood her province?'

'I meant what I said, my dear, as I generally do.'

'It is true that I give less time to these children than I gave to the elder ones,' said Eleanor.

'Why do you, Mother?' said Luce, transferring her eyes.

'I seem to have less to give. You are in so many different stages. And I may have lost my knack or my zest as the years passed,' said Eleanor, who spoke of herself with the same honesty as of other people. 'And when the habit is broken, there is little to be done. My younger children are shy of me.'

'No, Mother, I don't think they are.'

'They behave as if they were.'

'Mother, I think it is better to be at your best with your elder children,' said Luce. 'It is when they are older that they need understanding. There is little that cannot be done by nurses for young children.'

'That is assumed in our class,' said Fulbert.

'You sound as if you do not approve of it, Father.'

'I don't know that I know much of the subject,' said Fulbert, with a suggestion that further knowledge would hardly add to him.

'Graham has always had his mother's influence,' said Daniel. 'It almost seems a case where nothing can be done.'

'Boys, you might be monotonous,' said Luce. 'I don't know how you contrive to be amusing.'

'I do not either,' said Sir Jesse. 'You might have the goodness to inform me.'

'Grandpa, you have had enough of them,' said Luce, with swift compunction. 'We forget we are not natural members of your house.'

'Indeed you are,' said Regan.

'Grandma has said one of those little words that will be remembered,' said Graham.

'As neither of you seems about to leave the table, I will do so myself,' said Sir Jesse.

'No, Grandpa, you will not,' said Luce, leaning forward and putting a hand on his arm. 'You will stay here and have your smoke and talk with Father.'

'A strong man is checked in his course by a woman's hand,' said Graham.

'Will you both be silent?' said Eleanor.

'Boys, you are upsetting Mother,' said Luce.

'I was always afraid that Graham would grow up to be a grief to her.'

Sir Jesse rose and walked from the room.

'Boys, look at that,' said Luce.

'I saw it myself,' said Fulbert.

'Do you hear what I say, or do you not?' said Eleanor.

'Graham, answer your mother,' said Daniel.

'You can answer me yourself,' said Eleanor.

'No, you are mistaken, Mother. I am at a loss.'

'This is one of your worse moments, my boy,' said Fulbert, with his air of enjoyment.

'He can easily put an end to it,' said Eleanor.

'Why am I not struck dead,' said Daniel, 'if that is a thing that has happened to people?'

Regan's deep laugh sounded through the room.

'I wish Grandpa had stayed to hear that laugh,' said Luce.

'I wish he had done so for any reason,' said Daniel.

'Daniel, I am waiting to be answered,' said Eleanor.

'Surely not still,' said her son.

'You have staying power, my dear,' said Fulbert.

'I forget what you asked now, Mother,' said Luce.

'Oh, you are not equal to your mother, child,' said Fulbert.

'Your brothers do not forget, and it was to them I spoke,' said Eleanor.

'Mother, when you speak in that tone, I defy anyone to face you without flinching,' said Luce.

'I do not accept the challenge,' said Daniel.

'There is no real cause for annoyance, Eleanor, my dear,' said Fulbert.

'I hope your father is of that opinion.'

'I am sure he is,' said Regan, in an easy tone.

'Yes, Grandma, so somehow am I,' said Luce.

'In case he is not, it may be as well to avoid risk in future,' said Fulbert.

'Yes, Father, I would not put it more strongly than that,' said Luce.

'I think I would,' said Eleanor.

'Mother, do thaw,' said Luce. 'Your sons are not a pair of criminals.'

'They are penniless boys, who are doing no good to themselves.'

Regan looked at her grandsons almost with compunction, as if it were a natural ground for resentment, that other people should have more than they had.

'Yes, I suppose that is an accepted handicap,' said Luce, in a musing tone. 'To be penniless. And yet I would not have people modify their actions too much because of it. I do not think I would.'

'There is no harm in young men's being well-behaved to an old one,' said Fulbert.

'No, Father. But is it a fair accusation? What exactly is the boy's misdeed? I mean essentially. Not at the moment.'

'The fact of their existence,' said Fulbert. 'The sins of the fathers are visited upon the children.'

Luce gave a series of slow, little laughs, keeping her eyes from her mother.

'Their grandfather wants what is best for them,' said Regan.

'Graham, Grandma has dropped her handkerchief,' said Luce, without a break in her tone, and hardly changing the direction of her eyes. 'Are we to expect Grandpa to take the same attitude towards the other boys?'

'The younger ones often remain the younger ones,' said Eleanor.

'That sounds a cryptic remark, my dear,' said Fulbert, 'but I recognize the truth it contains.'

'Are not the schoolroom children coming down today?' said Luce.

'I have just sent word that they need not come,' said Eleanor. 'Missing their grandfather would only lead to questions.'

'Their yoke is easy and their burden light,' said Graham.

'Mother, I will try again with Graham,' said Daniel. 'It cannot be that I shall always speak in vain.'

'It is a fact that you do so at the moment, my boy,' said Fulbert, in mingled enjoyment and apprehension.

'Mother dear, relax,' said Luce. 'It is not good for you to remain in that wrought-up state.'

'Come, come, my dear, things are not so bad,' said Fulbert.

'I cannot bear the ignorant quoting of sacred words.'

'We see that you can't, and so the lads will remember it.'

'That should not be their reason for avoiding it.'

'It should be one of them. And they know the others.'

'Father, is Grandpa by himself?' said Luce.

'I daresay he is. Indeed he must be.'

'Don't you want to go to him, Father?' said Luce, looking at Fulbert with mild amusement.

'I have never heard that the sins of the children should be

visited upon the fathers. But I can't leave the old man to simmer on the hob, when he is in danger of boiling over.'

'Grandpa is not a kettle, Father,' said Luce, in a quiet tone.

Regan laughed, and Fulbert ran round the table and gave her a kiss, and then did the same to his wife and daughter, and seemed about to run from the room, but did not do so.

'I wonder if we shall realize that Grandpa is human, before – while we are all young about him,' said Luce.

'Before he becomes more than human,' said Graham.

'Yes, before that, boys,' said Luce, in an unflinching tone.

'It will be wasted when Grandpa understands all,' said Graham.

Regan rose and rustled from the room in some personal pre-occupation. Eleanor dropped her eyes and remained still. Fulbert's eyes flashed with rallying apprehension round the table. The silence held until it reached the stage at which it is impossible to break.

'Graham, I do not remember that I forbade you to speak,' said Daniel.

Graham emitted a sound.

'Cry, Graham, if you must. We shall understand.'

Luce made an involuntary sound that served as a signal, and the brothers and sister rocked in mirth, or in some emotion that bore the semblance of it.

Eleanor had her own reaction to such proceedings. She rose and appeared to engage herself with a bowl of flowers.

'You boys can go and sit with your grandfather,' she said, inserting a hand to gauge the depth of the water. 'I want your father to myself for a time.'

'Mother, do not hold yourself aloof,' said Luce, in a voice that had not quite regained its steadiness. 'Magnifying a matter is not the way to mend it.'

'That sort of laughter is very easy to catch,' said Eleanor, in a condoning manner that did her credit, considering that she had hardly found this the case herself. 'But your father and I will be left to ourselves. We have many things to discuss.'

'Well, let us begin on them, my dear,' said Fulbert leaning back in his chair.

Eleanor was silent for a moment.

'It is strange that we can get so vexed with people who are so much to us.'

'Not at all, when they give us cause. It was a good move to send the young jackanapes to their grandfather.'

'Do you think it was a mean thing to do, that I was retaliating on them?'

'No doubt you were, my dear. And it was the right thing. Why shouldn't they learn that they get as good as they give?'

'They ought not to learn it from their mother.'

'They are happy to have from anyone what is best for them. And that is what a dose of the old man will be. I hope they are not queering their pitch with him.'

This question was answered by the opening of the library door and the sound of Sir Jesse's voice.

'So I am held to be short of company. If you are engaged with your wife, I will have my own. I prefer a woman to half a man. I have sent the pair about their business, and I hope they will follow it.'

'I will fetch Grandma for you, Grandpa,' said Luce, coming forward. 'Father thought it would be good for the boys to talk to you.'

'So I shoulder the responsibility,' said Fulbert, with an amused air.

'I daresay,' said Sir Jesse to his granddaughter, without a hint of disputing the idea. 'But where is the benefit for me? I get my share of them.'

'It is not the boys' fault that they are not quite up to you, Grandpa.'

'Nor mine either, as I see it. And I put it to their account that they are so far behind. We are all of us human or should be. In their case I begin to have doubt. Grinning and chattering like apes and costing like dukes!'

'I wish you could forget how much they cost you, Grandpa,' said Luce, fingering Sir Jesse's coat.

'I wish the same, but I get too many reminders. Other people seem to bear it in mind.'

'It will not be for much longer, Grandpa. They are both in their last year at Cambridge.'

'And where will they spend the next ones? Behind bars, I should think. I hope that will be less expensive.'

'I should think it would be, Grandpa,' said Luce, in a demure tone, making a little grimace and curtsy for the eyes of her brothers.

'If we are fed by the public through a grating,' said Daniel, 'it will take our keep off Grandpa.'

'We should still carry our debt to the grave,' said his brother. 'Or to Grandpa's grave we should.'

'Why does he mind supporting us, so much more than the others? I suppose because we are adult and male. None of the others is both.'

'It seems odd that I should be both,' said Graham. 'Neither seems suited to me.'

'It is true of Grandpa and Father. And they have never earned a penny. We belong to the new generation that has to gain its bread.'

'It is a poor position not to be entitled just to that,' said Graham, with a faint smile. 'Think what Grandpa is entitled to!'

'I do not envy him,' said Daniel.

'You mean he is old and you are young,' said Graham, looking into his brother's face. 'You think he will soon die. But he sees his death as too far distant to count. So that takes away your advantage.'

'He can't think he is a god.'

'We have done what we can to foster the belief. And I have almost come to accept it.'

'He insists that we shall do so,' said Daniel.

'That is the way to make himself into one. And I feel he has succeeded.'

'He thinks that youth is a time for mischief and the conceal-ment of it,' said Daniel. 'I expect he remembers that it is. And he knows that mischief costs money.'

'I have heard him observe that everything does that,' said Graham.

'The inheritance must vanish with so much division,' said Daniel. 'Father is the last to anticipate it. I am a poor sort of eldest son. Grandpa rightly despises me.'

'Father says he will not see the time when it is gone,' said Graham, smiling. 'By claiming extinction for himself, he puts any experience of life in a favourable light.'

'He does not think he is immortal, as Grandpa does.'

'He does not need to yet. He has too good a span of life before him.'

'The girls will share equally with us,' said Daniel. 'There is not enough for anything else.'

'I see you do not think that Father is immortal.'

'I feel that I am, and that I shall have to support myself through that eternity.'

'And you think you will do it by coming out high on college lists.'

'Well, what are your own anticipations?'

'They are of an uneasy nature,' said Graham. 'I tell myself that the time of reckoning will be short; and I know that is said when things are very bad. But I would not change my last three years for yours.'

'The moments to be exchanged are not yet.'

'Moments instead of years. I hold to my opinion. And when people hold to things, they have not always lost them. Most great men have failed at the university.'

'I do not miss the implication. But other kinds of men have done the same.'

'What are you discussing?' said Eleanor, coming into the hall.

'Our own prospects,' said Daniel.

'Do you think you have good ones?' said Eleanor, while Luce walked up with a noiseless step, and placing her hand on her mother's shoulder, followed her eyes.

Eleanor had ambitions for her sons, and found herself assailed by doubts whether they were justified. She felt the position to be difficult for her, but had no uneasiness lest it might be the same for them.

'If not, what have we?' said Daniel.

'You will make your mother proud of you?' said Eleanor, who saw her preference for her eldest son as simple tribute to him.

'I believe you see it as a discredit to me, that I have not won your interest in equal measure,' said Graham.

34

Eleanor looked at him in faint surprise.

'Do you think your ability is equal to Daniel's?'

'Yes, but different in kind.'

'Any sign of self-respect is a good thing,' said Daniel. 'The respect of others may follow.'

'I think it often comes first,' said his brother.

'Mother,' said Luce, looking after the two young men, 'do you know that you treat those boys quite differently?'

'A mother often has an especial feeling for her eldest son.'

'Isn't that hard on the second one? It does not follow that he is inferior.'

'He does not think he is,' said Eleanor, in a tone of seeing a new light on the position. 'So it has not had much effect on him.'

'It may have had the more for that, Mother.'

'I must try to be more impartial. I see that Graham has developed a good deal lately.'

'Mother, you do honestly try to put right anything that is wrong,' said Luce, looking at Eleanor with gentle appraisement.

'I know you think my heart is in the right place,' said Eleanor, with a note of dryness.

'And why is that a poor compliment? It is the most fundamental of all things, in the sense that nothing counts without it.'

'Perhaps that is why we never hear that a heart is anywhere else.'

'Mother – you are a truer parent of your sons than you know,' said Luce, going into silent laughter, with her eyes on Eleanor.

CHAPTER TWO

'HATTON in a big bed, Nevill in a little bed,' said Nevill Sullivan surveying the scene of which he spoke.

'Lie still and go to sleep,' said the nurse.

'Hatton get up,' said Nevill, in a tone of agreement.

'Shut your eyes and try to sleep.'

'Shut his eyes,' said Nevill, keeping them shut with a trembling of the lids.

'Don't take any notice of me while I dress.'

'Watch Hatton,' said Nevill, turning on his side with the purpose.

'Now you are wide awake. You must rest until I am ready. You went to sleep very late.'

'As late as Hatton.'

'Yes, nearly as late.'

'As late as Hatton,' said Nevill, on a higher note.

'Yes, as late as that. That means you are tired this morning.'

'He is tired,' said Nevill, leaning back on his pillows.

'Here are Honor and Gavin coming to see you.'

'No,' said Nevill, in a tone of repudiating the prospect.

'Don't you want to see them?'

'No. Just Hatton and Nevill.'

'They have come to say good-morning.'

Nevill looked his question of this purpose, and his brother and sister ran into the room at a halt in their morning toilet, followed by a nursemaid baulked in her intention of completing it. The girl was a solid, lively-looking child of ten, with a fair, oval face, observant, grey eyes made smaller by the roundness of her cheeks, thick bright hair, small hands and feet, and a benevolent, interested, rather complacent expression. Her brother was a ponderous, drab-coloured boy a year younger, with blunter features and large, pale, steady eyes; and Nevill was a brown-eyed, flaxenhaired child of three, with an ambition to continue in his infancy and meet the treatment accorded to it.

'He is tired this morning,' he said, looking at the others with an eye at once pathetic and observant. 'He went to sleep as late as Hatton.'

'And what does that signify?' said Honor, giving a spring.

Gavin looked at her and followed her example, the method by which he gave the normal amount of activity to his life.

'They shake the room,' said Nevill, uneasily, to Hatton.

Honor and Gavin leapt about the floor, less damped by Hatton's indifference than spurred by the nursemaid's protests. Bertha Mullet was a freckled, healthy-looking girl of twenty-two, with eyes and hair and brows of the same fox-red colour, and something foxlike in the moulding of her face. She would sometimes push up her cheeks towards her eyes, and entertain the children with a representation of this creature, regarding the power as a simple asset, and supported in the view by Honor and Gavin, and more dubiously by Nevill, who found the performance realistic. Emma Hatton was a short, square woman of an age which had never been revealed, but revealed itself as about fifty-five, with a square, dark face, large, kind hands, deep, small, dark eyes, stiff, iron-grey hair, and a look of superiority, which was recognized and justified. She was a farmer's daughter, who saw the training of children as her vocation and therefore pursued it. Honor and Gavin regarded her as the centre of their world, and Nevill expended on her the force of a nature diverted by nobody else. Her assistant looked up to her and bowed to her rule, but found in Honor a more equal, indeed a completely equal companionship.

'Leap into the air,' chanted Honor, proceeding by this method round the room.

Gavin repeated the words and the action.

'Leap into the air,' said Nevill to Hatton, in a tone that made his words a request to be assisted to follow the example.

'No, you must rest a little longer.'

'He must rest,' said Nevill, in an explanatory tone to the others.

'Why don't you think of something to do yourself, Master Gavin?' said Mullet, who had viewed the proceedings with a serious eye.

'Because I don't want to,' said Gavin, giving an extra jump, by way of displaying a certain initiative.

'He will think of something,' said Nevill, nodding to Hatton in encouragement upon his own future.

'How old are you, Hatton?' said Honor, in an incidental tone.

'Older than you, but not a hundred,' said Hatton, automatically.

'Hatton is a hundred,' said Nevill, with pride. 'Not yet, but very soon.'

'Here is the mistress on the stairs! Here is your mother come to say good morning to you,' said Mullet, in a rather bustling manner.

Honor began to fasten her garments, as if to be employed would give a better impression; Mullet drew her towards her and took the task into her own hands; Hatton and Nevill were unaffected; and Gavin's unconcern was so marked that it became a positive condition.

'Well, my little ones,' said the voice that hardly varied with the people it addressed, 'so you are back from the sea. Did you have a happy time? Are you tired after your journey? Is no one going to answer me?'

Nevill laid hold of Hatton's dress and raised eyes of disapprobation and apprehension to her face.

'Are you coming to kiss me, my boy?' said Eleanor.

Gavin approached and suffered an embrace, and Honor followed his example.

'It was a pity I had to be out last night. It was a dull homecoming for you. I wish I could have helped it.'

'Mother couldn't help it,' said Nevill, in a condoning manner.

'We had Grandma,' said Gavin.

'But that was not the same,' said his mother.

'No, it was different.'

'It was better, wasn't it?' said Nevill, in an obliging tone.

'Honor kissed me, as well as letting me kiss her, Gavin,' said Eleanor.

Gavin did not answer, and his mother turned to Nevill's bed, as though she felt it hardly fitting that he should receive her under such conditions.

'Is anything the matter with him, Hatton?'

'He is only tired, madam. He went to sleep very late.'

'As late as Hatton,' said Nevill.

'Was he not in bed at the usual time?'

'We were at home too late for that, madam. And he could not sleep in a strange room.'

'A strange room? It is his own night nursery.'

'Yes, but he had forgotten it.'

'He had forgotten it,' Nevill explained to his mother.

'Could not someone sit with him?'

'Mullet and I were unpacking, madam. And no one else would have done.'

'No one but Hatton,' said Nevill.

'He hardly looks as if he had been to the sea.'

'People would not look different,' said Gavin.

'Hatton did sit with him for a little while,' said Nevill, more in condonation of Hatton than in information to his mother.

'Don't cover your face, dear,' said the latter, drawing down the clothes.

'No,' said Nevill, in a sharper tone, pulling them back.

'You will not be able to breathe properly.'

'He never breathes,' said Nevill, and closed his eyes.

'Isn't he growing rather a wilful little boy?'

'He is tired, as you say, madam. He will soon be himself.'

'Mother didn't say so,' said Gavin.

'You had better keep him in bed,' said Eleanor, suggesting an uncongenial course both for Hatton and her son.

'He will get up now, madam, and rest before his dinner.'

'In his little bed,' said Nevill, and changed his tone the next moment. 'Get up now.'

'Then I will go downstairs and come up when they are up and dressed.'

'We are up now,' said Gavin.

'Will you come again to see us?' said Nevill, leaning out of the bed to take hold of his mother's skirt and raise his eyes to her face.

'Yes, of course Mother will come to see her little boy.'

'Now she has gone,' said Nevill, in a satisfied tone, as the door closed.

'Oh, and you said you wanted her to come again,' said Mullet, with reproach.

'Nevill fawns on people,' said Honor.

'He doesn't,' said Nevill. 'He won't marry Honor when he is grown-up.'

Nevill's consistent use of the third person for himself suggested a cultivation of infantine habit.

'You can't marry your sister,' said Gavin.

'He can marry who he wants to. And he will marry Hatton.'

'Hatton and Nevill are engaged!' said Honor, with more contempt for the condition than for the unsuitability of the parties.

'Hatton will like it,' said Nevill.

'Why can't brothers and sisters marry?' said Gavin.

'Because they have to start a family,' said his sister. 'If they married people in the same one, there would never be any new ones. But they can live together.'

'Do they have any children then?'

'I don't think they do so often. But they can adopt some.'

'He will be your little boy,' promised Nevill in full comprehension.

'Nevill is one of the baser creatures,' said Gavin.

'He isn't,' said Nevill, clutching at Hatton's skirt and pointing to his brother. 'He is the same as him.'

'If people knew we had a baser creature, we should be prosecuted,' said Honor.

'What is prosecuted?' said Gavin.

'Put in prison.'

'They will be put in prison,' said Nevill, in a comfortable tone to Hatton. 'It is because they don't like him to be best.'

'Why should we mind what he is?' said Gavin.

'I wish you did not mind so much,' said Hatton, causing Mullet some amusement. 'It is past the time for your breakfast. Nevill must come in his dressing-gown.'

'Not much appetite,' said Nevill, leaning back in his chair.

'You will eat like a baser creature,' said Gavin.

'He was sick in the train,' said Nevill, disposing of the suggestion.

'So was Honor.'

'But he wasn't,' said Nevill to Hatton, indicating his brother.

'No, Gavin was my choice at that moment,' said Hatton.

'No, he was,' said Nevill, clutching at her arm and speaking in reference to what had taken place.

'We were all rather uncivilized,' said Honor.

'He was too,' said Nevill, nodding.

'You are three children come back to your home after a period of exile,' said Mullet, speaking as if she were beginning a tale.

'We haven't got a home,' said Gavin. 'This home is Grandpa's. It is because we are poor.'

'You are not,' said Mullet, in a sharper tone.

'Mother said we were.'

'That sort of poorness in your kind of family is different.'

'It is better, isn't it?' said Nevill, in a consoling tone.

'It is considered superior to the money of ordinary people.'

'Why aren't we ordinary?' said Honor.

'You are, until you prove you are not,' said Hatton.

'Youngest are best,' said Nevill.

'You won't be the youngest, if there is another baby,' said Honor.

Nevill regarded her for a moment.

'He will,' he said.

'That can be his distinction for the present,' said Hatton, leaving the table on some errand.

'I do think Hatton does talk beautifully,' said Mullet, in a tone that seemed a reproach to the existing social order. 'As pointed and as finished as any lady.'

'Pointed?' said Gavin.

'To the point,' said Honor.

'Hatton does it, doesn't she?' said Nevill, looking up into Mullet's face.

'Now we must not let time steal a march on us,' said Hatton, returning and using a rather conscious tone.

'Why mustn't we?' said Nevill. 'Why mustn't we, Hatton?'

'There is a lot to be done by tomorrow, when the new governess comes.'

'Not for him is she coming?'

'Not for you as much as the others. You will go in for half an hour.'

'She will like him, won't she, when he goes in?'

'Nevill says she will like him!' said Honor.

'I daresay she will at this stage,' said Hatton. 'It is later that the crux comes.'

'Crux?' said Gavin.

'Crisis,' said his sister.

'Hatton will come and fetch him,' said Nevill.

'I have had two governesses,' said Honor. 'I know the tricks of the trade.'

'Yes, you know, we know them,' said Gavin.

'He doesn't want to,' said Nevill.

'And the nature of the beasts,' said Honor.

'And the snares of the way and the obstacles of the race and all of it,' said Hatton, in an easy, rapid tone, keeping her eyes from Mullet and her hands employed. 'But that does not prevent you from attending to your breakfast.'

'It does do it,' said Nevill, putting his hand on her arm. 'It does, Hatton.'

Eleanor's voice came again at the door.

'Well, are you happy to be at home? Have you begun to feel brighter for your time at the sea?' she said, with a suggestion that this reaction had as yet been prevented in her children.

It seemed to her that it was still delayed.

'I think they do look better, Hatton. Honor was well before, but the boys were too thin. Now tell me how you enjoyed your holiday. Did you like it, Honor dear?'

'Yes, thank you, Mother.'

'Haven't you any more to say about it than that? Why, you went to the sea, and had rooms taken for you, and Hatton and Mullet there to take care of you, and had three weeks in a lovely place by the sands and waves. Now didn't you enjoy it all, and find it a treat?'

'It wasn't a lovely place,' said Gavin. 'It was all houses and streets. And we always have Hatton and Mullet.'

'But there had to be houses, or there wouldn't have been one for you to stay in.'

'There could have been just that one house.'

'But how would you have got anything to eat, if there had been no shops?'

'There could have been one like the one in the village, that sells most things.'

'It sells string,' said Nevill.

'But you wanted things to eat like those you have at home. And they don't come from the shop.'

'We didn't have them even as nice as that,' said Honor.

'You don't know when you are well off,' said Eleanor, laughing before she knew. 'I suppose all children are the same.'

'Well, the same and different,' said Honor.

'Hatton buy him a ball,' said Nevill.

'Why, you have one there,' said Eleanor, looking at some toys on the ground.

'No,' said Nevill, in a tone of repulsing her words.

'You don't want another, do you?'

'No,' said Nevill, in the same manner, shaking his head and a moment later his body.

'What does he want, Hatton?'

'Ball of string,' said Nevill, in a tone that suggested that the actual words were forced from him.

'Oh, that is what you want. Well, I daresay you can have one.'

'There is a kind that only costs a penny,' said Gavin.

'It costs a penny,' said Nevill, in a grave tone. 'But Hatton buy it for him.'

'Well, Honor dear, tell me about the holiday. What did you like best?'

'I think the beach,' said Honor.

'That was all there was,' said Gavin. 'The lodgings weren't nice.'

'Weren't they? What was wrong with them? Were they not good ones, Hatton?'

'Yes, madam, they were clean and pleasant. The children mean that the rooms were smaller than these.'

'This home will be a disadvantage to them. It will teach them to expect too much. Now have you really nothing to tell me, but that the rooms here had spoiled you for others?'

'We didn't tell you that,' said Gavin.

'He found a little crab,' said Nevill. 'It was as small as a crumb.'

'Well, that was something,' said Eleanor. 'You played on the beach, and found crabs, and found a lot of other interesting things, didn't you?'

'Not a lot,' said Gavin. 'We found an old net and a piece of wood from a ship.'

'We weren't sure it was from a ship,' said his sister.

'From a little boat,' suggested Nevill.

'And didn't you find seaweed and shells, and wade in the sea and build castles and do things like that?'

'We did when it was fine,' said Honor.

43

'And was it often wet?'

'No – yes – two days,' said Honor, meeting her mother's eyes and averting her own.

'Well, that was not much out of three weeks. They do not seem to appreciate things, Hatton. When I was a child, I should have remembered the holiday for years.'

'They will do the same, madam. And it has done what we wanted of it. But the truth is that children are happier at home. And it is fortunate it is not the other way round.'

'We found one shell that was not broken,' said Nevill, in further reassurance.

'So you love your home, my little ones,' said Eleanor, making the best of her children's attitude. 'Of course you are glad to be back again. And you have Father and Mother to welcome you. You have been without them all the time. So it couldn't be perfect, could it?'

'We have Grandpa and Grandma too,' said Nevill. 'And Grandma wasn't out, was she?'

'Yes, you have Mother and Father and Grandma and Grandpa,' said Eleanor, adjusting the order of these personalities. 'And your brothers and sisters, and your new governess coming tomorrow.'

'He has Hatton,' said her youngest son.

'It is the same nursery as Grandpa had, when he was a little boy like you.'

'Not like him,' said Nevill.

'Well, when he was as small as you. He used to play in it, as you do.'

'Not as small as him; as small as Gavin.'

'Yes, as small as you, and even smaller. He was here when he was a baby. You like to think of that, don't you?'

'He couldn't come in it now,' said Nevill. 'Hatton wouldn't let him.'

'Now, Honor dear,' said Eleanor, turning from her son to her daughter, perhaps a natural step, 'I hope you will try with this new governess, and not play and pay no attention, as you did with the last. You are old enough to begin to learn.'

'I have been learning for a long time.'

'It keeps Gavin back as well as you. And we should not do what is bad for someone else.'

'It is only being with me, that makes Gavin learn at all.'

'Well, well, dear, do your best. That is all we ask of you. But if you have such an opinion of yourself, we can expect a good deal of you.'

'I only said I didn't keep Gavin back, when you said I did.'

'Dear me, Hatton, girls are even less easy than boys,' said Eleanor, with a sigh.

'It is the person you are talking to, that you don't think is easy,' said Gavin.

'I daresay it sums up like that,' said his mother.

'Father likes girls better,' said Honor.

'He is a girlie,' said Nevill, recalling his father's attitude to his sisters. 'He likes Father better too.'

'You are a boy,' said Gavin. 'As much a boy as I am.'

'No, not as much. He is a little boy.'

'Yes, yes, a little boy,' said Mullet, taking his hand and speaking for Eleanor's ears. 'And now the little boy has had his breakfast, he must come and put on his coat for the garden.'

'Like a girlie,' said Nevill, in a tone of making a condition.

'Yes, like that. And when you come in, I will tell you a story about some children who had a new governess. You will all like that, won't you?'

'I would rather have one about a wrecker,' said Gavin, who had hardly done justice to the influence of the sea.

Eleanor looked after Mullet and Nevill with a smile for Hatton.

'You don't give me much of a welcome,' she said to the other children. 'Do you think of me as an ordinary person, who may come in at any time?'

'You do come in often,' said Gavin.

'You must remember I am your mother.'

'A lot of people are mothers. Hatton's sister is.'

'My honest boy!' said Eleanor, suddenly kissing her son. 'Now what is it, Honor dear? You seem put out about something. Do you know what it is, Gavin?'

'It is when you make me out better than she is.'

'Well, she does not always think people just alike, herself.'

'I do when they are,' said Honor.

'Well, I expect you are tired by your journey. Were they upset by the train, Hatton?'

'Honor and Nevill were, madam. Gavin never is.'

'I was sick almost the whole time,' said Honor.

'Dear, dear, poor Hatton and Mullet!' said Eleanor, in a bracing tone. 'Well, I must go and see if the others have anything that does not please them. We must not give all the attention to one part of the house.'

'We didn't say we were not pleased,' said Gavin, when his mother had gone.

'Neither did Mother,' said Honor. 'But she palpably was not.'

Hatton dispatched the three to the garden in the charge of Mullet, who walked up and down telling stories, with them all hanging on to her arms. When the time for exercise was over, she was the only one who had had any exercise, and she had had a good deal.

Eleanor went to the schoolroom to visit the next section of her family. She found two girls and a boy seated at the table with their governess, engaged in scanning an atlas, which could only be surveyed by them singly, and therefore lent itself to slow progress. This was their customary rate of advance, as Miss Mitford was a person of easy pace, and it was the family practice to economize in materials rather than in time. It seldom struck Eleanor or Regan that a few shillings might be well spent. Shillings were never well spent to them, only by necessity or compulsion. Two governesses came under the last head, and money was allotted to the purpose, but to do them justice in the smallest possible amount.

'Well, my dears,' said Eleanor, her tone rendered warm by her sense that these children probably differed from the others, 'you have not been to the sea. You have been at home and been bright and happy all the time. I believe it never pays to do too much for children.'

'No,' said James, the youngest of the three, making an accommodating movement.

'You would just as soon be at home, wouldn't you?'

'Yes.'

'Wouldn't you, Isabel?'

'Yes.'

'Wouldn't you, my Venice?'

'I am not quite sure. No, I don't think I would.'

'You would like to go to the sea?' said Eleanor, with a surprise that would have seemed more natural to a witness of the late scene. 'We must see about it next year. What do you think, Miss Mitford?'

Miss Mitford looked up in response, but not in response of any particular nature. She was a short, rather odd-looking woman of fifty, looking older than her age, with calm, green eyes, features so indeterminate that they seemed to change, and hair and clothes disposed in a manner which appeared to be her own, but had really been everyone's at the time when she grew up. It had seemed to her the mark of womanhood, and it still served that purpose. She was a person of reading and intelligence, but preferred a family to a school, and knew that by taking a post beneath her claims, she took her employers in her hand. She held them with unflinching calm and without giving any quarter, and criticism, after she had met it with surprise and had not bent to it, had not assailed her. Eleanor was hardly afraid of her, as she did not feel that kind of fear, but she hesitated to judge or advise her, and seldom inquired of her pupils' progress except of the pupils behind her back.

James joined his sisters on such days as a recurring and undefined indisposition kept him from school, occasions which did not involve his dispensing with education. They were actually the only ones when he did not do so, as he was a boy who could only learn from a woman in his home. The stage at which he could learn, but only under certain conditions, had never received attention. He was a boy of twelve, with liquid, brown eyes like Nevill's, features regarded as pretty and childish, and vaguely deprecated on that ground, and a responsive, innocent, sometimes suddenly sophisticated expression. His dependence on Hatton at Nevill's age had exceeded his brother's, and still went beyond anyone else's. If Hatton could have betrayed a preference, it would have been for him; and it sent a ray of light through his rather shadowed life to remember that at heart she had one.

Isabel was a short, pale girl of fifteen, with a face that was a gentle edition of Fulbert's, delicate hands like Honor's, a humorous expression of her own, and near-sighted, penetrating eyes; and Venetia, known as Venice, was a large, dark, handsome child a year and a half younger, with a steady, high colour and fine, closely-set, hazel eyes, and an amiability covering a resolute self-esteem, which was beginning to show in her expression, though only Isabel was aware of it. The two sisters lived for each other, as did Honor and Gavin; and James lived to himself like Nevill, but with less support, so that his life had a certain pathos. He would remedy matters by repairing to the nursery, where Hatton's welcome and Honor's inclination to a senior brought Nevill to open, and Gavin to secret despair. The suffering of his brothers was pleasant to James, not because he was a malicious or hostile, but because the evidence of sadness in other lives made him feel a being less apart. He showed no aptitude for books, and this in his sex was condemned; and he carried a sense of guilt, which it did not occur to him was unmerited. It was a time when endeavour in children was rated below success, an error which in later years has hardly yet been corrected, so that childhood was a more accurate foretaste of life than it is now.

'So you are not at school, my boy?' said Eleanor.

'No,' said James, giving a little start and looking at Isabel.

'He does not feel well,' said the latter.

'Doesn't he?' said Eleanor, with rather dubious sympathy, as if not quite sure of the authenticity of the condition. 'The unwellness seems to come rather often. It is kind of Miss Mitford to let you be in here. Have you thanked her?'

'No.'

'Then do it, my dear.'

'Thank you,' said James, without loss of composure, having no objection to being treated as a child, indeed finding it his natural treatment.

'He is not much above the average, is he, Miss Mitford?' said Eleanor, not entertaining the possibility of an absolutely ordinary child.

'No, I don't think he is.'

'You think he is up to it at any rate?'

'Well, I did not say so. Perhaps it was you who did.'

'Do you think he would learn more with his sisters at home?'

'You mean with their governess, don't you? Well, a good many boys would.'

'But I suppose we cannot arrange it?'

'No, you must be the slave of convention.'

'I suppose most boys are backward.'

'Well, some are forward.'

'You must make Miss Mitford think better of you, James.'

'I hope you do not think I take an ungenerous view,' said Miss Mitford.

'Do you never alter your opinions?' said Eleanor, with a faint sting in her tone.

'I seldom need to. My judgement is swift and strong,' said Miss Mitford, with no loss of gravity.

'Could you not help James, Isabel?'

'Not as well as Miss Mitford.'

'Could you, Venice? You are nearer his age.'

'Is that a qualification?' said Isabel.

'It would help her to see his point of view.'

'It might make her share it.'

'You think the girls are intelligent at any rate, Miss Mitford?' said Eleanor, seeking to turn this readiness to account.

'It is a good sign that they think so.'

'Do you never praise anyone?'

'I am rather grudging in that way. It is a sort of shyness.'

Venice gave a giggle.

'Are you not going to say a word to me, Venice?' said Eleanor.

'Yes,' said Venice, in a bright, conscious tone, turning wide eyes on her mother. 'I was thinking about the sea. I should like to go next year.'

'And so you shall, my dear. I wish I had arranged it. I ought to have thought of a change for you. And I could have sent James with Hatton. It would have done him good. Don't you think it would, Miss Mitford?'

'Yes.'

'But you did not suggest it.'

'No.'

'Miss Mitford knows that suggestions cost money,' said Isabel.

'They cost nothing, my child. I am always pleased to have them. It is carrying them out that costs.'

'My suggestions are not any good, when they are not carried out,' said Miss Mitford, in a faintly plaintive tone.

'Well, I hope you will make them another time. Good-bye, my dears; I will come up again and see you. James, do you forget again to open the door?'

James could not deny it.

'Does he generally, Miss Mitford?'

'Yes.'

'Does he not open the door for you?'

'No.'

'You must remember you are not a baby, mustn't you, James?'

'Yes,' said James, who had little chance of thinking he was, as the family steadily combated the supposed conviction.

'Could you remember to tell him, Miss Mitford?'

'Well, my memory is no better than his.'

'Then the girls must remember. Will you think of it, my dears? Now, my boy, if you are to be at home today, you must have tea in the nursery and go early to bed. When we are not well, we must not behave quite like well people, must we?'

'No,' said James, who had no great leaning towards the routine of the healthy, which he found a strain.

'Why is he to have tea in the nursery?' said Miss Mitford, as the door closed.

'The tea there is earlier than ours,' said Venice.

'Mother hasn't a favourite in this room,' said Isabel.

'I somehow feel it is not me,' said Miss Mitford. 'And my instinct is generally right in those ways.'

'I don't want to be one of her favoured ones,' said Venice, who had a familiar sense of meeting too little esteem.

'She only likes two people in the house, Daniel and Gavin,' said Isabel.

'And I like so many,' said Miss Mitford. 'I must have a more affectionate nature.'

'She likes Father and Luce,' said James, just looking up from his book.

'That is true,' said Miss Mitford. 'I hope it is the history book that you are reading, James.'

'Yes,' said James, who was perusing a more human portion of this volume, indeed an intensely human one, as it dealt with the elaborate execution of a familiar character. When any trouble or constraint was over, he allowed it to drift from his mind.

'What is the time?' said Venice.

'Two minutes to your break for luncheon,' said Miss Mitford, in an encouraging tone.

'You like your luncheon too, Mitta.'

'You must not call me Mitta except in a spirit of affection. And it is not often affectionate to tell people they like their food.'

'Here it comes!' said James, throwing his book on the table and himself into a chair.

'I am punctual today,' said Mullet, entering in understanding of the life she interrupted, and viewed with sympathy as inferior to that of the nursery. 'And Hatton says, if Master James has a headache, he may ask Miss Mitford to excuse his lessons this morning.'

James at once rose, selected some biscuits and a book and arranged a table and the sofa for the reception of them and himself. He did not look at Miss Mitford nor she at him. Hatton's word was law in the schoolroom, as Miss Mitford chose to accept it as such, pursuing with it the opposite course to that she took with other people's.

'Miss Isabel, look at your hair,' said Mullet, as if the vigour of the enjoinder rendered it possible.

'Hatton said I was not to touch it myself, because I tear at it.'

'Then you should come upstairs to have it done. I wonder the mistress did not notice it.'

'How do you know she did not?' said Miss Mitford.

'She would have sent her up to have it done,' said Venice, who managed her own with care and competence.

'Perhaps that is why it is shorter than Venice's, because you pull it,' said James, turning a serious eye from the sofa.

'You pull it often enough yourself,' said Isabel.

'I never pull any out,' said James, in defence of his own course, returning to his book.

'Why should we go down to dessert twice a day?' said Venice.

'Just to make the household as odd as possible,' said Isabel.

'You get twice as much dessert,' said Miss Mitford.

'Will you have tea or coffee after your dinner, ma'am?' said Mullet.

'I think coffee is more sustaining, as I don't have dessert.'

Mullet laughed, and the children did so with more abandonment, taking the chance of venting their mirth over Miss Mitford's practice of broaching private stores while they were downstairs. It merely made her meal correspond with theirs, but they thought it a habit of a certain grossness and never alluded to it to her face.

'Shall I tell Cook to send up the things you like?' said Mullet.

'It might be suspected that we had asked,' said Isabel.

James raised his eyes in survey of the situation.

'The little ones are going down before their dinner, so you won't have them,' said Mullet, in encouraging sympathy with intolerance of the creatures to whom her own life was given. 'The nursery dinner is late. And now I must take my tray.'

'I will go up to Hatton about my hair,' said Isabel.

'Don't put off your lessons longer than you must,' said Miss Mitford, in a tone of rejoinder.

'There is only one book,' said Isabel, implying a sacrifice of opportunity to her sister.

'Why don't they do different lessons at the same time?' said James, without moving his eyes.

'We might find it a strain,' said Miss Mitford.

Mullet went to fetch the children from the garden, and Eleanor met her coming up the stairs, with the three of them clinging to her.

'Dear, dear, can't any of you walk alone? Mullet will need to have several pairs of arms and legs.'

'Mullet help him,' said Nevill, with a note of defiance.

'She seems to be helping the others too. I think you must all have a rest this morning.'

'Hatton sit on his little bed,' said Nevill, as he entered the nursery.

'I have not time this morning. Mullet will stay with you for a while.'

'Mother likes us to be alone while we go to sleep,' said Gavin.

'Her standard is too high for Nevill,' said Hatton. 'And I notice it sometimes is for you.'

Honor broke into mirth.

'Don't you mind what she says?' said Gavin, with a note of respect.

'Hatton doesn't mind,' said Nevill, with tenderness and pride.

'The mistress said they were all to rest,' said Mullet.

'Well, that is not beyond us,' said Hatton. 'And there need be no delay.'

Presently Gavin awoke with a cry, and Eleanor came to his bedside. She found him sitting up, in the act of receiving a glass of water from Hatton, his demeanour accepting his situation as serious, and this view of it in others.

'What is it, my boy?'

'I want Honor to wake.'

'Did you have a dream?'

'No.'

'Tell Mother what it is.'

'It is nothing.'

'Is it burglars?' said Honor, suddenly sitting up straight.

'No, Gavin has had a dream and wants to tell you.'

'I don't,' said Gavin, turning away his head.

'What is it?' said his sister, in a rough tone that cleared his face.

'It was a sort of a dream.'

'Were you afraid?'

'No.'

'Will you tell me after dinner?'

'Yes.'

'It was kind of Honor to wake,' said Eleanor.

Gavin did not reply.

'Don't you think it was?'

'She thought it was burglars,' said Gavin, and turned on his side.

'What is wrong with them, Hatton?' said Eleanor.

'Only the journey, madam. They will be themselves tomorrow.'

'I wonder the human race has been so fond of migrations, when the young take so hardly to travelling,' said Eleanor, with her occasional dryness.

Mullet fell into laughter and hastily left the room, as though feeling it familiar to meet an employer's jest with the equal response of mirth. Honor looked at her mother and laughed in her turn, and Gavin surveyed them with a frown.

CHAPTER THREE

ELEANOR went downstairs to the dining-room, where her husband, his parents and his three eldest children were assembled for luncheon.

'Hatton continues to manage the little ones in her own way. I suppose it would do no good to interfere.'

'What is wrong with the method?' said Fulbert, seeming to gather himself together for judgement.

'A good many things that only a mother would see.'

'Then we cannot expect Hatton to be aware of them.'

'Nor the rest of us, Mother dear,' said Luce. 'You must not look for sympathy. I am always thankful that I had the same nurse when I was young. It takes any anxiety for the children simply off me.'

'Hatton will rule the house in the end,' said Eleanor.

'A good many of you seem to be doing that,' said Sir Jesse. 'But if too many cooks spoil the broth, the right number make it very good.'

'It is a real achievement, the way you all work together,' said Fulbert. 'I mean to pay you a serious compliment.'

'You talk as if you were a creature apart,' said Eleanor.

'Yes, you do, Father,' said Luce.

'Have you two lads forgotten your tongues?' said Fulbert.

'I had a hope of it,' said Sir Jesse.

'I don't think I forbade you to speak, Graham,' said Daniel.

'Did you change your room, Luce, my dear?' said Regan.

'Yes, I am having Graham's, Grandma.'

'What is this about changing rooms?' said Eleanor. 'It is the first I have heard of it.'

'Luce wants more light,' said Daniel. 'So we are arranging for Graham to do without it.'

'Well, what use is it to him?' said Sir Jesse, who resented any aspersion on his house. 'To look at himself in the glass? He can give way to his sister there.'

'I was the natural person to consult,' said Eleanor.

'Well, Mother dear, Grandma seemed just as much so,' said Luce. 'Perhaps more, as the house is hers.'

Eleanor was silent, submitting to the place she had accepted, and Regan gave her an almost sympathetic glance.

'The children are on the stairs,' said Daniel. 'They will have their dessert at an odd time today.'

'They had better dispense with it,' said Eleanor.

'That is seldom a happy solution,' said Fulbert. 'Things in the wrong order won't hurt them for once.'

Nevill ran into the room in the manner of a horse, lifting his feet and head in recognizable imitation.

'So you are a horse today,' said his mother.

'A charger, a little charger.'

'Chargers are big,' said Gavin.

'No,' said Nevill, shaking his head in a manner at once equine and negative; ' a little charger.'

'A pony,' suggested Daniel.

'A pony,' agreed Nevill.

'Ponies are always small,' said Regan.

'Always small,' said Nevill, on a contented note.

'Do you want me to go on with the tale?' said Luce.

Nevill trotted to her side and stood with his hand on her knee, and his eyes on her face.

'I don't remember if I like it,' said Gavin.

'It is Nevill's tale,' said Honor.

'But you can all listen,' said Eleanor.

'His tale,' said Nevill, throwing them a look.

'Can you tell me where we left off?' said Luce.

'No,' said Nevill, rapidly moving his feet. 'Don't let Gavin tell you. Luce tell Nevill.'

'Don't you remember yourself?'

'No.'

'And it is your tale,' said Eleanor.

'He doesn't remember,' said Nevill, striking Luce's knee.

'Read us a piece out of the book,' said Gavin.

'Well, get it and find the place,' said Luce. 'We have only a few minutes.'

Honor obeyed with speed and success, and Gavin waited while she did so, and joined her to listen.

'Why do you leave it all to Honor?' said Eleanor, who was not happy in the child whom she singled out for achievement.

Gavin kept his eyes on his sister's face. Nevill turned away and resumed his imitation of a pony, trying to distinguish the movements from those of a horse.

'Well, is no one coming to talk to me?' said Eleanor. 'Why did you all come down?'

Gavin did not allow his attention to be diverted, and Luce read on, as if she would not undertake a thing and not accomplish it.

'I must ring for Hatton to fetch you, if you haven't any reason for being here. Luce can read to you upstairs.'

'She never does,' said Gavin, in a parenthetic tone.

'We can't have your mother left out in the cold.'

Nevill paused in his prancing and glanced at Eleanor; Sir Jesse and Regan remained aloof, claiming no part in the separate family life; Fulbert beckoned to Honor and lifted her to his knee; Gavin did not move his eyes and frowned at the interruptions.

'Now we don't want any fallen faces,' said Eleanor, putting her arm round Nevill, and looking for the change which she described, or rather suggested. 'You will know how to stay another time.'

'Go with Hatton,' said Nevill, in an acquiescent tone.

'We should have had to go soon because of our dinner,' said Honor, in a confident manner from Fulbert's knee.

'Don't you want to go, my boy?' said Eleanor to Gavin.

'I don't mind.'

'Well, run away then.'

Gavin looked at her and sank into tears.

'Honor, is Gavin quite well?'

'Yes, I think so, Mother.'

'Then what is the matter with him?'

Honor met her mother's eyes.

Daniel and Graham picked up Honor and carried her round the room. She put her arms round their necks and laughed and shouted in reaction. Eleanor looked on with an indulgent smile, and Gavin with an expectant one. Nevill beat his hands on his sides and moved from foot to foot; and when his brothers took Gavin in Honor's stead, broke into wails and maintained them until they came to himself, when he repulsed them and stood abandoned to his sense that nothing could wipe out what had taken place. When Eleanor and Luce had expostulated in vain, and Regan explained with some success, he raised his arms and allowed himself to be lifted, leaning back in his brother's arms with an air of convalescence. They tightened their hold and quickened their pace, and he held to their shoulders and accepted this compensation for what he had borne, while Honor watched with bright eyes, and Gavin with a smile of gentle interest.

'Give Gavin one little turn, and then that is enough,' said Eleanor.

Nevill stood with his arm on Regan's knee, and his eyes on his brothers with a watchful expression. Hatton arrived in response to the sounds that had reached her ears.

'Say "Thank you", Gavin dear. You heard Honor say it,' said Eleanor.

Gavin did so.

'And look at Daniel and Graham while you speak.'

Gavin turned his eyes on his brothers, content with fulfilling his obligations separately.

'It was him that ran,' said Nevill, with a sigh.

'I suppose it is still the journey, Hatton,' said Eleanor, with another.

'It was best to cry it out, madam, whatever it was.'

'He cried it out,' said Nevill, in information to Hatton.

'Come and give me a kiss, and then run away,' said Eleanor.

57

Nevill went to her with a trotting step, took Hatton's hand and proceeded in this way towards the door.

'So you are a horse again. Daniel and Graham have been your horses, haven't they?'

'Pony, little pony,' said Nevill, seeming oblivious of his brothers.

'Isn't the little pony going to trot to say good-bye to Father?'

'Only to Grandma,' said Nevill, and trotted past Regan and then through the door.

Honor and Gavin kissed their parents and frolicked from the room, their voices sounding high and continuous until they reached the upper floor.

Regan had witnessed the scene with interest, and Sir Jesse without attention. The latter seldom noticed children, rather because it did not occur to him to do so, than because he disapproved of the practice.

'Their new governess is coming tomorrow,' said Luce. 'I do trust she will be a success.'

'Why doesn't Miss – Miss who teaches the others, teach them?' said Sir Jesse.

'Grandpa, you must know Miss Mitford's name after all these years,' said Luce. 'I expect she knows yours.'

'Why, so do I, my dear. And in that case she does the better, as you say.'

'I don't know who would dare to make the suggestion,' said Eleanor.

'Why, is there any risk?' said Sir Jesse. 'If so, I beg no one will take it. But isn't teaching her business? What she does – what she chooses to do, I should say?'

'I doubt if there is so much choice about it,' said Regan.

'In so far as there is, she exercises it,' said Eleanor. 'Her pupils must be in a certain stage. James had to go to school, because she found him too young.'

'I daresay the girls give her less trouble,' said Sir Jesse. 'If she has the right to choose, let her use it. But wouldn't one woman for the lot cost less?'

'We should have to increase her salary by as much as we are to give the other,' said Regan.

'So the other has not much choice,' said her husband, with amusement and no other feeling. 'Have as many as you like, if it is all for the same expense. I would rather be in a place where I got it all. But as you say, or as Miss Mitford says.'

'Grandma does not shrink from exposing the whole of her mind,' said Graham. 'That is a very rare thing.'

Regan smiled at her grandson before she resumed the subject.

'Miss Mitford would never take a hint,' she said.

'I hardly like to do so myself,' said Daniel.

'She is quite right,' said Luce. 'If we are ashamed of what we ask, there is no reason to help us. And it would be more strain to teach three extra children.'

'I don't think Miss Mitford suffers much in that way,' said Regan. 'She takes great care of herself.'

'There is nothing wrong in that, Grandma.'

'We do find the habit unengaging,' said Fulbert. 'But in Miss Mitford's place I should recommend it.'

Regan gave her son a look of admiration for his freedom from her own failings.

'Isn't the little fellow too young to learn?' said Daniel.

'Why can't you call your brother by his name?' said Eleanor. 'He would not forget yours.'

'We have not had him long enough to get used to him.'

'It is not good for him to be actually kept young,' said Luce.

'He seems all in favour of it,' said Daniel.

'Gavin has the most in him of the three,' said Eleanor.

'You mean you think so, my dear, or perhaps that you hope so,' said Fulbert. 'And he has his own ways, I admit. Or rather he has not any ways, unless that constitutes one. But I put my Honor down as the highest type.'

'Girls are more forward than boys. Gavin has more to come.'

'I am only talking of what is there. I find that the most good to me.'

'You are a partial parent, Mother,' said Luce. 'It is a good thing Hatton is free from the failing, a serious one with children.'

'It was I who chose Hatton.'

'Fortune favoured you, my dear,' said Fulbert.

'My own sense and judgement did so.'

59

'Well, we cannot find a ground for disputing it.'

'You sound as if you would like to do so.'

'Well, I hardly support you, my dear.'

'Isn't that one of them crying?' said Regan.

'It is only Nevill,' said Luce. 'It does not mean much with him. And we can rely on Hatton's ever-listening ear.'

'If you begin on Hatton again, do not rely on mine,' said her mother.

Fulbert and his father laughed, and Eleanor looked rather gratified. She was unusually sensitive to approval or appreciation. The schoolroom children entered the room, in accordance with the custom that allowed or required their presence at dessert. They came to established places at the table. Only the nursery children were expected to stand, and they would presumably continue to do so, as there was no further provision of seats.

'Who came in last?' said Eleanor, almost at once.

'James,' said Daniel. 'He has reached that stage.'

'Then go back and shut the door, my boy. Doors do not shut themselves, do they?'

James was enabled by experience to agree.

'It is a pity they do not,' said Isabel. 'It is absurd not to invent one that does, considering how often the process takes place.'

'Well, you have done a good morning's work,' said Sir Jesse, disposing of this question for his grandchildren, and pushing a dish towards them, before withdrawing his thought.

'Grandpa means you to help yourselves,' said Eleanor, in almost disapproving congratulation.

'They are old enough, Mother,' said Luce.

'If they were not, I should not allow it, my dear. That was a needless speech. James, don't you want any?'

James hesitated to say that the delicacy in question upset him, and helped himself.

'Venice looks well, doesn't she?' said Eleanor, willing for notice of her daughter's looks.

Venice turned her eyes to the wall and struck the ground with her foot.

'What is there on the wall that interests you?' said her mother.

'I am looking at the pictures of Aunt Lucia and Uncle Daniel.'

'You must know them very well,' said Eleanor, forgetting that Regan would be moved to emotion, and Sir Jesse to consequent concern, and averting her eyes as the scene took place.

The portraits of the dead son and daughter were rendered with the simple flattery of mercenary Victorian art, and Regan accepted the improvement not so much because it had come to her to be the truth, as because nothing seemed to her to be too good for the originals. That a portrait of Fulbert had a less honourable place, was due less to its obvious discrepancy with truth, than to the fact that he was not yet dead. Regan carried the loss of her children as she carried her body, always suffering and sustaining it.

'James,' said Eleanor, taking any chance to end the pause, 'you must not put things in your pocket to take upstairs. That is not the way to behave. Take what you want and no more. Grandpa did not mean that.'

'Isn't that the thing that makes him sick?' said Graham.

'Is it, James? Then why did you take it? You must know when you do not want something. What was your reason?'

James had several reasons, a reluctance to appear to fuss about himself, a fear lest allusion to his health should in some way expose his morning's leisure, a purpose of transferring his portion to his sisters, and a hesitation to meet his grandfather's kindness with anything but gratitude. He did not state them, though some were to his credit, but some of his experience, of which there was enough and to spare, welled over into his eyes.

'You are not crying!' said Eleanor, honestly incredulous. 'Crying because you have too many good things! Well, what a thing to do.'

'He has had one thing that is bad for him,' said Graham.

'If good things bring tears, he is better without them,' said Eleanor, giving James a sense that a general impotence did not preclude a mental advantage. 'And I think they had better go to the schoolroom. Perhaps there are fewer there.'

'There are fewer bad ones anyhow,' said Venice, under her breath.

'What did you say, dear?' said Eleanor.

'I said we had not been down here very long.'

'No, you have not, dear child,' said Eleanor, changing her tone. 'But luncheon is dragging on very late. That is why I am asking you to go. Not for any other reason.'

'Why do you state other reasons, if they do not hold good?' said Fulbert.

'Because I am a feeble, querulous mother. So my good children will leave us. I am afraid Grandpa will be getting tired of us all.'

'Door for the girls,' muttered Graham, without moving his eyes.

'What a little gentleman James grows!' said Regan, as this warning took effect.

'He is really a dear, well-behaved little boy,' said Eleanor, as if evidence had been accepted for another conclusion.

'A nice, mannerly lad,' said Sir Jesse.

James lingered at the door, prolonging his only moment of enjoyment, and free from any sense that he was not responsible for his own success.

'If James could purr, he would,' said Daniel, and sent his brother from the room.

'You are up very soon,' said Miss Mitford, raising her eyes from her book.

Her pupils dispersed about the room without replying.

'A good dessert?' said Miss Mitford.

'For Venice and me,' said Isabel. 'That thing that James does not like.'

'And what did James have?'

'Oh, nothing,' said Venice, turning her back before she answered.

'I ended up in favour anyhow,' said James, throwing himself on the sofa and taking up his book.

'It is no good to settle down,' said Miss Mitford, speaking as though she must reduce him to hopelessness. 'We have to go for our walk.'

'It is a completely fine day,' said Isabel, in the same tone.

James did not move his eyes, for the reason that he was not yet obliged to.

Eleanor appeared at the door.

'Isabel, don't you remember anything about this afternoon?'

'No, Mother.'

'Surely you will, if you think.'

'You were going out with your father,' said Miss Mitford, turning away her head.

'Oh, I was going out with Father!' said Isabel, in glad recollection. 'Of course I was. He promised to take me for a walk. I will go and get ready.'

'It was a strange thing to forget, when he has to leave us so soon.'

'Oh, I had not really forgotten,' said Isabel, on her way to the door, affording her mother satisfaction on her mental process, though no impression of it. 'I will be ready in a few minutes.'

'Would Venice like to go too?' said Eleanor, speaking as if this would be almost too much at her daughter's stage.

'It would be nice for us both to go,' said Venice, as though this would be the normal arrangement.

'Oh, would it?' said Eleanor, in half-reproving sympathy, as her daughter left the room.

James remained upon the sofa, hesitating to draw attention to his recumbent position by relinquishing it.

'And James? What about him?' said Eleanor, using an almost arch manner, as she made this unparalleled suggestion.

'Yes,' said James, sitting up straight, and using the movement to hide his book under the cushion. 'All three of us.'

'Well, run away then. Don't keep Father waiting. What is that book?'

James took it up and surveyed it as if for the first time; and indeed it presented a different aspect to him, seen under his mother's eyes.

'Is it a book to be about in a schoolroom?' said Eleanor, in a rapid, even tone to Miss Mitford, handing the book to her without seeming to look at it.

'I can keep it in my own room,' said Miss Mitford, in her ordinary manner. 'If there is any harm in it, you will not mind it for me.'

'Either schoolroom stories or instructive books are best. But you weren't reading it, were you, James?'

'Oh, no,' said James, with so much lightness that he hardly seemed to grasp the idea.

'You were reading it, my boy,' said Eleanor, in a deeper tone, taking a step towards him. 'There is your penknife in it, keeping the place.'

James took up the knife, propped it against the book, and moved a piece of cardboard up and down against the blade, as if the arrangement were necessary to his purpose.

'Oh, that is what you are doing,' said Eleanor, without more idea than James of what this was. 'But you will spoil books if you do that. Did Miss Mitford know you were doing it?'

'No,' said James, with an habitual movement of nervous guilt that came in well.

'Give it back to her, and go and get ready to go out with Father. Ah, that sends you off like an arrow from the bow.'

Eleanor smiled after her son, whose movement did suggest this simile, and turned to the governess.

'He is developing better now, isn't he, Miss Mitford?'

'Yes, he is, in his own way,' said Miss Mitford, meaning what she said.

'It is a pity he is not better fitted for school,' said Eleanor, unaware that some of her son's tendencies stood him in good stead there. 'I wish I understood children as you do. It would be such a help to me.'

Miss Mitford smiled in an absent manner, thinking of the shocks that Eleanor would sustain if this could be the case, and wondering if she had forgotten her own childhood or had an abnormal one. Eleanor saw her children's lives as so much fuller and less constrained than her own, that her own early temptations could have no place in them.

'Well, I must go down to my husband. I seem to spend my life in moving from one department of my family to another,' she said, smiling at Miss Mitford with a suggestion of the difference between their lots. 'I hope you will do as you like this afternoon, Miss Mitford.'

Miss Mitford did not reassure her, though she might have done so. She settled herself with a book which she did not leave in the way of her pupils, and a box of sweets which she dealt with in the same manner. She was a fairly satisfied person, with a knowledge of books which was held to be natural in her life, and a knowledge of people which would have been held to be impossible, and was really inevitable. She had a carelessness of opinion which protected her against the usual view of her life, and had pity rather than envy of Eleanor, whom she saw as a less contented being. Her influence over her pupils was not much the worse, that she accepted life as it was, and allowed them to see it. She would not speak to James of his duplicity, but he would derive some discomfort from her silence.

Eleanor went to the study she shared with her husband, and waited for the latter to join her. He was still at the luncheon table, whence Regan had departed and her grandsons been dismissed. An allowance of talk without boys or women was Sir Jesse's acknowledged right, and was daily accorded him. When Fulbert left his father for his wife, he was reminded of his promise to his daughter and informed of the extension of the scheme. He took his stand in the doorway, with his watch in his hand, possibly having faith in the theory that the memory is stronger in youth.

'They should not keep their father waiting,' said Eleanor, moving to the bell. 'They must not take your attention as a matter of course. Why should you think about them?'

Fulbert could produce no reason why he should give a thought to his offspring, and the summons brought them running downstairs in a manner that suggested that this was not a mutual attitude.

'Why are you so late?' said Eleanor. 'I should have thought you would be anxious to start, when you were to go out with Father.'

'We have been ready for some time,' said Venice. 'We did not know when we were to come down.'

'Oh, that is what it was. Well, another time it will be better to be in the hall. Then there will be no question about your being ready and waiting.'

The capacity for waiting assumed in the children, perhaps without much attention to heredity, was proved for some minutes longer; and then the party set off, with the girls on their father's arms, and James capering about them in a manner that baulked their progress and brought him steady reproof, but was the only means by which he could join the talk.

'Well, so you are glad to be rid of your father,' said Fulbert.

'No,' said Venice, with the strong protest suggested.

'No,' said Isabel, in a weaker tone and with the tears filling her eyes. She depended on her father and dreaded the house without him.

'No,' said James, in a tone that seemed an echo of the others.

'We shall write to each other, you and I,' said Fulbert, pressing Isabel's arm. 'Every week a letter will come for you, and nobody else shall read it.'

Isabel appeared as gratified as if this were a possible prospect, and her sister looked baffled by the comparative failure of her own more normal effort.

'You shall share the letter,' said Fulbert, with no feeling that his first promise was affected. 'I shall write a letter to my two middle girls, and it shall be just for themselves. Unless they like to show it to Mother.'

James curveted in the consciousness evoked by being left out of the attention, which indeed was becoming general.

'It shall be for my boy too,' promised Fulbert, with a sense purely of further magnanimity. 'My schoolroom party shall have their own letter, and show it to everyone else at their own discretion.'

A tendency to frolic indicated the view of this prospect.

'Don't be always under my boots, my boy,' said Fulbert, throwing up his feet to render this position untenable, and also slightly painful.

'What is it like in South America?' said Venice.

'Now you are putting the cart before the horse. This is the wrong occasion for that question. I like to give you that sort of information at first hand.'

'Grandpa knows,' said James. 'He said that the trees and flowers were quite different.'

'It can hardly be as it was when he was there,' said Fulbert, not surrendering the position of coming authority, though the changes might hardly extend to the vegetation. 'You must wait for my return.'

'Don't walk in front of me, James,' said Venice, in an amiable tone.

'Nor of me,' said Isabel, speaking with more sharpness.

'Keep to the side, my boy,' said Fulbert. 'What exactly do you want to know? Tell me and I will remember.'

James was obliged to return to his place to make this clear, and Fulbert paused and listened with patience, before he allowed the party to proceed.

'What does Isabel want to hear about South America?' he said, in a gentle tone. 'That the whole continent is at the bottom of the sea?'

'Yes,' said Isabel, quickening her pace.

Fulbert bent and whispered in her ear, and Venice suffered from her failure to produce feelings on the unknown continent on this scale.

'Do countries have the sea underneath them?' said James. 'Or does the land go right through?'

'It is the sea above them that Isabel wants,' said his father.

'But do they really, I mean?'

'People's thoughts and feelings are just as real, my boy.'

'Yes,' said James, in a lighter tone.

'Now we will all race to that tree and back,' said Fulbert, deciding that interest and entertainment should remain in his children's memory. 'Take your stand and start fair. We must all run right round it.'

The children braced themselves for the effort, James in a serious spirit, Venice in a semi-serious one, and Isabel with an appearance of sprightly interest which she could hardly feel, as she was of weaker build than the others, and though unconcerned for success in the contest, counted the cost of her father's sympathy.

'Well done, Venice!' said Fulbert, as he reached the goal, second to his daughter and a tie with his son, but prevented from yielding a place to his other daughter by the transparence of the manoeuvre. 'Well done, my boy. And so my Isabel is last, and tired into the bargain.'

'I am a poor athlete, Father.'

'Are you, my dear?' said Fulbert, putting his cheek against hers. 'Your strength has gone into other things, Better ones for your father.'

Venice again had a feeling that she met the more ordinary kinds of success. It was hardly weakened when Fulbert gave a shilling to each of them, in reward for their respective achievements. When the walk was over, it was found that it had occupied an hour. Fulbert and James would have guessed it an hour and a half, Venice somewhat longer, and Isabel had lost all count of time. Eleanor came into the hall to receive them.

'Why, Father looks quite tired, and so do you, Isabel. He has some reason, with the weight of two of you on him, but you seem to tire very easily.' Eleanor was at once moved and vexed by sign of weakness in her children; it seemed to threaten her possession of them. 'Venice looks as fresh as when she started. I think Isabel is depressed by the thought of your going, Fulbert.'

Isabel turned at once to the staircase; Venice followed in a rather disheartened manner; and James gave a jump and looked up at his mother.

'We had a race, and Venice won, and I was second, and Father gave us all a shilling.'

'That was a treat, wasn't it? But all this running and jumping for a little boy who cannot go to school! What does that mean, do you think? And now you had better all be off to the schoolroom. We don't want tears and tiredness on Father's last days.'

The children, uncertain of their mother's exact leanings, went upstairs, and Fulbert entered his study and threw himself into a chair.

'You know, Eleanor, or rather I suppose you do not, that you treat your children as if they were men and women.' Fulbert had a right to make this criticism, as he did not fall into the error.

'I am simply myself with them. It is best to be natural with children.'

'You overdo it, my dear. You prevent them from being the same. And each child needs a separate touch and a separate understanding.'

'I doubt the wisdom of making any sort of difference.'

'It needs to be done in a certain way,' said Fulbert, feeling that there was an example before his wife.

Eleanor gave a little laugh.

'I wonder you like to leave them with their feeble mother.'

'You are not without support, my dear.'

'I feel I could not leave them for any reason.'

'It is a good thing I can do so for the right ones. I am going for their sakes. I am sure you will give yourself to them. I can only put you in my place.'

'There is no one whom I could leave in mine,' said Eleanor, believing what she said. 'No one else would have the nine of them always in her thoughts. I ought to be saying good night to the three youngest at the moment.'

'That is a duty I shall be pleased to share with you. And I do not pity you for being left with it.'

They mounted to the nursery and found its occupants nearing the end of their day.

'You will soon be in your little bed,' said Eleanor to Nevill.

'By Hatton.'

'Yes, unless you would like to begin to share a room with Gavin.'

'By Hatton,' said her son, looking puzzled and uninterested.

'Yes, for a little while you can stay with her.'

'All night. Stay with Hatton all night.'

'How soon are you going away?' said Gavin, to his father.

'In about seven days.'

'That is a week,' said Honor.

'All night, all night,' said Nevill, beating his hand on his mother's knee.

'Yes, yes, all night. Honor, talk nicely to Father about his going. Tell him how you will miss him.'

Honor began to cry; Fulbert put his arm about her; Nevill gave her a look of respectful concern; Gavin surveyed her with a frown.

'There, dry your eyes and don't lean against Father,' said Eleanor. 'He is as tired as you are, at the end of the day. She was hiding her feelings, poor child.'

'She didn't hide them,' said Gavin.

'She tried to; she did not want to upset Father. You mind about his going too, don't you?'

'If we say we mind, he knows,' said Gavin, who was successfully hiding his own jealousy of his sister's interest.

'Father will be gone away. Gallop-a-trot,' said Nevill, illustrating this idea of progress.

'Nevill doesn't know much,' said Gavin.

'Well, he is only three,' said Eleanor. 'Neither did you at that age.'

'Father come back soon,' said Nevill, showing his grasp of the situation.

'I think I knew more,' said Gavin.

'We shall expect good reports of your lessons, if you talk like that.'

'It is boys at school who have reports,' said Gavin, mindful of James's experience.

'Mother meant a verbal report,' said Honor, causing her parents to smile.

'You will soon be able to go to school,' said Eleanor, to her son. 'You won't always have a governess.'

'James sometimes has Miss Mitford. I could always have her.'

'Do you mean you want to learn with Honor?'

'No,' said Gavin, true to his principle that real feeling should be hidden.

'Good night, Mother,' said Nevill, approaching Eleanor with small, quick steps.

'Good night, my little boy. So you are a horse again.'

'Puff, puff, puff,' said Nevill, in correction of her idea.

'He has passed to the age of machinery,' said Fulbert.

'Is that age three?' said Gavin.

'Father means to a different date,' said Honor.

'The boy may be right that he can be educated at home,' said Fulbert.

Eleanor made a mute sign against such reference to Honor, which she believed to be lost upon her daughter, though the point at issue was the latter's intelligence.

'I don't feel I have a great deal in common with Mother,' said Honor, as the door closed upon her parents.

Mullet looked at her in reproof and respect.

'In common?' said Gavin.

'You have had enough education for tonight. There must be something left for the governess to teach you,' said Hatton, producing mirth in Mullet. 'Now I am taking Nevill to bed. You must not stay up too long.'

'Will you tell us about when you were a child, while you do Honor's hair?' said Gavin to Mullet.

'Yes, I will give you the last chapter of my childhood,' said Mullet, entering on an evidently accustomed and congenial task, with her eyes and hands on Honor's head. 'For I don't think I was ever a real child after that. You know we lived in a house something like this; a little smaller and more compact perhaps, but much on the same line. And I was once left behind with the servants when my father was abroad. Not with a grandpa and a grandma and a mother; just with servants, just with the household staff. And I found myself alone in the schoolroom, with all the servants downstairs. I was often by myself for hours, as I had no equal in the house, and I preferred my own company to that of inferiors. Well, there I was sitting, in my shabby, velvet dress, swinging my feet in their shabby, velvet shoes; my things were good when they came, but I was really rather neglected; and there came a ring at the bell, and my father was in the house. "And what is this?" he said, when he had hastened to my place of refuge. "How comes it that I find my daughter alone and unattended?" The servants had come running up when they heard his ring, when his peremptory ring echoed through the house. "Here is my daughter, my heiress, left to languish in solitude! In quarters more befitting a dog," he went on, looking round the rather battered schoolroom, and saying almost more than he meant in the strength of his feelings. "Cast aside like a piece of flotsam and jetsam," he continued, clenching his teeth and his hands in a way he had. "When I left her, as I thought, to retainers faithful to the charge of my motherless child. Enough," he said. "No longer will I depend on those whose hearts do not beat with the spirit of trusty service. People with the souls of menials," he went on, lifting his arm with one of his rare gestures, "away from the walls which will shelter my child while there is breath within me." And there he stood with bent head, waiting for the servants to pass, almost bowing to them in the way a gentleman would, feeling the wrench of parting with people who had served him all his life.' Mullet's voice changed and became open and matter-of-fact. 'And there we both were, left alone in that great house, with no one to look after us, and very little idea of looking after ourselves. It was a good thing in a way, as the crash had to come, and I think Father felt it less than he would have in cold blood. He was a man whose hot blood was often a help to him.' Mullet gave a sigh and moved her brows. 'But I think his death was really caused by our fall from our rightful place.'

'So then you were left an orphan,' said Gavin.

'Yes, then came the change which split my life into halves.'

'Would your father have liked you to be a nurse?'

'Well, in one sense he had the gentleman's respect for useful work. In another it would have broken his heart,' said Mullet, hardly taking an exaggerated view, considering her parent's re-action to milder vicissitudes.

'What happened to the house?' said Honor.

'It was sold to pay debts. My father was in debt, as a man in his place would be.'

'He really ought not to have kept all those servants.'

'Well, no, he ought not. But he could hardly change from the way his family had always lived.'

'Were they all paid?'

'If a farthing to a dependent had been owing, Miss Honor, I could never have held up my head,' said Mullet, straightening her neck to render further words unnecessary.

'You told us you had a maid of your own. But you didn't have one then.'

'My last nurse was on the way to a maid. But I was quite without one on that day when my father came home; absolutely without,' said Mullet, with evident attention to accuracy. 'I was entirely at the mercy of all those servants downstairs.'

'Is Grandpa in debt?' said Gavin.

'Now if you talk about what I tell you, I shall only tell you the tales I tell to Nevill.'

'You ought to say Master Nevill.'

'Well, so I ought in these days. But the old days drag me back when I talk about them. Now remember these things are between ourselves.'

'Wouldn't people believe you?' said Honor.

'I daresay they would not,' said Mullet, with a little laugh at human incredulity.

'I don't think Mother would.'

'Sometimes I can hardly believe myself in my own early life,' said Mullet, fastening Honor's hair with a rapid skill acquired in a later one, and using a sincere note that was justified.

'There are Daniel and Graham on the stairs,' said Gavin.

'Your big brothers have come to see you,' said Mullet, in a rather severe tone. 'And you can put things like stories out of your head.'

This was hardly the purpose of the newcomers, who had found their study occupied by Luce and a friend, and hoped to find the nursery free at this hour of its occupants.

'You are going to bed, I suppose?' said Daniel.

'When we do go,' said Gavin.

'Well, that is now,' said Daniel, supplanting him in his chair.

Gavin recovered it; his brother displaced him and he returned; Graham and Honor enacted the same scene; the struggle resulted in screams and mirth, and in the course of it Honor knocked her head and wept with an abandonment proportionate to her excited mood. Hatton arrived with her fingers to her mouth, and Nevill under her arm, and made warning movements towards the floors beneath. Gavin was checked in a disposition to maintain the sport in spite of the consequences to his sister, and Nevill from under Hatton's arm made a hushing sound and raised his finger with the appropriate gesture.

Hatton became oblivious of her late anxiety, and directed Mullet's attention to Honor.

'If you put on a handkerchief soaked in water, there won't be much of a bruise in the morning.'

'Then Mother won't know, will she?' said Nevill, in a comforting tone.

'Why do you hold that great child?' said Honor, seeking to counteract the impression she had given.

'Hatton carry him,' said Nevill.

'Honor will have a pigeon's egg on her head tomorrow,' said Daniel.

'Not pigeon's egg tomorrow,' said Nevill, in a troubled tone. 'A nice handkerchief wet with water.'

'We will come and rock you to sleep,' said Graham.

'Hatton will sit on his little bed,' said Nevill, in a reassuring manner.

'Be a pony and trot away to it.'

Nevill agitated his limbs in rebellion against his bondage, and on being set down, trotted round the room and out of it, accepting the opening of the door as necessary and natural.

'Will Honor have a headache in bed?' said Gavin to Mullet.

'If she does, you must come and fetch me.'

'She can fetch you herself, when she has only knocked her head.'

'The nights are not cold yet.'

'I like cold; I like even ice.'

'He is afraid of the dark,' said Honor, stooping to gather her belongings. 'He is almost as afraid as I am. But my head doesn't hurt any more; I can dispense with this handkerchief.'

'You can dispense with it,' said Gavin, with more than one kind of admiration.

'Open the door for me. Because I am carrying so much,' said Honor, indicating that she did not require it on other grounds.

The pair departed without taking leave of their brothers, who neither noticed nor offered to remedy the omission. They were succeeded by the schoolroom party, who entered the room without any sign of interest as if the change meant nothing to them. They were marshalled by Luce, with the air of a benevolent despot.

'Can we be of any use to you?' said Daniel.

'Luce said the schoolroom must be aired before supper,' said Venice.

James went to a chair and resumed his book.

'Is Miss Mitford proof against chill?' said Graham.

'She has gone to her room,' said Isabel.

'I have been wondering if Graham ought to be handed back to her,' said Daniel.

'Well, she likes her pupils to be of advanced age,' said Graham.

Venice laughed.

'Now why is it amusing?' said Luce, leaning back and locking her hands round her knees. 'Miss Mitford is older and wiser than Graham. Why should he not learn from her?'

'She is a woman,' said Venice.

'But knowledge is no more valuable, coming from a man.'

'It is held to be,' said Isabel. 'Men are more expensive than women.'

'Isn't Mitta expensive?' said Venice, surprised.

'She still seems to me in her own way a person born to command,' said Luce.

'Few of us can so far fulfil our destiny,' said Graham.

'I wonder if anyone is born to obey,' said Isabel. 'That may be why people command rather badly, that they have no suitable material to work on.'

'I wonder if we are a commanding family,' said Luce.

'I expect Isabel is right that most families are,' said Daniel.

Venice came up as if wishing to join the talk, but at a loss for a contribution.

'So James has learned to read,' said Graham.

'You are less forward for your age,' said Daniel.

'Mitta forgot to put that book away,' said Venice.

'Isn't James supposed to read it?' said Luce. 'Let me see it, James.'

James passed the book to his sister with disarming obedience.

'An instance of the normal reluctance to obey,' she said, raising her brows and returning the book.

Miss Mitford opened the door.

'I have had to come up for you,' she said.

'True, Mitta,' said Daniel.

'Supper has been brought in.'

'What is it?' said Venice, while Isabel turned in milder interest.

75

'Something made with eggs,' said Miss Mitford, on a plaintive note.

'It seems that Mitta is old enough to dine downstairs,' said Graham, as the door closed, or he thought it did.

'The bread of dependence is generally eaten upstairs,' said Miss Mitford.

'So your speech could not wait for a moment,' said Daniel.

'It is a pity it did not, Graham,' said Luce.

'It is not so long since we were Mitta's pupils,' said Graham.

'Does that make it better to see you turning out so awkwardly?' said his brother.

'It may have prepared her for it.'

'And you have been other people's pupil since.'

'But no one ever taught me as much as dear old Mitta,' said Graham, in a tone of quotation.

'It will soon be recognized that you have not made suitable progress since.'

'Oh, you and your coming school success!'

'Now why do people despise that kind of achievement?' said Luce, again with her hands about her knees. 'Why belittle any kind of gift?'

'We certainly never have any other kind,' said Graham, as if he were speaking to himself. 'People who have that sort of success never do anything in after life, but neither do the other people. No one does anything in after life. I see that my only chance has been missed.'

'Be quiet for a moment, boys,' said Luce, raising her hand. 'I want to listen to the wheels of the house going round. Yes, Mother is going into the schoolroom to say good night. That means that the dinner gong will soon sound.'

'And Graham will be indulging his vice,' said Daniel. 'Can nothing at all be done?'

Eleanor had entered the room below.

'Well, my dears, have you had a happy day?'

'It has been much as usual,' said Isabel.

'Well, that is happy, isn't it? Could you have any more done for you? And you have been out with Father. Surely that prevents the day from being ordinary.'

'Yes, of course it does.'

'And has James had a good day at school?'

'Yes,' said James. 'No, I have not been to school.'

'Then weren't you to have tea in the nursery and go early to bed?'

'Oh, yes,' said James, in a tone of sudden recollection.

'You must not forget what we arrange, my boy. Your eyes look tired. What have you been doing?'

'Nothing,' said James, in an almost wondering manner.

Eleanor left the subject. Her son's recent practice of reading had escaped her. She thought of him as a child, to whom a book was a task, a thing he had been long enough for her to form the habit.

'You had better run upstairs, as you don't seem to have much appetite. Are you too tired to eat? Why, you are sitting on a book.'

'Oh, that chair always seems lower than the others.'

'There are plenty of other chairs. Why choose one so low that you have to put something on it? And surely a cushion would be more comfortable than a book.'

James looked as if this were a new idea.

'What things boys do! Now kiss me and be off to bed.'

James embraced his mother with zest, and ran from the room with the lightness of one with no interest behind.

'He is a dear little boy,' said Eleanor, in the tone of voicing a recent conclusion, which marked her approval of James. 'Did not anyone – did not either of you girls remember that he was to go to bed?'

'We all four forgot,' said Miss Mitford. 'That seems to show it was not an easy thing to remember.'

Eleanor smiled only to the extent required.

'He is young to remember everything for himself, with several people – with two sisters older than he is, in the room.'

'I am older than he is too,' said Miss Mitford.

'This is a thing that only concerned himself,' said Isabel.

'My dear, the little boy's health is a matter of equal concern to everyone. I am sure Miss Mitford agrees with me.'

'Not that it is of equal concern,' said Miss Mitford.

'So you will remember another time, my dear,' said Eleanor, not looking at the governess. 'Come now and say good night, and then have a happy hour before you go to bed.'

'What is to make our happiness?' said Isabel. 'I wish Mother had told us.'

'She could have done so,' said Miss Mitford.

'I don't wish she had told us anything more,' said Venice.

'There are no books I have not read,' said Isabel.

'You must fall back on your old, tried favourites,' said Miss Mitford. 'There is no pleasure equal to it.'

'You don't think so yourself. You know you would rather have new ones. You have them from the library every week.'

'Yes. One of my few extravagances.'

'One of her two extravagances,' murmured Venice.

'Mother says she wonders you have time to read them all,' said Isabel.

'Does she?' said Miss Mitford, gently raising her eyes. 'I never forget the claims of my own life.'

'You would not like to be a child again.'

'No, not at all.'

'I would rather be a woman, even if I had to be –'

'You will be able to be one, without being a governess,' said Miss Mitford, in an encouraging tone, beginning to cut the leaves of a volume that required it.

'Didn't you want to be a governess?'

'Why is it said that people judge other people by themselves? It is the last thing they do.'

Isabel was silent and Venice drew near to listen.

'Of course I am different,' said Miss Mitford, keeping her lips steady.

'I meant there were other things you might have been,' said Isabel.

'I do not see what they were.'

'I should think there are worse things.'

'Yes, so should I, but I believe it is not generally thought.'

'What would you have liked to be?' said Venice.

'What I am, with enough money to live on.'

There was silence.

'Just my plain, odd self,' said Miss Mitford.

'You would not have liked to be married?'

'No, I never wanted a full, normal life.'

'I don't think I do,' said Isabel. 'Do you, Venice?'

'I don't know; I am not sure.'

'You would pay the price of full success,' said Miss Mitford, in a tone of understanding.

'I don't see why spinsters have any less success,' said Isabel.

'Well, they have no proof that they have been sought,' said Miss Mitford.

'Have you ever been sought?' said Venice, in a tone that recalled Honor's when she asked Hatton her age.

'You must not probe the secrets of a woman's heart,' said Miss Mitford, putting down the knife and taking up the book.

The door opened and James entered in his dressing-gown, and leaving the door ajar to indicate a transitory errand, began to collect his possessions. He picked up his book, put it under his chin and piled other objects upon it, and using it in this way, went from the room.

'He will think about it more, if he does not finish it,' said Miss Mitford. 'It is better to fulfil the spirit than the letter of your mother's wish.'

'James is fortunate in getting the first,' said Isabel. 'There is nothing in the book that I did not know.'

'James will not understand it,' said Venice.

'People do understand things when they read them for the first time,' said Miss Mitford.

'Yes,' said Venice, who had been struck by this herself.

'In a year I shall read what I like,' said Isabel. 'When we are sixteen, we can choose from the library.'

'You will browse on the wholesome pastures of English literature,' said Miss Mitford. 'Browse is the wrong word. But it is right to tell us they are wholesome.'

'Well, they are,' said Isabel.

'Yes, that is why it is well to know.'

'I wonder if Mother knows,' said Venice, laughing. 'I hope she will not go up to see if James is all right.'

Miss Mitford raised her eyes.

'Won't he think of it himself?' said Isabel, meaning that there were precautionary measures.

'You are as afraid of Mother as we are, Mitta,' said Venice.

'Not quite. She has no affection for me, and that puts me outside her power. But I am afraid of her, of course. I am a sensitive, shrinking creature at heart.'

'Would you mind if she – ?'

'Dismissed me? Yes. This is to be my last post. I shall retire when Honor grows up.'

'What will you do then?' said Isabel.

'I can live with my relations, if I pay them.'

'But you don't like being with them. You are always glad to come back.'

'And yet I think I shall enjoy living with them. What an odd incalculable person I am!'

'You ought not to have to pay relations.'

'Well, the English have no family feelings. That is, none of the kind you mean. They have them, and one of them is that relations must cause no expense.'

'Perhaps they are poor,' said Venice.

'Not as poor as you think, considering that I am a governess.'

'Perhaps they are not near relations.'

'Yes, they are. It is near relations who have family feelings.'

'You might as well live with friends,' said Venice.

'Well, there is the tie of blood.'

'What difference does that make, if people forget it?'

'They know other people remember it. That is another family feeling.'

'I shall not let Isabel work, when I am married. She will always live with me.'

'I may be married myself,' said Isabel. 'I am not quite sure that I shall not.'

'You will have enough money to pay your sister, without working,' said Miss Mitford.

'I should not want her to pay,' said Venice.

'People with families often need money the most,' said Isabel. 'You might be dependent on my contribution to the house.'

'That is another set of family feelings,' said Miss Mitford.

There was silence.

'We know things we should not know, if we had not had you, Mitta,' said Isabel.

'That is the purpose of my being with you.'

'I meant things apart from lessons.'

'Well, you know them sooner,' said Miss Mitford.

CHAPTER FOUR

'WE have not tidied the nursery,' said Honor, in a nonchalant tone to the new governess. 'Hatton told us to do it, but we took no notice.'

'Then you had better do it now. The room is not in a suitable state for lessons.'

The pupils exchanged a glance over this unforeseen attitude.

'Why don't you do it?' said Gavin, in a just audible tone.

'I did not make the room untidy.'

Honor kicked some toys towards a cupboard, and Gavin idly seconded her. Both had an air of putting no value on the objects that had engaged them.

'Why were you playing with the toys, if you do not care about them?' said Miss Pilbeam.

'We didn't say we didn't,' said Gavin.

'We have nothing else to play with,' said Honor.

'Will she give us some more?' said Gavin, with a nudge to his sister.

'I am here to help you to work, not to play. Why do you use your feet instead of your hands?'

Miss Pilbeam was a large, pale woman of twenty-seven, with rather solid features, small, honest eyes, large, white hands, a sober, reliable expression, and a smile that seemed a deliberate adaptation of her face. Her qualification for teaching was her being presumed to know more than young children, and she was required to produce no others.

'That will do for a summary clearance,' said Honor, drawing Miss Pilbeam's eyes.

'Yes, it will do,' said Gavin.

'Now come and show me if you can use your hands as well,' said Miss Pilbeam, putting a smile on her features and some copy-books on the table.

'We don't begin with writing,' said Honor.

'What do you usually do first?'

'Spelling or history or French or sums. That is all we learn, except a little Latin,' said Honor, in an easy tone that forestalled a possibly slight opinion of these studies.

'Well, we will begin with writing today.'

'Why should it be different?' said Gavin.

'Because I wish it to be.'

'Is that a reason?'

'You will have to learn that it is.'

Honor thrust her pen into the ink so sharply that it spluttered.

'The poor, old cloth!' she said, indicating another slight opinion.

'It is a pretty cloth. It is a pity you have made it so dirty.'

Honor took up a corner of it and wiped her pen, in further suggestion of her attitude.

'It is really to protect the table,' she said.

'Well, it must save it a good deal,' said Miss Pilbeam.

Honor laughed.

'Haven't you a pen-wiper?' said the governess.

'No.'

'A thing to wipe pens?' said Gavin.

'Of course,' said his sister.

'I will make you one,' said Miss Pilbeam.

'Oh, you don't have to buy them,' said Gavin.

'They have them in shops, but I can make you one quite well.'

'Why don't you buy one?' said Gavin in a rough tone.

'Because it is not necessary.'

'We always buy things,' said Honor.

'I will teach you how to make some.'

'What will you teach us to make?'

'Pen wipers and needle-cases and blotters and several other things.'

'Is she supposed to teach us that?' said Gavin, aside to his sister.

'I am not obliged to,' said Miss Pilbeam, 'but perhaps you would like to learn.'

'I don't want to learn things I don't have to,' said Honor.

'Would she be allowed to teach us them in lesson-time?' said Gavin, in another aside.

'I should not let you do it then,' said Miss Pilbeam making the necessary adjustment. 'We will remember at some other time.'

'Do you know how to make a bow and arrow?'

'Yes, I can teach you that.'

'I only asked if you knew.'

'A bow and arrows,' said Honor.

'Would you like to make them too?' said Miss Pilbeam.

'Yes, I think I should.'

'Then we will make some one day after lessons.'

'Don't you go home then?' said Gavin.

'Yes, as a rule. But sometimes I can stay with you for a little while.'

'Do you have to?'

'No, but sometimes you might like me to.'

Honor and Gavin looked at each other, and broke into laughter at the assumption of welcome.

'You can go on with your writing now. We shall not talk so much another day.'

'It is you who are talking,' said Gavin.

'Well, I must stop now.'

'Are you going to stay today?'

'No. I must go home this morning. My father wants to see me.'

'Oh, has she got a home?' said Gavin, to his sister, turning his thumb towards Miss Pilbeam.

'Yes,' said the latter, smiling. 'Where should I live, if I had not?'

'You might live in the streets.'

'Do you know many people who do that?'

'No, but we don't really know you.'

'Do you have to do what your father tells you?' said Honor.

'I like to when I can. So do you, I suppose.'

'Why does he want to see you?'

'He will like to know how I have got on.'

'With us, do you mean?' said Honor, surprised at this question's having any interest outside.

'Yes, and that reminds me that we are not progressing very fast. Let me see your copies.'

Honor slapped her book down in front of Miss Pilbeam.

'It is not very good, and you have smudged it.'

'It is as good as I care to do it,' said Honor, leaning back.

'Haven't you got to see mine?' said Gavin, thrusting it forward.

'Yes, I want to see yours too. This is not good either. I think you can both do better.'

'We might with an effort,' said Honor.

'Then you must make the effort in future. Now we will go on to history.'

'Do you want ordinary string for a bow and arrow?' said Gavin.

'No, a special kind. We might have to buy that. How much pocket money do you have?'

'Oh, about threepence a week,' said Honor, casting a vagueness over the insignificance of the sum.

'That is what we have,' said her brother.

'You can do a good deal with threepence a week,' said Miss Pilbeam.

'Did you have as much when you were a child?' said Gavin.

'Yes, that is what I used to have.'

'Could your father afford to give it to you?'

'Yes he used to manage that.'

'Then why do you have to be a governess?'

'Well, I want more than that now.'

'How much do you have?' said Honor, with her eyes and her hands engaged with her pen, and her voice sounding as if it barely detached itself.

'You know you should not ask that question.'

'You asked us how much we had.'

'That is quite different. Get out your history books.'

'We only have one book. Nevill will have to share it too.'

'Is that your little brother? He looks such a dear little boy.'

'He isn't,' said Gavin. 'He keeps doing the same thing.'

'Well, I shall judge for myself. Now I will read you a chapter and ask you questions afterwards.'

Honor rose and threw herself on the sofa.

'You must not sit there, Honor. Come back to your place.'

'I always do when I am being read to.'

'This is not a story book. Sit up and pay attention.'

'Is reading teaching?' said Gavin.

'Yes, when I am going to ask you questions. It is all a part of our work.'

'But we shall be telling you; not you us.'

'I hope that is how it will be.'

'Is teaching work?' said Honor.

'Yes, and learning too, when they are both done as they should be.'

'Will her teaching be done like that?' said Gavin, to his sister.

'I hope it will be; I shall do my best,' said Miss Pilbeam, choosing to use a simple, sincere tone, as she sometimes chose to wear a smile. 'Now will both of you listen?'

Miss Pilbeam read, while her pupils occupied themselves with the only thing in front of them, the tablecloth. Gavin plaiting the fringe, and Honor drawing out threads and weaving a string. When Eleanor entered, Miss Pilbeam was the only one who continued her employment, and she pursued it as if unaware of interruption, until the visitor spoke.

'Well, how do you find the new little pupils, Miss Pilbeam?'

Miss Pilbeam raised steady eyes.

'I hardly know what to expect of them yet.'

'What lesson are you doing?'

'We are beginning history.'

'They have done a good deal of that, I think.'

'I shall soon find out what stage they are in.'

'She has to read it out of the book herself,' muttered Gavin.

'What did you say, dear?' said Eleanor. 'What did he say, Honor?'

'He said Miss Pilbeam was reading from the book. We are to answer questions afterwards.'

Miss Pilbeam glanced from one of her pupils to the other, without raising her eyes. She was perhaps the first to begin to make progress.

'That is a good way of using the book,' said Eleanor. 'I will come in another day to hear how they acquit themselves. How is your father, Miss Pilbeam? He must miss your mother very much.'

'Yes, he does. He is in better spirits, but he is very dependent upon me.'

'You are a useful person in two households. I hope this little woman will grow up to be like you.'

Honor looked surprised.

'Don't you hope you will, dear? You would like her to, wouldn't you Gavin?'

'No, I don't think so. If people are useful, it is only nice for other people, and not for them.'

'She is safe with her brother, isn't she, Miss Pilbeam?' said Eleanor, smiling as she left the room, and unconscious of any implication upon Miss Pilbeam's lot.

'Has your mother gone away?' said Gavin.

'She is dead. She died over a year ago.'

Gavin and Honor looked at each other and broke into awkward mirth.

'Then why don't you wear black?' said Honor, as if this excused their outbreak.

'I have just gone out of it.'

'Then you don't mind any more.'

'Of course I do. Clothes do not make any difference.'

'Then why do people wear black? Isn't it to show that they mind?'

'It is just a custom.'

'Does your father wear black?' said Gavin.

'He wears a black band on his arm. That is what men do.'

'Then he minds more than you do?'

'Yes, I am afraid he minds even more than that.'

'Would he rather you had died?'

'Yes, perhaps he would.'

'I should hate anyone who wanted me to die,' said Honor.

'Is he glad you have stopped minding?' said Gavin.

'You know I have not stopped. Now we will go on with the lesson. I hope I shall not have to tell your mother that you are inattentive.'

Honor and Gavin shared the hope to the point of allowing the lesson to proceed to its end. Then Gavin resumed the talk.

'What is your father, Miss Pilbeam?'

'He is a veterinary surgeon.'

'What kind of a surgeon is that? An ophthalmic surgeon is one who cures people's eyes.'

'Yes. A veterinary surgeon is one who cures animals.'

'Animals? Just horses and cows?'

'All kinds. Hunters and hounds and everything,' said Miss Pilbeam, carrying the subject into its higher sphere.

'Then your father is not a real doctor?'

'He is something different and something the same as well,' said Miss Pilbeam, in a tone of throwing full light on her pupils' minds.

'Then he is not a gentleman?'

'He is an educated man. He passed very hard examinations.'

'As hard as those for people like Daniel and Graham?'

'Yes, I should think nearly as hard.'

'But he doesn't earn enough for you not to be a governess.'

'He likes me to do something useful.'

'But teaching isn't useful unless you know enough to teach.'

'I know enough to teach you.'

'But you had to read the history out of a book. You didn't know it in your head.'

'I could not make a second book, could I?'

Honor broke into laughter.

'You will soon cease to expect duplicates in this house,' she said.

Miss Pilbeam looked at her in silence.

'Then we can answer out of the book,' pursued Gavin.

'We will see what your mother says.'

'We do sums now,' said Honor, recognizing the end of the matter.

'Give me the arithmetic book.'

Gavin handed it with a look at his sister, and a snake wriggled out over Miss Pilbeam's hands.

'What a babyish toy to play with!' she exclaimed, as she realized its nature, and her pupils' faces showed the fulfilment of their hopes.

'It is Nevill's,' said Gavin, in explanation. 'I just put it inside the book. I thought that, as your father was a surgeon of animals, you might like it.'

Miss Pilbeam laughed before she knew, and general mirth ensued.

'It is a realistic object,' said Honor.

'Yes, it is very simple,' said Miss Pilbeam. 'Now take down this sum.'

'We always have our sums put down for us.'

'And I don't do the same as Honor,' said Gavin. 'She has harder ones. Farther on in the book.'

'Well, show me the ones you do have.'

Honor did so, and Miss Pilbeam dictated the examples, and worked Honor's herself, to be ready with her aid. Honor soon gave the correct answer.

'Let me see your book.'

Honor tossed it forward.

'Yes, that is good. You have been very quick. How about you, Gavin?'

'I only do one sum. Honor does three.'

'And there are only eleven months between you. You must catch up, Gavin. Do you ever help him, Honor?'

'No, I don't teach people,' said Honor, implying a difference between her experience and Miss Pilbeam's.

'She is a year older than me,' said Gavin. 'Her birthday is on the second of July, and mine is on the last day in June. It is a year all but two days.'

'I think you must be better at mathematics than you seem,' said Miss Pilbeam, smiling.

'We are the same age for two days,' said Honor, hardly doing herself the same justice. 'This sum is wrong, but I see where. I always find my own mistakes.'

'You are good at arithmetic,' said Miss Pilbeam.

'Better than you are, isn't she?' said Gavin.

'I think she is for her age.'

'She is apart from that. You have not done the first sum yet.'

'I have not been trying. I saw she did not need my help.'

'You seemed to be trying.'

'Appearances are deceitful,' said Miss Pilbeam, with a pleasant note that was only fair on appearances, as she had this point in common with them. 'I shall expect Honor to get on very fast. I can always prepare the lesson, if necessary.'

'You will have to do that at home, and your father will know that you can't do Honor's sums.'

'Well, that will not matter,' said Miss Pilbeam, laughing amusedly. 'I think this is your luncheon.'

'It is your luncheon too.'

'Yes, I think we are to have it together.'

'Does she have to pay for it?' said Gavin, aside to his sister.

'Master Gavin, that is very rude,' said Mullet. 'Miss Honor must be quite ashamed.'

'I am not,' said Honor.

'Can I get you anything else, miss?'

'She would not dare to say "Yes",' said Gavin.

'Now I shall tell Hatton,' said Mullet.

'I can talk to Honor, if I like.'

'Hatton would wish to know.'

'Then she will be pleased about it.'

'I think he is not himself,' said Miss Pilbeam. 'He may be shy. Perhaps we might pass it over this time.'

'Now isn't that kind of Miss Pilbeam?'

'She is trying to curry favour.'

'You can leave him to me, Mullet. We will see what your mother says presently, Gavin.'

Mullet took her tray, and Gavin swung on his chair to show his indifference, a state which certainly could not be deduced from his expression.

'Mother does not like to be worried about little things.' said Honor.

'Rudeness is not a little thing.'

'Pretence rudeness is,' said Gavin.

'Why do you pretend anything so babyish and silly?'

'Honor and I always pretend.'

'Well, if you pretend rudeness again, I shall ask your mother what to do about it.'

Gavin ceased to swing, the purpose of the process being over.

'She can't stand on her own legs,' murmured Honor.

Miss Pilbeam fixed her eyes on Honor's face, kept them there for some moments, and withdrew them with an air of ruminative purpose.

'We have Latin now,' said Honor, in a pleasant tone. 'We are doing a book called Caesar. We have only read one page.'

'Well, in that case we will not go on with it today. I will take the book home and read it to myself, so that I can tell you the story. That will make it easier.'

'Graham has a translation of it,' said Gavin. 'But Miss Mitford reads Latin books without.'

'Oh, we won't talk about translations,' said Miss Pilbeam, justified in her protest, as she was going to make no mention of one she had seen at home.

'Why can't we just read the translation?' said Honor. 'We should know what was in the book.'

'Because that is not the way to learn Latin,' said Miss Pilbeam, who meant to use it only as a way of managing without having done so. 'We will do some Latin grammar this morning.'

'We don't much like doing that.'

'But think how useful it will be in reading the books,' said Miss Pilbeam, with earnestness and faith.

'Latin is a dead language,' said Gavin.

'Yes, it is not actually spoken now,' said Miss Pilbeam, confirming and amplifying his knowledge. 'But it is nice to be able to read it. It is the key to so much.'

'The key?'

'Yes, it opens the gates of knowledge,' said Miss Pilbeam, laying her hands on the table and looking into Gavin's face.

'Miss Pilbeam is speaking metaphorically,' said Honor.

'Yes, I was; I am glad you understood.'

'I didn't,' said Gavin.

'We must make allowances for those twelve months,' said Miss Pilbeam, smiling. 'Here is your little brother.'

Nevill left Hatton in the doorway, ran twice round Miss Pilbeam, paused at her knee and raised his eyes to her face.

'He is the youngest, miss. These are his first lessons.'

'Hatton teach him,' said Nevill, on a sudden note of apprehension.

'No, Miss Pilbeam can teach better than I can.'

'Not as well as Hatton,' said Nevill, his tone changing to one of resignation and goodwill; 'but very nice.'

'I will leave him, miss. If he is not good, send one of the others to fetch me.'

'We can ring for Mullet,' said Honor.

'No, Mullet has other things to do.'

'We might refuse to go,' said Gavin.

Hatton left the room in a smooth manner, suggestive merely of concern that Nevill should not notice her going.

Miss Pilbeam bent towards the latter.

'Can you say A, b, c?'

'A, b, c,' said Nevill, looking up.

'He doesn't know anything,' said Honor.

'He does,' said Nevill, not taking his eyes from Miss Pilbeam's face.

'Well, I will teach you four letters, and show you how to make them,' said Miss Pilbeam, lifting him to her knee.

'A chair like Gavin.'

'No, a chair would not be high enough.'

'Shall he paint?' said Nevill, who sat on Mullet's knee for this purpose.

'Well, you may colour the letters.'

'A paint box,' said Nevill, to Honor.

'No, I can't go and get one. Here are some crayons.'

'That is better,' said Miss Pilbeam. 'There will be no mess. And you can make the letters coloured from the first.'

'He will make them all coloured,' said Nevill, looking round.

'Let me hold your hand and make an a.'

'A red a,' said Nevill, putting his eyes, his mind and a good deal of his strength on the crayon.

'A red a, a blue b, and a green c,' said Miss Pilbeam, guiding his hand.

'A is red, b is blue, and c is green,' said Nevill, in a tone of grasp and progress.

'It does not matter which colour each letter is.'

'It does,' said Nevill, suspecting an intention to smooth his path.

'You can make each letter in any colour. You can have a green a, and a red b, and a blue c.'

'But always coloured,' said Nevill.

'No. Letters can be black.'

'No, not black.'

'Yes, that is what they generally are.'

'Black,' said Nevill, looking for a crayon of this kind.

'You will never teach him anything,' said Gavin.

'It would have been better not to have colours,' said Honor.

'I shall teach him easily. He is very quick. You try to get on with your declensions,' said Miss Pilbeam, implying that her confidence did not extend indefinitely.

'Quick,' said Nevill, pushing his crayon rapidly about.

'No, that is not the way. You must make the letters as I showed you. Now we will make d.'

'D is – pink,' said Nevill, after a moment's thought.

'Yes, d can be pink.'

'A is red, b is blue, c is green, and d is pink,' said Nevill, in a tone of concluding the subject, preparing to get down from Miss Pilbeam's knee.

'No, I want you to make them all again.'

'He will make them all again,' said Nevill.

The lesson proceeded until Eleanor entered with some friends. She was accustomed to conduct her guests round the departments of her house, as she felt that in these lay the significance and the credit of her life. Nevill left Miss Pilbeam's knee and ran to meet her.

'A, b, c, d,' he said, looking up towards her, as if he were not quite sure of the position of her face.

'That is a clever boy. I am very pleased. So he has made a beginning, Miss Pilbeam.'

'A, b, c, d,' said Nevill, in a sharper tone, indicating the superfluity of the question.

'You know it all, don't you?'

'He knows it all,' said her son, with a faint sigh.

'There are a lot more letters,' said Miss Pilbeam, addressing her words to Nevill, and her tone to everybody else.

'There are four,' said her pupil.

'No, there are a great many. You have learnt the four first ones.'

Nevill looked up with comprehension dawning in his eyes.

'What are you doing?' said Eleanor, to the other two.

'Latin declensions,' said Honor, not taking her eyes from her book.

'Aren't they almost too wonderful?' said a woman guest. 'I thought it was only backward children who ever fulfilled any promise. But these have fulfilled the promise already, so it is all right. I always find it a test to be with a woman with nine children. I find I am inclined to feel that she has more than I have. Of course one ought not to feel it, but I almost think she might agree. It somehow seems nice of Miss Mitford to have that small one on her knee, so unembittered.'

'This is Miss Pilbeam,' said Eleanor.

'Of course, I felt I knew her face. I knew it was a different face from Miss Mitford's. It is much younger, isn't it? And Miss Mitford's face is quite young enough.'

'I think we sometimes pass in the village,' said Miss Pilbeam.

'Yes, that would be it,' said Mrs Cranmer, shaking hands. 'When we learn faces, it is in the village. There don't seem to be so many outside. You knew my face was not Miss Mitford's. Of course all our thoughts might be hers. And I hope they are. Miss Mitford would have such deep thoughts.'

Hope Cranmer was a small, vital-looking woman of sixty, with strong, grey, springy hair, a straight, handsome nose, clear, brown eyes, an openly curious and critical expression, and a voice so strong and sudden and deep that it took people by surprise. Her stepdaughter stood behind her, a tall, slightly awkward woman of thirty-six, with pale, hazel eyes, a long, stiff nose and chin, an oddly youthful expression, and an obstinate, innocent, complacent mouth, which did not open as much as other people's, when in use. The husband and father was a short, solid man of sixty-eight, with a heavy, hooked nose, bright, dark eyes with a look of benevolence and scepticism, and an air of humorous content with part of life, and gentle regret for the rest of it.

'Paul is always with me now,' said Hope. 'He has saved some money and inherited some more, and he is going to devote himself to leisure, because he likes it so much. He has even given up the work he loved, because of it. And he has not aged or soured or gone to pieces or anything.'

'I think he deserves a rest now, Mother,' said Faith.

'But then he would be one of the people who are lost without their work. Or who would those people be?'

'I enjoy leisure the more for not deserving it too well,' said Paul. 'People who have hardly earned it, are past its use.'

'And I can't help thinking we ascribe too much to leisure,' said his wife, 'that even if people do spend their lives in useful effort, they may age a little sometimes. It seems hard, when they have done all they can to prevent it. Up with the lark, a hard day's work, and going to bed healthily tired; what more can people do?'

'We confess to a suspicion of your good faith, Mrs Cranmer,' said her stepson, who completed the family.

'We should follow the golden mean,' said Faith.

'I dislike the mean,' said Paul, 'and anything else that prevents our going the full length with things.'

'You will follow that principle in your pursuit of leisure, Father,' said Ridley.

Ridley Cranmer was a tall, large, almost commanding-looking man of forty-three, with a broad, full face and head, large, expressionless eyes, whose colour could not be determined, and cannot be recorded, a rather full and fleshy, but not ill-modelled nose and chin, and a suave, appreciative, and where possible chivalrous manner. He was a lawyer in London, as his father had been before him, and spent his spare time at home; where the spectacle of Paul's freedom chafed him with its reminder that his inheritance might have been increased, an attitude which his father found unfilial, which he did not mind, and unreasonable, which he did.

Ridley and Faith were on terms of inevitable intimacy. Ridley understood his sister, and neither liked nor disliked the character he accepted; and Faith, who was used to vague conceptions, had a feeling that it was as well not to understand her brother. Hope said it was absurd that she and her stepdaughter should be called Hope and Faith, and that she admired Paul for not betraying embarrassment, and sympathized with Ridley when he did. Ridley treated his stepmother with formally affectionate concern, and Faith tried to be a daughter to her; and these efforts increased her tendency to admit acid undertones into her apparently inconsequent and genial speech.

Faith's name had been chosen by her own mother, in spite of, or perhaps because of, her father's lack of the attribute. It was said to suit her, and she had been heard quietly to observe that she hoped it did. Paul viewed his daughter's religion with a smooth consideration, and Hope with an indifference changed to impatience by Faith's conscientious concern for herself. Whether or not Ridley had a religion was not known, as he evinced one or not according to his company, a course which he pursued with many things.

'Fancy having to sit on someone's knee to learn!' said Hope.

'You mean, Mrs Cranmer, fancy learning when you have to sit on someone's knee!' said Ridley.

'I am sure the lessons are very interesting,' said Faith.

'They are bad things for the young,' said Paul. 'We don't choose the right time for them.'

'They will come to appreciate them later, Father.'

'You both seem to think the same,' said Hope. 'And that happens so seldom that I am sure you must be right. But we are supposed to see them appreciating them now.'

'You must be very gratified, Mrs Sullivan,' said Ridley, in an almost emotional tone.

'Haven't we any more rooms to see?' said Hope. 'I look forward to going from floor to floor, and seeing people younger and

95

younger on each. Isn't there anyone smaller than that little one? I am sure there used to be. I do hope this house is not going to be that depressing thing, a home without a baby.'

'The person smaller than Nevill was probably Nevill himself,' said Ridley.

'Yes, he is the last,' said Eleanor. 'This is the first day he has had lessons.'

Ridley shook his head with no change in his eyes, and his sister gave him a glance with one in hers.

'Do you remember me, Honor?' she said.

'Yes, you are Miss Cranmer.'

'Yes, my name is Faith Cranmer.'

'Isn't she Miss?' said Gavin to his sister, with a gesture towards Faith.

'Yes, that is what you would call me,' said the latter.

'She is only Miss, isn't she?' said Gavin to Honor, in a more insistent tone.

Faith gave a smile to Eleanor, with reference to this childish view.

'No one thinks it better to be Mrs, dear,' said Hope.

'I think I do,' said Honor.

'Why do you think so?' said Eleanor, with a smile.

'Well, it is better to have a house and a husband and children, than not to have anything.'

The laughter that greeted the answer mystified Honor.

'Why isn't it better?' she said.

'It is in some senses, of course,' said Faith.

'I think it is difficult for Honor,' said Hope. 'I am almost finding it so myself.'

'Do you think you are an advantage?' said Eleanor, to the child.

'She does sums better than Miss Pilbeam,' said Gavin.

'That settles it,' said Paul.

'Now isn't that a little bit of an exaggeration?' said Faith.

'No, it really is not this morning,' said Miss Pilbeam, in a tone of full tribute. 'I was very pleased.'

Eleanor laid a hand on Honor's head.

'Now what about the question of the advantage, Mrs Sullivan?' said Ridley.

'We have seen a rare caress,' said Hope. 'And it is true that it means more than frequent ones. Though perhaps the frequent ones together may mean more still. But of course it means enough.'

'Some more letters,' said Nevill, striking Miss Pilbeam's knee.

'No, you have had enough for today. I am afraid you will forget them.'

'There are a lot,' said Nevill in recollection.

'He thirsts to learn,' said Hope. 'You need do nothing for your children, Eleanor. And people say you do so much.'

'I do nothing for anyone else, I suppose they mean.'

'Well, if they do, it is not nice of them, dear. I shall know what they mean, another time.'

'Some more letters,' said Nevill, with increasing urgency.

'How many do you think there are?' said Miss Pilbeam, bending towards him.

'A hundred.'

'No, there are twenty-six.'

'There are twenty-six,' said Nevill, in an impressed tone. 'And he will learn them all.'

'The next one is called e.'

'A white one,' said Nevill, looking about for the crayon.

'Yes, if you like. The letters are called the alphabet.'

'They are called letters.'

'Yes, they are called that too.'

'He calls them that,' said Nevill.

'He is the first person I have met who really said "Let me know all",' said Hope. 'And at his age too! I suppose the others do know all by now.'

'They are just beginning Latin,' said Miss Pilbeam.

'Well, isn't that knowing all? People don't begin Latin until then. And now we go down and meet those who have been learning even longer. I see it is true that the whole of life is education.'

'That is a happy thought,' said Faith, as she turned to follow. 'It makes me feel less regret that so far I have learned so little.'

'I am sure you mean you have had no advantages,' said Hope. 'And I believe they were equal to Miss Pilbeam. And you have only just begun to want to know all. I don't know how it is you are so late.'

'Would you prefer this chair, Mother?' said Faith at the table, suggesting that she harboured no ill feeling.

'No, guests always think everything is perfect. Isn't it nice of her to go on calling me Mother? I always think it is so daughterly.'

'You are the only mother I can remember.'

'I appreciate your not recalling other examples of what I am. Your father and Ridley both do it, and it seems such a double course.'

'Ridley does not do you the same honour,' said Fulbert.

'It is a little different,' said Faith. 'He is older and a man.'

'It seems to be quite different,' said Hope.

'How was Nevill managing his first day in the schoolroom?' said Luce.

'Managing is the word,' said Hope. 'He was giving directions and having them followed.'

'Is Miss Pilbeam a success?'

'Yes, indeed. They were doing Latin and the alphabet. And those are the foundations of all learning.'

'I am so glad,' said Luce. 'I suggested Miss Pilbeam, because I knew she really needed the employment. It is a relief that the arrangement is a success.'

'You are unPlatonic, my child,' said Fulbert. 'The work does not exist for the man, but the man for the work.'

'I know nothing about Plato, Father,' said Luce, illustrating the methods of education in her family. 'But I do know when a kindness needs to be done. And this was a clear case of it.'

'I am so glad Miss Pilbeam has a post that suits her,' said Faith. 'I have been so sorry for her and her father since Mrs Pilbeam died.'

Fulbert threw his quizzical glance from one young woman to the other.

'You need not worry about your children's education, Fulbert,' said Hope. 'I saw it going on on every floor. There is a room on each on purpose. I am glad we never go round our house; the difference would strike us too forcibly. I daresay Paul and Ridley go sometimes, to hear the echo of a voice that is still.'

'Mrs Cranmer, there is room in my heart for more than one person,' said Ridley.

'Yes, that is what I was saying, dear.'

'And I am sure I may say the same of my father.'

'No, you may not,' said Hope; 'I forbid it.'

Faith turned grave, neutral eyes on her stepmother.

'You will miss the hunting this winter, Fulbert,' said Paul.

'I shall, and other things as well.'

'Yes, that would not be the first thing on his mind, Father,' said Faith with a smile.

'We do not talk of the things that go too deep for words,' said Hope. 'I suppose it would really be no good.'

'Will you be hunting, Daniel?' said Paul.

'There are other things that he must do,' said Eleanor at once.

Regan turned eyes of troubled sympathy on her grandson.

'It is a thing he should not have begun,' said Sir Jesse.

'You forget, Paul, that they do nothing but learn,' said Hope. 'A person has only to need a post, to be accommodated as a teacher here. I think it is wonderful of Luce to lift weights off people's minds. If we had not provided for Faith, it might be such a relief.'

'I am far from regarding myself as fit for such important work as teaching, Mother.'

'But Luce would regard you as fit, dear. That is what I mean. I said it was wonderful of her.'

Regan laughed in enjoyment of the joke, quite free from uneasiness about her grandchildren's advantages.

'I don't think you hunt, Faith?' said Fulbert.

'No, I do not,' said Faith, in a quiet, pleasant tone.

'You are like Luce and uncertain of your nerve?'

'Yes, I make no claim to that kind of courage, Father,' said Luce, smiling and saying nothing of other kinds.

'It is not the highest sort,' said Fulbert.

'I wonder if there is any other,' said Graham. 'I felt it was the lack of the whole of courage that prevented my hunting.'

'My nerve is quite good,' said Faith, in the same tone.

99

'She thinks it is cruel to the fox,' said Hope. 'Isn't it imaginative of her? She puts herself in his place.'

'We must set the pleasure to human beings on the other side of the scales,' said Sir Jesse.

'She thinks the fox doesn't count that, or not enough to find it any compensation. She believes he only thinks of himself. And yet she thinks of him. She is a wonderful character.'

'She thinks of the fox and not of men and women.'

'No, she thinks of them too. She says that hunting degrades them, that they should get their pleasure in other ways. She wants them to have pleasure.'

'Hunting takes a lot of qualities,' said Sir Jesse.

'Grandpa speaks after a lifetime's practice of it,' said Daniel.

'A way you will never speak,' said his grandfather.

'Is this being cruel to be kind?' said Hope. 'Or is it just being cruel?'

'It is being honest,' said her host.

'It is showing moral courage,' said Graham. 'In other words yielding to temptation.'

'The qualities might surely be put to better purpose than hounding to death an innocent creature,' said Faith.

'Hounding is a good word,' said Hope. 'It seems such a right use of it.'

'I do think, Mrs Sullivan,' said Ridley, bending towards Eleanor, 'that there is something repellent in the idea of a little, terrified creature being driven to exhaustion and death. How would any of us like it?'

'The fox has his own chance,' said Sir Jesse.

'He would prefer the one that we have,' said Daniel. 'Not that I consider his preferences.'

'You may do so,' said his grandfather.

'You are hunting as usual, Paul?' said Fulbert, regarding Faith's scruples as things to be necessarily passed over.

'More than usual, now that I am my own master.'

'Can I pass you the sugar, Father?' said Faith.

'Isn't it selfless of Fulbert to take an interest in what he will miss?' said Hope. 'It is people with emptier lives like mine who ought to go away.'

'It is because of what my life holds, that I am going.'

'Yes, it would hardly be worth while for me to go.'

'Take what you can get out of it, my boy,' said Sir Jesse, almost harshly. 'You are not a woman.'

'Father knows that, Grandpa,' said Luce, in her demure tone.

'I think he is one of those men who do,' said Graham.

'Do men get more out of things than women?' said Faith. 'I should hardly have thought so.'

'I would not exchange my life for a man's,' said Regan.

'You would be an odd person if you would, Lady Sullivan,' said Ridley, in an earnest tone.

'I always think I should have been more of a success as a man,' said Eleanor.

'Mrs Sullivan, you do not wish for the change?' said Ridley, in an almost stricken manner.

'Well, not at this stage, I suppose.'

'Would you be rid of us all, Mother?' said Luce.

'Well, I might prefer to be your father.'

'That would be giving up a good deal of us.'

'It would be gaining some more,' said Fulbert. 'I admit no belittlement of fatherhood.'

'We must acknowledge the woman's part as the deeper and fuller here,' said Ridley.

'In most cases,' said Faith. 'And exceptions prove rules.'

'They seem to break them,' said Graham. 'But what does it matter?'

'Would you be a woman or a man, Luce, my dear?' said Regan.

'A woman, Grandma,' said Luce, simply, turning her eyes full on Regan's face.

'Which would you choose to be, Father?' said Faith.

'Well, I think a man gets more and gives less.'

'You have not answered my question, Father.'

'He has in his own way, Faith,' said Luce, in a low, amused tone.

'It would be no advantage not to give,' said Faith. 'One would not wish to give that up.'

'It would be shocking to ask Faith what she gave,' said Hope to her husband. 'She can only give intangible things, and no one can speak of those. And I did feel the impulse.'

'Few normal people would wish to belong to the opposite sex,' said Daniel.

'It would mean they were different,' said Graham. 'And that would seem to them a pity.'

'A human being is a wonderful thing,' said Faith.

'Then of course it would be a pity,' said Paul.

'A human being is in some ways a melancholy thing,' said Ridley, glancing at Eleanor.

'People often make their own troubles,' said Faith.

'Well, it does seem shallow to be fortunate,' said Hope.

'We don't all have to make them,' said Regan.

'I wish I had had as much sorrow as you have, Lady Sullivan,' said Hope. 'I am really ashamed of having been through so little.'

Regan laughed.

'I don't know anyone with such an infectious laugh as Grandma, when she really gives it,' said Luce.

'I daresay the experience behind it only adds to it,' said Faith.

'Can't we even laugh properly without having trouble?' said Hope. 'Then it is true that laughter is near to tears. Is this six or seven children coming in?'

'You know it is six, Mother.'

'I knew it ought to be. But it did seem to be more. And surely these children ought to count more than one.'

Nevill ran up to Regan and stood by her knee.

'A, b, c, d,' he said.

'What a clever boy! I did not know you could learn so fast.'

'A is red, b is blue, c is green, and d is pink,' said Nevill watching her face for the effect of this knowledge.

'Does Miss Pilbeam colour them?'

'No, he does. There are twenty-six.'

'Twenty-six what?'

'Twenty-six a, b, c, d,' said Nevill, rapidly moving his feet.

'Letters,' said Honor.

'Letters,' said Nevill, a calm overspreading his face.

'And you will learn them all?' said Regan.

'He will learn twenty-six.'

'And what colours will they be?'

'White, purple, brown, crimson lake,' said Nevill, with very little pause.

'Does it confuse him to have the colours?' said Eleanor. 'I should have thought it would make it harder.'

'It does make him think each letter has its own colour,' said Honor. 'But he asked to have it like that. He really wanted to paint them.'

'Aren't they wonderful to have to have things made harder?' said Hope. 'And to ask for it too. I have never heard of it before.'

'You must have heard of children who wanted to colour things, Mother,' said Faith. 'I always did myself.'

'Yes, dear, but I thought it was to make them easier.'

'We can't catch my stepmother out, Mrs Sullivan,' said Ridley.

'That was the last thing I wanted to do,' said Faith, in a quiet tone.

'We know quite a lot about Faith,' said Hope. 'Most people are so secretive about themselves.'

'I hope I do not talk about myself,' said Faith. 'Not that there is anything I wish to hide.'

'I want to hide almost everything,' said Hope. 'Some of it must leak out, but I do trust not all.'

'Did you like your lessons with Miss Pilbeam, Gavin?' said Eleanor.

'I didn't mind them.'

'Did you, Honor?'

'Yes, thank you, Mother.'

'He liked it too,' said Nevill, turning his eyes rapidly from face to face.

'Don't they think or talk of anything but learning?' said Hope.

'This is an exceptional occasion,' said Eleanor. 'They have a new governess.'

'Yes, the one that was not Miss Mitford. Have you got rid of her? I mean, have they grown beyond her? Of course they would have.'

'No, they are not up to her yet.'

'Who is up to her?'

'These two,' said Eleanor, indicating Isabel and Venice.

'And does James have someone in between?'

'No, James goes to school.'

'The school is between Miss Mitford and Miss Pilbeam. And Daniel and Graham are at Cambridge, and there is no more for Luce to learn. I see I denied my stepchildren every opportunity.'

'Have you little ones finished your dessert?' said Eleanor. 'We don't want much of you today.'

Nevill forced the remainder of his portion into his mouth and prepared to leave.

'The child will choke, my dear,' said Fulbert.

His son ran towards the door, with a view to dealing with his situation in his own way.

'Honor, tell Hatton to see that Nevill does not choke,' said Eleanor.

'Is that what Hatton does?' said Hope. 'And the other nurse and Miss Mitford and Miss Pilbeam all do their own things. Suppose something unforeseen should arise? I suppose you would have someone else. I am so glad this was not unforeseen.'

'Civilization has its weaker side,' said Fulbert.

'It seems a strong side, so well supported,' said Graham.

'It is more difficult to make other people do things than to do them yourself,' said Eleanor.

'It seems a foolish way of arranging matters,' said Daniel.

'What a family for liking difficult things!' said Hope. 'Always choosing the harder part.'

'You would not suggest, Daniel, that your mother should be a slave to all the departments of her house?' said Ridley, in some consternation.

'Yes, I would, if it would save her any trouble.'

'Isn't anyone going up with Nevill?' said Eleanor. 'I am so afraid he will choke.'

'Are you really?' said Hope. 'I do sympathize with you. You make me very anxious, myself. Can't we send for the person who deals with it? You would want to get that off your mind.'

Sounds came from the hall that disposed of the question, and Venice hastened to her brother's aid.

'That is a good sister,' said Eleanor, as her daughter returned, leading Nevill, who capered forward in open relief. 'Is there anything to be done out there?'

'Mullet heard and came down,' said Venice.

'It was Mullet, was it?' said Hope. 'Not Hatton; you were wrong, Eleanor; but it is a good deal to keep in your head.'

'You are laughing at us as a family, Mrs Cranmer,' said Luce.

'I am only jealous of you for being one, dear.'

Nevill ran up to Regan.

'He ate it all at once,' he said, looking at the table. 'But not do it another time.'

'No, no more today,' said Eleanor. 'People who are sick have had enough.'

Nevill turned and ran to the door, the purpose of his presence being over. A maid opened it and he went out.

'You should say, "Thank you",' called Eleanor, who though providing attendance as a matter of course for her children, did not approve of their accepting it in the corresponding spirit.

Nevill ran back and up to the maid, and taking her apron, looked up into her face.

'Thank you,' he said, and dragged her from the room.

'He did want someone else,' said Hope. 'And they say that children left to scramble up anyhow, do better.'

'Honor and Gavin can run away too,' said Eleanor. 'The elder ones at the table can stay.'

'Why don't they all do the same?' said Hope. 'Because it would be easier?'

'They would not like it. The same things are not suited to them.'

'Do you understand them like that? And I thought that parents always misunderstood their children.'

'The very strength and possessiveness of a parent's feelings may prevent easy understanding,' said Luce.

'Is that what I said?' said Hope. 'I am glad. It sounded like something not so nice.'

'Is James at home today?' said Eleanor, looking at her son.

'Do a parent's feelings render a child actually invisible?' said Graham.

'But is he at home? You know what I mean. Is he not well?'

'It seems that children understand their parents,' said Paul, laughing.

'Sons understand their mothers, we know,' said Hope. 'But is it a thing we talk about?'

'There is a holiday at the school,' said Isabel, while Faith gave a glance at her stepmother.

'Oh, that is what it is,' said Eleanor, as if this were a more venial circumstance than indisposition. 'But the holidays seem to come rather often. It is early in the term.'

'It is the schoolmaster's wife's birthday,' said James.

'Is it?' said Paul. 'Or is it out of the Bible or the grammar?'

'Either is very suitable for a school,' said his wife.

Faith gave another glance at her.

'Would the master give a holiday for his own birthday?' said Daniel.

'He never does,' said James.

'It seems a reversal of the usual theories with regard to ladies' birthdays,' said Ridley.

'It is nice of him to choose his wife's,' said Hope. 'It makes him seem so glad that she was born.'

'I don't know why the rest of us should rejoice,' said Regan.

'It is James who is doing so, and he knows her,' said Hope. 'One sees what the master means, and I think it is very nice.'

'I never see her,' said James.

'Well, that does make him seem rather absorbed in his own point of view. But it is pleasant to keep birthdays, Lady Sullivan, and he will give James a holiday on yours, if you wish.'

'James takes a holiday on mine anyhow,' said Regan, smiling.

'Well, that is the birthday to be kept,' said Sir Jesse. 'That, if no other.'

His wife looked deeply moved.

'I think you are even better than the schoolmaster, Sir Jesse,' said Hope.

'Now, Isabel and Venice, let us hear your voices,' said Eleanor.

For a moment no sound at all was heard.

'Do you have a holiday on Miss Mitford's birthday?' said Paul.

'We don't even know when it is,' said Venice.

'An unjust distinction between educationists,' said Daniel.

'We should not despise people who are employed in the house,' said Hope.

'Miss Mitford is a very well-read woman,' said Faith.

'Yes, that is not at all like despising her, dear.'

'Books seem to come for her by every post,' said Regan.

'I think that is rather like it,' said Paul.

'Miss Mitford has been with us for seventeen years,' said Luce.

'I hope it is not a tragedy in a phrase,' said Graham, his tone not betraying that he really hoped it.

'She would be well-read by now,' said Isabel. 'The books do come twice a week.'

'Grandma was not exaggerating as much as I thought,' said Daniel.

'Ninety-six times a year, if we do not count her holidays,' said Isabel.

'I do not wonder you wanted them to talk, Eleanor,' said Hope. 'It would have been a great pity to miss it.'

'Now we know the length of Miss Mitford's holidays,' said Daniel.

'I do not,' said Paul, while Fulbert rapidly and openly calculated on his fingers.

'Four weeks,' said Faith, in a slightly breathless tone, outstripping him by a tense and covert effort.

'You see I did have her educated,' said Hope.

'Now I think Miss Mitford will be expecting you,' said Eleanor to the children.

'Let them stay for a while,' said Fulbert. 'I will have them while I can.'

'Yes, I am to lose my son, Cranmer,' said Sir Jesse, who was inclined to refer any subject to himself, and to address his words to men. 'I ought to say I may never see him again. But somehow I feel I should not mean it.'

'People would think you did,' said Regan.

'I should not,' said Hope; 'I am sure he is immortal.'

'I am seventy-nine,' said Sir Jesse.

'There, I said you were.'

Regan laughed.

'But I must not depend on my father,' said Fulbert. 'And I

should make my plans to meet the event of anything's happening to me. The one thing's happening, of course I mean. I only have the normal chance.'

'I daresay there are plenty of risks out there,' said Regan.

'Someone must break it to my mother and my wife,' went on Fulbert, with the faint unction that marked his utterance of anything that bore on himself. 'Someone must share the guardianship of my infant children. My sons are young, and younger to my wife than they are. I am dependent on someone outside. Paul, will you face the risk of another man's burdens?'

'I am no good at other people's affairs. I don't take as much trouble with them as I do with my own. I don't even take enough trouble with those.'

'Then, Ridley, I must turn to you,' said Fulbert, doing as he said. 'We have never been close, or even perhaps congenial friends; but I depend on your character; you have our affairs in your hands; you would work well with my wife. Will you undertake the trust?'

Ridley rose to his feet.

'I will undertake it, Fulbert. And from the bottom of my heart will I regard it as a trust.'

'It is not as if it would ever happen,' said Regan.

'Lady Sullivan,' said Ridley, turning quickly to her, 'do you think we should be calmly discussing it, if we thought it would?'

'I don't know what else you could do.'

Ridley looked round, allowed his face to relax into a smile and resumed his seat.

'Well, there is an end of that,' said Fulbert. 'I can return to my own character. There is something unnatural in making plans for one's own end.'

'It is too necessary for us to like it,' said Regan.

'It is very brave,' said Graham. 'But people think so, and that is something.'

'I think we ought to go, Mother,' said Faith.

'You mean we are constraining their last hours?'

'I have not seen any sign of constraint.'

'We are happy to be helped over them,' said Sir Jesse. 'It is hard to talk to my son, with this in front. And most of what I have to say can wait for his return. He must have heard it many times.'

'He will not be in the same position, Sir Jesse,' said Ridley, speaking with easy confidence in the future. 'He will have much to relate, that is entirely unfamiliar.'

'We know he will come back, if he is alive,' said Regan. 'It will be a good thing when he is gone now.'

'What are you children doing, listening to grown-up talk?' said Eleanor.

'You have stated our occupation,' said Isabel. 'And it is hard to see our alternative.'

'You can all run away to the schoolroom.'

'You do mix the sexes,' said Hope. 'I was wondering if I had been wrong in keeping Ridley and Faith together.'

'Brothers and sisters are separated soon enough.'

'Ridley and Faith were not. We only found it out when they were.'

'Ridley was always a very masculine type,' said Faith. 'And he was some years older than I was, and I think more developed for his age.'

'You must remember you are speaking of your brother, dear,' said Hope.

'I said nothing against him, Mother.'

'You were damning him with faint praise; I think with almost no praise at all. I believe you were just damning him.'

'I am not always thinking of praising people or not praising them.'

'It would be nice to think of the first, dear.'

'You don't often do it yourself, Mother.'

'Well, I so seldom see any cause for praise. And when I do, I am so often upset about it. So it is not very easy for me.'

'I shall be quite an important person for the next months,' said Fulbert. 'I daresay you all think it will be a change.'

'It had not crossed my mind, Father,' said Luce, with a smile.

'Other things will be that, my boy,' said Sir Jesse. 'My advice is to make the most of them.'

'Away, away, you children,' said Luce, gently clapping her hands.

'Yes, Miss Mitford will be expecting them,' said Eleanor.

'Miss Mitford's heart must grow sick with hope deferred,' said Graham.

'You have taken a weight off my mind, Ridley,' said Fulbert.

'There is happily no need to regard it as transferred to mine.'

'I wish I could sometimes meet a mark of confidence,' said Hope.

'Different people are suited to different things,' said Faith.

'I don't think that is a better way of putting it, dear, or anyhow not nicer. I ought to go away like Fulbert, and let absence make the heart grow fond.'

'Such a step would be fraught with danger for many of us,' said Ridley, shaking his head.

'I don't mean I should dare to go.'

'Ridley does not mean in Mr Sullivan's case,' said Faith. 'He was thinking of ordinary people like ourselves.'

'Being coupled with you, dear, makes up for everything,' said Hope.

'I think the gap must tend to get a little narrower,' said Fulbert, in an unflinching tone.

'It is a good thing if it does,' said Regan; 'I am sure I hope it will.'

'What should we talk about, if it disappeared?' said Graham.

'Do you think you will miss your father less, as time goes on, Graham?' said Eleanor.

'I hope my elders are right. I want to be saved all I can.'

'Do you, Daniel?'

'I will take Grandma's word for it.'

Eleanor looked round in an instinct to pass on to James, but realized that he was gone.

'You ought to bear your own testimony, my dear,' said Fulbert, 'if you require it of other people.'

'I think you ought, Mother,' said Luce.

'I shall miss your father more with every day.'

'I am sure that is the truth, Mother. And very few people could say it unflinchingly like that.'

'I am glad Grandma set the fashion, and not Mother,' said Graham.

'This is excellent for the gap,' said Daniel. 'Father may have been getting anxious about it.'

'How wonderful heroism is!' said Hope.

'I think we ought to leave them, Mother,' said Faith.

'To wallow in our family miseries,' said Regan, in a tone of contempt for the prospect.

'I have never seen the courage of despair before,' said Hope.

'I can quite understand it,' said Faith. 'It does not show any lack of feeling.'

'We shall be outstaying our welcome,' said Paul.

'And doing other things to it,' said his wife. 'Good-bye, Fulbert; we shall meet you again before you go, and again when you come back; it will be nothing but meeting. I am hiding everything under a cheerful exterior, as that seems to be the kind that is always used.'

'You put rather a strain on our patience, Mrs Cranmer,' said Ridley, as they left the house.

'But not too much for it, dear. You mean that too.'

'You can talk with more sense, Ridley,' said Paul.

'I do see what Ridley means, Father,' said Faith, in a tone so quiet as to be almost an undertone. 'I cannot say I do not.'

'Then we won't expect it, dear,' said Hope. 'I wonder if I shall be the means of binding you and Ridley together.'

'Do you ever show your true self, Mrs Cranmer?' said Ridley, who was proceeding in a state of exaltation produced by the trust reposed in him.

'I hope not often. I do my best to conceal it.'

'Our true selves should not be anything to be ashamed of,' said Faith.

'I don't think it would be nice not to be ashamed of them,' said Hope. 'I am ashamed and terrified of mine, and even more of other people's.'

'Other people's are the thing,' said Paul.

'There are people in whom I would place an absolute trust,' said Faith.

'We won't ask you to mention them, for fear they are not us,' said Hope.

'I think one of them is Mrs Sullivan.'

'Oh, so they are not us,' said Paul.

'I confess that the inner truth of people tends to elude me,' said Ridley. 'Penetration may not be one of my qualities.'

'Well, that was not mentioned,' said Hope. 'But I daresay it does not matter. You are able to think the best of everyone; and as people live up to our conception of them, that would improve them.'

'Here we are at home,' said Faith, in a bright tone, as if welcoming an end to a conversation she regretted. 'It is nearly time for tea.'

'I am glad to hear it,' said Paul. 'A woman's life is giving me a woman's ways.'

'That may not be the explanation, Father. I also feel ready for it,' said Ridley.

'And your life is a man's, a hero's really,' said Hope.

'That is perhaps an exaggeration, Mrs Cranmer.'

'Talking to the old man is a tax,' said Paul. 'He is like a volcano that is quiet at the top.'

'Then he is like a real one,' said Hope, 'and that must be alarming. I sympathize with him, if he has to pretend to be better than he is. I know what a strain it can be.'

'Did you adopt the course today?' said Paul, laughing.

'No, I was dreadful, wasn't I? Absolutely myself. To think that Fulbert will have to remember me like that!'

'It is better to be oneself, whatever impression one gives,' said Faith.

'But we are told to conquer ourselves,' said Hope.

'The process was perhaps incomplete, Mrs Cranmer,' said Ridley.

'Well, we are not to mind about success. It is only the effort that counts.'

'To disguise one's real nature seems such a second-rate instinct,' said Faith.

'I suppose all instincts are,' said Hope. 'That is why they have to be overlaid by reason. I know I am inconsistent, but it upsets me to visit the Sullivans. It is because their house is so much better than mine.'

'The Sullivans have a place, Mother. This is just a comfortable home.'

'I know you do not mean to be unkind, dear.'

'I do not indeed; I was only speaking the truth.'

'There isn't much difference. Brutal frankness is an accepted term.'

'I think this is a very restful room.'

'Yes, you know just what I mean.'

'We should not be any happier in a better one.'

'Well, it would not be true happiness. But I like the other kind. And having a dozen children would be the first kind, wouldn't it?'

'You know Mrs Sullivan has nine children, Mother.'

'Yes, but easy exaggeration glosses it over, and makes it seem more trivial and vague. I could not bring myself to say nine; I am such a coward.'

'Have you not found two stepchildren enough?' said Ridley.

'Oh, of course, dear. You have given me the duties and responsibilities of motherhood. I ought not to want any more.'

'We know it has not been the same, Mother,' said Faith, in a quiet tone.

'Oh, well, dear, I am not one of those women who have never heard themselves called Mother.'

'I wonder how much feeling those youngsters have for their parents,' said Paul.

'Paul, that is kind. I do feel that perhaps I am making a fuss about nothing. Faith and Ridley think I am. Now I have had some comfort, I will show my better qualities for the rest of the day. I will be one of those rare people who keep them for their families. I am glad I have not expended them on anyone else.'

'Are you jealous of the whole brood?' said Paul.

'I am jealous of Nevill,' said Faith, lightly.

'The one who choked?' said Hope.

'You know that was Nevill, Mother.'

'There is my worse nature again. It really seems the only one I have.'

'I should like him to stay always as he is now.'

'Why, he would be bound to choke sooner or later, if it went on.'

'Venice will grow up a handsome girl,' said Ridley.

'The one who prevented the choking? But wouldn't she have to remain in the same stage too? Because it couldn't be allowed to happen. Eleanor saw it herself.'

'There are seven more,' said Paul.

'Are there?' said Hope. 'There it is again.'

'I should like to see more of the girls,' said Faith.

'Surely a wish you can gratify,' said Paul. 'That is the best thing to do with wishes.'

'I think I like girls better than boys.'

'Then you need only be jealous of four,' said Hope. 'But of course you are too young for such feelings. People would be jealous of you. Where is Ridley going?'

'To London,' said her stepson, slightly drawing himself up.

'Of course, you are indispensable there. And here too, as we know. You are not without honour anywhere.'

Faith glanced at her parents, and as they made no movement towards the hall, accompanied her brother herself.

'Do you like Faith the better of your children?' said Hope, to her husband.

'Oh, well, yes, a father takes to his daughter.'

'I like her better too. And you would expect me to be a woman who never preferred her own sex.'

'I should have said you generally did so.'

'Most people do. It is a thing that has not been noticed. People know too much about their sex, to think it possible to prefer it, when really they find it familiar and congenial.'

'Faith seemed to feel that she preferred it,' said Paul.

'Yes, but Faith knows nothing about it. And I could pay her no greater compliment. Self-knowledge speaks ill for people; it shows they are what they are, almost on purpose. And I am not speaking against her the moment her back is turned. I am not at all what I am supposed to be.'

'That would perhaps be the safest moment to choose,' said Faith, returning and speaking with a smile. 'But it is better to be open and aboveboard with everybody.'

'But we could not speak evil to their faces,' said Hope.

'Well, it is not a thing we are obliged to do, Mother.'

'I like my friends best when they are doing it. It makes them so zestful and observant. Original too, almost creative. You see I am speaking good behind their backs. And you don't seem to like it much, but I suppose no one likes to hear other people always praised.'

'I think that would be very pleasant,' said Faith.

'Well, let us all praise Ridley.'

'He has met a great mark of confidence today.'

'That is not praise. You must say you think he deserved it.'

'I think that trust often makes people worthy of it.'

'Faith, I like to hear people speak evil. You know I have admitted it. But you must remember that Ridley is your brother.'

CHAPTER FIVE

'SIR JESSE says we must continue to practise economy,' said Priscilla Marlowe, lifting her eyes without warning from her book. 'He says it need not interfere with our comfort. I could see he knew it prevented it.'

'People used to talk about elegant economy,' said her sister, also looking up from a book. 'I suppose they meant unobtrusive expenditure.'

'Sir Jesse says our interests lie in things of the mind,' said Priscilla, in an absent tone that suggested that this was the case. 'And they do cost less than other things.'

'I wonder why he chose such interests for us,' said the third member of the group, relinquishing the same occupation as his sisters.

'Because it would be an economy,' said Priscilla; 'perhaps an elegant one in this case.'

'I hope he is not thinking of reducing our allowance,' said her brother, in a shrill, anxious voice. 'Because we have cut things to their finest point.'

'It was in his mind, but it did not come out. He would have found it too embarrassing. We hardly know what we owe to his dislike of discomfiture. I wonder why I have to see him alone. I suppose so that he may have only one third of the discomfiture that is rightly his. I ought to be sacrificed as the eldest sister, but it seems that I have three times as much as is mine.'

'It is awkward that I am assumed to earn so much more than I do,' said Lester. 'My last book brought in sixty pounds, and it took two years. And I am ashamed to confess how poorly my work is paid. It would make him think it was poor work and despised. And so he believes I spend money on myself, a thing I should never do.'

'It would be a selfish course,' said Priscilla. 'But Susan earns a good deal at her school, and he does not separate our incomes. He assumes that you earn the most, as the man.'

'I do not mind being helped by my sister. I must grant her the superior place, when it is justly hers. But I wonder why Sir Jesse despises me for earning so little, when he believes it is really so much.'

'He is used to thinking in large sums,' said Susan.

'He breaks the habit when he comes here,' said her sister. 'Perhaps that is why he never seems at ease. He does think in very small ones then.'

'We ought to be grateful to him for saving us from penury,' said Susan. 'And giving us an education that makes us self-supporting.'

'In your case,' said Lester, gravely. 'I could not be a schoolmaster because of my voice and manner. The boys would be amused by me.'

'And we are grateful,' said Priscilla. 'I never know why people say they ought to be. Of course they ought.'

'It is hard to be beholden to him,' said Lester.

'We have been glad of the chance,' said Priscilla. 'And it is one that people always take.'

'We had no alternative,' said her brother.

'None but perishing of want,' said Susan. 'Three orphans from South America, the children of Sir Jesse's friends, but having no other claim. That is what we were.'

'And see what we are now,' said Lester, with a crow of laughter. 'Still orphans, but having established a claim.'

Priscilla, Lester and Susan Marlowe were aged thirty-five, thirty-four and thirty-two. They had pale, oblong faces, tall angular frames, round, grey, short-sighted eyes, peering through cheap, round glasses, and seeming to peer considerably beyond, heavy, shelving brows, from which curly, colourless hair receded, and in Lester's case had disappeared, and features so little conforming to rule, that they differed equally from other people's and each other's. Priscilla's voice was slow and apparently serious, Lester's shrill and uneven, and Susan's rapid and deep.

Sir Jesse gave them a cottage on the place, the services of an old couple whom he wished to support, and did so in this way, and an allowance to eke out what they earned. He never asked them to his house, seldom visited them and passed them abroad with acknowledgement but without a word; a course which people attributed to embarrassment at his generosity, though the feeling arises more easily from the consciousness of other qualities. They were used to his ways, hardly knew his wife, unaware that her hostile indifference embraced others besides themselves, had an almost surreptitious acquaintance with Daniel and Graham; and lived in their interests and anxieties and each other, with as much satisfaction as most people and more enjoyment.

'I have a month at home,' said Susan, looking round the low, cramped room with an expression that hardly suggested its character. 'How did we get all that wood for the fire?'

'We collect it in the park,' said her sister. 'We go after dusk, so that we shall not be seen. We are not ashamed of our poverty, but we know Sir Jesse is; and it might look as if we were short of fuel.'

'It would look so,' said Lester. 'And we do not want to suggest that he might provide it, when he does so much for us.'

'It is a good method of making him do so,' said Susan. 'Do you suppose he knows you get it?'

'He must know that the coal he sends is not enough,' said Priscilla. 'And I expect he would know if we were cold. He seems to know everything about us.'

'He must know that we have thin walls and no damp course,'

said Lester, in a serious voice. 'He may think we don't feel the cold.'

'What could you do with the cold but feel it?' said Susan. 'How else would you know there was such a thing?'

'People seem to think other people don't feel cold or grief or anything,' said Priscilla. 'I don't think they mind their feeling the heat. It seems a more comfortable thing, and it does not require any fuel.'

'Why are we having so much to eat?' said Susan.

'I am afraid not because it is your first day at home,' said her sister. 'Mrs Morris has to nurse her husband, and cannot cook tonight.'

'It is only old age,' said Lester, with simple reassurance. 'Nothing infectious.'

'Well, not immediately,' said Priscilla.

Lester gave a laugh.

'I am thankful to be at home,' said Susan. 'We can never be at ease except with each other. No one would understand our life, who had not lived it. A past without parents or a background is as rare as being brought up in an orphanage.'

'Is that rare?' said Priscilla. 'The papers always say how many thousands of inmates are admitted every year. It shows how few people behave as well as Sir Jesse.'

'That is why we have to contribute to such institutions,' said Lester.

'Do you?' said Priscilla, astonished. 'How you prevent the left hand from knowing what the right hand doeth!'

'Not I myself,' said Lester, opening his eyes. 'I never spend money without saying so.'

'We are the last people to support orphanages,' said Susan. 'They are fortunate in not having had to support us.'

'I suppose Sir Jesse has been father and mother to us,' said Lester, as if the thought amused him; 'though no one would think it, who saw him pass us without a word.'

'Family life seldom gets to that,' said Priscilla, 'or not with both the father and the mother.'

'We have never lisped our prayers at our mother's knee,' said Susan. 'What can be expected of us?'

'Hard work and reasonable success,' said Lester, in an almost wondering tone.

'Criminals are always told to look back on the time when they did that,' said Priscilla. 'It does not seem to be an auspicious beginning.'

'Our parents were friends of Sir Jesse's,' said Lester. 'And they lived in South America. I do not want to know more about them.'

'It seems to stamp them,' said Priscilla. 'I should not dare to ask. If it were anything that could be borne, Sir Jesse would have told us. And he would not mind our bearing a certain amount.'

'He seems to avoid contact with their children,' said Susan. 'We should never forgive ourselves, if we exerted any untoward influence on him. I wonder he allows us to mix with each other.'

Lester raised his eyes at this train of thought.

'It is the cheapest way of disposing of us,' he said. 'He gives us a house and a little money, and we provide the rest.'

'You would not think we had such large appetites, to look at us,' said Susan.

'I should have thought we were rather hungry-looking,' said Priscilla. 'As though we hardly knew where our next meal was coming from. And we do know. From Sir Jesse and our own hard earnings.'

'Well, Mrs Morris,' said Lester, 'I hope Morris is better.'

The housekeeper closed her eyes and kept them closed, while she placed the teapot with her usual precision.

'He must have a very good appetite.'

'What makes you say that, sir?' said Mrs Morris, performing an action that seemed unnatural to her, and looking at the speaker.

'You cook so much for him, that you have no time for us.'

'I hope to give you your usual dinner, sir.'

'If we have this tea and our usual dinner, Morris must be very bad.'

'He could not eat what I cooked, sir,' said Mrs Morris, arranging the table for those who could.

'Would he like anything special?' said Priscilla.

'He is not used to having what he fancies, miss.'

'There he is, going down the path,' said Susan.

119

'He can get about, miss.'

'He is going to the inn.'

Mrs Morris just cast a glance after her husband, as if his errand meant too little to warrant attention.

'Not used to having what he fancies!' said Susan, as the door closed. 'He gets more and more used to it.'

'Well, it means we can do the same,' said her sister.

'I am glad Morris has his own life,' said Lester, gravely.

'Lester talks quite like a man to Mrs Morris,' said Priscilla.

'Mr and Mrs Cranmer,' said Mrs Morris.

'Well, my dears,' said Hope. 'Are you expecting friends to tea, or is this your ordinary standard?' Her tone had a slight difference from the one she used to the Sullivans.

'It is Susan's first day at home,' said Paul, whose tone was always the same.

'I do respect the power to spend on things that did not meet the eye of outsiders. I don't believe they are even glad we have come on them in their luxury. And I should think it such a happy coincidence.'

'We are glad you are to share it,' said Lester.

'And now you do not pretend that you take it as a matter of course. I can't tell you what I think of you. I almost wish Faith were here; Paul will never appreciate the position.'

'Did she know you were coming?' said Lester, simply.

'What insight you have into our family life! No, I did not tell her.'

'I expect she is just as happy at home.'

'No, she likes nothing better than a little change, and she really needed it. But I needed it more, because compared to her as a companion I am a Cleopatra in my infinite variety. How few people would dare to say that!'

'How many of us think it of ourselves?' said Paul.

'Do not be foolish, Paul. Very few of us.'

'Very few,' said Priscilla.

'Have you been to the big house to say good-bye to Fulbert?' said Hope.

'No, his going makes no difference to us,' said Susan. 'We see none of them but Sir Jesse and the two elder boys.'

'Has Sir Jesse been to see you lately?'

'He came this afternoon.'

'And you were not going to mention it! I should take the first opportunity of bringing it in. Why did he come to see you? I must ask, Paul. They don't mind my knowing, and it would never occur to them to tell me.'

'Partly because a visit was due,' said Priscilla, 'and partly to hint that we might be more economical.'

'Even more than we are,' said Lester, seriously.

'Well, there is always something that can be cut off,' said Hope. 'But I wonder how Sir Jesse knew.'

'He didn't; he only hoped so,' said Priscilla. 'And when he saw the cottage, he thought he was wrong and took his leave.'

'But what about the tea? Did you expect him to stay?'

'To tea here?' said Lester.

'Yes.'

'And have it with us? Sir Jesse?'

'Yes. Is it impossible?'

'All things are possible,' said Susan. 'It is unthinkable.'

'We thought Mrs Morris could not cook tonight, because Morris is ill,' said Lester.

'Thank you so much; I am glad you do not always live like this. I don't like to think I am a stingy housekeeper. I am mean in so many matters; all the others, I think; and I hoped I made an exception of little, material things. The larger ones just can't be helped.'

'They never can,' said Lester, gravely.

'Sir Jesse said that he would miss his son,' said Priscilla. 'It seemed odd that he should have ordinary human feelings.'

'I shall have to do my best for him,' said Paul. 'He must have men about him, and he will not suffer his grandsons.'

'He does too much for them,' said Susan. 'Even what he does for us, makes him think we are on a different level.'

'Well, the things he does, giving us a cottage and a small allowance, keeps us on one,' said Priscilla. 'But isn't it wonderful that he does it?'

'Sometimes I feel I am an able-bodied man, accepting help

from another,' said Lester, expecting and meeting sympathy for this trick of his imagination.

'We are told that giving has the advantage over receiving,' said Paul.

'We should have to be told,' said Priscilla. 'Whoever said it, must have thought so.'

'You don't find it so in your experience?'

'We never give,' said Lester. 'It would not be fair on Sir Jesse.'

'I always feel that being here is a lesson,' said Hope.

'In rising above disadvantages, do you mean?' said Susan.

'Well, dear, I suppose I did. But I also meant in depending on your own qualities.'

'We are not going to disclaim them,' said Priscilla. 'It would be less awkward to mention them.'

'Do mention them, dear,' said Hope. 'I don't think anyone else has done so.'

'Intellect, individuality, our own kind of charm,' said Priscilla, with her lips grave.

Her sister laughed.

'Why is it amusing?' said Hope. 'I call it almost solemn. I feel inclined to rise. And now anyone could just rattle them off.'

'We could all have done so,' said Paul.

'I am glad you are a gentler creature than I am, Paul. I should hate you to be as hard as a woman. A husband ought to have some masculine qualities.'

'We are quite content,' said Lester.

'I see you are,' said Hope; 'and though I can't understand it, it makes me appreciate my easier lot.'

'I should have thought it was more difficult,' said Lester.

'I don't know whether to be annoyed or flattered by that. I like to feel I am in a hard place, but somehow any kind of difficulty seems a humiliation.'

'I believe you look down on us,' said Susan.

'Well, one does despise poverty and dependence,' said Hope, in a sharper tone. 'You did not speak in praise of them yourselves. But I pity them too, and I never feel that pity is such a dreadful thing. It is absurd to say it is the same as contempt. It even leads to kindness, and contempt never does that.'

'People even pity themselves,' said Priscilla. 'So the two feelings must be quite separate. People call contempt pity. That is how the confusion arises.'

'What is that parcel, Priscilla?' said Lester.

'Oh, I had forgotten. Sir Jesse brought it this afternoon. It is a photograph of our mother. He said he came across it. It seems strange to think of Sir Jesse going through his odds and ends. One would think that sort of thing would be done for him. It must be one of those wrong ideas that the poor get about the rich. I did not dare to open it by myself.'

'No, of course not,' said Lester, looking at the parcel as if he would hesitate under any circumstances.

'What are you afraid of?' said Hope. 'I know it is an insensitive question, but nothing brings out my better qualities today. If your first meeting with your mother fails to do so, nothing can be done.'

'It seems strange that most people know their mothers from the first,' said Priscilla.

'Now we shall be able to trace our odd physiognomy to its source,' said Susan.

'We shall have to,' said her sister.

'I don't mind what she is like,' said Lester.

'We see the strong feeling of the son for the mother coming out,' said Hope.

'I am sure Lester is not a man who would ever be ashamed of his mother,' said Priscilla.

'I have always thought it silly to say that photographs seem to be looking at us,' said Susan. 'But it does seem that this one would have the impulse.'

'I am glad it sees us with the condoning eyes of a mother,' said Priscilla, holding the photograph out of her own sight.

'I am sure her ugly ducklings are swans to her, dears,' said Hope.

'She is tall,' said Lester.

'I don't know why,' said Hope, 'but I suddenly feel inclined to cry.'

'And as plain as we are,' said Susan. 'Or not quite.'

'No, not as plain,' said Lester.

'Of course a mother is always beautiful to her son,' said Hope. 'There was no reason for Lester to be afraid. It was different for his sisters.'

'It is a good face and a good head,' said Paul.

'I do congratulate you all,' said Hope. 'And her as well, of course. I have never seen such a family.'

'I wonder why she made a friend of Sir Jesse,' said Lester.

'Is that the only thing you know against her?' said Paul, laughing.

'It is all we know about her,' said Susan. 'Perhaps she felt he would be a friend to her children.'

'We see where Susan gets her practical side,' said Priscilla. 'From Mother. This is the first homecoming when she has been here to welcome her.'

'So Sir Jesse did not bring a photograph of your father,' said Paul.

'I am rather glad,' said Priscilla. 'These family reunions are rather a strain.'

'We must have the photograph framed,' said Susan.

'Don't go yet, Paul,' said Priscilla. 'Sit down here by Mother.'

'I feel ashamed that the meeting has been witnessed by our idly curious eyes,' said Hope.

'I think you ought to share Mother with us, Lester,' said Priscilla. 'Mothers are not quite indifferent to their daughters. Perhaps Mother would not change me for all the sons in the world.'

'How much does a frame cost?' said her brother.

'There is Mother coming out.'

'It depends on the quality,' said Susan.

'In both of you,' said Priscilla. 'But ought the first economy we make after we have known Mother, to be on her? Though of course mothers do not like their children to spend their money on them.'

'I will subscribe to the frame,' said Lester, who could not always take this course with the family expenses.

'There are Ridley and Faith,' said Susan. 'How did they know you were here?'

'Just what Mother would have said!' said Priscilla.

'Something must have told them,' said Hope. 'It was not me.'

'We guessed you would be here,' said Faith, as she entered with her brother. 'We thought we might as well walk home together.'

'Need you have walked home at all, dear?' said Hope.

There was a pause.

'We have had tea,' said Faith, as if they would not impose this demand on the house.

'I hope we are not intruding,' said Ridley, with a smile for his suggestion.

'I hope not, dear,' said Hope.

'Have you been turning out old albums?' said Faith, looking at the table. 'I think the old-fashioned photographs are often so interesting.'

'They certainly throw a vivid light on the past,' said Ridley.

'Who is the lady?' said Faith, with the sprightliness that does not suggest high or serious anticipations.

'It is our mother,' said Lester, handing her the photograph. 'Sir Jesse brought it today. We had not seen it before.'

'Oh, I did not know,' said Faith, taking a step backwards with her eyes on his face.

'I think that was natural,' said Paul.

'It shows that one should be careful what one says,' said Faith, lightly. 'But I did not say anything derogatory, did I? And I had not looked at the photograph.'

'Your opinion would not have been of value,' said Paul.

'It must be quite a significant occasion,' said Ridley. 'I can picture the flights of imagination that the sight must produce.'

'It seems to render them for the first time unnecessary,' said Priscilla.

'Do you see any likeness in her to any of you?' said Faith. 'Or in any of you to her, I should say?'

'I think Lester is a little like her,' said Susan.

'They say that sons take after their mothers,' said Faith.

'We shall be four instead of three in future,' said Priscilla, putting the photograph on the chimney-piece.

'There is a photograph at home that I shall destroy,' said Hope. 'I want Faith to be sincere when she says I am the only mother she has known.'

'I have always been so,' said Faith. 'It is not my habit to say things I do not mean.'

'Then I hope we have never been five.'

'I think that photographs are chiefly useful for recalling people to those who knew them,' said Faith.

'Then they are not of great use,' said Paul.

'They are better than nothing for those who did not,' said Lester.

'As you say, Lester, nothing is not much to depend upon,' said Ridley, in a tone of sympathy.

'Has Sir Jesse a photograph of your father?' said Faith.

'Not to our knowledge,' said Susan.

'Have you not asked him?' said Faith, with a smile for this indifference.

'We don't often ask him questions.'

'I don't think he would mind one on that subject.'

'It might not be the exception,' said Paul.

Faith gave her father a glance, as if perplexed by his attitude.

'Would it help you if I were to ask him?' she said to the Marlowes. 'I could just put a casual question, and pass on to something else, and give you the result later. I think I am at the house rather oftener than you are.'

'We are never there,' said Lester.

'I expect that is just a custom that has grown up.'

'It is, dear, no doubt,' said Hope.

'You don't want to go,' said Paul, his bright eyes scanning the Marlowes' faces.

'We don't wear their kind of clothes,' said Susan. 'And we should feel we were dependants.'

'Then wouldn't the clothes be all right?' said Hope.

'I think that dress is very becoming to Susan,' said Faith.

'She has to have things for outsiders,' said Lester.

'People look themselves in whatever they wear,' said Faith.

'It is a good thing they don't know that,' said Hope. 'And I am not going to believe it.'

'We should have to look like other people,' said Priscilla, 'and that costs money.'

'I think you would find it a little change to go now and then,' said Faith.

'Daniel and Graham come here sometimes,' said Susan.

'Do they? I did not know that.'

'I wonder how it escaped your notice, dear,' said Hope.

'I expect Mrs Sullivan is glad for them to have the break, Mother.'

'It is their own feeling that brings them,' said Paul.

'Yes, they come to see us,' said Priscilla. 'It is one of those cases of people's finding their happiness in humbler surroundings.'

'I don't suppose they even notice the surroundings,' said Faith, showing that she was more observant herself.

'We owe too much to Sir Jesse for our intercourse with him to be natural,' said Lester.

'That does not argue any lack of generosity on either side,' said Faith.

'It does not on Sir Jesse's,' said Priscilla.

'I know that the little discomforts of any unusual position are often very hard to get over,' said Faith.

'They must be,' said Hope, 'because any embarrassment is bad enough.'

'We have got away from the subject of your father's photograph,' said Faith.

'And now you have led us back to it, dear,' said Hope.

'Very few people never have their photographs taken, Mother.'

'We have never done so,' said Priscilla. 'Perhaps it runs in the family.'

'Your mother's was taken,' said Faith.

'Well, people do sometimes take after one side.'

'Do people have their own photographs taken?' said Paul. 'Other people want a record of them.'

'And then they have to be told to look pleasant,' said Hope. 'If anyone wanted one of me, I could not subdue my elation.'

'I am touched by people's wanting a record of Mother,' said Priscilla. 'It says so much for them and for her.'

'I do not believe I have ever been immortalized in that way,' said Ridley.

'But think of the other ways, dear,' said Hope. 'I have not been taken since I was married. Your father was in the mood for wanting a record of me then. People do want them of people when they are about to spend their lives with them, though it is difficult to see what use they will be.'

'Sir Jesse will miss his son very much,' said Faith. 'It will make a third empty place in the house.'

'Are there any others?' said Hope. 'I know there are a great many full ones.'

'Lady Sullivan has lost two children, Mother.'

'The house never strikes me as empty somehow. There are plenty of little, pattering feet. I mean there are eighteen.'

'I suspect it has its own emptiness for her, Mother.'

'Well, you would understand. Our house must have its own for you.'

'You have your own place, Mrs Cranmer,' said Ridley, with a note of reproach.

'Yes, it is mine now.'

'Sir Jesse's is the perfect place,' said Susan.

'I think I would vote for Eleanor Sullivan's,' said Ridley, looking about with a grave eagerness. 'All the advantages of a married woman, and none of the care and contrivance.'

'I thought those were dear to a woman's heart,' said Hope.

'I am sure I do not want any place but my own,' said Faith, contracting her brows at the thought of other people's.

'I want any place that is better than mine,' said Hope.

'Do people's places mean their endowments?' said Paul.

'No, our characteristics in their places,' said his wife. 'Everyone is content with his own endowments. The Marlowes' are things one could hardly speak about. I have never heard anyone but them do so.'

'I have heard many people.'

'You need not pounce on the one touch of meanness in my speech.'

'I am afraid I am not content with my endowments,' said Faith, with a wry little smile.

'Don't you think there is something about you that no one else has?' said Hope. 'Because I am sure there is.'

Faith raised her eyes and looked into her stepmother's.

'I know you think I cannot meet your eyes,' said the latter. 'And that being so, why do you put me to the test?'

'I think we had better be going, Mother.'

'We were all to go together. But as Priscilla cannot spare your father and me, the rest of you must go by yourselves.'

'That is only Ridley and me, Mother.'

'Is that all, dear? Then there are not any more.'

'I think that is a hint of whose breadth we need not be in doubt,' said Ridley, rising and going into mirth. 'We have no choice but to withdraw with as good a grace as possible.'

Faith stood for a moment, irresolute, and then went from one Marlowe to another in quiet and pleasant farewell, and led the way from the house.

'Of course stepmothers are cruel,' said Hope, 'but then so are stepchildren, though they don't have any of the discredit. We all have a right to survive, and only the fittest can do so, and it seems that a struggle is inevitable.'

'I wonder why we are all entitled to life,' said Susan. 'But I am glad Sir Jesse accepted it in our case.'

'We have a right to work for our bread,' said Lester, almost wonderingly.

'We have so many rights,' said Priscilla, 'but they don't seem such very good ones.'

'Will you come home with us, now that we can't overtake the others?' said Hope.

There was a silence.

'Well, it is Susan's first day at home,' said Priscilla.

'She would have to walk back,' said Lester.

'You know you would have the carriage,' said Hope. 'You should not stoop to falsehood to avoid an invitation.'

'What alternative is there?' said Paul.

'Are you so fond of your life in this cottage?' said Hope.

'Yes, we are,' said Priscilla. 'Our odd, isolated experience has drawn us so close.'

'The cottage is our home,' said Lester. 'Sir Jesse gave it to us.'

'I have always felt a little sorry about that,' said Hope. 'But there is never any need to worry about people. They are always so satisfied.'

'A poor thing but our own,' said Susan.

'I quite agree, dear. But why put it in the form of a saying? They don't contain the truth.'

'They call attention to it,' said Priscilla. 'Of course it is there without them.'

'I am glad it is there,' said Lester, with great content. 'Of course people do not see the cottage with our eyes.'

'Books and a fire,' said Priscilla, looking at these things. 'What more could we have?'

'I see you haven't any more,' said Hope, with some exasperation. 'But does that prevent your having dinner with a friend? You could have that as well.'

'We know about the other things,' said Susan. 'Cushions and flowers and things that shimmer in the firelight.'

'We like the firelight better by itself,' said Priscilla.

'I can see you do,' said Hope. 'And I like the things that go with it. I don't even want a mind above material things; I enjoy having one on their level.'

'I have never seen better firelight,' said Paul.

'It is the beech from the park,' said Lester.

'Does Sir Jesse send it to you?' said Hope.

'No, we have his tacit permission to gather it.'

'Are you proud of the mark of intimacy? Or humbled by being in need of fuel? I must remember that beech makes a fire like this. I want one to play on my possessions. I don't care if it is a nasty use for it. I don't want it for anything else.'

'It is a mistake to make the lily gild other things,' said Susan.

'If you liked me a little better, I should not be so petty,' said Hope. 'What is the good of striving to be worthy of your friendship, when I have no chance of it? You know how I long for your affection; people always know the things that add to themselves; I expect you exaggerate my desire for it. Of course I don't show it in public, when you are so neglected and eccentric. You could not expect it of a petty person, or what is your reason for thinking her petty? But you might save me from spending all my evenings with the family. I love to do it for Paul's sake, but I like to have things for my own sake as well, and I believe you know that I do.'

'Well, Susan only came home today,' said Lester.

'And I came thirty years ago. I do see she doesn't need a change so much. And of course I like her to be considered first. So I will leave you to look at the firelight playing on nothing. Though if you won't exert any influence over me, I don't see how I can improve.'

'We like you as you are,' said Lester.

'That is a crumb of comfort for me to take with me. I do hate going empty away. Would you like me to send you a load of beech?'

'Yes, if you will,' said Lester.

'How people do jump up and pin one down! Now we are committed to it. Well, it will come with love from us both, and I hope it will be all right by itself.'

'We know it will,' said Paul.

'Hope does not respect us as much as if we had the usual position,' said Susan, when they were alone. 'Her referring to it openly does not alter it.'

'Is it one reason why we do not respect ourselves?' said Lester, in simple question.

'The only one, I think,' said Priscilla.

'Ridley and Faith seem to respect us,' said Lester.

'Faith respects her fellow-creatures,' said Susan. 'And Ridley is a lawyer, and knows how common it is to be penniless; and he respects us for having a little money from Sir Jesse, and being able to earn a little more.'

'How I respect us!' said Priscilla.

'Do we respect other people?' said Lester.

'I do very much indeed,' said Priscilla. 'They seem to have so much of everything. Think of Faith, and her charitable nature and her comfortable home and her life of ease. I think a human being is remarkably well equipped. Kind hearts are more than coronets, but so many people seem to have them both.'

'A good home is not a coronet,' said Susan.

'Well, I should have said it really was.'

'It is odd that we cannot ask Sir Jesse about our parentage,' said Lester.

'It is because he has never told us,' said Susan.

'It seems a pity that one should preclude the other,' said

Priscilla. 'One does not see what can be done. He hardly spoke of the photograph when he left it.'

'Perhaps he was thinking of what it could tell us, if it could speak,' said Susan.

'He was quite sure it could not do that. And I should hardly dare to listen. And I don't suppose it would.'

'We ought to imagine things about ourselves.'

'If they were true, Sir Jesse would not have had to bring us up,' said Lester.

'He never seems proud of what he has done,' said Priscilla. 'He almost draws a veil over it.'

'Over us, I think it is,' said Susan. 'He does not require us to go to church, because he would have to recognize us.'

'It would be a great waste of our Sunday,' said Lester, in a startled tone.

'I wonder if we are as odd as we think we are,' said Susan.

'We can only hope so,' said her sister, 'and continue to do our best.'

'There is Daniel's voice,' said Susan. 'And I expect Graham is with him.'

'That would not mean a voice,' said Lester, in a tone of stating a fact.

'You do not mind my bringing Graham,' said Daniel. 'I find it best to keep him under my eye.'

Graham took a seat.

'Has your father gone yet?' said Susan.

'No, or I should be at home, taking his place,' said Daniel.

'I wish I had just enough money to live on,' said Graham, looking round the room.

'Why do people wish that?' said Priscilla. 'Why not wish to have enough and to spare?'

'They mean they do not ask much,' said Graham. 'But of course they are asking everything.'

'A thing is more desirable when it is unattainable,' said Daniel.

'And how reasonable that is,' said Priscilla, 'when nothing comes up to expectation!'

'This would,' said Graham, 'to anyone brought up as an obligation.'

'We have been brought up like that too,' said Susan, 'but it has sat on us more lightly.'

'Sir Jesse seems to have formed the habit,' said Priscilla. 'And it is a very useful one.'

'I wish you could sometimes come to the house,' said Graham.

'Sir Jesse is ashamed of us,' said Susan. 'We never quite know why.'

'We will not pretend to see any reason,' said Priscilla.

'I wonder if we shall ever know,' said Lester.

'Grandma is the person to ask you,' said Daniel, 'and she never welcomes outsiders.'

'Then how do your friends get to the house?' said Susan.

'They do not,' said Graham. 'We have no friends.'

'The iron has entered into the boy's soul,' said Daniel.

'Graham and Lester both have a squeak in their voices,' said Susan.

'Lester must unconsciously try to catch a note from a different and more spacious world,' said her sister.

'I have very simple tastes,' said Graham.

'You have had little chance of acquiring others,' said Daniel.

'That is said to give people expensive ones,' said Priscilla.

'Has it in your case?' said Graham.

'No, but we are unusual. It is no good to say we are not.'

'Is that why Hope is uneasy about knowing us?' said Lester.

'It is only because we are not known,' said Priscilla. 'It is nothing personal.'

'There is something second-rate going through Hope,' said Susan. 'She thinks she makes it better by joking about it.'

'And so she does,' said her sister. 'She makes it very good indeed. You don't mean you do not like it?'

'I wish the next six months were over,' said Graham.

'I do not,' said Lester. 'It would mean that all three of us had six months less to live.'

'It would mean it for us too,' said Daniel, 'and for everyone.'

'I suppose it would,' said Lester, after a moment's thought.

'Oh, let me introduce Mother,' said Priscilla, taking up the photograph. 'My long struggle to take her place is over. She is here to fill it herself. I almost feel jealous of her, but I suppose that is usual with eldest daughters. Sir Jesse came this afternoon and filled the blank in our lives.'

'Grandpa did not say he was coming,' said Graham.

'Is it the first time you have not had his confidence?' said Daniel.

'I am so grateful to Mother for my existence,' said Priscilla. 'I believe that is very unusual, but I enjoy existence very much. I do agree that life is sweet.'

'You are more like your mother than you are like each other,' said Graham.

'She must be in all of us,' said Lester.

'So she has really been here all the time,' said Priscilla. 'That makes me feel rather foolish.'

'Who will miss your father the most?' said Susan.

'Grandma,' said Graham, 'and then I suppose Mother, and then one or two of the girls. But no one will like the house without him. He seems to lift some blight that hangs over us.'

'I hardly know him,' said Lester.

'You must feel you are beginning to do so,' said Priscilla. 'And you must find it a privilege?'

'We shall have to settle down,' said Daniel. 'We can't remain in a state of tension for six months.'

'It does sound dreadful,' said Priscilla, looking at Graham's face. 'To settle down for six months, when youth is such a sad time. Not that I did not find it very pleasant. I always wonder why people cling to it, when they find it so uncongenial. I get to like it more and more. You see I still think I have it.'

'I could like it,' said Graham, again looking round the room.

'Books and a fire,' said Priscilla. 'You can have nothing more. I am not one of those people who belittle the things they have. I daresay you think I do the opposite.'

'People pity us,' said Lester to Graham, in a tone of information.

'Because we have the bare necessities of life,' said Priscilla. 'And that is foolish, when necessities are so important. They would hardly pity us any more for not having them.'

'They pity you and not me,' said Graham, in an incredulous tone.

'Well, you live in Sir Jesse's house, and we live here,' said Susan.

'I have a seat at the table and a room on an upper floor.'

'And what do you do at the table, Graham?' said Daniel.

'You cannot have pity as well,' said Priscilla. 'And it would not be much good to you.'

'We know about it, though we do not mind it,' said Lester.

'You know nothing of self-pity,' said Graham. 'And that is the only sort that counts.'

CHAPTER SIX

'DOES no one want to say good-bye to Father?' said Eleanor, in a high, incredulous voice from the hall, with her face held towards the upper landings. 'Do you not want to see the last of him? Or have you all forgotten he is going?'

'Our minds may be so weary of the image that they have yielded it up,' said Isabel, as her feet kept pace with her sister's on the stairs.

'Are you just going on with your life in your ordinary way?' said Eleanor, in the same tone and with her brows raised. 'Is this day just the same as any other to you?'

'It is an odd person who can suggest that,' said her daughter. 'We thought you might want to say good-bye to Father by yourself, that that was perhaps why he came to see us last night.'

'Oh, that is what it was. But I do not want to keep him to myself at this last stage. He will want to remember us all together,' said Eleanor, with her querulous honesty. 'I am not the only person he has in his life. Run up and see that everyone is here. He will be going in half-an-hour.'

Isabel mounted a flight of stairs and raised her voice in a message to Hatton.

'From the way Isabel moves, you would think your father had a month to be here,' said Eleanor.

'He has almost,' said Isabel, in a low voice to Venice, as she returned. 'Thirty minutes, and we have had one!'

'Shall I go and fetch Luce and Daniel and Graham?' said James, hovering near his mother.

'Yes, tell them all to come. I cannot understand this lacka-daisical attitude. You might not have a father. I simply do not feel I can explain it.'

Eleanor was released from this effort by the appearance of her sons and daughter from their study, with Luce holding her father's arm, and her brothers wearing the look of the final advice and farewell. Sir Jesse and Regan came from the library, the former resolute and almost urbane, the latter ravaged and fierce. Hatton appeared on the landing with the children, put Nevill's hand into Honor's, and withdrew round the balusters to await events.

'So we are here to get all we can out of it,' said Regan. 'It shows it is not too much for us; that is one thing.'

'It ensures that it shall be,' said Graham.

'Trouble shared is trouble halved,' said Fulbert, in a cheerful tone. 'It will be disappearing amongst a dozen, and I shall leave dry eyes behind.'

'Grandma, Luce, Daniel, Grandpa,' said Nevill, seeming to fol-low out his father's thought. 'Venice, Father, Graham, Isabel. And he is here too, and Hatton. And Mother and James.'

'Father is the important person today,' said Eleanor.

'We are all Father's,' said her son, supporting her view.

'And he is obliged to leave us.'

'No,' said Nevill, in a light tone. 'Father is not going away any more.'

'He has heard too much of it,' said Fulbert.

'We have all done that,' said Regan, rapidly blinking her eyes.

Luce put a chair for her grandmother and stood stroking her shoulders, and Nevill ran to another chair and climbed on to it, and keeping his eyes on Regan, pulled out his handkerchief and retained it in his hand.

'Why are you in out-of-door things, Luce?' said Eleanor, sur-prised by any sign of personal pursuits.

'Because I am going to the station, Mother.'

'As well as the boys?'

'Yes.'

'Will there be room in the carriage?'

'Yes.'

'Won't it upset you?'

'Yes,' said Luce, smiling, 'but that need not be taken into account.'

'But won't that be depressing for your father at the last?'

'No, Mother, he will not be conscious of it.'

'But is there any point in your going?'

'Yes,' said Luce, now with a note of patience. 'Father will have a woman to see him off, as well as young men.'

'I should find it too much.'

'I am in my way a strong woman, Mother.'

'And I am a weak one, I suppose.'

'It is the first time I have heard a woman make that claim, without any sign of satisfaction,' said Graham, who had been watching his mother.

'I have no fault to find with the strength or the weakness,' said Fulbert. 'They are both after my heart.'

Luce moved her hands more rapidly on Regan's shoulders, as if to stave off any impending emotion.

'I hope the occasion may prove a turning point in Graham's life,' said Daniel.

Venice laughed, and Eleanor glanced at her in mute question of such a sound.

'Mother,' said Luce, in a low tone, 'let Father leave us in a happy atmosphere.'

'It can hardly be that, my dear, when he is going for six months.'

'Not after he has gone. But while he is here, let us stand up to the test.'

'Isabel looks as if she were at a funeral,' said Eleanor, as if this were going beyond the suitable point.

'She may be right,' said Regan.

'I don't want her father to remember her like that.'

'Why is it assumed that people forget all moments but the last?' said Daniel.

Isabel broke into tears; Fulbert put his arm about her; she could not control her weeping, and it became almost loud. Hatton came round the staircase and stood with her eyes upon her, as if debating her course.

'Isabel dear, if you cannot control yourself, Hatton must take you upstairs, as if you were one of the little ones,' said Eleanor, speaking as though her daughter were nearer to this stage than she was.

'She will come and sit by Grandma,' said Regan, using the same manner, but also the gift for doing so.

Isabel sat on the floor at Regan's feet; the latter began to stroke her hair, and Luce noted the action and glided away, seeing her own ministrations rendered unnecessary by this transference of thought to another.

'What are you doing, Gavin?' said Eleanor.

'Drawing,' said her son, continuing the occupation.

'Isn't that rather a strange way of spending your last half-hour with Father?'

'No.'

'What makes you do it just now?'

'Nothing.'

'Let me see what you are drawing.'

'No,' said Gavin, pocketing the paper.

'That is not nice behaviour. But I expect you are upset by Father's leaving us.'

'No, I am not.'

'He will draw,' said Nevill, throwing himself off his chair and running to his brother.

Gavin turned aside.

'Let him do it, Gavin,' said Eleanor.

Gavin pursued his way.

'Let him have a piece of paper.'

'I only have the one piece.'

Nevill stood with his feet apart and his arms at his sides, on the point of surrendering himself to a lament of frustration.

'Will my good, useful girl get him a pencil and paper?' said Eleanor.

Venice recognized herself in the description, and was in time to prevent Hatton, who had partly descended the stairs, from coming further. Nevill put the paper on a chair, and stood, pushing the pencil rather violently about it, as if he were unfitted by emotional stress for normal application.

'What is the mystery about Gavin's drawing, Honor?' said Eleanor.

'There isn't one, Mother.'

'What is he drawing?'

'A portrait of Father.'

'Oh, that is what it is; that is very nice,' said Eleanor, as though finding herself wrong in some surmise to which this adjective could not be applied. 'That was the right thing to think of, wasn't it?'

'I didn't think of it. It was Honor,' said Gavin.

'Poor little girl, she wanted a portrait to keep,' said Eleanor, making a statement that was natural to the circumstances, but caused her daughter to fall into such violent weeping, that the services of Hatton were called upon and she was led from sight.

'Here is a dear, bright face for Father to remember!' said Eleanor, taking Venice's cheek in her hand.

Venice stared before her and struck her side, and Eleanor turned to her sons, baffled by her daughter's various responses to the occasion.

'Have you asked your father if you can do anything for him, as the eldest son?' she said to Daniel, with her vague note of reproof.

'Yes, I have, and been answered.'

'And you, Graham?'

'Yes, with the same result.'

'I am sure I can depend on my two tall sons.'

'A conviction that seems to be born of the moment,' said Daniel.

'Mother, you haven't much hope of your children, have you?' said Luce.

'I am so used to training and guiding them, that I forget the time has come for results.'

'The results do not remind you, Mother?'

'I wish they could sometimes be allowed to appear.'

'Graham need not be self-conscious about his little efforts at improvement,' said Daniel.

'Let me see your portrait of Father, Gavin,' said Eleanor, simply passing from her elder sons.

Gavin took the paper from his pocket and handed it to Graham, as if in a near enough approach to obedience, and Eleanor looked at it without moving, seeming to accept this method of putting it at a convenient level.

'Anyone can see it is a man,' said Graham.

'That halves the number of people it may represent,' said Daniel.

'It is a grown-up man,' said Gavin. 'It has wrinkles.'

'Perhaps that quarters them.'

'Let me see myself in my son's eyes,' said Fulbert. 'I admit the wrinkles, both here and in the original. There is a framed photograph in my dressing room that may pass into Honor's possession, if she so desires.'

Honor, who had been led back in a state of pale calm, raised a lighted face.

'It has the advantage of having no wrinkles, as the less honest artist took them out.'

'If the frame is silver, Honor could sell it for a lot of money,' said Gavin.

'But she will want to keep it,' said his mother. 'It is a picture of Father.'

'Can I have it even after Father comes back?' said Honor.

'It is your very own,' said Fulbert, 'and the lack of wrinkles will become a more and more distinguishing feature.'

'Now you feel quite cheered up, don't you?' said Eleanor.

'Yes,' said her daughter, agreeing that this was a natural result.

'You will feel you have a little bit of Father always with you.'

'It is all of him down to his hands,' said Gavin.

Nevill, who had been making rapid but considered marks on the fair side of his paper, now approached and proffered it for inspection.

'It is Luce; it is Grandma,' he said.

'It is differentiated to about the same extent,' said Daniel. 'It indicates age and sex.'

'It does, Daniel,' said Luce, as if this were an all but incredible circumstance.

'It is Hatton,' said Nevill, in a settled tone.

'Poor Father!' said Luce, half to herself. 'He stands amongst his family on a day when he should be the hero, and everyone seems more in the foreground than he.'

'He is the basis that everything is built upon,' said Graham. 'Surely that is enough.'

'Well, it cannot go on much longer, boys.'

'If there were any reason why it should stop,' said Graham, 'surely it would have operated by now.'

'The train will become due,' said Luce.

'I suppose it has always been expected at a certain time,' said Daniel. 'Was no account taken of it, when we assembled for the final scene?'

'We could have acted a play in the time,' said his brother.

'We have done so, Graham,' said Luce.

'Father's wrinkles can hardly be getting less,' said Venice.

'We have stood and striven faithfully,' said Graham; 'we have jested with set lips; two of us have wept. Have we not earned our release?'

'We will act no more,' said Sir Jesse, suddenly striding forward with a scowl on his face. 'We will cease to parade the tears of women and teach young men to make a show of themselves. My son can go to his duty without that. I have left my family in my time, and without exposing them to this. Does no one think of anything but disburdening himself? Let him think of other things.'

He drew back, breathing deeply. Fulbert looked up with an expression that made his face a boy's; Regan surveyed them both with a look that also came from the past; and in the silence that followed, Luce approached her mother.

'Mother, I am going to end the scene. For the sake of Father and ourselves. It is losing weight and meaning. It will be less significant, not more, for being prolonged. I take it upon myself to say that time is up.'

'Time, is it?' said Fulbert, turning and beginning on the round of his farewells, as if seeing the mistake of prolonging them. 'Time for me to enter on the months which are to restore me to you. I am like a criminal anxious to begin his sentence; I am one, in that I should have served it years ago.'

He went the course of his family with a sort of resolute ease, embraced the women and girls with a suggestion of an especial meaning for each, and left before emotion could be manifest. Regan stood and stared before her with a face that was suddenly blank and old, and Sir Jesse was silent and almost absent, as if withdrawing from further part in the scene. Eleanor was pale and controlled; Isabel and Honor were lost in the struggle with their tears; Venice and James were conscious of themselves and nervous of the attention of others; Gavin appeared to be unaffected; and the two young men devoted themselves to the duties of the moment.

Nevill ran up to Fulbert as he reached the door, and thrust his paper into his hand.

'A picture of Father,' he said.

'Nevill has made the supreme sacrifice, that of Hatton,' said Graham, and brought a smile to Regan's face.

Luce stood in the hall and motioned her father onward in a manner that gave no quarter, and as Daniel held open the carriage door, entered almost with alacrity and took her seat. Fulbert followed with his usual springy gait; the brothers sat at the back; Fulbert raised his hand to his mother and his wife, or to one or the other, as each took the salute to herself. Of the group in the hall Regan was the first to speak.

'Well, the children will be back, I suppose. There is no danger of our losing them.'

Sir Jesse turned and walked to the library, with a lack of expectance about him, that sent his wife after him with an altered face. Eleanor was the next to utter her first words.

'James, I do not believe you uttered a syllable during the whole of Father's last half-hour with us.'

James looked at his mother and maintained this course.

'Why did you suppose you were here?'

'Hatton told us to come down.'

'Then did you not want to say good-bye to Father?'

'Yes, but we did it last night.'

'But wouldn't you have liked a last word?'

'Well – but we had it last night – it was better – then we had it by itself,' said James, in a barely articulate tone.

'Oh, that is what it was. Well, I can understand that.'

James simply relaxed his body and his face.

'You did not speak to Father, either, did you, Gavin?' said Eleanor, in an almost expressionless tone, as if she hesitated to commit herself on her sons' motives.

Gavin looked at her in silence.

'Of course you were making a picture of him,' said Eleanor, seeking his corresponding justification.

'He was too,' said Nevill, beginning to look about for the paper, which he knew his father had not taken.

'We can't help Father's going to America,' said Gavin.

'No, but it is because of you in a way,' said Eleanor, at once. 'It is because he wants to make the future safe for us.'

'Then it is because of you too.'

'Of course, it is especially because of me. But I did not think it was not.'

Gavin considered for a moment and then left the subject.

'Isabel, you seem in a state of utter exhaustion,' said Eleanor, in a sharper tone. 'How you are upset by any little strain! Everything seems too much for you.'

'The last half-hour has been,' said Isabel, for her sister's ears.

'Venice, take her upstairs, and tell Miss Mitford that I said she was to go to Hatton and lie down.'

Isabel proceeded to her rest; the circuitous method also disposed of Venice; James stood with a sense of personal justification; Nevill ran up to Eleanor and offered his paper.

'A picture of Mother,' he said.

'My dear, little, comforting boy!'

'A picture of Mother; Father come back soon; all gone away, but come back tomorrow,' said Nevill, rapidly enumerating grounds of consolation.

'Luce and Daniel and Graham will come back in a few minutes,' said Gavin.

'Come back in a few minutes,' said Nevill, passing on this information to his mother before he left her.

'Honor, hadn't you and Gavin better have some game?' said Eleanor, looking at the silent children.

'He will be a horse,' suggested Nevill.

'Would you like to get that photograph from Father's room?' said Eleanor, seeing the need of another solution.

Honor and Gavin sprang towards the stairs, and Nevill gave them a glance and continued his exercise.

James made a movement of sudden recollection and ran up after them, producing in his mother the impression that he had some object in view, and no curiosity concerning it, which were results that he had intended.

Nevill suddenly realized that he was alone with his mother in the hall.

'Go with Hatton,' he said, in a tone of giving the situation one chance before he despaired of it.

'I will take you to her,' said Eleanor, offering her hand.

Nevill accepted it and mounted the stairs with an air of concentrating all his being on one object. When they reached the nursery, he looked up at his mother.

'Father come back tomorrow, come back soon,' he said, and ran through the door.

Eleanor satisfied herself that Isabel was asleep, and paid a visit to Venice and Miss Mitford as she passed the schoolroom.

'Are you standing about doing nothing, dear? Is she, Miss Mitford?'

'Yes.'

'Is that the way to keep up her spirits?'

'I do not think she is in spirits.'

'Cannot she find some occupation?'

'Girls of her age have no pursuits.'

'Could she not make something to do?'

'That is beneath human dignity.'

'Is it so dignified just to stand about?'

'It is more so. And she is accustoming herself to the change in the house. Surely that is quite reasonable.'

'I think we shall have to let time do that for us.'

'Well, that is what she is doing. Half-an-hour cannot do much.'

'Is James anywhere about?'

'He is with the children in the nursery. He had a holiday because his father was going.'

'He will no doubt have one when he comes back. I don't know

how he makes any progress. I don't suppose he does make much. Are the girls resting too today? Isabel is asleep.'

'I hope that is resting,' said Miss Mitford. 'I hope it is not one of those heavy, unrefreshing sleeps.'

'Can Isabel and I have a photograph of Father, like Honor and Gavin?' said Venice, in a sudden tone.

'Yes, of course you can, dear child. I will put one out for you. There is sure to be a frame that will fit it.'

'Is there?' said Miss Mitford, seeing this question in Venice's eyes. 'I should think that is unusual.'

'I don't know of one, certainly. But we shall find one.'

'I should not know where to look for such a thing.'

Eleanor's face revealed that this was the case with herself.

'I have a pair of frames that I do not want,' said Miss Mitford.

'Whom have you had in them?' said Venice.

'My father and mother. But I am inclined to take them out, because they stir the chords of memory.'

'Venice dear, do not ask questions,' said Eleanor. 'Just say you will like to have the frames, if Miss Mitford has no use for them. And then you may come and get the photograph.'

'Whom will you put in the second frame?' said Miss Mitford. 'I could give you a photograph of myself, to balance your father's.'

Venice hesitated with a half-smile, and Miss Mitford suddenly gave a whole one.

'Come with me and I will give you one of my own photographs,' said Eleanor. 'Then you can have your parents on either side of your fireplace. It is kind of you to amuse them, Miss Mitford. She is quite cheered up.'

Isabel awoke to find her sister disposing the photographs on the mantelpiece.

'What are those?' she said, and heard the account. 'I would as soon have had Mitta as Mother,' she said.

'We could not put her to correspond with Father,' said Venice, not criticizing the view on any other ground.

'I think I shall say I am too tired to come down to dessert.'

'Can you be as tired as that, after your rest? Mother saw you were asleep.'

'I can after these last days.'

'Well, if you want to explain that!' said Venice, causing her sister to rise from her bed.

'Now remember,' said the latter, as they left the schoolroom later, 'I am quite myself and not at all depressed, and I wanted to come downstairs. I was only tired and upset by Father's going.'

'And what if I am asked what you ate at dinner?'

'Oh, just tell a fib,' said Isabel, as if her previous injunctions had not involved this step.

'Well, my weary girl,' said Eleanor, 'are you quite yourself again?'

'Yes, thank you, Mother.'

'Did she have a good luncheon, Venice?'

'Yes.'

'And James? How is he? Doesn't he think he might go to school this afternoon, and do some hours of work? It would be a little thing he could do for Father.'

'When we have a holiday, we are supposed to have one,' said James in a faint voice.

'Do you mean you would find it embarrassing to go back?'

'No,' said James, who would have found it even more so to admit this.

'What does he mean, Isabel?'

'Well, he is not expected, and they are supposed to keep to what they say.'

'Mother, I think Father has unwittingly put enough on the children today,' said Luce, with an unconscious glance at Sir Jesse.

'The boy is right that he should do one thing or the other,' said the latter, with a suggestion of seeking to counteract his outbreak. 'If he has begun the day in one way, let him finish it.'

'Then he must have a walk and a rest,' said Eleanor, who seemed to consider widely varying courses adapted to her son. 'He is not having a holiday in the ordinary sense.'

'James would not dispute it,' said Graham.

'I don't think he ever has one,' said Isabel. 'Does he know what an ordinary holiday means? To him a holiday must be a sort of tribute paid to other people's experience.'

James gave his sister a look of seeing someone familiar passing out of his sight.

'Wouldn't any of you like to hear about your father's last moments?' said Eleanor.

Her chance use of words with another association caused some mirth.

'What an odd thing to laugh at, if you really took the words as you pretend!'

'It is their bearing that interpretation that constitutes the joke,' said Daniel.

'Joke!' said his mother, drawing her brows together.

'We had an ordinary little talk,' said Luce, in a tone unaffected by what had passed. 'We found ourselves discussing the best time for leaving England. The last moments' – her voice shook on the words – 'tend to lack vitality and interest.'

'Why did you insist on being present at them?' said Eleanor.

'To prevent them from being worse for Father than they had to be, Mother.'

'Sit on Grandma's knee,' said Nevill.

Regan lifted him and he settled himself against her in dependence on the effort to support his weight, and closed and opened his eyes.

'He has missed his sleep,' said Venice. 'It was because of saying good-bye to Father.'

'Sleep, school, everything missed,' said Eleanor, with a sigh.

'Good-night, Grandma,' said Nevill, meeting Regan's eyes with a smile.

'The child will be a burden. Can't somebody fetch him?' said Sir Jesse, seeming to find no fault with a burden, if it were suitably disposed.

'Let him lie down, Grandma,' said Luce, with her eyes on the pair.

'No,' said Nevill, struggling to his former position.

'Hatton can carry him without waking him, when he is once asleep,' said Venice.

It was decided to rely on this power, making a temporary sacrifice of Regan, and Eleanor turned to her sons.

'Have you your father's directions clear in your minds?'

'Yes. Habit has not yet overlaid them,' said Graham.

'I wish he had told you to learn to answer a serious question. It grows wearisome, this taking everything as an excuse for jauntiness. It will become a recognized affectation.'

'We will not look at Graham at his hard moment,' said Daniel.

'I am glad to bear it for us both,' said Graham.

'Mother, that is too severe,' said Luce, laughing. 'It is natural to the boys to be as they are.'

'We cannot always leave our natural selves unmodified, and expect other people to bear with them.'

'It is about what most of us do,' said Sir Jesse, with some thought of his own illustration of the point.

'I suppose it is,' said Eleanor, with a sigh that seemed to refer to herself.

'Are our natural selves so bad?' said Isabel.

'More petty and narrow than bad,' said her mother. 'Not that that is not poor enough.'

'Mother, you have your own opinion of yourself and other people,' said Luce.

'Do you show your natural self, James?' said Eleanor, with one of her accesses of coldness.

'No; yes; I don't know,' said James, looking surprised and apprehensive.

'Do you pretend to be different from what you are?'

'Oh, no,' said James, suddenly seeing his life as a course of subterfuge.

'Do you, Venice?'

'No, I don't think so.'

'Do you, Isabel?'

'I don't know. I have not thought. And I do not intend to think. Probably most of us do the same thing.'

'That is not a gracious way to talk.'

'It was not that sort of question. It was one to make people admit what they had better keep to themselves.'

'You have answered it more plainly than you know.'

'Well, I suppose that was your object in asking it.'

'You think people do disguise themselves?'

'Up to a point, of course. We should be sorry if they did

not. I should be grateful if you would resume your disguise.'

'Isabel, you must remember you are speaking to your mother.'

'It is not a moment when I should choose to do so.'

'My dear, I know you are tired and upset, but there is reason in everything. Do you think it is nice to take advantage of Father's going at once like this?'

'No, not at all, but you were the first person guilty of it. And in James's case you wreaked your feelings on a helpless child.'

Graham rested his eyes on Isabel, as if he thought these words did not only apply to James.

'Isabel, I shall have to ask you to go upstairs,' said Eleanor.

'I have not the least wish to remain.'

'Then do not do so, my dear.'

Isabel rose and bursting into tears, ran out of the room. Luce rose at almost the same moment and went with a movement of her shoulders after her.

'Well, what a lot of smoke without any flame!' said Eleanor, not looking into anyone's face.

'There was a certain amount of flame,' said Daniel. 'And you put the match, Mother.'

'It was very inflammable material.'

'That did not make it wiser.'

'Venice, go and see what is happening,' said Eleanor.

Venice went out and found her sister weeping on the stairs, with Luce standing over her; and not being inclined to return and describe the scene, she simply joined it. The same thing happened to James, who was the next emissary, and to Honor, who succeeded him. Gavin was the first to report on the situation.

'Isabel is sitting on the stairs, crying, and the others are standing near.'

Nevill struggled to the ground and ran up to Eleanor.

'Isabel is crying, but stop soon, and Father soon come back and put his arm round her.'

Eleanor stroked his hair.

'Do you think you can go to Isabel, and try to bring her back to Mother?'

Nevill ran to the door, waited for it to be opened without looking at the operator, mounted the stairs to his sister, took her hand and tried to drag her to the dining-room. Luce came behind, as if not yet relaxing her vigilance, and Venice and James and Honor rather uncertainly followed. Sir Jesse put some viands on a plate and pushed it towards his granddaughter, who was moved to uncertain mirth by this method of encouragement, and Nevill took his stand at her side, with his eyes going from the plate to her face.

'Now you had better go upstairs and enjoy your good things there,' said Eleanor. 'Here is another plate for the nursery children.'

Honor took it and Nevill ran by her side, openly yielding himself to the occasion. Hatton appeared in response to a summons, took both the plates in one hand, and Nevill's hand in the other, and led the way from the room. The other five children followed. Luce lay back in her chair and gave a sigh.

'Dear, dear, the miniature world of a family! All the emotions of mankind seem to find a place in it.'

'It was those emotions that originally gave rise to it,' said Daniel. 'No doubt they would still be there.'

'What a thing to be at the head of it!' said Eleanor.

Sir Jesse looked up, but perceived that the reference was not to himself.

'I think it is the place I would choose,' said Daniel.

'I would not,' said his brother.

'Isabel has a very deep feeling for Father,' said Luce, looking round the table. 'It seems to be something altogether beyond her age.'

'It is unwise to imagine the months ahead, if that is her trouble,' said Graham.

Regan covered her face and sank into weeping. Luce left her chair, and with a movement of her brows in reference to the consistent nature of her offices, went to her relief. Sir Jesse beckoned to his grandsons to follow him in Fulbert's stead, and left the women to their ways, as his expression suggested. Luce stood a little apart from Regan, as if the moment to officiate were not yet at hand, and touched her shoulders from time to time in token of what was in store. Eleanor looked at her mother-in-law with guarded eyes, and Regan felt the gaze and returned it almost with defiance.

'Don't try to control yourself, Grandma. Let yourself go; it will do you good,' said Luce, taking a sure, if unintended method of inducing recovery.

'So your grandfather has gone,' said Regan. 'Men don't feel things like women.'

'Well, perhaps they don't, Grandma,' said Luce, giving her hands a regular movement. 'Do you know, I think Isabel is very like you in some ways?'

Regan's face and Eleanor's responded to this suggestion in a different manner.

'Mother, I don't believe you like people to show their feelings,' said Luce.

'It depends on their age and other things.'

'Age hasn't much to do with it, if we are to judge from Isabel and me,' said Regan, with a smile.

'Grandma, you are yourself again,' said Luce.

'Shall we go to the drawing-room?' said Eleanor. 'If we are to support each other, we may as well do it at ease.'

As Regan led the way into the room, Hope sprang from the hearth.

'I told them I would wait for you. I know I ought not to have come. We do not intrude upon family privacy at such a time. But I know what such a condition can be, and it did seem I ought to prevent it, if I could. If I only annoy you, it will take you out of yourselves. That always seems to have to be done in some unpleasant way. I do want to sacrifice myself for you. I have sacrificed the others by leaving them at home. No sacrifice is too great.'

'You have made Grandma laugh, Mrs Cranmer,' said Luce, in the tone of one pushing up with an assurance.

'That shows I have forgotten myself, for I was really out of spirits. I see why the jesters of old were such sad people. If their profession was cheering people who needed it, it would have been unfeeling not to be. They couldn't have had enough sadness in their own lives to account for their reputation.'

'Comic actors and writers and all such people are said to be melancholy,' said Luce. 'And they do not come in contact with the people they cheer.'

'Well, it may just be the contrast of their professional liveliness with their normal human discontent. We might say that wrestlers and acrobats are lazy, because they sit on chairs at home. People do give their spare time to complaining. Well, I saw you and your brothers driving with your father to the station, and I said to myself. There are those dear children facing the hardest moments, and here am I, just running the house, that is, giving spare time to complaining. So I have come here to be rejected and unwelcome, because that will give me a hard moment, and I really cannot go on any longer without one.'

'Mother is laughing now,' announced Luce. 'And I did not think that would be contrived today.'

'I have been a sad, sour woman for a good many hours,' said Eleanor.

'Well, you have not been yourself,' said Hope. 'So that shows how different you really are.'

'There is not much in my life that I can look back on with pride.'

'What an odd thing to think of doing! I thought people looked back with remorse, and thought of the might-have-beens, and how it was always too late. I should never dare to do it at all.'

'I have had such sad, little faces round me today, and I have not done much to brighten them.'

'I am quite above minding the number today, my dear.'

'They will all be six months older before their father sees them again.'

'Yes, they will, but does that matter? It is not like being ill or an anxiety.'

'Nevill will be three and a half,' said Luce, in the same regretful tone.

'Will that be a disadvantage to him? Is there something about age that I don't understand?'

'Their childhood is slipping away,' explained Luce.

'Yes, but it won't do that any more quickly because Fulbert is gone. I expect every day will drag. And doesn't time always stand still in childhood? I thought it was always those long, summer days.'

'It has been a chill enough day today,' said Eleanor.

'So I have come to bring it a little ordinary warmth. I know it is ordinary; I am not making any claim. I enjoy having a talk with women, and I know you will like to give pleasure to another in your own dark hours, because that would be one of your characteristics. I will begin by saying that Faith is so forbearing that it is impossible to live with her.'

'You go on managing it,' said Regan.

'Another laugh, Mrs Cranmer!' said Luce.

'I do it by being always in the wrong. And though that is not much to do for Paul, it is the little, daily sacrifices that count. They are so much more than the one great one.'

'I wonder if people would recognize that one, if they saw it,' said Eleanor.

'There, see how much good I am doing you! It is a healthy sign to see the inconsistencies in others. It seems fortunate that it is almost universal.'

'Does Ridley make any sacrifices?' said Regan.

'Well, he may be waiting for the one great one.'

'I hope we are not putting too much on him,' said Eleanor.

'I don't think you could have thought I meant that, dear,' said Hope.

Regan went into laughter and Eleanor looked puzzled for a moment.

'Fulbert may come back to do his own work,' said Regan, with a return of grimness.

'And Ridley will go on waiting,' said Hope. 'And I like my stepchildren to be frustrated. I can say it today, because it is to do you good.'

'Do you know, Mrs Cranmer, it does have that effect?' said Luce, bringing her brows together.

'Where is Sir Jesse?' said Hope. 'I keep being afraid he will come in.'

'He is with the boys in the library,' said Eleanor.

'I always say people prefer their own sex. It is such a tribute to everyone, when they understand it so well. It means they don't even mind being understood. I am glad Faith is not here, to look as if I were really saying something uncharitable.'

'Faith is here, Mrs Cranmer,' said Luce, in a just audible tone, glancing out of the window and trying to suppress a smile.

'I suppose she would be by now. So she has come to put me at a disadvantage.'

'I hardly think that is fair.'

'No, dear, but I am here to do you good. Being fair would achieve nothing, and being put at a disadvantage may. We will wait for Faith to do her part. If it is for your sakes, I mind nothing.'

Faith looked with gentle inquiry from face to face.

'I am afraid it is the last of all days to call.'

'I don't think you can be, dear,' said Hope.

'I feel I must be an unwelcome visitor.'

'I don't think you can feel that either.'

Faith brought her eyes to rest on her stepmother.

'You see it is happening,' said Hope, fidgeting. 'But I am only too glad to be of use.'

Faith's expression became one of inquiry.

'You must have some errand that you have not said,' said Hope.

'I did not like the idea of your walking home by yourself, Mother.'

'But when we walk together, we can't keep in step.'

'I will try and take shorter steps.'

'And if I do the opposite, we shall meet each other. It is quite a little parable for our daily life.'

'I am afraid I am rather tall,' said Faith, looking round with a deprecating smile. 'But I do not think it at all fair for the shorter person to adapt herself. It is for the taller one to do that.'

'It must be nice to give out of abundance,' said Hope.

'Or bearable anyhow,' said Regan.

Luce exchanged a glance with Faith, in smiling reference to the attitude of the older women.

'How are the children?' said Faith, turning to Eleanor.

'They have had a sad day, I am afraid.'

'Perhaps I may go and see them.'

'Well, it would be very kind.'

'Do let us go from floor to floor,' said Hope, incurring a glance from Faith, who had wished to go alone with Eleanor. 'I should not feel I had been here, if I had not done that. And it would be a pity not to take advantage of my unembittered mood. I must always have seen the children with a jaundiced eye.'

'I must just look in on my husband,' said Regan, as they crossed the hall.

'I see I have no conception of a true union.'

Sir Jesse was engaged on some game of his youth with his eldest grandson, while the second looked on. He had lost his skill with years, and Daniel was being hard pressed to give him play, and at the same time cover his lapses. Graham was pale with the effort of following and supporting the contest.

'Youth and Age,' said Faith, looking round with a smile. 'It makes me wish I were a painter.'

'That was a picture in words,' said Luce.

'Not a very elaborate one, I am afraid,' said Faith, looking down as she turned to the stairs.

'We see the older children first,' said Hope. 'The higher we go, the younger they get. It seems odd that the smaller ones should have to climb further. We read about little, sturdy legs toiling up the stairs, but why does it have to be like that?'

'The nurseries are always furthest from the lower floors,' said Faith.

'Yes, that is what I said, dear. But why?'

'We don't want too many nursery sounds,' said Eleanor.

'I thought they were the most beautiful sounds in the world. I don't seem to understand the things I have missed. But I dare-say that is natural.'

The schoolroom children were lying back in their chairs, listening to Miss Mitford reading aloud. They rose, looking rather conscious of their self-indulgence.

'So they are in spirits again,' said Eleanor, who took any form of recreation as a token of this.

'How do you know they are?' said Hope. 'Miss Mitford may be trying to distract them.'

'I hope she has met with a measure of success. They are themselves again, are they, Miss Mitford?'

'No.'

'Are they not? Why?'

'Because their father has left them.'

'But they are up to enjoying a book.'

'Anyone is equal to something done by someone else.'

'Well, I hope your time is not being quite wasted. What are you doing, James? You don't seem to be listening.'

James did not say he was sunk in the lethargy of exhaustion. He sat up and alertly indicated a box at his side.

'I am tidying my case of curiosities.'

'They do not look as if they had had much attention,' said Eleanor, smiling in the belief that a boy could pursue such an occupation without result. 'You had better ask Venice to help you.'

'Why Venice?' said Hope.

'She is our obliging little woman.'

'Miss Mitford said she would help me to put labels on the things,' said James.

'Well, that would bring order out of chaos. Why do you prop up the box on a book? I never knew a boy put books to such odd purposes.'

'It goes down without it,' said James, drawing out the book so that the box dropped with a crash, and taking the box into his arms as if to protect it.

'Where did you get the book?' said his mother.

'From the dining-room,' said James, in immediate, cordial response.

'I saw a space on the shelves. Did you take more than one?'

'Three all the same,' said James, holding the box with his chin, while he adjusted his hands beneath it. 'Two of them are in my room.'

'Then run and fetch them, my dear. They are not books you want to read.'

James looked for someone to whom to entrust his box, yielded it to Faith's ready hands, and scampered upstairs.

'What is the book?' said Hope.

Eleanor met her eyes, while she addressed a casual remark to Miss Mitford, and everyone knew that the subject was not one for Isabel and Venice, including the pair concerned. James returned and put the books into Eleanor's hands without looking at them, and carefully retrieved his box.

'Why did you take them?' said his mother.

'They looked as if they were interesting,' said James, in an almost confidential tone. 'They have covers like Miss Mitford's German fairy tales. And there were nine all alike. But perhaps the leaves wanted cutting.'

'And can't you do that?' said Faith, at once.

'I always tear them, if I do it,' said James, looking at her with frankness in his eyes, if in no other part of him.

'That would not do for the dining-room books,' said Eleanor. 'They must be left alone in future.'

'Would you like to have a paper knife?' said Faith.

'Is that a knife for cutting pages?' said James, with his customary unawareness of the purposes of things.

'Yes. I will bring you one next time I come.'

'Then I shall have one like Miss Mitford,' said James, betraying that he had seen this one in use.

'Isabel looks tired, Miss Mitford,' said Eleanor. 'And she has had a sleep. She cannot spend her life resting.'

'Certainly not, on such a day as this in her family.'

'Everything possible has been spared her.'

'I am sure it has. But that could hardly be much.'

'They would be better in bed,' said Eleanor, taking an accustomed outlet for her anxiety and other feelings.

'You need not stand, children,' said Luce. 'We know you have had a long day.'

'Need they sit either?' said Hope. 'I think they like to lie down. Are they prostrated by their father's going?'

'Yes,' said Miss Mitford.

'I expect they would like to be rid of us,' said Faith, going with decision to the door. 'After all, they did not invite us in here, did they?'

'You seemed to have a standing invitation, dear,' said Hope.

'What an open expression James has!' said Faith, when she gained the landing.

Luce touched her arm and her own lips, and motioned towards the open door, and Faith nodded and smiled in suitable dumb response.

'Well, that wasn't a very gracious welcome,' said Eleanor, to her children. 'It is kind of people to come and see you. Don't you think it is, Isabel?'

'I don't suppose so, or they would not come so often. People are not so fond of being kind.'

'I don't think you have any reason for saying that, my dear. You have had great patience today.'

'Oh, so have you,' said Isabel, raising her hands to her head.

Miss Mitford made as if to resume the book, and Eleanor left the room without requiring James's offices at the door, indeed shutting it herself with a certain sharpness. Her expression for the moment resembled Isabel's. Her daughter was at the end of her tether, and so was she.

The party went upstairs to the nursery, where Honor and Gavin were employed at the table, and Nevill was sitting on Hatton's lap, looking flushed and rumpled.

'Too tired to sleep,' he said, as he turned to the guests.

'Is he, Hatton?' said Eleanor, with a certain weariness in her own manner.

'He missed his rest, madam. He will be all right in the morning.'

'But not go to bed yet,' said Nevill, in a sharp tone.

'I hope he isn't sickening for anything,' said Eleanor.

'You must hope so,' said Hope. 'I am sure I do too. Indeed I hope no one is.'

'What are the others doing?' said Faith.

'We are painting arrows for our bows and arrows,' said Gavin. 'Miss Pilbeam helped us to make the bows. The arrows were in the shop.'

'He has a bow-and-arrow,' said Nevill, pronouncing the last three words in one, and indicating a production of Mullet's on a chair.

'That is not a real one,' said Gavin.

'A little bow-and-arrow,' said Nevill, in a contented tone.

'What will you shoot with them?' said Faith, with some misgiving in her tone.

'Oh, birds and animals and things,' said Gavin. 'They are not toys. They could give a mortal wound.'

'I don't suppose we shall hit much,' said Honor. 'And they are not poisoned arrows.'

'He will shoot a bird,' said Nevill, his voice rising with his thought. 'He will shoot a chicken; he will shoot a cock.'

'A duck would be easy to shoot,' said Gavin.

'A duck,' agreed Nevill, settling down on Hatton's lap.

'They must not make havoc among the poultry, Hatton,' said Eleanor.

'Then how are they to manage?' said Hope.

'Why don't they have a target to shoot at?' said Faith.

'What is a target?' said Gavin.

'A piece of wood made on purpose for shooting,' said Faith, with mingled eagerness and precision. 'It has holes or marks on it, so that people can aim.'

'I would rather shoot at something alive. I expect I shall shoot at wild birds.'

'He will too,' said Nevill.

'But suppose you hit one and hurt it?'

'It wouldn't know it was hurt; it would be dead,' said Gavin. 'Grown-up men shoot birds.'

'And animals too,' said Honor. 'They shoot big game.'

'What would you do with a dead bird?' said Faith.

'Cook it and eat it,' said Gavin.

'Or have a funeral,' said Honor.

'And say prayers,' said Nevill, in a lower tone, with a movement of his hands towards each other.

'But it might be hurt and not dead,' said Faith.

'Then I would shoot it again and make it dead,' said Gavin.

'Well, if you can depend on your aim like that!'

'He doesn't,' said Honor, defending her brother from this charge. 'If he shot a bird once, he could do it again.'

'We might stuff a bird, to give to Father when he comes home,' said Gavin.

'How would you do that?' said Faith, believing the process to involve objections.

'Take out the inside and fill it up with something else. Fred knows about it. He is the gardener's boy.'

'Fred is a nice boy,' said Nevill.

'Wouldn't a live bird be better than a stuffed one?' said Faith, looking at Nevill with disagreement.

'It wouldn't be your own,' said Honor. 'It couldn't belong to anyone. It wouldn't be different from other birds.'

'Father likes stuffed birds. There is one in his dressing-room,' said Gavin.

'A little, red bird,' said Nevill. 'He will shoot a robin for Father.'

> '"A robin redbreast in a cage
> Puts all Heaven in a rage,"'

quoted Faith, with rising feeling.

'Faith does have points in common with Heaven,' said Hope.

'Not a cage,' said Nevill. 'A nice, glass *case*.'

'We needn't kill a robin,' said Honor. 'Father kills other birds.'

'All hang down,' said Nevill. 'Poor birds!'

'Yes, that is what I mean,' said Faith. 'Poor birds!'

Nevill beat his hands together and uttered the sounds he made when chasing the fowls.

'The bird couldn't run, if it were stuffed and dead,' said Gavin.

'It sings,' said Nevill. 'Father's bird sings in its case.'

'I don't think it can do that,' said Faith.

'Tweet, tweet,' said Nevill, in disproof of this, assuming a listening air.

'I don't think they are very cruel to anything,' said Eleanor.

'Well, only to Faith,' said Hope: 'I think they are to her. It is three against one.'

'I do not feel that at all,' said Faith.

'We only don't think the same as she does,' said Honor.

'We can't all think alike, can we?' said Faith. 'But I hope we shall agree about this some day.'

'Some day he will shoot a little bird for you,' promised Nevill, in vague amendment, as Faith bent to bid him good-bye.

CHAPTER SEVEN

'HAVE you all read Father's letter?' said Eleanor. 'It is meant for us all. There is a note for me, that I have taken.'

Regan put aside a note for herself, with a look of promise at her husband.

'Here is a letter addressed to Isabel,' said Eleanor, turning out the envelope. 'I had better see if there is anything in it, before it goes upstairs.'

'No, Mother,' said Luce, putting out a restraining hand, 'that is not the way to deal with letters. Let Isabel have it intact, as she would expect. That will teach her how to treat correspondence.'

'Does she not know?' said Daniel. 'Has she never seen any letters?'

'I daresay not addressed to herself,' said Graham. 'As she has no friends, she can only hear from her family. And they generally shares one's life. In her case they always do.'

'Your father may have put in something as an afterthought,' said Eleanor, still handling the letter.

'Then Isabel will tell you of it,' said Daniel.

'I don't know that she will. She is a strange, independent child. And her father may not have thought to give a definite direction.'

'He would put any message for you into your own letter,' said Graham.

'Not certainly. Things so often occur to him at the last. He may even have written this note on purpose to include something, and thought he would give Isabel pleasure at the same time.'

'There is no ground for that assumption,' said Sir Jesse, in an easy tone.

'More than anyone would think, who did not know Fulbert.'

'Would you say that, Mother?' said Luce. 'I think it is more like Father to have his own message for each of us. I can often tell to which one he is speaking, by his voice and words.'

'But not by his notes,' said Eleanor, smiling. 'You have never watched him write them, if you think that.'

'We generally communicate by word of mouth, as we share our home,' said Daniel.

'But he has to deal with people outside,' said his mother. 'His family is not the whole of his life. He has a good deal of correspondence.'

'Then I suppose he addresses his letters to the people who are to read them. And this one is addressed to Isabel.'

'A letter written by my own husband to my own child and enclosed in a letter to me, is not a secret from me,' said Eleanor, tearing the envelope.

'We see it is not,' said Graham.

'You talk as if we all lived in a state of estrangement.'

'Two of us will now do so.'

'No, my boy, Isabel will hardly notice that the envelope is broken.'

'Father seems anyhow to have wasted an envelope,' said Daniel.

'A weak yielding to curiosity, Mother, that is unworthy of you,' said Luce.

Eleanor looked surprised by the charge. She had felt no interest in Fulbert's word to his daughter, and had given the true account of her motives.

'You don't keep the children apart in your mind, as Father does, Mother.'

'They don't need all that differentiation. I am tired of hearing about it.'

'It is well that they should not need it,' said Sir Jesse.

'It teaches them to be touchy and exacting.'

'You do not expect those qualities in Isabel,' said Daniel. 'I trust that your method will prove its success.'

'There is nothing in the letter,' said his mother, putting it down. 'Isabel can have it when someone goes upstairs.'

'Who will be the bearer of it?' said Graham.

'None of you need be. I will take it myself when I go to the schoolroom. For the matter of that, the girls will be passing in a minute.'

'You might put it in a fresh envelope,' said Graham.

'I am not ashamed of anything I do,' said Eleanor, raising her brows. 'I should not dream of hiding it. I have opened Isabel's letter, and she may know I have done so.'

'I am sorry for that,' said Daniel.

'I never know why revealing baseness makes it better,' said Graham.

'People do not reveal such a thing,' said Sir Jesse.

'Isabel,' said Eleanor, raising her voice, as footsteps sounded in the hall, 'come in and say good morning to us. Are you all there?'

Isabel and Venice and Miss Mitford entered the room.

'Good morning,' said Miss Mitford, looking at Eleanor and using a tone of compliance with an injunction.

'Good morning, Miss Mitford; good morning, my dears. I want to read you Father's letter. Come and hear it.'

The two girls listened to the letter, put the normal questions and comments, and were about to go.

'Here is a note put in for you, Isabel,' said Eleanor, handing it to her daughter.

'Thank you. Father said he would write to me,' said Isabel, turning to show the letter to her sister.

'It came inside my letter,' said her mother.

'Who opened it?' said Isabel.

'Now, who had the right to do that?' said Eleanor, stroking her hair. 'No one touched it, who had no business with it. I should not have allowed that. I wanted to see if there was any message for me. There is one for all of you in my letter.'

Isabel looked at her mother's note, as it lay on the table.

'You have not let anyone see that.'

'Well, naturally not, my dear. Father would not have liked it.'

'Would he have wished you to see mine?'

'Think for a moment and tell me.'

'It is a pity you do such second-rate things,' said Isabel, in a slow voice. 'It is a mean way of using power.'

'What other second-rate thing have you known me do?'

'You do not deny the term. And these things are never isolated.'

'Come, come, my child. You would have shown me the letter, would you not?'

'I might have had no choice. But I should have read it myself first. There would have been a semblance of free will. Decency would not have been outraged.'

'What a term to use of a mother's overlooking her child's correspondence!'

'The thing's being between a mother and child, or rather its coming from a mother, adds to the ugliness.'

'Do you think it so important that a little girl's letter should be private? It clearly cannot be so in itself.'

Isabel deliberately took up her mother's letter and tore it open. Eleanor took no notice, as if regarding such an incident as too trivial to heed.

Isabel glanced down the letter and then opened her own. A faint smile crept round her lips as she scanned it, and she put it in her pocket and relinquished the first. Fulbert's attitude to writing was as his wife had suggested. He had done the duty amid a pressure of work. It had been convenient to him that his sentiments as a husband and father should be the same. The two letters were identical in wording, except for the beginning and end. Isabel looked round the room.

'Father draws no distinction between Mother and me,' she said, with a touch of satisfied pride. 'He has copied one letter from the other. I don't know which was the original.'

Eleanor took up her own note and found that this was the case. Regan tore open hers and looked in appeal at her granddaughter. Isabel yielded her own letter, and Regan made a swift comparison and smiled her relief. Graham, who had been watching his grandmother, relaxed his expression.

'You meant to sacrifice me, and you have sacrificed Father,' said Isabel to her mother. 'You thought I should look childish and foolish, and you have contrived that he does. You can deal as you will with people who are away. He and I were both in your hands.'

'I did not think how you would appear,' said Eleanor. 'It is not a question that would enter my mind. I thought there might be a message from Father, as I said. And you must see that the letter did not apply especially to you.'

'You see the same about yours. And you would not have let me read it, if you had not read mine. You only did that to make the whole matter seem nothing.'

'Well, I am glad it has come to seem so,' said Eleanor, finding that she matched her power against her daughter's, as she could not otherwise withstand her. 'It did not take much to make it.'

'You know you will not mention to Father that the two letters are the same.'

'I should hardly think of it. And you give the message to yourself too much of a place. He wrote it separately to give you pleasure. He had no idea it would be pushed into this sort of prominence.'

'Doubtless he had not,' said Sir Jesse.

'None at all. That is clear,' said Isabel. 'He meant it to be private.'

'I have written the same letter to different people,' said Daniel. 'But never to people under the same roof. Separation struck me as the first condition.'

'So an idea came to you,' said his grandfather.

'Your father was very much occupied,' said Eleanor.

'A very disorganizing circumstance,' said Graham, sighing.

'Well, Isabel will be able to write him a nice, long, amusing letter in exchange,' said Eleanor, with a hint of revenge on her daughter. 'She has no duties and she can give plenty of time to it. Will you see that she does it, Miss Mitford?'

'Well, it is nothing to do with me.'

'That seems to be the case,' said Sir Jesse.

'Then she can attend to it herself,' said Eleanor. 'She is old enough to write her own letters.'

'And also to read them. The one thing follows from the other,' said Isabel. 'People's correspondence is their own affair.'

'Is that quite the word for this little message?'

'You used it yourself. And you talk about a long, amusing letter in return. If I describe this scene, I might write one. Perhaps I shall.'

'I don't think you would like to make Father feel even a little uncomfortable. It was not a very unnatural thing to model a letter on one already written, when he was pressed for time.'

'I think I could give the scene without referring to that. That does not seem to me the point of it.'

Eleanor gave a glance almost of apprehension at her daughter, and turned to the governess.

'So James is at school today.'

'Yes.'

'He could find no excuse for staying at home. If he had known that Isabel was to have a letter from her father, he might have used that.'

'It seems to be an event of a portentous nature,' said Sir Jesse.

'Venice must write a letter to Father, and then perhaps she will have the message next time,' said Eleanor, smiling at her daughter.

'Father might have some copies of a note printed off, so that we could all have one,' said Graham. 'Then he could reap a good harvest in exchange.'

'What a lot you make of the little circumstance of the notes being worded in the same way!' said Eleanor, in a wondering tone.

'It is true that they do so,' said Sir Jesse.

'You were led further by your assumption that they were different, Mother,' said Daniel.

'Oh, don't let us go on harping on one little point. Pray let us change the subject. Do you feel that you have lived these weeks since Father left us, as he would like? Do you feel that, Isabel?'

'I have no choice how to live them. The question is more pertinent for you. What do you feel about the weeks, including this morning?'

'I have done my best,' said Eleanor. 'I daresay he would like me to do better.'

'Shall we stamp off a dozen impressions of a creditable letter, and all sign it?' said Daniel. 'Nevill could put a cross.'

'You have been helped to a subject for a jest,' said Eleanor. 'And between you, you will make the most of it.'

'They generally share such things,' said Sir Jesse.

'I hope Father will not stay away long,' said Isabel.

'What an odd little speech!' said her mother. 'You would surely not hope the opposite. And you know that he must stay for six months.'

'Mother, Isabel is younger and more helpless than you,' said Luce, in a low tone.

Eleanor looked at Isabel, and suddenly covered her face in her hands and broke into tears.

Sir Jesse rose and walked from the room, holding the paper before him with an effect of being absorbed in it. Regan smiled on the family in simple affection. She thought little of the opening of the letter, and assumed that trouble had arisen because the moment was ripe. Her son had left his family, and it was brought to this.

Miss Mitford sat down to await the end of the scene. She did not leave it, because of its human appeal. She was the happiest person present, as she was more often than was suspected. She did not let pity for her employer or pupil mar her interest. Pity had come to be the normal background of her mind, and other feelings arose irrespective of it.

'Did we know what Father did for us by his mere presence?' said Luce. 'We think of service as coming from definite action. This is a lesson.'

'He will come back and find himself a god,' said Daniel. 'That will make a hard demand on him.'

'I only want him as he is,' said Eleanor, raising her eyes. 'Miss Mitford, you must think this is a strange scene to arise out of nothing.'

'I don't know how it could do that.'

'Well, to develop from a trifle, or to have the trifle made the reason of it. No doubt the emotions were there, and had to come out.'

'I hope it has been a relief,' said Miss Mitford.

'Yes, I think it has. I believe I feel the better for it. Do you, my Isabel?'

'No, I don't think so. I had no emotions until the scene made them. I think I feel the worse.'

Regan gave a kind laugh.

'I don't expect you understand yourself,' said Eleanor, gently. 'Your father is the person who understands you. Poor child, you are one of the greatest sufferers from his absence.'

Isabel naturally began to cry. Venice glanced about in some discomfort at having no ground for tears. Miss Mitford rose from her seat.

'Yes, run out into the air,' said Eleanor, as if the movement suggested a solution of all questions. 'Take your letter, Isabel dear. You will like to have it.'

Isabel looked at the note with an uncertain smile.

'Yes, it is funny, isn't it?' said Eleanor. 'Poor Father! He must have been very busy. Well, he meant to send you your own message. You know that.'

'And Mother will know it in future,' said Isabel, as she left the house. 'I think she has had a lesson, and one she needed.'

'I wish it were time for me to give your father an account of my stewardship,' said Eleanor, to her elder children. 'I dread the prospect of guiding you all for so many months. You do not respond to the single hand.'

'A good deal is to your credit, Mother,' said Luce.

'You make an exception of this morning. But I only ask that there should be honesty between us.'

'I would ask rarer and better things,' said Graham.

'People take perfection as a matter of course,' said Daniel. 'Anything else affronts and enrages them.'

'I have learnt not to look for it,' said Eleanor.

'You make your own demand, Mother,' said Luce.

'Miss Mitford and the girls are coming back,' said Eleanor. 'Of course it has begun to rain. It is to be one of those days when every little thing goes wrong. Perhaps they would like to sit with us until their lessons.'

'Is that a risk, if the day is of that nature?' said Graham. 'It has so far been true to itself.'

'Come in, my dears, and take off your things,' said Eleanor. 'You can stay with us for a time. It will make a change for you. I expect Miss Mitford would like an hour to herself.'

'Do I not also need the change?' said Miss Mitford.

The laughter that greeted the words sowed that it did not even now occur to anyone, and Miss Mitford went to the door, striking everyone as a mildly ludicrous figure, with the exception of Graham, who saw her as a sad one. It would have been cheering to him to know her view of herself.

'Well, what is a subject fraught with no danger?' said Luce.

'Hardly that one perhaps,' said Daniel.

'Let us talk in our own way,' said Eleanor. 'The subjects will arise of themselves. We are seldom at a loss for them.'

The minutes passed and this did not come about. Eleanor took up her needlework, as if it were a matter of indifference. When Venice giggled she looked at her with a smile.

'The five of them ought to be photographed,' said Regan, surveying her grandchildren.

'We ought to have a group of them all, to send to their father,' said Eleanor. 'They have not been taken together since Nevill was born.'

'How sincerely they speak, considering that they do not consider spending the money or the effort!' said Daniel, to his brother.

'We must be grateful for the thought,' said Graham. 'I see how real a thing it is.'

'Father will no doubt appreciate it when it reaches him,' said Isabel.

'It is a photograph of Mother that Father would want,' said Luce.

'He took one of me with him,' said Eleanor.

'And one of Grandma too, I suppose.'

'No, I did not load him up with one,' said Regan.

'He asked me for one of myself,' said Eleanor. 'Or rather he was packing a clumsy one, and I gave him another.'

'He will not forget us,' said Luce, in a peaceful tone.

'No, dear, but that is not the point of a photograph,' said Eleanor. 'It gives a sort of companionship, an illusion of the presence of the person.'

'The real presence must be a shadowy one in that case,' said Regan.

'Is it better to have a photograph of oneself packed or not?' said Graham.

'I see it as a tribute,' said Daniel.

'It is in a sense, of course,' said Eleanor.

'I expect there was one about the room,' said Regan.

'There were photographs of all of us,' said Eleanor. 'Of everyone in the house.'

'Mother said a subject would arise, and it has arisen,' said Graham.

Regan laughed and went to attend to her housekeeping.

'It does not often occur to your grandmother that I may like to be left with my children,' said Eleanor.

'It strikes few of us that people want to be rid of us,' said Daniel. 'I do not remember having the feeling.'

'I feel a temptation to mark time until Father returns,' said Luce.

'The house is even duller, the house seems duller than it was,' said Isabel. 'And that produces a sense of waiting for something.'

'You cannot be dull when there are so many of you together,' said Eleanor, with simple conviction. 'You have your own rooms and your own interests. And Miss Mitford gives all her time to you, and you seem to find her amusing.'

'Another subject has arisen,' said Graham.

'I am not going to have any more of them,' said Eleanor, shaking her head. 'We must not make Father's absence an excuse for complaint and indolence. I see the rain has stopped, and there is time for a run before lessons. I wonder if Miss Mitford has noticed it.'

'She does not notice anything when she is reading,' said Venice.

'Does she do nothing but read? I hope she will not teach you to be always poring over books. There are other things in life.'

'Not in every life,' said Graham.

'That is what she does teach us in our lesson hours,' said Isabel. 'We thought she was supposed to, and so did she. At other times she does not interfere with us.'

'I should think Isabel is the last girl to be dull in herself,' said Eleanor, looking after her daughters. 'She is always amusing and amused. And Venice is the easiest child. I should think no schoolroom could be happier. It is nice for James to come home to all of it.'

'So it all works round to James's advantage,' said Graham.

'You talk as if he were a pathetic character,' said Eleanor. 'He could not have more than he has.'

'Graham dear,' said Luce, in a low tone, 'things can only be done by us according to our nature and our understanding. It is useless to expect more. We can none of us give it.'

'That does not take from the pathos. Indeed it is the reason of it.'

'It is partly the ordinary pathos of childhood, Graham.'

'Of childhood in the later stage, when it is worked and confined and exhorted. For its weakness the burden is great.'

'James has his own power of throwing things off,' said Luce.

'Of course all my children are tragic figures,' said Eleanor.

CHAPTER EIGHT

'Two for Mother, and four for Father,' said Faith, disturbing the letters at the breakfast table. 'And three for Ridley.'

'And how many for you?' said Paul.

'Seven, Father,' said Faith, in an unobtrusive manner.

'And were they less worthy of mention?'

'Well, there was no need to speak of them, Father.'

'Why not as much as the others?'

'Well, one does not want to draw attention to one's own things, when they are more than other people's.'

'I did not know that,' said Hope.

'Faith had a fair method of attracting the general interest,' said Ridley.

'They are only to do with oneself, after all,' went on Faith, as if her brother had not spoken.

'I wish I had more than two letters,' said Hope. 'It makes it seem as if only two people were thinking of me.'

'It was very nice of seven people to be thinking of me,' said Faith, in a light tone.

'It is even better to be the sort of person to be in their thoughts.'

'I did not mean to suggest that, Mother.'

'Well, it was not necessary, dear.'

'Faith is an inveterate correspondent,' said Ridley.

'Letter writing is not a vice,' said his father.

'I think in this case it has become a habit. And people are obliged to write letters in answer to those they receive.'

'I see. It is a good idea to put oneself in their thoughts,' said Hope.

Faith looked down at her letters, as if she would like to make a protest concerning them, but was silent.

'Faith keeps up with everyone who has crossed her path,' said Ridley.

'I see no reason for dropping people, when once I have known them,' said his sister.

'I can't understand people's not seeing those reasons,' said Hope.

'I never lose my interest in anyone I have known.'

'I like to hear about them, and the different ways in which they have gone downhill.'

'They have not always done that, Mother.'

'Then I think I correspond with them. Two people write to me, to every seven to you. That shows the proportion.'

'I think Faith's correspondents are often a good way down the hill, when she first meets them,' said Ridley, laughing.

'I see no reason for only being interested in fortunate people,' said his sister.

'You are not good at seeing reasons, dear,' said Hope.

'I like people for their personal qualities.'

'If they have many of those, they are not objects for letters,' said Paul. 'They would have their own way about them.'

'I suppose Faith won't tell us who her correspondents are,' said Hope.

'Well, I see no point in doing that. It is not quite the sort of atmosphere in which I should choose to reveal them.'

'I am sure they would be very uncomfortable, dear,' said Hope.

'What is that letter, Ridley?' said Faith, looking past her stepmother. 'You look as if you had had bad news.'

Ridley kept his eyes on the letter and did not speak. His parents turned their eyes on him, and he remained as still as if he were on the stage. Something about him suggested that he felt he was on it.

'Mrs Cranmer,' he said, partly rising from the table, 'may I ask you for a moment of your time?'

'You may have it all. I cannot do anything with it until I know the subject of that letter.'

'I would willingly postpone your knowing.'

'But do not do so, dear.'

Ridley sat down again and appeared to be lost in thought, and his father rose and read the letter over his shoulder.

MY DEAR RIDLEY,

I must depend on you to fulfil your word. I am so sick a man that when this reaches you, I shall be a dead one, unless a cable has come to you earlier. There is no need to hasten hard news to innocent people, and the word of my death can come to my family through you. All to be told will follow by a later mail. I have written this letter with my own hand. I know you will serve my wife to the limit of your power. And I will end to you, as you are to be to me,

Your friend,
FULBERT SULLIVAN.

The family stood in silence. Paul was sunk in thought. Faith put her handkerchief to her eyes. Hope rose with an almost energetic movement.

'Well, someone has to be the first to speak. And I can see you expect it to be me. I am the one whose feelings don't have to be too deep for words.'

'We can't help having the feelings, Mother,' said Faith.

'What have you to do, Ridley?' said Paul.

'To go to Mrs Sullivan, Father, to go to Eleanor Sullivan, and break to her the truth. And from my heart do I wish that this cup might pass from me.'

Faith looked at her brother with open eyes.

'I must not delay,' went on Ridley, as if unconscious of his last words. 'I can only make the blow as swift and merciful as possible. I can only do my best.'

'Do you think that perhaps a woman might do it better?' said Faith.

Ridley turned and looked into her face.

'It was not so that Fulbert left it. And it is not so that it shall be. I do not break my faith with the dead.'

'I only made the suggestion for what it was worth.'

'And Ridley has told you what that was, dear,' said Hope.

Ridley looked at his stepmother as if he thought she misused the occasion.

'Of course all the best in people will come out now,' she said. 'It is true that the accompaniments of grief are the worst part. I am always uneasy when people show the best that is in them. I am not talking about Ridley's best, as that is indispensable, but on the whole I prefer people's dear, faulty, familiar selves.'

Faith looked up as if she hardly saw herself in these last words.

'It is something that we don't seem to be drawn closer,' went on Hope. 'That is what is done by the most distressing things. I am glad we don't feel it to that extent.'

'There seems no urgency to break the news,' said Paul. 'But Ridley will have to get it behind.'

'I can hardly face the family, Father, with this between us. Even my lawyer's training in inscrutability does not prepare me for that.'

'You will tell me if I can be of any use to you, Ridley,' said Faith, in a gentle tone, after a moment's communing with herself.

'Faith's best seems to improve with every moment,' said Hope. 'And Ridley has only to use his as it is. He will have to decide when to do it.'

'That was not left to me, Mrs Cranmer. If it had been, I fear I might have taken some way out. As it is – ' Ridley straightened his shoulders and made his way from the house.

'Ridley's best is rather unfitted for daily life,' said Hope. 'This is the first time I have seen it in thirty years. It might be better to have one that came in oftener. But I suppose it is meant for an emergency.'

'We must hope it will do its work on this occasion,' said Faith. 'After all, Mr Sullivan depended on it.'

'I am sure it will,' said Hope. 'You see that my best is as good as yours.'

'Are we not rather running this idea to death, Mother?'

'My best is better than yours. It is never used for people's embarrassment. My worst is used for that. I am right not to like the best in people. Why should I, when it is put to a mean purpose? And I believe it generally is.'

'I hope my worse side did not creep out for the moment,' said Faith, in a lighter tone.

'I don't think so, dear; I am sure you were at your very best.'

'Father,' said Faith, 'I think Mother is much more upset by this news than she shows.'

'She has shown it to me,' said Paul.

'The best in you both is better than I have ever imagined,' said Hope. 'I am really comforted by it, and I did not know it ever did that. If Ridley's is doing the same for Eleanor, I see what Fulbert meant.'

'Well, now don't you think we might consider if there is anything we can do, Mother?'

'I think we might; I should agree with anything you said. If we don't put ourselves forward, and don't fancy we are the sort of people who could be tolerated at such a time, I think we might do what we can. But I don't quite see what that is.'

'Need we be quite so unsure of ourselves? If we took that line, we should never do anything for anyone.'

'And that is too high a standard for us. So we will go and do the womanly duties that are borne at these times. I suppose people do put up with them. It is known that the well-meant offices aggravate sorrow, so no doubt they must. And we will leave your father to suffer in a man's simplicity. I feel rather anxious about him, and it is the irritation in anxiety that is the worst part.'

'I am coming with you,' said Paul.

'Now I can throw myself into serving others. I will make it all as easy to bear as possible. Ridley must be breaking the truth by now. I have heard that that is harder than hearing it, but I do not agree.'

Ridley had reached the Sullivans' house and asked for Eleanor. He was shown to the drawing-room, where she was with Luce and Regan. He had depended on seeing her alone, and had to adjust his words. He met her eyes and then advanced and laid a hand on her shoulder. She looked up, alarmed, but her voice was forestalled by Regan's.

'He is dead, is he? He has gone after the others. Well, I can live in peace now. There is no one else.'

Eleanor was standing, pale and still, heedless of those about her. Luce took the letter from Regan's hand, and went and put her arms about her mother. Regan spoke again, neither to herself nor the others.

'It wasn't much good to have them, for my husband to be left without a son. We have wasted it all, our time and our feeling. All our feeling has gone. And we have only each other at the end.'

'Lady Sullivan,' said Ridley, in a low tone, 'we have to tell your husband.'

Regan made a movement that would have been a spring, if she had had youth and strength, and was gone from sight. It was not from Ridley's lips that Sir Jesse would hear of the death of his son.

Daniel and Graham came from their grandfather, with the truth in their faces, and the thought in their minds that they were tied to Sir Jesse now. They gave their attention to their mother, while they imagined their own future; the full manhood, the loss of their father, the service to two generations; and saw the truth of their father's life, which they had deemed so easy.

Eleanor looked up and spoke in her natural tones.

'We had better send for the children. It is no good to put off their knowing.'

Her words revealed herself, and her children confronted their knowledge of her. She felt real grief, made no pretence of despair, tried to face her loss and her duty, could not follow children's suffering. Luce looked in mute appeal at Ridley.

'Mrs Sullivan,' he said, bending towards her, 'would you not leave them a while in their happiness? That is the way to spare yourself.'

'I must not think of that. The thing will have to be done.'

The schoolroom children were summoned. They caught the threat in the message, and came with fear in their eyes. Their mother put her arms about them.

'My little son and daughters, there is a great sorrow come to us today. Father will not return to us. We are to be alone.'

The children broke into weeping, at first without character or difference. James was the first to recover, and to try to realize his new life. Venice looked at her mother, as though with an instinct to help her. Isabel stood as if she were alone. Ridley remained with his eyes on Eleanor, and wore a look of venerating sympathy.

Regan returned to fetch the letter for her husband, took it from Ridley and went from the room. As she passed, she cast on the group a glance without hope or gentleness, almost without pity, a glance of hard resignation to the helpless suffering.

'My children,' said Eleanor, 'will you do your first thing for your mother? Will you break it to the little ones for me? Will you begin to help?'

Venice went to the door, as if to fulfil the request. James made a movement to follow her, glancing at his mother. Isabel met her eyes, but seemed not to hear what she had said.

'Is it too much for you, my dear?' said Eleanor, looking at Isabel. 'Then I will do it myself. Why should I put my duty on to those weaker than I? It is for their mother to spare them. James, will you bring them to me?'

James began to run from the room, checked himself and subdued his pace, and looked in appeal at his brothers.

'I can go and tell them, Mother,' said Graham.

'No, Graham,' said Luce, moving forward with her eyes on her mother. 'It is natural for them to hear the truth amongst us all. It will make one shock and one memory, and will spare them the meetings afterwards. We must think of the things that make children suffer.'

'We cannot save them the one thing,' said Eleanor, with a faint smile. 'I should not think those will count beside it. But do as you will, my dear. I am grateful for any help.'

A message was sent upstairs. Hatton entered with the children, and remained in the room, as though she would not withdraw the protection of her presence. James seemed to drift towards her, and stood at her side, suggesting the sphere with which he identified his life. Eleanor drew the children to her, and said the words she had said to the others. Honor wept in startled despair and grasp of a changed life; Nevill in abandonment to the general sorrow, and sympathy with it; Gavin did not weep, and looked at the older faces in resentment and question. Daniel put a hand on his head and said an encouraging word. His mother looked up, unsure of this line, but let her eyes fall, as if offering no judgement. Sir Jesse and Regan entered and went to their chairs by the hearth, acquiescing once again in the old customs in a different life. Sir Jesse laid his hand on Eleanor's shoulder as he passed, and Regan gave her grandchildren a smile that did not touch her own experience beneath. Luce waited for the tension to relax, and then moved towards Daniel, who knew that she put him in his father's place.

'We must make an effort, Mother,' he said. 'It is the only thing. We must leave this moment behind. Life will not wait for us.'

'When life has done what it has, it might have the grace just to do that,' said Graham.

Gavin gave a loud laugh, and his mother turned her eyes on him. She did not know that he was hailing the first break in the oppression. Nevill left Hatton and went up to Daniel.

'He won't cry any more,' he promised, and looked round the room. 'All stop now.'

Venice took his hands as if in play, but he seemed to feel some lack in her, and returned to Hatton. Eleanor gave Venice the smile of approval that she gave to this child's courage.

'Did Father have an ordinary illness like an English one?' said Gavin. 'Or are the illnesses different there?'

'We do not know yet, my boy,' said Eleanor. 'I think it was different. We shall hear soon.'

'How do we know he is dead?'

'He is not dead, my child. He is more alive than he has ever been.'

'But how do we know he is what we call dead?' said Gavin, with a faint frown.

Eleanor explained and Gavin listened until he understood, and then moved away.

'What is the good of his being more alive, when he is not with the people who belong to him?' said Honor, in a tone that seemed to anticipate a mature one of the future. 'And he is always more alive than other people. He ought not to be even what we call dead; he ought not to be.'

'Mrs Sullivan,' said Ridley, as if the words broke from him, 'what a duty you have to live for! We see how much your husband had.'

'I am not a person fitted to carry such a burden.'

'I have my grandchildren,' said Sir Jesse's voice from the hearth. 'I do not go empty to the grave.'

Nevill looked in the direction of the voice, and going to a vase on a table, drew out some flowers and thrust them towards his grandfather.

'They are all for Grandpa.'

'Won't you bring me some flowers too?' said Regan, turning more slowly than usual, as if her response were feebler.

Nevill returned to the vase, looked back at the flowers in Sir Jesse's hands, and ran and transferred them to Regan's.

'All for Grandma,' he said, wiping his hands down his garments, as though the office were distasteful.

'Isabel dear, sit down and try to stop crying,' said Eleanor. 'You know you do not help us by making yourself ill.'

Isabel obeyed as if all things were indifferent, and her mother gave a sigh as she withdrew her eyes.

'I wonder when I shall be able to get to my own sorrow,' she said to Ridley, with a faint smile.

Ridley met her look and swiftly touched his eyes, and Nevill ran up to him and looked up into his face.

'All stop now,' he told him for his guidance.

Ridley gave a smile at Eleanor.

' "*O sancta simplicitas*",' he said.

'What does that mean?' said Gavin.

'It means that childhood is sacred,' said Eleanor.

'You don't think it is, do you?' said her son.

'What will happen when they have all stopped?' said Graham to Daniel. 'Is there anything left?'

'Is there?' said Eleanor to herself, in a tone only partly designed for the ears of others.

Daniel led her to a seat; Ridley looked at him with a change in his face; Regan turned her eyes from the hearth, and rested them for a moment upon Ridley.

Gavin detached himself from the group and went towards the door.

'Where are you going, my boy?' said Eleanor.

'Upstairs.'

'But you will be alone up there.'

Gavin continued his way.

'Wouldn't you rather stay down here with all of us?'

'I don't much like seeing people when they are like this.'

'We cannot help being sad for Father. But we are going to do our best to be brave.'

Gavin waited as if to weigh the evidence of this, and then proceeded.

'Don't you mind being alone?'

'I shouldn't be alone, if Honor came with me.'

'Do you want to go up, Honor?'

'I don't mind.'

'It is all too much for them,' said Luce.

'Of course it is, my dear,' said her mother, with a sharper note. 'How could it not be?'

'Always cry now,' said Nevill, sadly. 'It is because Father goes away.'

'Mother, I think we must release them,' said Luce. 'It is all beyond their age.'

'If release is the word, let them go, my dear, of course. But Nevill is the only one who is too young to understand.'

'That does not make it better for them, Mother.'

'It is him that is young,' said Nevill.

'We are so glad you are what you are,' said Eleanor, smiling at him.

'So better now,' said Nevill, in a tone that lost its cheerfulness as he looked at Regan. 'But not poor Grandma.'

'Can't you go to her and do something to make her better?' said Luce.

Nevill went up to Regan and paused at her knee, while he considered his course. His earnest eyes fixed on her face made her smile and finally give a little laugh, and he ran back to Luce to report on his success.

'Grandma laugh now. All laugh now,' he said, looking round to witness the change.

Sir Jesse beckoned to him and lifted him to his knee.

'What should we do without our little lad?'

'Grandpa loves him too,' said Nevill, in some surprise.

'Hatton, I think you can take them,' said Eleanor. 'I am not being much help to them.'

Nevill ran towards the door with a feeling of achievement; Gavin walked out of the room and towards the stairs; Honor looked round as if she hardly realized what was happening, and got off her chair in a dazed manner and followed.

'Come and kiss your mother, Gavin,' said Eleanor, as if this observance might be omitted with the others.

Gavin returned, took a passive part in the embrace, and retraced his steps.

'You will like to think of Father when you are upstairs.'

Gavin paused at a distance and looked into his mother's face.

'We don't any of us seem much to like it.'

'Of course it will make you sad. But we can hardly remember him unless we are that.'

Gavin paused for thought.

'I think I can.'

'Well, remember him in your own way. Good-bye, my Honor; you will think of Father too.'

'I shan't ever think of anyone else now.'

'You will think of your mother too, and remember that she is alone.'

'We are all alone now. Father was the person who held us together. It is the father who does that.'

'I know your father did. But you still have your mother.'

'And you have Luce and Daniel and Graham. And Grandma has Grandpa. We all have someone. But it doesn't make it different. Father was the person who protected us.'

'Take her upstairs, Hatton,' said Eleanor. 'I can feel they are safe with you.'

'Hatton will take care of her,' said Nevill, running at Honor's side. 'He will too.'

James, with an almost capering movement, came to take leave of his mother, with a view to establishing a precedent of following Hatton himself.

'Are you going with them, my boy?'

James made another movement.

'Do you want to go?' said Eleanor, in a gentle, condoning manner.

'No,' said James, in a light tone.

'You would rather stay down here with me?'

'Yes, I would.'

'Then stay, my little son. I shall like to have you. You can leave him with me, Hatton.'

'I should like his help with Honor, madam. She needs to have one of them older than herself. She can't take the lead today.'

'Then go up, my boy, and comfort your little sister, and remember that you do it for your mother.'

James withdrew with a sense of having satisfactorily and even with credit laid the foundation of his future.

Mullet was awaiting the stricken group, and began at once to talk, as if she had been summoning her powers for their benefit.

'Now here you are, safe and sound. And you have your home and Hatton and me. Some children lose it all when their father dies, but it is different with you.'

'Why is it different?' said Gavin.

Hatton withdrew to liberate Mullet's gifts, and James quietly followed and went to his room.

'Because this house belongs to your grandpa, and you will still live here with him. You won't have to move into a small house and face a changed life.'

'Why do people do that?' said Gavin.

'A dear little house,' said Nevill, coming up to Mullet.

'Dear, dear, the collapses and crashes there have been in my family! You would hardly believe the tale of them. First prosperity and luxury and leisure, and then downfall and poverty and trouble. Poverty in a sense of course I mean; all things are comparative. And desertion by friends is always part of it. I am thinking of a cousin of my father's, who was a well-known physician and lived in Harley Street, which is an address for people of that kind. And they kept a butler and a cook and the usual complement of under servants. And they did much as the mood took them. Yes, their lot was cast in pleasant places. And then the curse that was hanging over them gathered and fell. There has always been this something ill-fated about our family. My uncle died, and the end of it all came. They had to take shelter under a humble roof, and keep one servant; well, one good servant from the old days, and one or two young ones it really was, though to hear the family talk, you would have thought it was a state of penury; and move out of society and face a different future. Yes, I often think of them, moving in their shabby gentility about their second-rate social round, always with that air of having come down in the world, which a truer dignity would lay aside. A morning of trivial shopping, after an interview with the rather tyrannical cook; a dose of cavalier treatment from the tradesmen instead of the accustomed respect, for that class of person is the first to show a sense of difference; an afternoon over a dreary fire, missing the friends who used to attend their frequent functions; that is my cousins' life. I often think I have been wise in cutting right adrift from the past, that I have chosen the better part.'

'I don't think you have,' said Gavin. 'You don't have even as much as they have. And perhaps that is why they don't write to you.'

'It may be; there are more unlikely things. I often think of those people who used to cross our threshold and accept our hospitality. How many friends have I from my old life? None. But I would not thank them to darken my horizon. They were fair weather friends.'

'How do you pronounce horizon?' said Gavin, Mullet having put the emphasis on the first syllable.

'Horizon,' said Honor, in a mechanical tone, placing it on the second.

'Well, there are different pronunciations in different circles. And my education was broken off too soon for me to have the usual foundation. And my father never did believe in much learning for girls. It was one of those old-fashioned ideas he had inherited from his ancestors. I was never to do anything, and what was the good of so much training? And there it was.'

'But you might have been a governess instead of a nurse,' said Gavin.

'It would have been all the same to him,' said Mullet. 'A dependent position is a dependent position. That is what it would have been.'

'I think your father was a rather foolish man.'

'He had his vein of foolishness, according to modern ideas. But I could not help loving him for it,' said Mullet, bearing out the theory that people love their creations. 'And, after all, I owed him my being.'

Honor got off her chair and came up to Gavin with a faint smile.

'Perhaps it is the other way round,' she said, as if feeling that the day broke some bond upon her tongue.

Gavin seemed puzzled, and at that moment Hatton returned to the room and at once looked at Honor's face.

'Well, now,' she said in a cheerful tone, while her eyes met Mullet's, 'it is time for you to have your dinner. I expect Mr Ridley is staying, and you will see him when you go downstairs.'

'We have seen him,' said Gavin.

'I don't want to go down,' said Honor.

'It will make a change for you,' said Mullet.

'It won't,' said Gavin. 'We go down every day. It will be the same as usual.'

Honor raised her eyes to his face, dumbfounded by a knowledge that went no further.

'Well, you will soon come up again,' said Hatton. 'Now Gavin will have some meat, won't he?'

'Yes.'

'That is my sensible boy.'

'He will eat it all up,' said Nevill, in a vigorous tone.

'So I have two sensible boys.'

'But he will eat the most.'

'I shall see which of you does that. Now Honor will come and have her dinner on my knee.'

Honor went at once to Hatton.

'Sit on Hatton's knee,' said Nevill.

'No, Honor is my baby today.'

'No, he is.'

'You are my baby boy, and Honor is my baby girl.'

'He is a girlie,' said Nevill, holding his knife and fork idle.

'Poor Gavin can't be anything,' said Mullet.

'Not anything,' said Nevill, sadly surveying his brother.

'Honor is going to sleep,' said Gavin, in a rough tone.

'She is tired out,' said Hatton.

'He is tired,' said Nevill, laying his head on the table.

'I am not,' said Gavin, loudly.

'You are a brave boy,' said Mullet.

'He is brave,' said Nevill, leaning towards Hatton, 'a brave soldier boy.'

Honor sank into weeping, cried to the end of her tears, and stood pale and barely conscious while she was made ready to go downstairs. Hatton took them to the door and stood outside, with her ears alert. Mullet remained with her, as if any demand might arise.

'Miss Luce will be a second mother to the children,' she said.

'They will be the better for another,' said Hatton.

'Don't you think the mistress does her part by them?'

'She does all she can, but children hardly want what she gives them. In a way they need very little. They want at once more and less.'

'Master Nevill will hardly remember his father.'

'He has not been able to do much for them lately,' said Hatton, with a sigh. 'And he can do nothing more.'

The children entered the room and stood aloof and silent. Nevill looked about for some employment. Honor was exhausted and Gavin in a state of inner tumult. Eleanor was talking to Ridley, and Regan was lost in herself. Honor sent her eyes round the faces at the table, and went and stood by Isabel. Fulbert's absence of the last months saved his family an empty place. Sir Jesse made a movement from habit towards the things on the table.

'Can they eat them today?' he said, in a voice that simply implied that the day was different.

Gavin came up to the table.

'Yes,' he said.

Sir Jesse pushed a dish towards him and seemed to forget his presence, and Nevill came to his brother's side. Eleanor turned her eyes on them.

'You are having dessert, are you?' she said, in a tone that added nothing to her words.

'Yes,' said Gavin.

'Yes,' said Nevill, standing with his eyes and his hands at the edge of the table.

'Would you like some, Honor?'

'No, thank you.'

'Have it, if you like, dear.'

Honor did not reply.

'James, did you try to take care of Honor?'

James looked at his mother, with a wave of recollection sweeping over him.

'Did you do what you could for her, my boy?'

James met his mother's eyes, and moisture came into his own.

'She – I don't think – she didn't seem to want me.'

'Never mind, dear,' said Eleanor, kindly. 'She could not help it. I am sure you did your best.'

James looked at Honor, saw that she had hardly heard, and realized that even a fatherless boy might continue to have escapes.

'Gavin, tell Hatton when you go upstairs that Honor is to lie down,' said Eleanor.

Gavin made no sign.

'Do you hear me, my boy?'

'Honor can tell her herself.'

'But I asked you to.'

'He will tell her,' said Nevill, to his mother.

'Gavin, do you want to be less useful than Nevill?'

'It is not useful when she can do it herself. And lying down doesn't make any difference. You always think it does.'

'Not to Father's having left us. But it will make Honor's head-ache better.'

'Have you got a headache?' said Gavin, to his sister.

'No.'

Nevill looked round the table over his hands.

'Poor Honor!' he said, in a rapid tone. 'Poor Isabel! Poor Grandma!' He returned to his plate and looked up to add an afterthought. 'Poor Luce!'

'Nevill admits only feminine feeling,' said Daniel.

'He has met more of it,' said Graham. 'And there may be more.'

'Poor Graham! Poor Daniel!' said Nevill, in an obliging tone.

'Poor Mother!' said Eleanor, gently.

'Poor Mother!' agreed her son. 'But Father come back after a long time, and Mr Ridley stay till then.'

'He must not eat too much,' said Venice, in a lifeless tone.

'Not much today,' said Nevill, in grave tribute to the occasion.

Hatton opened the door and stood with her eyes on her charges. Nevill looked at her and back at the table, supplied his mouth with a befitting moderation, and went to her side; Honor slowly followed; James glanced from Hatton to his mother; Gavin continued to eat.

'Go with Hatton, my six poor children,' said Eleanor. 'She can do more for you than your mother. Go, James dear, if you want to.'

James could only hesitate at this imputation, which he realized was to be a recurring one.

'Have you had your dessert?' said his mother, misinterpreting the pause.

'Oh, no,' said James, with a lightness that disposed of the idea.

'Did you not want any?'

'No.'

'Would you like some now?'

'No, thank you.'

'You weren't thinking about it today?'

'No,' said James, as if his thoughts were still absent from it.

'Then go, my little son. You will be safe with Hatton.'

Ridley waited until the door closed, and bent towards Eleanor.

'There is something particular in our feeling for these old attendants, who have spent their lives in our service. They, if any, have earned our affection.'

'My children have much more feeling for Hatton than they have for me.'

'Mrs Sullivan!' said Ridley, a smile overspreading his face at this extension of the truth.

'Hatton is not so much older than Ridley,' said Daniel.

'He is not an attendant,' said his brother. 'Attendants may age earlier. There are reasons why they should.'

'I was older than most of these children when my feelings transferred, or rather extended themselves to my parents,' said Luce.

'And we must not say that was long ago,' said Ridley.

Regan left the room, as if she could sustain her feeling only by herself. Ridley hastened to the door and stood, as she passed through it, with an air of putting the whole of himself into his concern.

'There seems a hopelessness about the grief of the old,' he said, as he returned to Eleanor. 'In proportion as it lacks the strength of our prime, it is without the power of reaction and recovery.'

'You none of you think you do anything like the old,' said Sir Jesse. 'You feel things in the same way as they do, just as you feel them in the same way as the young. We suffer according to ourselves.'

Ridley gave an uncertain glance towards the end of the table, where he had believed Sir Jesse to be sitting, lost in his grief.

'All real sorrow must last to the end,' said Eleanor.

'Mrs Sullivan, you do indeed think so now,' said Ridley, in earnest understanding.

A message was brought and delivered to Ridley.

'Mrs Sullivan,' he said, with a rueful smile, 'my family seek admittance, but are prepared to be denied.' His tone suggested that he also was ready for this climax.

'Let them come in, Mother,' said Luce. 'The boys would be better for a change. And we need not repel kindness.'

'If anyone will benefit by it, my dear, let them all join us.'

'It is a case of pure friendship,' said Daniel, 'for it is clear that the advantage will not extend to the guests.'

'Why are we the ones not satisfied with the situation?' said Graham. 'Would the others ask nothing better?'

Hope went in silence to her usual place; Paul walked to Sir Jesse and sat down by his side; Faith stood apart, as if she would put forward no personal claim, even for a seat.

'I hope it does not look as if Paul were trying to take Fulbert's place,' murmured Hope.

'There would be no possibility of his doing that, Mother.'

'No, dear, that is what I meant.'

'Mrs Cranmer is ill at ease because of our trouble,' said Luce, for her mother's ears. 'It must be accounted to her for friendship.'

'I hope no one is looking at me,' said Hope. 'I am so ashamed of not being dead. It is the valuable lives that are cut off, but one does not like to acquiesce in it. How does one seem as if one really wished one had died instead?'

'How are all the children?' said Faith.

No one answered her, as she addressed no one in particular.

'I knew you would come, Mrs Cranmer,' said Luce. 'I don't know how, but I did.'

'I think Luce had grounds for expecting it,' said Daniel.

'And you did not give orders that we were not to be admitted,' said Hope. 'I know now that I have never appreciated anything before.'

'No, Mrs Cranmer, we omitted to do that,' said Luce.

'How are all the children?' said Faith.

'It is something to feel we have friends in the stretch of darkness before us,' said Graham.

'I know that nothing equals the despair of youth,' said Hope. 'I am almost as much ashamed of being middle-aged as of being alive, and no doubt you see less difference than I do.'

'Faith, are you not going to sit down?' said Daniel, who with his brother was standing by his seat.

'No, I don't mind standing,' said Faith.

'But I do,' muttered Graham.

'Faith dear, sit down and let the boys do the same,' said Luce. 'The main trial is enough, without little extra ones.'

Faith gave a slight start and walked to a seat, and at once looked round, as if her mind had not left the question on her lips.

'How are all the children?'

'My dear, would you ask again?' said Hope. 'Perhaps they are all so stunned by grief, that it is not referred to.'

'They are in different states, Mrs Cranmer,' said Luce. 'It is asking about them together that precludes an answer. James and Gavin and Nevill are not giving anxiety; Honor and Isabel are; Venice is in a state between. That is all I can tell you. It is all I know.'

'Poor little things!' said Faith.

'I can see Ridley being a support to your mother, and Paul to your grandfather,' said Hope. 'I don't think I need be ashamed that they have not died.'

'Mrs Cranmer,' said Luce, as if speaking on a sudden impulse, 'Would you go and do the same for Grandma? She is alone in the library, and I don't feel I can undertake it.' She gave a little smile. 'My strength is giving out.'

'I am sure that is the bravest smile I have ever seen,' said Hope, hurrying to the door. 'It is shocking of me to have any strength left, and I will go and expend every ounce of it. The sooner it is used up, the better.'

'Luce seems to be different,' said Graham, looking at his sister. 'We ought none of us to be the same again. I hope I shall not be found to be the only one unchanged.'

'I hope you will be among them, Graham dear,' said Luce.

Hope crossed the hall and found Regan sitting by the library fire.

'Don't take any notice of me,' she said. 'You would be hardly conscious that I have entered. I know that all real experience has passed me by. But I have heard that a mother's feelings are the deepest, and so I have come to you.'

Regan raised her eyes.

'I heard you all come,' she said.

'Don't talk in that unnatural way; it makes me feel even more inferior. I have never been in an unnatural state; I have never had the chance of getting into one. I suppose this is the third time for you.'

'The third time,' said Regan. 'I only had three.'

'I am not being of any use at all. My words ought to have brought a flood of tears.'

'Crying does no good.'

'And I thought it was an outlet and a safety-valve. I thought, if people cried until they could cry no more, the worst was over. How do all these wrong reports get about? Is there no healing power in tears?'

'I ought to know,' said Regan, with a faint smile. 'The worst comes to stay, when it comes. But I expect you think I can live in the past, like other old people.'

'I have heard that report about them. Is it another wrong one?'

'They live more in the present, which is sensible of them; and in the future, which perhaps is not, though it is the only share they will get of it.'

'Then it is simply a mistake about their living in their memories?'

'Memories only have a meaning, if they lead up to the present. This sort of thing takes the life and heart out of them.'

'Is there no satisfaction in the dignity of deep experience? I should really like to know that.'

'Depth is no help in trouble. And why is it dignified to be battered? It might be more so to get your own way.'

'I am doing you a great deal of good. I call that quite natural. But you look down on me for my superficial life.'

'Some people seem to skate on the top of things,' said Regan, in a tone of agreement.

'I think I have done you enough good now. There is reason in everything. People can be too natural. I suppose most people are.'

Regan laughed.

'You are not one of those people who see nothing and hear nothing and know nothing,' she said. 'I never thought you were.'

'That is the word I needed. To think of your fulfilling my need at such a time! You have come out of your own sorrow. And that must show the worst is over. Or is it another error?'

'The worst comes back,' said Regan.

'But gradually with less force?'

'Well, it gets dulled.'

'But isn't that an improvement in a way?'

'A great one. People who don't think so, have not been through much.'

'But I think so; I said it of my own accord. I need not be so ashamed of my easy experience, if it hasn't done me any harm.'

'Well, there is no good in weeping here alone,' said Regan. 'I may as well put myself on my family. It is better for me, if not for them.'

'Well, Grandma, I was waiting for you,' said Luce. 'It is not in you to remain at a standstill. I knew you would move forward.'

'Not a useful habit at this stage. It won't come in very well.'

'Mrs Cranmer, I am grateful,' said Luce. 'You have restored to us the real person and the real voice. We are all taking our first steps on our new path. It is more difficult for us in a way, that we shall not have the usual observances. They make a barrier between the first shock and the beginning of the future. It will be left to us to help ourselves.'

'That is a good way of saying there does not have to be a funeral,' said Graham.

'I agree,' said Daniel, 'now that I know what it is.'

'So do I,' said Hope. 'I will never call a funeral gruesome and obsolete pageantry again. No wonder the custom survives. Now I will take my family away. I suppose Ridley is not going to live with you now?'

'I believe Nevill did suggest it,' said Daniel.

'He has been here long enough for you to judge of his presence. And I can see you have done so. Paul, we must go. We have done all we can; I mean, no one can do anything.'

'May I see the children?' said Faith.

'No, Faith,' said Luce, in a quiet, almost ruthless tone. 'They have borne enough today. I mean' – she gave a smile without moving her head – 'even the most well-meant and careful touch might be too much. I want them to face nothing more at all.'

'I hope Faith is really one of those people who forgive anything,' said Hope. 'Or even one of those who forgive big things and not small. That would do.'

'I would not touch on anything sad,' said Faith, hesitating near the door.

'Faith, will you accept what I say?' said Luce. 'Whether you agree with it or not? I know it is one of those things that do not carry their evidence, but I will rely on your understanding.'

'Of course, I see what you mean,' said Faith.

'Dear me, does she really?' said Hope.

'Thank you, Faith,' said Luce.

'The children always take the initiative with me,' said Faith. 'I am never the instigator of the proceedings.'

'Can it be that Luce's words have had no effect at all?' said Hope.

'Well, go and do your worst, Faith,' said Luce, with another smile.

'I did not know that people spoke true words in jest, on purpose,' said Hope.

Faith left the room with a smoothness that seemed to draw a veil over the proceeding, and mounted the flights of stairs to the nursery, her expression becoming resolute as her breath failed.

'Well, what are you all doing?' she said, putting her head round the door, as if to surprise and engage the occupants.

Isabel and Venice and Honor were doing nothing; James was reading on the sofa; Gavin and Nevill were playing on the floor, at a similar game but separately.

'Boys should get up when a lady comes into the room,' said Hatton. 'James, bring a chair for Miss Cranmer.'

James did so, placing his open book on a table in readiness for his return.

'So you are not painting arrows today,' said Faith, taking the chair as if it were her due.

There was silence.

'You are not, are you?' said Hatton.

'No,' said Gavin, 'we are playing at soldiers.'

'He is too,' said Nevill, placing one in position.

'And what are the soldiers doing?' said Faith. 'Are they having a great battle?'

'Say what they are doing,' said Hatton, who did not know what this was.

'They are having a military funeral,' said Gavin, not moving his eyes from the floor.

'Bury a general,' said Nevill, in a solemn tone, with his arm poised for another adjustment. 'Bury a tall, big man like Father. Poor Father is all buried in a far land. But he is like a soldier now.'

There was silence.

'Do you have a coffin?' said James, in an awkward manner.

'No,' said Gavin. 'Just his martial cloak around him.'

'Just his cloak,' said Nevill, picking up a soldier and beginning to wrap something about it.

'And what are the rest of you doing?' said Faith.

'James is reading – was reading,' said Hatton, 'and the others are not up to much today.'

'There is a difference between boys and girls, isn't there? This seems an illustration of it.'

'You should not talk about children as if they were not there,' said Gavin.

'Gavin, that is rude,' said Hatton.

'Not any more rude than she was.'

'He is not himself today, miss.'

'I am,' said Gavin.

'He is too,' said Nevill, in an absent tone.

'One does not know what to say to them,' said Faith.

'She needn't say anything,' said Gavin, addressing Hatton.

'You will excuse him today, miss.'

'I don't care if she doesn't. Then I needn't excuse her.'

'Well, I think I must say good-bye,' said Faith, as if she were uttering a threat.

'Come again soon. Good-bye. Come again to see him,' said Nevill, glancing up from the floor.

Faith looked at the three girls, and after a second's hesitation walked towards them and stooped and gave a kiss to each, smiling gently and fully into their faces. Then with a slightly heightened colour she turned to Nevill.

'Are you going to give me a kiss?'

Nevill sat up and raised his face, and when Faith had knelt down and embraced him, resumed his game.

As Faith closed the door, Honor uttered her first word since her coming.

'Not a high type,' she said.

James gave Honor a look he sometimes gave Isabel, and returned to his book.

'I was not very proud of any of you,' said Hatton.

'Well, no one would be proud of her,' said Gavin.

'I was quite ashamed of you, Gavin.'

'I am glad.'

Faith went down to the drawing-room, and spoke in a cheerful, satisfied tone.

'Well, I was glad to get a glimpse of them. I remembered the instructions to make it no more than that.'

'That was understanding of you, Faith,' said Luce.

'We had better go,' said Hope. 'I simply don't know what Luce will say next.'

'Did you think that they seemed themselves?' said Eleanor.

'I would hardly say that of the girls. The boys seemed in better spirits.'

'I hope they weren't too unkind to you,' said Hope.

'Why should they be, Mother?'

'There is no reason, dear. That is why I hope they were not.'

'Nevill was very friendly, and so was James. The girls were not equal to so much; things go deeper with them. Gavin is a rougher diamond altogether. I have promised Nevill to pay another visit soon.'

'Were they all together?' said Eleanor.

'Yes, in the nursery with Hatton.'

'I suppose they cannot bear Miss Mitford's touch in sorrow,' said Hope.

'I wish I had gone in and said a word to Miss Mitford,' said Faith.

'Why should you do that?' said Hope.

'Well, it is always nice to see a friend, Mother,' said Faith, her tone somehow making a point of the equality and friendship.

Sir Jesse and Paul came from the fire, continuing to talk. Paul went at once from the house, giving his family no chance to linger. Ridley bent over Eleanor's hand, and followed his father with an expression of controlled feeling.

'I wish we had only to sustain grief,' said Graham, when the family were alone.

'So do I, Graham,' said Luce. 'But we have to support many burdens. I cannot say I don't see them as such, that I would not rather sorrow in peace. But there is no choice before us.'

'And not much else,' said her brother.

'No, Graham, not much else.'

'The way you dealt with Faith gave me a gleam of comfort, Luce,' said Daniel.

'I could hardly put my mind on her. I see what people mean by the selfishness of sorrow.'

'I take exception to the phrase. It suggests some personal advantage.'

'If it means that people who are sorrowing, should give their attention to those who are not, it is a wicked thing to say,' said Graham.

'And why shouldn't we be absorbed in our own trouble?' said Luce.

'If we were not, we should be called shallow,' said Daniel.

'People are indeed wicked,' said Graham.

'Mother,' said Luce, as Eleanor passed them, 'had you not better sit down and rest?'

'I am not tired, my dear.'

'Honest, as usual, Mother. But it may be the false energy of exhaustion.'

'I wish exhaustion had that effect on me,' said Graham.

'I don't even feel it,' said Regan, in a tone that did not bear out her words.

Luce sat down at her grandmother's side, as though without the power to aid her further.

'We have all to move forward,' said Sir Jesse. 'Some of us can only go slowly, but our direction is the same. And my son left sons behind him.'

'You talk as if women did not exist, Grandpa,' said Luce.

'It is a pity men do not manage to do so,' said Regan.

'They are more exposed to risk than women, Grandma. It is a thing that has its brighter side.'

'For them perhaps.'

'Yes, only for them, Grandma.'

'I belong to the sex that encounters perils,' said Graham. 'That does not seem very suitable somehow.'

'It does not, Graham dear,' said Luce.

'We must manage to keep him from them,' said Regan, in a tone that did not grudge her grandson the life her son had lost.

'He does not strike me as a person who will incur them,' said Sir Jesse.

'It is a pity that Grandpa has ever had to meet us,' said Graham. 'The mere idea of us seems to be satisfying to him.'

'Ridley has done a great deal for us today,' said Eleanor. 'I dare not imagine what things would have been without him.'

'We should not have known what had happened,' said Graham. 'I shall always see him as the bearer of ill tidings.'

'I wonder if we shall,' said Luce.

'I am afraid I am very restless,' said Eleanor, who was moving about the room. 'I suppose I am in an unnatural state. I hope I shall be able to do my duty by you all. I don't seem to be able to reach my own sorrow. I am simply oppressed by a fear of the future.'

'We all tremble a little before that, Mother,' said Luce.

'It was good of Hope to come at once,' said Regan.

'Grandma, you don't often say a word in favour of anyone outside,' said Luce.

'She is a deal better than most people.'

'I like her very much, Grandma, but is she *better*? Is that quite her word?'

'It does as well as any other.'

'Grandma, I should never have suspected you of making a woman friend.'

'I have to do what I can with the people left. And it seemed to me that I had one.'

A silence fell on the family.

'Mother,' said Luce, 'shall we give ourselves a little help on this first day? Shall we have Nevill brought down to say good night?'

'Ought we to make a sacrifice of him?' said Graham.

'We shall not do that, Graham. We will not take him beyond his scope.'

Hatton obeyed the summons and led Nevill into the room. She had an air of disapproval and gave him no injunctions. He seemed preoccupied and stood waiting for what was required of him, before returning to his own sphere.

'So you have come to say good night,' said Eleanor.

'Good night, Mother,' said Nevill, going up to her to get the first step over.

'He has come to give us a glimpse of him,' said Regan.

'Good night, Grandma,' said Nevill, doing the same to her, and then sending his eyes round the room and speaking more quickly. 'Good night, Luce; good night, Grandpa; good night, Graham; good night, Father; good night, Daniel.'

He turned and looked up at Hatton in inquiry as to the moment of withdrawal.

'Father is not here, my little one,' said Eleanor.

'Yes, he is here,' said Nevill, in an absent tone. 'Father has come back today.'

'No, he cannot come back to us, my little boy.'

'Good night – Grandpa,' amended Nevill, looking about for a substitute for Fulbert.

'How strange that he should say that, on this day of all days!' said Luce.

'He has heard his father's name a great deal,' said Regan, in simple explanation.

'That is all of his father he has left,' said Eleanor, sighing.

'When people accept the death of someone, are they always staggered by the general results of it?' said Graham.

'Well, what have you been doing upstairs?' said Eleanor to Nevill.

'He played at soldiers. And Gavin did too.'

'Did you play together?'

'No, he did it all by himself.'

'What did the soldiers do?'

'Bury a general,' said Nevill, in a deepening tone. 'Bury a soldier man like Father. Beat the drum and make a thunder noise.'

There was a pause.

'How did he think of that?' said Eleanor, to Hatton.

'I don't know, Madam. We can never tell how ideas come into their minds.'

'It came into his mind,' said Nevill, with a pride that protected his brother.

'Was Gavin playing too?' said Eleanor, in a sudden tone.

'No,' said her son, 'Gavin played all by himself.'

'Was Honor?'

'No, poor Honor sat on a chair.'

'And James was not playing either?'

'Oh, no,' said Nevill, in a virtuous tone. 'Not talk to James when he is reading.'

'Well, good night, my little son.'

Nevill accepted this sign of release, but on his way to the door he returned to Regan.

'Not a drum was heard,' he began, and paused as his memory failed him, and turned and ran from the room.

'It is a good thing some amusement can come out of it,' said Regan.

'We do not realize the gulf between children and ourselves,' said Eleanor.

'We do now,' said Daniel.

'That is true of Mother,' said Graham.

'Well, Father used to say so,' said Luce.

'What used your father to say?' said Eleanor.

'That you did not realize the gulf between yourself and your children, Mother,' said Luce, in an open, deliberate tone. 'What you say of yourself. What no doubt he often said to you.'

'I shall have to do so now. I daresay it will be borne in upon me.'

'Why will it be different?' said Regan.

'Well, I shall have to fulfil two characters.'

Regan was silent.

'Say what is in your mind, Grandma,' said Luce. 'That is not a fair way to deal with anyone.'

'If we could be other people as well as ourselves, it would not matter what happened to us. And a loss does not give us other qualities.'

'I suppose the days will pass,' said Eleanor, as though to herself.

'There is little suggestion of it about this one,' said Graham.

'Would it be better if we were apart for a time?' said Daniel.

'Why should it?' said Eleanor, with a change in her eyes.

'We shouldn't have each other's feelings on us, as well as our own.'

'I should have yours. They wouldn't be off my mind for a moment. You could all forget mine, could you?'

'We might have more chance of it, if we were separated. We shall have to learn to spare ourselves.'

'Well, I will go to my room and give you a rest,' said Eleanor.

'And have a respite from us, Mother dear,' said Luce.

'You can put it as you like, to hide the truth from yourselves. You do not hide it from me.'

Luce stood still with her eyes down, as her mother left the room.

'It has to be,' she said, lifting her eyes. 'It is no use to disguise it.'

'We might have postponed it,' said Graham, with a look of trouble.

'It would have done no good, Graham. The little, subtle miseries of sorrow have to be faced. I don't think they are the least part of it.'

'I think they should be,' said Graham.

'Go after your mother,' said Sir Jesse, roughly, to his grandsons. 'What do your personal pains matter, since they only do so to yourselves? Go and do what you can to help a burden heavier than yours. What else should you do? What is your opinion of yourselves and your use in this house?'

His grandchildren left the room, Daniel with an expression of almost amused submission, Graham with a look of relief, and Luce with an air of resigning herself to service. Regan looked after them with compassion.

'There is nothing you want of them, is there?' said Sir Jesse, with a note of excuse in his tone.

'I want nothing that anyone can give me; I could do with my three children.'

An almost humble expression crossed the husband's face.

'Things are not the same to men,' said Regan. 'Their family is only a part of their life.'

'I would have given my remaining years to save my son.'

'Why should you?' said Regan. 'They are all you have left. He had no more to lose than you.'

A note was brought in, addressed to Eleanor, and put on a table to await her.

'From Ridley,' said Regan, looking at the envelope. 'He will always be thrusting himself in now.'

'There was no other way. I might not have been alive. We could not foretell the future.'

'It seems that Fulbert did so.'

'He provided against its risks.'

'What does Ridley want to say to Eleanor? He has been with her half the day.'

'You cannot see through the envelope,' said Sir Jesse.

Regan took up the letter, as if she were inclined to do her best.

'I have a good mind to open it.'

'So I see. But must you not come to another mind?' said Sir Jesse, with a smile that suggested that he and his wife were both in their youth.

'If Ridley wrote me a letter, I should not care if Eleanor read it.'

'You would be surprised if she did. And you know she would not.'

'It must be in a way a message to us all.'

'In that case we shall hear the gist of it. It may be to say that he cannot come tomorrow.'

'I am sure it is not that. It is probably a piece of palaver.'

'You do not seem to need to open it. And it sounds as if it might be awkward if you did. He has to explain Fulbert's affairs. They are not much, as I am still alive, but she is new to such things.'

'It is a good thing Fulbert lived long enough to have a family,' said Regan, again at the end of her control. 'Or it would have been as little good to have him as the others.'

'We have our memories,' said her husband.

'Yes, you can add them to a stock of those.'

Eleanor came into the room and looked about for the letter.

'They said there was a note for me.'

'They should have taken it to you,' said Sir Jesse, seeming to welcome another subject.

'Luce and the boys were with me,' said Eleanor, as though to counteract the last impression given by her children. 'The servants would guess we did not want to be disturbed.'

Regan met Sir Jesse's eyes, but the latter's face told nothing.

Eleanor opened the letter and sat down to read it.

MY DEAR ELEANOR,

I could not let this day pass without expressing to you what I could not say to your face, my deep admiration for your selfless resolution and courage. Much will depend on your strength and wisdom, and I shall work with you with a growing sense of privilege.

Yours in sympathy and gratitude,
RIDLEY CRANMER.

'Does Ridley call you Eleanor now?' said Regan, in comment upon the only part of the letter she had seen.

'He does here. I always use his Christian name.'

'He is a good deal younger than you.'

'Only about five years.'

'Is there any message for the rest of us?'

'No. It is just a word about our working together.'

'Why couldn't it wait until tomorrow?'

'I suppose some things are better written,' said Eleanor, going to the door with the letter.

'Well, there wasn't room for much more than that,' said Regan. 'It hardly went down the first page. I wonder why she kept it to herself.'

'She seems hardly to have done so,' said Sir Jesse.

CHAPTER NINE

'YOU did not expect me today,' said Sir Jesse, entering the Marlowes' cottage.

'No,' said Lester, 'or you could have seen Priscilla by herself.'

'I am glad to see you all. I should be happy to have young friends. I am now a childless man.'

There was a pause.

'Your son had a happy life,' said Susan.

'You see that a reason for his losing it? People state it as if it were.'

'We have to think of reasons,' said Priscilla. 'It is too shocking that there shouldn't be any. When people have had a sad life, we say that death is a release. It is to prevent things from being without any plan.'

'It is unwise to criticize one of you in the presence of the others.'

'And we do not spoil it by criticizing each other to our faces, in the accepted way,' said Priscilla.

'You hardly knew my son.'

'We met him a few times.'

'I should have liked you to know him better, and him to know you.'

'We did not realize that,' said Lester, looking surprised.

'We did our best to know him to the extent you desired,' said Priscilla.

'I wish I had died instead of him,' said Sir Jesse.

'Why do people wish that?' said Priscilla. 'Instead of wishing that no one had died.'

'I should have liked to see you all together. I believe I never did.'

'It could have been arranged. I think you could not have wanted it very much.'

'You have your son's children,' said Susan.

'Susan does offer conventional comfort,' said Priscilla. 'But what other kind is there? She does not like to offer none at all.'

'There is none,' said Sir Jesse.

'That is where she is in a difficult place.'

'You take my trouble lightly.'

'We do not feel close enough to take an intimate view of it,' said Lester, at once.

'I have not done much for you. You might have asked much more.'

'We should not have expected anything,' said Priscilla. 'But we have been the more glad to have it.'

'You are a generous girl, my dear. And not without knowledge of life.'

'Then we have some points in common.'

'That may be,' said Sir Jesse, looking into the fire. 'That may be.'

'I wish he would not keep gazing at the fire,' said Priscilla, aside to the others. 'People are supposed to see faces in it, but I am so afraid he will see wood.'

'You are not afraid of me,' said Sir Jesse. 'You would ask me for anything you wanted.'

'Does that mean he knows we take it without asking?' said Priscilla.

'We are not in need of anything,' said Lester.

Sir Jesse gave him an almost gentle look, that seemed to make some comparison.

'You do not see much of my family?'

'Daniel and Graham come in sometimes.'

'Luce does not come?' said Sir Jesse, on his suddenly harsher note.

'No, she never does,' said Lester, in simple assurance.

'Why are we pariahs?' said Susan, looking Sir Jesse in the eyes.

'It is your own word,' said the latter.

'It is yours,' said Priscilla, 'though you have not used it. And we have no right to object to it. We know nothing about ourselves, except that you knew our parents.'

'That is my reason for concerning myself with you.'

'It was a fortunate friendship for us.'

'That is for you to say.'

'That is what I must have felt,' said Priscilla.

'I must go,' said Sir Jesse. 'I am glad I have seen you. I hope you don't think hardly of me. I have had your welfare in my mind.'

He left the house with his head bent, as though feeling he would not be seen by those whom he could not see, and raised his head as he passed into another road.

'What would he have done, if we had not been grateful for bare necessities?' said Susan.

'He knew just how much he meant to do,' said Lester.

'He knows why people dislike their benefactors,' said Priscilla. 'It is because they expect them to share equally with them, when of course they do not. That is why he expects us to dislike him.'

'We are never to know our story?' said her brother.

'I feel that is confirmed today,' said Susan. 'Something made him go as far as he would ever go. It may be a good thing.'

'It gives us a feeling of security,' said Priscilla. 'I daresay it would be too much for us to know. We might not be able to forgive Mother.'

The housekeeper entered the room.

'Sir Jesse spoke to me today, miss. He has never done it before. He said he hoped I was taking care of you all.'

'Why does he break his records all of a sudden?' said Susan.

'His son has broken one by dying,' said Priscilla, 'and that has put him on the course.'

'How shall we behave when Sir Jesse dies?' said Lester. 'Shall we have to go to the funeral?'

'You will have to represent us,' said Susan.

'What a good thing Susan knows these things!' said Priscilla. 'I could not answer such a question.'

'I hope he will leave us as much as he allows us,' said Lester, in an anxious tone. 'He must know he will cause us great trouble if he does not.'

'It is wonderful of people to think of other people's needs after they are dead themselves,' said Priscilla. 'I always feel it is too much to expect.'

'People don't find it so,' said Susan.

'And we must not talk as if people were about to die, because they are old.'

'There is something in the view,' said Lester gravely.

'It is too ordinary for us,' said Priscilla. 'We have tried to get our own touch, and we must not dispel it through carelessness.'

'It does not sound as if it were natural,' said Susan.

'Well, things must often owe as much to art as to nature. I dare say the best things do.'

'Does Sir Jesse respect or despise us?' said Lester.

'It is possible to do both,' said Susan.

'One feeling must get the upper hand,' said her sister. 'And though it is extraordinary, when he supports us, I believe in his case it is respect.'

'He has quite an affection for you,' said Lester.

'Well, I have done much to earn it. They say that a conscious effort is not the best way to win affection, but it seems a fairly good way, and often the only one.'

'We cannot deal only in the best methods,' said Susan. 'What would be the good of the others? And now they are so much good.'

'We have got Sir Jesse's visit over,' said Lester. 'He won't come again for months.'

'This is an extra visit, caused by the death of his son,' said Susan.

'You need not see him when he comes,' said Priscilla.

'It gives us a feeling of strain,' said Lester. 'We know we are in his power.'

'I see how real the trouble has been, that I thought I had taken off you. But Sir Jesse does not resent our being alive when his son is dead. He seems to think he has something left in us. He must love us better than we deserve, or his grief draws him closer to us. It is strange to see these things really happening.'

'Especially between Sir Jesse and us,' said Lester.

'Would he mind if one of us were to die?' said Susan.

'He would wish he had made things easier for us,' said her sister. 'People always wish they had given more help, when people are beyond it. Wishing it before would mean giving it. One does see how it gets put off.'

'We shall never have to wish we had given help to Sir Jesse,' said Lester, in a musing tone.

'If one of us were to marry, would he reveal our parentage?' said Susan.

'I could not support a wife,' said Lester, in a startled manner.

'If we cannot find out by less drastic means, we will leave it,' said Priscilla.

'If only the photograph could speak!' said Susan. 'Sir Jesse never looks at it. It is not of much interest to him.'

'He is careful never to look at it,' said Lester.

'Why are inanimate things supposed to be so communicative?' said Priscilla. 'It might tell us nothing. And it may be on the side of Sir Jesse.'

'To think what we could tell the photograph!' said Susan.

'Well, not so much,' said Lester.

'There isn't so much to be told,' said Priscilla. 'Photographs would find that.'

'Mr Ridley Cranmer,' said Mrs Morris at the door.

'You are satisfactory friends to call upon,' said Ridley, pausing inside the room, as if its size would hardly allow advance. 'We can rely on finding you at home. It is not easy for an occupied man to appoint his time.'

'I wonder if Mother likes to hear that about us,' said Priscilla.

'You still find that your mother's photograph adds an interest to your life,' said Ridley, resting his eyes on the chimneypiece. 'I can understand that it suggests many pictures of the past. I wonder Sir Jesse did not grant it to you before.'

'He only found it by accident,' said Susan.

'Is that the case?' said Ridley. 'I believe Sir Jesse has paid you a visit this afternoon?'

'Yes, he has just gone.'

'I saw him coming away from the house.'

'Then you would believe it,' said Priscilla.

'Does he often honour you in that way?'

'No, very seldom,' said Susan.

'It is sad to think he is now a childless man.'

'He said that of himself,' said Lester.

'Did he?' said Ridley, with a look of interest.

'Does it strike you as a curious thing to say?'

'I can hardly imagine our friend, Sir Jesse, making such an intimate statement.'

'The news had leaked out,' said Priscilla.

Ridley threw back his head and went into laughter.

'I wish I could have relied upon that process for making it known to the family. But it fell to me to reveal it by a more exacting method, by word of mouth.' His tone became grave as he ended.

'It must have been a hard moment for everyone,' said Susan.

'But I had my reward in the courage and resolution displayed by them all,' went on Ridley, 'especially by the chief character in the scene, Eleanor Sullivan. She indeed rose to the heights. No yielding to personal feeling or thought of self. A calm, firm advance into the future. It was an impressive thing.'

'She will have a difficult life,' said Lester.

'Lester, it seems almost too much,' said Ridley, turning in sudden feeling. 'It seems that something should be done to ease so great a burden.'

'She has three grown-up children.'

'And the word relegates them to their position, points out how much and how little they can do. To her they are her children. Nothing can make them less; nothing can add to their significance. Nothing alters the deep, essential, limited relation.'

'She has her husband's parents.'

'Rather would I say, Lester, that they have her.'

'So that is how Mother feels to us,' said Priscilla. 'I feel half-inclined to take her away from the chimneypiece.'

'Leave her,' said Ridley, in a rather dramatic manner, resting his eyes again on the photograph. 'Nothing was further from me than to belittle the relation. She is your mother. You bear the traces of her lineaments. She is in her place.'

'People say we are like her,' said Susan.

'That is what Ridley meant,' said Priscilla.

'I must leave you now,' said Ridley, seeming not to hear the words, and perhaps not doing so in the stress of his feelings. 'My duties call me. I have more in these sad days. I hardly know why I came in. I happened to be passing.'

'Why do people give that reason for calling?' said Susan. 'They can't drop in on every acquaintance they pass.'

'They imply that they would not call at the cost of any trouble,' said Priscilla. 'They mean to give the impression of not wanting much to come. And really they give one of wanting to come so much, that they are embarrassed by the strength of the feeling. Sir Jesse called because that was his intention. We will always call in that spirit.'

'It is not like Ridley to call by himself on people of no place and parentage.'

'He had his own reasons,' said Lester.

CHAPTER TEN

'WELL, my boy, I must solicit your help,' said Ridley, entering the Sullivans' hall. 'I have come to seek a moment with your grandfather.'

'I don't know where he is,' said Gavin.

'Can you find out for me?'

'We never do find out things about him.'

'Grandpa is in the library,' said Honor, coming up. 'Couldn't you go and see him?'

'So I am to beard the lion in his den.'

'Grandpa is a big lion,' said Nevill, pausing by the group. 'He can roar very loud.'

'He can at times,' said Honor, making a mature grimace, and glancing to see if Ridley had had the advantage of it.

'Do you often play in the hall?' said the latter.

'Sometimes when it is wet,' said Gavin.

'Shall I play at lions with you?' said Ridley, looking at a skin on the floor, and seeming to be struck by an idea that would serve his own purpose.

'Yes,' said Honor and Gavin.

Nevill turned on his heel and toiled rapidly up the staircase, and paused at a secure height in anticipation of the success of the scene. Ridley put the skin over his head and ran in different directions, uttering threatening sounds and causing Honor and Gavin to leap aside with cries of joy and mirth. Nevill watched the action with bright, dilated eyes, and, when Ridley ran in his direction, fled farther upwards with piercing shrieks. Hatton descended in expostulation, and Miss Mitford in alarm, the latter not having distinguished between the notes of real and pleasurable terror in Nevill's voice. Regan hustled forward in the same spirit as Hatton, and smiled upon Ridley in a rare benevolence.

'I plead guilty, Lady Sullivan,' said the latter, standing with outspread hands, and the rug in one of them. 'I am caught redhanded.'

'You have had a good game,' said Regan, to the children.

'We did while it went on,' said Gavin.

'I fear we do not receive encouragement to prolong it,' said Ridley.

'Grandma could hide behind the staircase,' suggested Gavin.

'He will kill the lion,' said Nevill, coming tentatively down the stairs. 'He won't let it eat poor Grandma. He will kill it dead.'

'There, it is dead,' said Ridley, dropping the skin on the floor. 'You see you have killed it.'

'It is quite dead,' said Nevill, in a regretful tone, descending the rest of the stairs and cautiously touching the skin with his foot, before trampling freely upon it. 'But he will make it alive again.'

'It was dead before,' said Gavin.

'But once it was alive. It was in a forest and could roar.'

'It was in a jungle,' said Honor.

'A jungle,' said Nevill, in reverent tone.

'It is a lioness, not a lion,' said Gavin. 'It has no mane.'

'It is really a tiger,' said Honor.

'Which is more fierce?' said Nevill.

'A tiger,' said his sister.

'Then it is a tiger, a great big tiger. No, it is a lion. A lion is more fierce.'

'I fear I am in disgrace, Lady Sullivan,' said Ridley. 'And it is not a day when I should choose such a situation. I am here to make an appeal to your favour.'

'He is a lion,' said Nevill, thrusting his head under the rug and making a charge against Ridley as vigorous as possible, considering its weight.

'I wish I could say the same of myself,' said Ridley, gently repulsing the attack. 'I am feeling the reverse of lion-hearted. I had come to ask a word with your husband, and my attention was distracted by these would-be inhabitants of the jungle. I fear I helped them to realize their ambition.'

'It sounds as if you were easily distracted,' said Regan.

'So much did my errand mean to me, that I found myself postponing the risks that it involved.'

'And how long do you want to keep on that line?'

'No longer, if you will make it easy for me to do otherwise.'

Regan met his eyes in silence, not fulfilling this suggestion, and suddenly turned and led the way across the hall.

'Poor Mr Ridley has to go and see Grandpa,' said Nevill, with eyes of concern.

'He wants to,' said Gavin.

'No, he didn't like it.'

'He said he did.'

'Hints are in the air,' said Honor, swinging one leg round the other. 'Hatton and Mullet are big with them.'

'What?' said Gavin.

'Hatton is big,' said Nevill. 'But not as big as Mullet. Hatton is rather big.'

'A cloud no larger than a man's hand,' said Honor.

'Why do you talk without saying anything?' said Gavin. 'It makes talking no good.'

'All in its own time,' said his sister.

'You think you are grand,' said Gavin, and ended the conversation.

The schoolroom party came down the stairs. James took a seat on the lowest step and opened a book; Isabel leaned against the balusters; Venice came up to Nevill with a view to his entertainment.

'Why have you all come down?' said Gavin.

'We are to play in the hall, because we are not getting any exercise,' said James, just raising his eyes.

Isabel laid her head on her arms, in personal discharge of the obligation.

'There is something heavy in the atmosphere in these days,' she said.

'You have said it,' said Honor, nodding.

'Play at lions like Mr Ridley,' said Nevill, struggling under the rug.

'So that is what the noise was,' said Isabel.

'It sounded as if someone was hurt,' said James, in an incidental tone.

'The screams of the damned,' said Honor.

'Don't let her talk like that,' said Gavin, with a note of misery.

'There are breakers ahead,' said Honor.

Gavin walked up to her and gave her a kick.

'Gavin, that is very unkind,' said Venice. 'And you should never kick a girl.'

'Ought I to kick Nevill then?'

'No,' said Nevill, flying into Venice's arms.

'You must never be rough with girls, or boys younger than yourself.'

'Then I can be rough with James.'

Honor went up to Gavin and returned the kick. He took no notice beyond rubbing his leg, and they resumed their normal relation.

'They didn't mean to hurt each other,' said Nevill, withdrawing a long gaze.

Sir Jesse and Regan and Ridley came from the library, continuing their talk. They gave no attention to the children, who did nothing to attract it.

'I shall always be grateful, Sir Jesse, for the hospitality of your house.'

'You did not come here for your own purposes.'

'I have confessed that I began to do so, as time passed. How many months is it since the death of your son?'

'We know,' said Regan. 'And no one who does not, needs to be told.'

'I do not forget what is due to the memory of a man who was my friend.'

'He depended on you to be his,' said Sir Jesse, in a grave manner.

'And to the end of my power did I fulfil that trust,' said Ridley, in a suddenly full tone. 'If feelings arose to the overthrow of a simple spirit of duty, I was helpless as a man and a friend. The emotions of manhood carried me away. I regret if my words are crude; I have no others.'

'Why are they so?' said Sir Jesse. 'Things are not that, because they are simple. They need no doctoring.'

'Eleanor was the wife of your son. She is the mother of your grandchildren. I have come to you and your wife, as those who stand in the place of her parents. I feel I have not been wrong.'

'She has had no family since we have known her,' said Regan. 'There is no demand on her, or on her family means.'

'We have not come to the discussion of such things.'

'A fact does not need discussion. No doubt you know it.'

'You came here in the service of our son,' said Sir Jesse. 'We continued to think of you as here in his interests. But I will leave our personal feelings; you are not concerned with them. I am prepared to wish you well. I desire no ill to befall you. I have been blind. I have not had my eyes on your life, but on my own.'

'I am glad the last half-hour is over,' said Ridley, speaking as if Sir Jesse's words had been lighter than they had. 'I have felt like a schoolboy making an awkward confession.'

'A schoolboy does not often have to confess a thing like this,' said Regan.

Ridley went into laughter, as though to propitiate Regan by appreciation of her words.

'What do you think of having nine stepchildren?' she said.

'I hope I shall never forget they are your grandchildren.'

'It would hardly matter if you did, as they will not.'

'I suspect they will not indeed,' said Ridley. 'I should be the last person to recommend their doing so. Not that they would appear to me to be the greater loss. And that brings me to the point of asking permission to fetch the other person most concerned.'

Eleanor was with her three eldest children in their study, and came out, accompanied by them.

'Well, my dear, we are to lose you,' said Sir Jesse. 'How much are we to lose with you?'

'I knew that would be the point,' said Eleanor.

'We have our lives,' said Regan. 'You have given your minds to yours.'

'They feel we have had them,' said Sir Jesse. 'But we have to get through the days we have left. We have a right to ask what remains to us.'

'There is a good deal that needs discussion,' said Eleanor.

'It has had it,' said Sir Jesse. 'Let us start where you left off. That is what we shall have to do.'

'We thought of several plans and discarded them.'

'Is there one you have not discarded?'

'The one that seems to us best,' said Eleanor, with an open, cold simplicity, 'is that Ridley and I should have a house in the village, and leave the children with you, on the understanding that I have daily access to them. We could not afford what you do for them, and it is best for boys to be guided by a man bound to them by blood. I would make the contribution to their expenses that I have always made. This seems best for the interests of us all.'

Regan drew a hard breath and sank into tears.

'Sir Jesse,' said Ridley, keeping his eyes averted from her, 'I should like to say how earnestly I will do my part under the new order; with what sincerity I will further the welfare of those to whom I stand in a semi-fatherly relation. If honest effort is of any avail—' He stopped as he saw Regan's face.

'Such a thing is never useless,' said Sir Jesse.

'I wonder what they will all have to say,' said Regan.

'We are all here, Grandma,' said Luce, in a low, clear tone.

'Our elders must soon have become conscious of the nine pairs of eyes,' said Daniel.

'They would have had that feeling that someone was looking at them,' said his brother.

'Lady Sullivan,' said Ridley, 'I do not desire to hear what that may be. I doubt if it will be for my ears.'

'What is your real word to us?' said Regan, suddenly to Eleanor.

Luce came forward and took her mother's hand.

'That I have felt myself unfit to be alone with my burden. I have never had faith in myself as a mother. My children will not suffer from not having me in their home. I wish in a way that they would. And I shall be at their service. I see no good in postponing a change that is resolved upon, and I am not troubled about making it so soon. I am marrying in distrust of myself, in despair at my loneliness, and in gratitude for a feeling that met my need. I was not in a position to reject it.'

'We wish you all that is good, my dear,' said Sir Jesse. 'You are doing your best for yourself and for others, and many people stop at the first.'

'And so may we say that the meeting is adjourned?' said Ridley, with a smile and a hand on Eleanor's shoulder. 'Or rather dissolved, as the business is concluded.'

Regan gave Eleanor a look of such helpless consternation at her acceptance of this caress for another's, that Sir Jesse took a step between them.

'You have other things to say to other people. You have done what you must by us.'

'It will be the same thing,' said Eleanor, 'but it will have to be said.'

'No, Mother dear,' said Luce, 'why will it? We know what there is to know. We do not need it repeated. We can bear to see you recede a little from us, if it is to result in your going forward yourself.'

'You have always made things easy for me, my dear.'

'And in this case you do so for me,' said Ridley.

'I don't think they are finding it very difficult themselves,' said Eleanor, looking at her children.

'It is not for you to see our problems, Mother,' said Daniel. 'They would not be any help to you.'

'No, do not ask for them, my dear,' said Sir Jesse.

'I should almost like to feel they were greater,' said Eleanor. 'Daniel, have you a word of your own to say to your mother?'

'I welcome anything that is for your happiness. And the feeling is not only mine.'

'So do I indeed,' said Graham, his eyes passing over Ridley.

'You are kind and just to me, my children.'

'He does too; he is too,' said Nevill, coming up to his mother.

'I did not notice you were all here,' said Eleanor, looking round the hall.

'It is a wet day, Mother,' said Luce, 'and you sent word that lessons were to be suspended.'

'Mother passed over six of her nine children,' said Venice.

'You are always in my mind, my child,' said Eleanor. 'I did not know you had come to the hall. Perhaps that is typical of my dealings with you.'

'We are in a way grateful to Ridley,' said Graham.

'Graham,' said Ridley, impulsively, 'I see that as an unspeakably generous thing to say. I hope I shall never forget it.'

'What has my Isabel to say to me?' said Eleanor.

'Simply what the others have said. We have not had time to prepare our speeches. You are spared an awkward opening to your new life.'

'The awkwardness would not have been chiefly Mother's,' said Venice.

Ridley looked at Eleanor in amusement, and with an air of being about to share the charge of the sprightly young of her family.

'Well, James, what have you to say to your mother?' said Eleanor.

James looked up from his book with a start.

'Have you not been listening, my boy?'

'No,' said James, rather faintly. 'Not to grown-up people's conversation.'

'That is a good rule on the whole, but you could have made an exception today. We have let you stay away from school to hear what we have to tell you.'

'If our family life were more eventful, James would face his future without education,' said Daniel.

'I think the strain on him would be as great,' said Graham. 'He, if anyone, must understand that life is one long training.'

'So you do not know what we have been saying, my little son. Well, something is going to happen that will make me happier. Can you guess what it is?'

'Father is not dead!' said James, jumping to his feet and standing ready to spring with joy.

'No, that is not it. You know that is not possible. But someone is going to take his place, is going to take care of me for him. Can you guess who it is?'

'It is not Mr Ridley?' said James, in a tone of getting through a step on the way to the real conclusion.

'Yes, it is he; it is Mr Ridley,' said Eleanor, looking past her son.

'He has been taking care of you for some time, hasn't he?'

'Well, now we are going to live together, so that he can do it better. You will be glad to feel I am not alone any more.'

'Is he going to live here?'

'Not in this house. He and I will have a house of our own quite near.'

'Where shall we live?' said Venice.

'Here, as you always have, with Grandpa and Grandma. And I shall come and visit you every day. You will see me as often as you do now.'

'But you won't be here in the evenings,' said James.

'I shall often be late enough to say good night. You need not be afraid you will lose your mother.'

'Will it always go on like that?'

'For as long as we need look forward.'

'Shall we come to your house too?' said Venice.

'Of course you will, my dear. As often as you like.'

'Then we shall really be the same as we are now.'

'Yes, except that you will be happier, because you won't feel that I am alone, while you are enjoying your work and your pleasures together.'

The children were silent, as these points were revealed in their life.

'And I hope I shall be a not unwelcome figure in the background,' said Ridley.

'Yes. No,' said James, with a caper. 'No.'

'What do you mean, dear?' said Eleanor.

'Not in the background,' said James, in a hardly audible voice.

'Of course not. That was a nice thing to say. And true and sensible too. And now my girls will come and kiss their mother, and show her they feel the same in their hearts, though they may be too shy to say so.'

'Perhaps I may myself make a similar claim,' said Ridley. 'I think I see signs of the acceptance of me in my new character.'

Isabel and Venice received his embrace, Venice glancing aside as his eyes dwelt on herself. James hovered in a half-expectation of a similar salute, and was rewarded by a pat on the shoulder.

'What are you thinking of, Isabel?' said Eleanor, catching an expression on her daughter's face, which she wished explained, or rather contradicted, before she left her.

'Nothing,' said Ridley, smiling as he quoted the coming reply.

'Isabel has got beyond that stage. Answer me, Isabel dear.'

'You should not want to know the things in people's minds. If you were meant to hear them, they would be said.'

'Do you often think of such things as are not said?' said Eleanor.

'Not in your sense. Though if I did, it might not be unnatural in a child of yours.'

Eleanor looked into Isabel's face, and walked towards her youngest children. Ridley followed, as if he had not observed the encounter. Mullet had brought the luncheon and was dispensing it. Hatton was aware of the scene in progress, and had directed that the children should remain downstairs.

'Is the whole of our family life to be enacted in the hall?' said Daniel. 'We only want the beds, to make things complete.'

James carried his book to his stair, and settled himself upon it. He had an air of entering upon a life in which this sort of thing would be easier. Isabel went to a window and stood, throwing the blind cord over her finger, taking no notice when the tassel struck the pane. James raised his eyes and rested them on her, and withdrew them in aloofness from what he saw, rather than misapprehension of it. Graham also observed her, and did not free himself so soon. Nevill, seated on Mullet's lap, surveyed his mother over the rim of a glass.

'Is it a nice luncheon?' she said.

'It is the same as usual,' said Gavin.

'Well, that is nice, isn't it?'

'He likes it,' said Nevill.

'Well, what do you think we have come to tell you?'

'Don't let Honor guess,' said Gavin, rubbing his feet quickly together.

'I have some news for you about myself. You don't often hear me talk about myself, do you?'

'You have done it since Father died,' said Gavin.

'Well, I have had myself in my mind. There has been no one else to think much about me. Have you ever thought about my being alone?'

'You are not,' said Honor. 'Not any more than we are. We have other people and not Father, and so have you.'

'Well, now I am going to have someone who will think of me as Father did, and will not feel I must only have the same as other people. Can you guess who it is?'

'It is Mr Ridley,' said Honor, at once. 'But you have him now.'

'Well, I am going to have him in a different way. We are going to belong to each other.'

'Are you going to marry him?'

'Yes, I am, my little girl.'

'It is not allowed by the law,' said Gavin.

'I think, young man, that I may be the judge of that,' said Ridley. 'The law happens to be my profession.'

'But you can't be Mother's real husband.'

'That is what I am going to be.'

'But a woman can't have more than one husband in a civilized land. It is only in savage countries that they do that. And then it is usually more than one wife.'

'In some countries polyandry is practised,' said Honor, in an easy tone.

'And you feel we are starting the custom in this country?' said Ridley, smiling.

'Say to Mother that you hope she will be very happy,' whispered Mullet.

'Why will you be happier, married to Mr Ridley, than just always being with him?' said Honor.

'An observant pair of eyes, Nurse,' said Ridley.

'We don't call her Nurse,' said Gavin.

'He calls her Mullet,' said Nevill. 'And sometimes he says, dear Mullet.'

'Here is a successful household character,' said Ridley, indicating Mullet to Eleanor.

'You shouldn't say things about her when she can hear,' said Gavin.

'I think I have upset him,' said Eleanor. 'I shall not leave you, my little son. I shall be coming to the house every day.'

'Won't you be in the house?' said Honor.

'No, I shall be in another house quite near.'

'With him?' said Gavin, with a gesture towards Ridley.

'Yes, he will be my husband then.'

'Is it because of the law?'

'What do you mean, my boy?'

'Is it because of the law, that he can't live here like Father?'

'The law has nothing to do with it. It seemed a good plan for us to have a home of our own.'

'I expect it is because of Grandma,' said Honor.

'What do you mean, dear child?'

'Grandma wouldn't have anyone here instead of Father.'

'The charm of childhood!' said Ridley to Eleanor, with a smile.

'You don't think that anyone is ever instead of anyone else, do you?' said Eleanor to Honor.

Honor raised her eyes and kept them on her mother's.

'I think that so it must seem to her in a way,' said Ridley, gently.

'He will have him instead of Father,' said Nevill, nodding his head towards Ridley.

'My poor little man, I fear you will have no choice,' said Ridley bending over him. 'No other father will have a place in your memory.'

'Honor won't cry any more, now you are instead of Father. Honor doesn't like Father to go away.'

'Does she cry?' said Eleanor, to Mullet.

'Sometimes when she is in bed, ma'am.'

'I should have been told.'

Mullet did not say that Honor had repudiated the idea with violence.

'Honor doesn't like people to talk about it,' said Gavin.

'I don't mind,' said his sister.

'Well, how are you enjoying your holiday?' said Eleanor, as if it might be realized that there was another side to life. 'I thought that, as I was happy, I should like you to be so too; so I said you were to have no lessons.'

'Lessons,' said Nevill, in a tone of glad anticipation, getting off Mullet's knee.

'No, Miss Pilbeam is not coming today,' said Mullet.

'She is.'

'No, today is a holiday.'

'This attitude does Miss Pilbeam credit,' said Ridley.

'He says all he can in favour of people,' said Gavin, to Honor.

'Not coming today,' said Nevill, in a doleful tone that cheered as he ended. 'But come again tomorrow.'

'He gets on very well,' said Eleanor.

'B, a, t, bat; c, a, t, cat; h, a, t, hat,' said Nevill, in support of this.

'He is forward for a boy. It is hard to judge of a young boy's promise,' said Eleanor, thinking of James and Gavin and postponing the difficulty.

'And yet I expect the boys rejoice in their sex,' said Ridley.

'What do they do?' said Gavin.

'They are glad they will grow up into men,' said his mother. 'Would you like to be a woman?'

'I would as soon be one.'

'I would rather be a man,' said Honor.

'He will be a lady,' said Nevill.

'You all seem to want what you cannot have,' said Eleanor. 'The children belong more to the mother, you know. Men don't have so large a share in them.'

'Father did,' said Honor.

'Well, but think for a moment. You were very sad when Father died, but you would have been even more sad if I had died.'

There was a pause.

'She couldn't have been more sad,' said Gavin.

'I shouldn't have minded so much about anyone grown-up,' said Honor, causing Gavin to turn aside with a flush creeping over his face.

'No doubt we are leading them out of their depth,' said Ridley.

'We are understanding everything,' said Honor.

'Not the things that lie underneath,' said Eleanor, in a musing tone, unconscious that she was taking her daughter on equal terms.

'Are there things like that, when people marry another man?'

'Now you are out of your depth indeed.'

'You only pretend that I am.'

'Of course one's children think one belongs entirely to them,' said Eleanor.

'You haven't ever done that,' said Gavin. 'Not like Hatton and people who really do. But you are supposed to belong to Father.'

'You know your father is dead, don't you, my child?' said Eleanor, in gentle bewilderment.

'You know I do. You couldn't be marrying someone else if he wasn't.'

'Well, well, we will begin to look forward. It is natural for you to be disturbed at first. But you are not going to lose me. You will hardly know I am not in the house.'

'Will you be there at dessert?' said Gavin.

'Not always, but I shall when Grandma asks me.'

'Will she have to ask you?'

'No, but I think she will like to sometimes.'

Nevill looked up with an arrested expression.

'Mother won't be there. Only Grandma and Luce,' he said, mentioning the other two who exercised supervision.

'Yes, as a rule, but you will come and have tea with me in my house.'

'Honor and Gavin will too,' said Nevill, in a tone that assured general goodwill.

'Will he be there?' said Gavin, glancing at Ridley.

'Yes, of course. It will be his house as well as mine. We shall share it.'

'They will share it,' said Nevill, in a tone that approved this course.

222

'Will you have any more children?' said Gavin.

'No, I don't think so,' said Eleanor.

'Why don't you?'

'Well, people don't generally have more than nine.'

'Queen Anne had eighteen.'

'Yes, but I am not a queen.'

'Do queens have more than other people?'

'It seems sometimes as if they do,' said Eleanor, smiling.

'If you had any more, would they live with you or with Grandma?' said Honor.

'With me,' said Eleanor, obliged to continue on the line.

'Would Hatton go to your house to take care of them, or would she stay with us?'

'She would stay with you. You will always have her.'

'Hatton will always stay here,' said Nevill. 'Not with those other children.'

'Here is Hatton coming to fetch you,' said Mullet, in the conscious tone of one whose presence has been forgotten.

'Perhaps with a true instinct,' said Ridley, smiling at Eleanor. 'I think our ordeal did not become less, with the age of those who sat in judgement.'

'Mr Ridley always take care of her, and Father coming back soon,' said Nevill, glancing behind Hatton's hand at his mother.

'Doesn't he understand any more than that?'

'He understands everything, madam. He gets into the way of saying things.'

'Father never come back any more, but Mr Ridley always stay with her,' said Nevill, with his ready proof of what was said.

'Well, you will all give me a kiss and tell me you are glad I am going to be happier,' said Eleanor, with a note of welcome for the end of her task.

'I will make the same request, as the congratulation applies to me,' said Ridley. 'And I hope to become a welcome nursery guest.'

Honor and Gavin bowed to circumstances, and their brother gave another backward glance.

'He will kiss him another day,' he promised.

Hatton let him mount the first flight of stairs, and then picked him up and carried him to the nursery, his expression undergoing no change. Honor and Gavin were in some discomfort at the end of the scene, and followed with high, conscious talk. Nevill ran round the nursery two or three times and paused at Hatton's knee, as if by chance.

'Go down to Grandma soon today. Mother won't be there any more.'

'Yes, Mother will be there. She is not going away yet. She will not be married for some time.'

Nevill cast his eyes over Hatton's face and resumed his running.

'Just fancy this change in the family!' said Mullet, in a low tone to Hatton. 'Who would have thought it, when the master died?'

'That would not have been the moment for picturing it, certainly.'

Gavin burst into a loud laugh.

'Did you have this kind of thing in your family, Mullet?' said Honor.

'Well, perhaps in a way I did,' said Mullet, in a constrained tone.

'I will go and get on with my mending,' said Hatton. 'I am not sharing the holiday.'

'Well, what was it?' said Honor, after waiting for the door to close.

'Well, something like this did happen to my relations,' said Mullet, folding up garments, as if fluency were more natural when her hands were occupied. 'It was a family of cousins who lived in London; well, an aunt and cousins it really was, but my aunt was a colourless sort of person, who attracted little attention, and it is my cousins whom I always think of as the victims of the stroke of fate.'

'Well, what happened?' said Honor.

'It is a little hard to describe,' said Mullet, with a natural hesitation, as she did not yet know what it was. 'I was never at close quarters with it. It was one of those things that cast their shadows before and aft, and no one could escape the repercussion of it. Well, after my aunt's bereavement there ensued a period of calm.

My aunt was disconsolate, of course, but she maintained the even tenor of her life. And then the change came. The man destined to be my uncle loomed into view.' Mullet's voice deepened at the mention of this destiny. 'A tall, sinister-looking man he was, with thin lips and a scar stretching across his face, and twisting in an odd way round his mouth. Handsome in a way, of course, with a kind of sinister charm, but a man whose very presence seemed to cast some primitive spell.'

'How did he get the scar?' said Gavin.

'It was never spoken of, Master Gavin. There seemed to be a sort of unwritten law that no word of it should pass human lips,' said Mullet, her voice gaining confidence. 'And none ever crossed my father's or mine. I daresay he thought it was hardly a subject for my ears.'

'He knew about it then,' said Honor.

'Well, Miss Honor, these things pass from men to men. I suspect he had his shrewd suspicions. He was a shrewd man in his way.'

'Well, what happened to the family?'

'In a way nothing, in a way everything. That is the best way to put it.'

'But what was it?' said Honor, not taking this view.

'A strange, uncanny atmosphere brooded over that house. Laughter never seemed to sound, and the sun never to shine in those rooms. And in the place of those happy children, who used to shout and play in that deep-vaulted hall, there were tall, grave men and women, with haunted eyes, and lips that had forgotten how to smile. And my aunt crept in and out, a sad, silent being, who seemed to have more in common with another world. That is how things were in that household.'

'But what did he do, the man with the scar?' said Gavin.

'You may well ask, Master Gavin. He did what he did. It is best not to say any more.'

'One of those things that children are not told,' said Honor.

'And those purposes needed money, whatever they were,' went on Mullet, hastening her words. 'In those days all the wife's money belonged to the man; and he used to dole her own income out to her in pence, or in pounds I expect it was, or in low banknotes, but in small enough sums, considering her worldly estate. Yes, she must have felt she had come on evil days.'

'And how are things now?' said Honor.

'As far as I know, as they were. I have no wish to hear. It could be no good news.'

'I should think it is better here than in that house.'

'Oh, so should I,' said Mullet, with a little laugh. 'And now we must remember that you are to be punctual downstairs today.'

Honor turned to the door, expecting to see Hatton, and confirmed in the anticipation.

'We shan't have to be so punctual when Mother is not here,' said Gavin, simply stating a fact.

'And why not, Master Gavin?' said Mullet.

'She will be with us often enough to keep us up to the mark,' said Hatton.

'It is funny that Mr Ridley and Mother should both want to live together,' said Honor. 'It is a coincidence.'

'A frequent one in marriage, I hope,' said Hatton.

Mullet laughed.

'This isn't a real marriage,' said Honor. 'The Queen wouldn't see Mother now. She wouldn't see either of them.'

'Don't talk nonsense, Miss Honor; of course she would,' said Mullet.

'Mr Ridley is the worst, because it is the man who asks the woman to marry him.'

'A woman is not allowed to,' said Gavin.

'Neither the mistress nor Mr Ridley is doing anything wrong.'

'Not so that they could be put in prison,' said Honor. 'But some of the worst wrong things are not like that.'

'You must have heard of people marrying twice. It is not like you to talk in such a silly way.'

'It is a thing that only unusual people talk sensibly about,' said Hatton.

'Honor is unusual,' said Gavin. 'Father said she was.'

'Well, she wants other people to think so too,' said Mullet.

'I don't care if they don't,' said Honor; 'I don't want them to think the same.'

'James doesn't mind if Mother marries Mr Ridley,' said Gavin. 'I don't mind either, if they like to do it.'

'That is a good reason,' said Hatton.

'He doesn't mind,' said Nevill. 'He is the same as James.'

'I know why Mother wants to marry him,' said Honor. 'I always understand things. It is because she hadn't anyone to think so much of her as Father did, when she had got used to it. But I shouldn't ever marry a second person, when the first one had done that.'

'I daresay the people won't ask you,' said Gavin. 'You are not allowed to ask them yourself.'

'He will marry her,' said Nevill, nodding at Honor.

'You won't be allowed to,' said Gavin. 'You are her brother.'

'He isn't allowed either,' said Nevill, pointing at Gavin.

'Now none of this talk downstairs,' said Hatton. 'Don't say a word about it, unless other people do.'

Her injunction was heeded by one of her hearers, who ran up to Regan as he entered the room.

'He won't talk about it,' he promised.

'What is the forbidden subject?' she said.

Nevill looked at her, as if he would explain, if he had the words.

'Mother and Mr Ridley marrying,' said Gavin, in a ruthless tone.

'A nurse's idea,' said Sir Jesse. 'We may have our own.'

'I have not avoided the subject today,' said Eleanor.

'Least said, soonest mended,' said Honor.

'There is nothing that requires mending,' said her mother.

'Nevill reminds me of James at that age,' said Luce, as if she had not heard what had passed. 'He has no touch of Gavin.'

'Not him and Gavin,' said Nevill. 'Him and James.'

'None of you seems like another to me,' said Eleanor. 'Perhaps Daniel and Gavin are a little alike.'

'And Isabel and Honor, Mother,' said Luce.

'Well, not so much alike, as with a good deal in common.'

'Soundly observed in a way, Mother, but Father used to say they were alike,' said Luce, her tone setting the example of continued easy reference to her father.

'Have you settled on a house, Eleanor?' said Regan. 'I suppose you have made a search for one.'

'We have done everything but sign the lease. I think we cannot do better.'

'It is a nice house,' said Nevill.

'What do you know about it?' said Gavin.

'Mother will live there with Mr Ridley.'

'What house is it?' said Honor.

'The square house near the church,' said her mother. 'It is called the Grey House.'

'Isn't it very small?'

'Not for the two of us. It has six bedrooms. This house has given you a wrong standard. I have always foreseen that you will have to modify your ideas.'

'It is a sort of grey,' said Gavin.

'No, not grey,' said Nevill.

'It has a green lawn,' said Luce.

'Where is the lawn?' said Gavin.

'In front of the house,' said his mother.

'I don't call that a lawn.'

'What do you call it?'

'A patch of grass.'

'You will all have to live in a castle.'

'A great, big castle,' said Nevill. 'He will live in one with soldiers in it. It is called a fort.'

'I must get you some toy cottages,' said Eleanor. 'I saw some in London.'

'When will you get them?' said Gavin, coming nearer.

'Ridley will bring them. They will be a present from us both. Perhaps he will bring them tomorrow.'

'No, today,' said Nevill, with rising feeling. 'Today.'

'Tomorrow will soon be here,' said Luce.

'It won't,' said Nevill, in a tone of experience.

'Is there anything joined to the cottages?' said Gavin.

'There is a little garden with a patch of grass,' said Eleanor, with a smile.

'A cottage with a hen,' said Nevill.

'Miss Pilbeam might help us to make a pigsty,' said Honor.

'The ideas for future establishments are suitably modified,' said Daniel.

'Mother dear, your scheme is crowned with success,' said Luce.

'We shouldn't want to live in the cottages,' said Gavin.

'He will live in a cottage,' said Nevill. 'With Hatton.'

'What would you have to eat?' said Daniel.

'A hen would lay an egg,' said Nevill, without hesitation.

'Who would eat the egg? You or Hatton?'

'One for Hatton and one for him.'

'But would one hen lay two eggs?'

'One, two, three, four, five, six, fourteen.'

'But you would be sick, if you ate so many.'

'Give them all to Hatton,' said Nevill, in a tone of suitably and generously solving the problem.

'Now you three can go upstairs,' said Eleanor. 'No one else can speak while you are here. Now, James, let us hear your voice.'

'Will you often be at luncheon after you are married?' said James, recalled by his predicament to the time when it might be less frequent.

'I shall be there when Grandma asks me. Now see if you can open your mouth without asking a question.'

'There is a monkey-puzzle tree in front of your house. On the piece of grass, on the lawn.'

'Do you think you will ever have a house of your own?' said Eleanor.

'Yes. Everyone is paid enough for that. Even a labourer has a cottage. And if he can't earn, he can go to the workhouse.'

'Constant stimulus has not been in vain,' said Daniel. 'Witness the gulf between James's ideas and those of the other.'

'With the children reconciled to cottages, and James to the workhouse,' said Graham, looking at the window, 'Mother need not be distressed about the notions of her family.'

'But it would be sad to be brought to the workhouse,' said Eleanor to James, fearing she had made such a prospect too natural.

'It is better than it was, more comfortable.'

'James has carried his concern to the point of investigation,' said Daniel. 'He can pass on to Graham anything that Graham needs to know. So all Mother's sons are provided for.'

'You will step into my shoes yourself?' said Sir Jesse.

There was silence.

'With their father in his grave, it is no wonder if it seems the natural place for his parents,' said Regan.

'There is no problem about our final accommodation,' said Graham. 'We have no anxiety there.'

'People in the workhouse can have a pauper's funeral,' said James.

'I think that is enough about the workhouse,' said Eleanor.

'What can a man do to earn the most?' said James, as if going as far as possible from the subject.

'We have reached that estate, and do not know,' said Daniel.

'Has Grandpa earned a great deal?'

'He has never needed to earn,' said Isabel. 'Things will be different for you.'

'Did Father earn very much?'

'Heredity seems to justify James in his perplexity,' said Daniel. 'And it throws no light for any of us.'

'The first thing to do is to work and get to Cambridge,' said Eleanor.

'But Daniel and Graham are there, and they don't know about earning. And that is the only thing that matters, isn't it?'

Eleanor was silent before this result of her admonitions.

'You have to be an educated man before you can do anything.'

'That does not seem to James the sequence of affairs,' said Graham.

'No,' said James, in a light but unshaken voice.

'Perhaps we will leave these problems to the future,' said Eleanor.

'You had better have done so, Mother,' said Luce, in a low, amused tone.

'James would never have objected to that arrangement,' said Isabel.

'If Ridley does not come to a meal, he loses no time afterwards,' said Regan, as she heard a bell.

'He is welcome,' said Sir Jesse. 'He comes to see one who has been a daughter to us.'

'Grandma, we shall dread to hear your voice,' said Luce.

Some minutes elapsed before Ridley's entering the room, and then he advanced in the wake of Hope, and spoke without emerging from this shelter.

'I am come to proffer another plea on my own account. I should have said it was a thing I seldom did, but I must seem to be making up for lost time. You will think it never rains but it pours. I have to beg that my marriage may be hastened. I find that the effect of delay on myself, on my work, and on my clients, will be such that it becomes imperative to avoid it. Some waiting correspondence has brought my position home to me. I have no choice but to beg permission to bring matters to a climax.'

'He does not know whose permission should be asked,' said Hope, 'and I do not either. I am glad he is so ill at ease. It may be one of those times when we feel we have never liked people so well.'

'Have I the sanction of the person who should give it?' said Ridley.

'It is your own affair,' said Regan.

'Thank Lady Sullivan, Ridley,' said Hope.

'I do so indeed,' said Ridley, 'for the freedom of action implied in the words.'

'Eleanor goes from our home, and shall go when and how she wishes,' said Sir Jesse.

'The condition of a honeymoon seems to be our taking it at once,' went on Ridley, in a more ordinary and open manner. 'And I confess to a natural reluctance to forgo one.'

'Well, there is not much gained by putting it off,' said Regan.

'I think there is not, Grandma,' said Luce.

'You would not like to have me for a little longer?' said Eleanor.

'We are depending on your assurance that we shall not lose you,' said Daniel.

'I suppose no one makes a success of the transitional time.'

'We are not criticizing you, Mother dear,' said Luce.

'I had better yield to the general opinion,' said Eleanor, with a touch of bitterness.

'I hope your own is not an exception,' said Ridley.

'Is it any wonder that I did not see what was coming on us?' said Daniel, in a low tone.

'I shall never prove that I saw it,' said Graham. 'It seemed that speaking of it would establish it. Luce did not say a word.'

'Somehow I could not, Graham.'

'We cannot yield to our instinct to rescue our mother,' said Daniel.

'It does not seem that she would give you much trouble,' said Isabel.

'Hush, boys, hush. Not before the children,' said Luce.

'Well, shall we put the marriage in a fortnight?' said Sir Jesse, trying to help his daughter-in-law.

'I am afraid I must press for it earlier, even in a matter of days,' said Ridley. 'But I thank you, Sir Jesse, for generously furthering my cause. I wish I could rid myself of the idea that I am carrying off my bride.'

'Why does one dislike the term, bride, as applied to one's mother?' said Luce.

'There are several reasons, and none of them can be mentioned,' said Graham.

'Not before the children,' said Venice.

'We seem to be giving rise to a good deal of confidential discussion, Eleanor,' said Ridley.

'Are you going to be married as soon as on Friday?' said James, in a high voice.

'I thank you, James,' said Ridley, 'for putting into words what I did not dare to myself.'

'Will you just go into the church and come out again, married?'

'I thank you again, James.'

'And then Mother will be Mrs Ridley Cranmer?'

'I thank you once more, my boy.'

'So you have thought out all the steps,' said Regan, in a cool tone.

'I fear that I stand exposed,' said Ridley.

'Shall we all come to the church?' said Venice.

'No, dear child,' said Eleanor. 'You will say good-bye to me here, and I shall come to see you on the day I come back from my honeymoon.'

'And then you will come every day,' said James.

'In this atmosphere of reconciliation I will take my leave,' said Ridley. 'I must betake myself to the duties that beset my remaining hours.'

'I will come to the door with you,' said Eleanor.

Regan gave her a swift look.

'It is strange that we resent Mother's treating Ridley as she treated Father,' said Luce.

'Surely it is not,' said Daniel.

'She does not do so,' said Isabel.

'That is true,' said Graham.

'How you all suppress your personal feeling!' said Hope. 'It is wonderful when you have so much. I somehow feel ashamed of Ridley, and yet he is only doing what your father did, and that must be a great and good thing, I suppose. I wonder if your mother knows her place in my life. I have only just found it out myself. Luce is too young to want me for a friend, and your grandmother would not be able to bear one.'

'You come nearer to it than anyone, Mrs Cranmer,' said Luce. 'Grandma does not shrink into herself or take the defensive when she hears your approach.'

'No, dear, but is that the test of real friendship? I feel it is generous of you to welcome Ridley. And it is a sensible idea to keep him in a house apart. I wonder I never thought of it. They say it is never too late to mend, but in this case it is. Your mother will be one of those people who really have two homes.'

'I wonder whom they will lose next. Their grandfather or me?' said Regan.

'The loss of your son has not killed you, Lady Sullivan. We must face facts,' said Hope.

Regan was laughing as Eleanor returned to the room.

'What is the jest?' said the latter.

'It was not one, Mother,' said Luce, 'and as far as it was, it would not gain by repeating.'

'What was it, my dear, nevertheless?'

'It was about Grandma's dying.'

'Not dying, dear,' said Hope.

'I warned you not to have it revealed, Mother.'

'But that is such a terrible solution,' said Graham.

'It is odd that old people think so little of their death,' said Regan.

'They make a good many false claims, in that case,' said Isabel.

'They would look foolish, if they forgot it,' said her grandmother. 'Other people never separate them from it.'

'I think they feel stoic and heroic when they talk of it,' said Graham.

'So it is true that human motives are mixed,' said Hope.

'I warned you not to have it revealed, Mother.'

'I must apply myself to my duties for the next days,' said Eleanor. 'There are things to be done for the children, before I leave them, I must take them into the town on Thursday, to get them some things that Hatton wants for them.'

'Don't they want them for themselves?' said Hope. 'I thought the child was father of the man.'

'I don't know how these duties get put off.'

'You had every excuse, Mother,' said Luce.

'Who is going into the town?' said James, in a casual manner.

'You and Honor and Gavin,' said his mother. 'Nevill can do with what is handed down.'

'I should think he can,' said Hope. 'I wonder it does not overwhelm him.'

'That means a holiday for James,' said Eleanor, sighing. 'And I suppose the wedding day does too.'

'I shall have to say good-bye to you,' said James, going on quickly to the next words. 'You won't mind living in the little house, will you?'

'No, not at all. It will be my own.'

'That will be a change for the better,' said Regan, in an almost cordial manner.

CHAPTER ELEVEN

'WHAT is the matter, Gavin?' said Eleanor, as she returned to the house with her children. 'Why are you staying in the carriage? You seem in such an odd mood.'

Gavin got out and walked up the steps without a word.

'What is wrong with him, Honor?'

'He wanted you to stop and listen to him in the street. And now he wants to go back again.'

'He must know he can't do that. We are later than we ought to be already. Grandma is waiting for us. It is tiresome of him to make my last day so difficult.'

James frolicked up the steps in the manner of a different and easier boy, and Honor followed in a neutral manner.

'Why do people speak to each other, if other people don't listen?' said Gavin, without looking back.

'I heard what you said,' said his mother. 'You remember that I answered. But you must know you made a mistake.'

'I know that I saw him,' said Gavin. 'All my life I shall know.'

'Children do fancy they see things, when they have them in their minds. Going where Father sometimes took you, reminded you of him, and you thought you saw him. That was all.'

'I wasn't reminded of him; I wasn't thinking about him. I haven't thought much about him for some time.'

'Honor, can't you persuade him that he must be wrong?'

'He really thinks he saw him. You can't persuade a person then.'

'Well, run upstairs and try to forget it.'

'I shan't ever forget it,' said Gavin, going heavily from stair to stair. 'I shall remember it every minute. I shan't ever remember other things.'

'Honor, tell Hatton what he thinks, and ask her to explain to him.'

'I shall tell her,' said Gavin.

'Perhaps you had better say nothing about it,' said Eleanor.

'I shall tell her,' repeated Gavin.

'No, you had better not, my boy. Do you hear what I say?'

'If I didn't hear, I couldn't answer.'

Eleanor sighed and went her way, prevented from pressing the point by the thought that it was her last day with her children.

Gavin went to the nursery.

'I saw Father,' he said.

'No, you are making a mistake,' said Hatton.

Gavin sat down to take off his boots, and wasted no further word.

'You have fancied it,' said Hatton, looking at his face, while Mullet, also observing it, came to his aid.

Gavin leaned back and accepted the latter's ministrations without attention to herself.

'Poor Gavin is not well,' said Nevill, glancing at his brother.

'He really thinks he saw him,' said Honor, to Hatton.

'Of course he does, or he would not say so.'

'He does do that sometimes,' said Nevill, in shocked condemnation of his brother's practices.

'It is easy to imagine things,' said Mullet, falling into the error of judging other people by herself. 'When he has had his dinner, he will see how it was. When we are hungry, our minds are out of our control.'

'I wasn't hungry,' said Gavin. 'We had things to eat at a shop. I am not hungry now.'

'Did he tell the mistress about it?' said Mullet to Honor.

'Yes.'

'And what did she say?'

'Something like what you and Hatton have said.'

'Did she mind his saying it?'

'Yes, I think she did rather.'

Gavin took no notice when his plate was set before him, but presently took up his knife and fork, to forestall the inevitable pressure. As he ate, his colour returned, and he went through the meal with his normal appetite. When his sister talked, he answered with his usual directness, and he followed the others down to dessert, as though neither expecting nor desiring anything else. Nevill ran into the room and spoke at once.

'Mother will be gone tomorrow,' he said, and rapidly corrected his tone. 'Poor Mother will be gone away very soon.'

'They like the constant holidays,' said Eleanor, with a smile and a sigh.

'It was a chance to give Miss Pilbeam a day to herself,' said Luce.

'I thought we need hardly trouble,' said Eleanor. 'Nevill had his lessons alone.'

'Just him and Miss Pilbeam,' said the latter.

'It was not worth Miss Pilbeam's while to come for half-an-hour,' said Luce.

'He had an hour,' said Nevill. 'Then Hatton came for him.'

'I should like to die,' said Gavin, looking round the table.

'Why would you?' said Regan and Graham at once.

'Because as long as you are alive, things can happen that you don't like. Even if you couldn't bear them, they would happen.'

'A good description of life,' said Isabel.

'It is too one-sided,' said Eleanor. 'And in your case it would be absurd. No children could be more fortunate.'

'We haven't any father,' said Honor. 'So they could be.'

'We could have one, if we liked,' said Gavin.

'Does he mean Ridley?' said Luce.

'He thinks he saw Father today,' said Honor.

'I did see him,' said her brother. 'In the town, when we were there with Mother.'

'It is a fancy he has had,' said Eleanor.

Gavin's face did not change.

'What makes you think so, my boy?' said Sir Jesse. 'Why did you not speak to him?'

'Grandpa, don't press it,' said Luce, in a low tone. 'It is not a matter to push to its logical conclusion.'

'He didn't want me to,' said Gavin. 'He didn't want us even to see him.'

'I should think that is very likely true,' said Eleanor, gently. 'So he would like you just to forget it. And that is what we will do.'

'Did you know he was there?' said Gavin, meeting her eyes.

'Of course she didn't,' said Honor. 'Or she wouldn't be going to marry Mr Ridley.'

'Then she won't be able to forget it. She says things that are not true.'

'So that is what you think of me,' said Eleanor.

'He will think of Mother always when she is gone away,' said Nevill.

'I seem to have chosen the right course,' said Eleanor. 'People have no trouble in adapting themselves to it.'

'I don't think I could ever come to a decision,' said Graham. 'I hope my life will not afford much power of choice.'

'I should say the hope is grounded,' said Sir Jesse.

'You are not going to live far away,' said James, to his mother.

'No, of course not, my boy. I could not bear to do that.'

'I should think you could,' said Gavin.

'My dear, I have just said I could not,' said Eleanor, in a tone of speaking to a much older person. 'You must let people give their own account of themselves. You can't know as much about them as they do.'

'You can think you do. You can be sure.'

'Then you should remind yourself that you are likely to be wrong.'

'I never remind myself of things. If I don't think they are true, why should I?'

'It is an office we do tend to reserve for other people,' said Isabel.

'Why does this luncheon feel like an anniversary?' said Graham.

'It is my last luncheon as a member of the household,' said Eleanor. 'I think I shall try to forget it.'

'You do forget things,' said Gavin.

'What kind of things?'

'Not little things.'

'So I forget big things, do I? Would you all say so? Would you, Luce?'

'No, Mother dear, I should not.'

'Would you, Daniel?'

'No, it seems to me an unwarrantable assertion.'

'Would you, Graham?'

'No, I should have thought you would have them written on your heart.'

'Would you, Isabel?'

'No, I should have thought the opposite.'

'Would you, Venice?'

'No, I shouldn't,' said Venice, opening her eyes.

'Would you, James?'

'No, I should have thought you would remember them.'

'Would you, Honor?'

'No, I shouldn't myself, but Gavin only means you forgot that you saw Father.'

'He wouldn't either,' said Nevill, excitably. 'He wouldn't let them say it.'

'My little boy,' said Eleanor, lifting him to her knee.

'He would kill them,' said Nevill, sitting compliantly on it.

Gavin appeared to be paying no attention.

'Are you all going to say your own word to me on my last day?' said Eleanor.

'You would not think Mother was a person in whom hope would die so hard,' said Graham.

'I should like to have one from each of you to carry with me.'

'Surely we have all said one,' said Daniel.

'And they will be easy to remember, as they are all the same,' said Isabel.

'It isn't our fault that it is her last day,' said Gavin.

'The boy is upset in some way,' said Sir Jesse.

'Yes, of course that is what it is,' said Eleanor.

'Come, let us all disperse,' said Luce. 'There is no need to make it a melancholy occasion. Mother has things to do before tomorrow. She and I are going to do them together.'

She left the room with her arm in her mother's. Isabel and Venice and James took the chance to disappear. Sir Jesse withdrew with his grandsons, as was his habit since the loss of his son. Mullet came to fetch the children and led Nevill from the room. Gavin appeared to follow her, but in a moment fell behind and walked up to his grandmother.

'I saw Father today,' he said.

'You are thinking of him, because Mother is leaving you. I am thinking of him too. So you and I are feeling the same.'

'You are not thinking of him because of that, are you?'

Regan laughed, and Gavin's face flushed and his eyes filled with angry tears, but he spoke in a simple, controlled manner.

'Perhaps he will come to the house.'

'It would seem quite natural, wouldn't it?'

'Are you saying what you think is not true?' said Gavin, looking into her face.

'No, I am not. I shall never get used to being without him.'

'This house is his home, isn't it?'

'Yes, of course it is, or was.'

'It is now,' said Gavin. 'He hasn't any other. I could tell he hadn't another one, like Mother.'

'How could you tell?' said Regan.

'By the way he looked. And by the way he looked at Honor.'

'Didn't he look at you too?'

'Not as much. He never does. That is how I first knew it was Father. And then I looked and saw that it was. And I called to Mother, and she went on. And when I looked back, he was gone.'

'Where did you see him?'

'In the dark street that goes from the big shops to the little ones. You know there are two inns there. Mother and Honor were in front of me, and Father came out of one of them. And he saw me first, because I was behind, and then he stood and looked at Honor.'

'Did he know you saw him?' said Regan, feeling it wise to draw out the child's impression.

'No, I don't think so. If people who are back from the dead, are the same as other people, Mother ought not to marry Mr Ridley. It is against the law. But perhaps this is different.'

'People can't come back from the dead, my child.'

'I think Father has. He looked like that. And he wouldn't be the very first, would he?'

'How did he look?' said Regan, in a gentle tone.

'Thin and pale, with a smaller face than he used to have. And his hands were small and pale, coming out of the sleeves of his coat. They looked like Mother's or Luce's. And he must be smaller himself, because his coat was so large. But I daresay he wouldn't be quite the same. It must have been cold where he was, because the coat had fur on it; and he had worn it often, because it was mended down the front, and one of the fur cuffs was partly gone.'

Regan's eyes were fixed on her grandson, and she kept them on his face as she slowly rose to her feet.

'Where did you say you saw him?'

Gavin told her again, hardly varying his words, and she suddenly took his hand and hurried to the door. In the hall she snatched the first garment she saw, and almost ran out of the house. She was like a person who feels she must get something over, before she can settle to her life. As they drew near the stables, Gavin dragged at her hand and spoke in a weaker voice.

'I don't think I need go with you. Father doesn't want to see me the most. Honor would be better, but one person is enough. It is best to be all together, when a person comes back from the dead.'

Regan threw a glance at his face and then at his house clothes, released his hand and pursued her way. He walked back to the house and mounted to the nursery.

'Grandma has gone to fetch Father. So Mother will know that I saw him. Everyone will.'

'What are you saying, Master Gavin?' said Mullet.

'Things will be like they used to be. Father will be here again, even if he isn't the same. And we shall get used to his being different. And I don't think he is so very. I don't know if Mother will be here. She may go with Mr Ridley. But Grandma will love Father, whatever he is like. And one person who really loves him, is enough.'

'I would rather have a father than a mother,' said Honor. 'I think all this family would.'

'He would rather have Father,' said Nevill. 'But he would rather have poor Mother too. And she won't come every day.'

The carriage was heard to pass the house on its way to the gates.

'It is Grandma going to the town to find Father,' said Gavin. 'I told her where I saw him, and what he was like. And she knew it was him.'

'You did not, Master Gavin!' said Mullet. 'It was a cruel thing to do. You don't mean her ladyship believed you? That you have sent her by herself to find him? It is a dreadful thing to happen. Whatever can we do?'

'I didn't send her. She went of her own accord. Children don't send grown-up people. You know that. She was glad that Father had come back. No one could have been more glad. She didn't mind going by herself. She didn't mind even if he was back from the dead.'

'Grandma loves people, doesn't she?' said Nevill.

'Well, you must play quietly this afternoon, if you really think what you say,' said Mullet.

'We ought to be glad he has come back,' said Gavin.

'Of course you would be. But it would be a solemn occasion.'

'Why should it? Solemn things are sad. We were solemn when he was dead. We ought not to be the same when it is the opposite. And Nevill is not being quiet.'

'He is a coachman,' explained the latter, handling imaginary reins and also impersonating the horse. 'He will drive Grandma to find Father. He will drive her fast.'

'He is too young to understand,' said Mullet.

'But if it isn't true, there isn't anything to understand.'

'And you pretended you thought it was true,' said Mullet, with reproach.

'He didn't pretend,' said Honor, in a tone that made Hatton turn and look into her face.

'People only pretend ordinary things,' said Gavin.

'They can make a mistake about the others,' said Hatton. 'And the cleverer people are, the sooner they see they have made one. And it is easier to see that out of doors.'

'I am going to stay in,' said Honor. 'Then I can go down, if Father comes back and sends for me. He will want to see me, even if he is back from the dead. If he is so very different, he wouldn't remember enough to come home. And I want to see him, whatever he is like. I don't mind if he is a ghost.'

'He is not a ghost,' said Gavin, in his ordinary voice. 'He is like he always was. Only he is pale and his face is smaller.'

'He couldn't be smaller, if he is the same.'

'He could, if he had got thin.'

'Would you like to go out, Gavin?' said Hatton, in an easy tone.

'I don't mind. I can see Father when I come in.'

'He will stay in,' said Nevill. 'No, he will go for a walk and hold Mullet's hand. He will find a little nest.'

Honor waited until Mullet and her brothers had gone, and then threw herself into Hatton's arms in a passion of tears.

'I don't want it to be a mistake. For a minute I thought it was true. I thought Father would come back.'

'You know he can't do that. You must know, if you think. But you have a great many people to love you.'

'I haven't. Only Grandma and Luce.'

'You know how Gavin loves you.'

'Does he?' said Honor, lifting her head at the idea.

'More than anyone else in the world. And you know that I love you.'

'Yes,' said Honor, relaxing her body against Hatton's.

'And Nevill loves you too.'

'I don't count Nevill. And James doesn't like people much better than they like him. I don't think people do. And that isn't very much.'

'You can't think that Isabel does not love you.'

'She would, if I were as old as she is. But I never shall be, shall I? Because she will get older too. And Venice only loves Isabel.'

'And there are your big brothers.'

'Do you mean Daniel and Graham?' said Honor, as if Hatton were hardly likely to mean these.

'And Mother loves you. You know that.'

'She feels I belong to her. Gavin is the one she loves. But Mother does her duty by her children.'

'Would you like me to read to you?'

'If you read a book I know. Then I can half listen to the reading, and half to hear if Father comes back.'

'Which is a book that you know?'

'I know them all,' said Honor. 'You won't read in a loud voice, will you?'

Hatton read, and Honor divided her attention as she had said, and presently slipped from Hatton's knee and stood with an air of intense listening.

'Father has come back,' she said, with a sigh of simple and great relief. 'Gavin did see him. I don't mind if he is back from the dead. I can hear his voice, and it is the same as it used to be. I don't mind anything as long as he is here.'

Hatton went on to the landing, and stood suddenly still, her face growing white.

'I shall go down,' said Honor. 'No, I shall wait until they send for me. No, I shall go down now. I have heard his voice, and now I have heard it, I must want to see him, mustn't I? I shall run straight up to him; I don't mind what he is like. He will lift me up as he used to, and if he can't do it like an ordinary man, if it is like a ghost, it will be the ghost of Father.'

She ran down the stairs and broke into the library, where Fulbert was standing with his mother. He turned and came to meet her and lifted and kissed her in his old way, and after the first onset of tears, she subsided in simple content.

'You are the same,' she said; 'you are not a ghost; you don't look so very different.'

'I am grateful for the assurance,' said Fulbert. 'I hardly know how to explain myself on any other ground. I must be prepared for people's coming to the opposite conclusion.'

'You will always be here now. It will be like it used to be,' said Honor, as she heard the old note. 'But if you were alive why didn't you come before?'

'Father has been ill,' said Regan, who was leaning back in her chair, pale and still but hardly spent. 'So ill that he could not remember anything. But he will soon be well now.'

'But that doesn't make him a ghost. He is only like other people who have been ill.'

'You tell people that,' said Fulbert, 'if they throw any doubt on my authenticity. I am of flesh and blood like themselves, even if a little less of them.'

'Do the others know?' said Honor, beginning to jump and quiver in anticipation. 'I will go and tell them; I am the one to know first. They won't think it is true at first. Only Gavin will believe it.'

'Gavin will have his own position in future,' said Fulbert.

Regan smiled as if she were apart from words.

Honor encountered Graham in the hall, and crying the tidings, went on to find Daniel. The young men entered, half-braced for the truth, half-prepared for some travesty of it.

'Honor should be here with her assurance,' said Fulbert, as he shook hands with his sons and then drew them into his embrace. 'She protested that I was not a ghost.'

Graham turned aside, white and shaken, and Daniel stood ready to give his support to any who required it. He glanced at his grandmother, but Regan had what she needed.

Luce entered, driven by Honor, started and paled, took some steps towards her father, and threw herself on his breast. Regan surveyed the scene in sympathy, almost at ease. Regan's tears had been shed.

'Grandma,' said Luce, in a hardly audible tone, as if compelled to the words, 'does Grandpa know?'

'Yes, he knows. He has seen your father. He will soon be here.' Regan needed to say no more of Sir Jesse's meeting with his son.

'Father,' said Luce, in a gentle tone, 'would it be too much for you to have Isabel and Venice and James? They are having needless moments of feeling they are fatherless.'

'It is too much, and it is not enough. Let them all come. It is the healthy and natural way.'

Honor rushed upstairs with the summons, and her sister went to the door.

'Children,' she said, 'your life is going to be whole again. The cloud is lifted. Honor has told you the truth.'

She led them to their father, Isabel white and trembling, Venice crimson and with staring eyes, James uncertain and almost afraid. Fulbert embraced them in a natural way, keeping his old manner with each. Isabel staggered and nearly fell, but recovered and sat with her eyes on her father, almost in the manner of Regan. Venice's face relaxed and her eyes began to glow instead of stare. Daniel gave them seats and treated Graham as one of them. James fidgeted round his father's chair in his old way, until, also in the old way, enjoined to be still, and the natural words seemed to break the tension and set on foot the old life.

'The chief actor must bear the heaviest part,' said Daniel. 'May we hear the tale to be told?'

'In a word,' said his father, while Regan's unmoved and satisfied face showed it had been put in many to herself. 'You read the letter I wrote to Ridley, and the other from my servant, confirming my death. I had no equals about me. The second was written and sent while I lay unconscious; they thought I was near enough to my end. I lived for months, remembering nothing, and when I came to myself and found that no letters came, I questioned the men and found how things had gone. They were in awe of your father and had not dared to confess. They had even sent my effects to your mother. I wrote and told Ridley to prepare you for the truth, followed the letter myself, and waited at the inn to recover and to hear that the way was clear. I dreaded the shock for your mother, for mine, and for you all. That letter cannot have reached him.'

'Grandma,' said Luce, in a desperate whisper, as if the words were wrung from her, 'does Father know about Mother and Ridley?'

Regan nodded almost with indifference, as though this were a secondary thing.

'I can face the natural results of my disappearance,' said Fulbert, turning on his daughter his old unflinching gaze. 'I should wish no one to go through life alone. But I hope my wife will find it a relief not to replace me after all.' He turned and put his arm round Isabel, as though here was someone who would never have done so.

'Father,' said Luce, in a faltering manner, 'Mother had her hard time after you had gone.'

'That was the trouble, no doubt,' said Fulbert. 'I wish I could have spared you all. But our life may be better, that we know what it is to lose it.'

'It is a method of enhancement I can only deplore,' said Daniel. 'You are yourself again, my son. You have had some hard months. Your own work must have suffered. I shall be thankful to take up my duty again and leave you to yours.'

'I hope that disgrace for failure will be balanced by credit for feeling,' said Graham.

'There is greater credit in the greater feeling, that made you go on as if I were here,' said Fulbert. 'I am touched by the signs of the unbroken life in my home. It has held as though my eyes were on it. I find no change in any of you. There is no gulf to be bridged. James does not open doors and he is remaining away from school. And I would have had it so. I have no sense of missing steps in my family history.'

James gave a little jump, uncertain whether he had met success or not.

'Grandma,' said Luce, in a low tone, 'the little boys have come in. Is it better for them to be prepared?'

'Gavin does not need preparation,' said Fulbert. 'He has done his best to perform the office for you all. And no doubt he has done so for Nevill. Let it happen in its own way. I ask nothing that is not spontaneous and natural.'

Nevill ran into the room and towards his grandmother, caught sight of his father, paused and rested his eyes on him, and then ran on and laid something on Regan's lap.

'A bird's nest,' he said. 'Where the little birds used to live.'

'What will they do without their home?'

'All fly away,' said Nevill.

'The little birds had a father and mother bird,' said Regan, guiding his head towards Fulbert. 'And the father bird has come back to the nest.'

Nevill cast his eyes about in quest of this visitor, and dropped them to the nest, in case Regan's words might be true.

'Where?' he said, bringing them back to her face.

'Look and see,' said Regan, turning his head again in the right direction.

'Outside,' said Nevill, as some sparrows chirped by the window. 'He has come back. Hark.'

'Nevill is showing to the same advantage as James,' said Daniel.

'Do you see who is standing by Isabel?' said Regan.

'Father,' said Nevill, in a light tone, as if he would not emphasize what might be in doubt.

'He would like to see his little boy.'

Nevill detached himself from Regan, as if this would aid his father's view.

Nevill detached himself from Regan, as if this would aid his arms and laughed and whimpered alternately, touching his cheek and withdrawing his hand, as though uncertain whether he caressed the authentic person.

'I have congratulated myself that my family has not changed,' said Fulbert. 'I must remember to wonder if the same thing can be said of myself.'

'Dear Father!' said Luce, for the guidance of Nevill.

'Dear Father,' he agreed, using a more confident hand, and allowing himself to look definitely into Fulbert's face. 'Dear Father has come back after a long time. He won't go away again today.'

'He will never go away again,' said Luce.

'Yes,' said Nevill, struggling down from Fulbert's arms and nodding his head. 'He will. But Mr Ridley will always stay.'

'I can't live down my bad name all at once,' said Fulbert. 'And now where is my son, who helped me to get to my home?'

Gavin approached and raised his face, as for a daily greeting.

'You knew I should come back one day, didn't you?'

'No. We thought you were dead.'

'You did not seem so very surprised to see me.'

'Did you know that I saw you?' said Gavin, lifting his eyes to his father's.

'I realized you had, after you had passed. You did not come back and speak to me.'

'You didn't speak to us. And it would be for people back from the dead to speak first. They might not still understand.'

'You were an observant boy to recognize Grandpa's old coat.'

'I didn't know it was his. It was Grandma who knew. I thought it was yours.'

'Father may get tired of this changelessness in his sons,' said Daniel.

'Poor Father is very tired,' said Nevill, casting a look at Fulbert. 'He won't be able to come back another day.'

'Grandma dear,' said Luce, 'Grandpa is crossing the hall. But I suppose he knows what he can bear.'

Sir Jesse entered and came up to his son, and taking both his hands, stood thus for some time, and then passed on to his chair and sank into it.

'Now I can say my "Nunc dimittis",' he said to himself, or rather to the assembled company.

There was a pause.

'What did Grandpa say?' said Gavin.

'They are Latin words,' said Honor.

'Grandpa can say them,' said Nevill, with pride in his relative.

'Would you like to be able to?' said Luce.

'Yes, but he will some day.'

'Ask Father if he will teach you,' said Luce, hoping to make a bond where one was needed.

'No, Miss Pilbeam will teach him.'

'Has Grandpa seen Father before?' said Gavin.

'Yes, but not for long,' said Luce.

'Grandpa is glad that Father has come back,' said Nevill.

'Grandma,' said Luce, in a shaken tone, 'it is on us, the desperate moment. Mother and Ridley are in the hall. What are we to do?'

'We can do nothing,' said Regan, seeming almost to repress a smile.

'One of you go and prepare your mother,' said Fulbert to his sons, in his old manner.

'We should have thought of that, if we were not petrified,' said Daniel.

'I will go, Father,' said Luce, and went swiftly from the room.

'The occasion of Ridley's discomfiture is spoiled by its tragedy,' said Daniel.

'It is hard on us,' said Graham. 'But nothing can spoil it for Grandma. And she has had few pleasures of late.'

'Hope and Paul are there as well,' said Regan, again with an unsteadiness about her lips.

'Another circumstance of our life unchanged,' said Fulbert.

'It is a good thing that family is not any larger,' said Isabel.

Regan laughed with noticeable heartiness, almost as though to cover some other cause for mirth.

'Faith is not there,' said Venice.

'She will remedy the matter,' said her sister.

'Will Mother be able to marry Mr Ridley now?' said James.

'Of course not,' said Isabel. 'Father was glad to see no change in you, but he will alter his mind, if you don't take care.'

Hope entered and began at once to talk, as if to give time to those who followed.

'Fulbert, I wish I could say I knew this would happen. But I did not know. I am afraid you will see signs of it.'

'I have found so few in my own home that I can hardly believe what is before my eyes.'

'I suppose I meant in our home. There are not so few there.'

'I know, I know,' said Fulbert; 'I am prepared.'

'And Ridley is not. Well, it is right that you should have the advantage of him.'

'I hope it is. For I have it.'

Hope sat down as if her limbs gave under her. Regan looked at her easily. The awaited group came into the room, Luce leading her mother. Eleanor walked forward with her usual step, and Ridley was drawn to his full height to face what was upon him.

'Fulbert!' he said, moving in front of the others. 'My friend.'

Fulbert accepted his hand, but went towards his wife, and it was not until they had exchanged an embrace that he turned his eyes on his face.

'My friend,' repeated Ridley. 'I trust that nothing will alter that for you. It will not for me.'

'It need not,' said Fulbert. 'A dead man cannot expect to be treated as a live one.'

'You left your affairs in my hands. If in the course of dealing with them, I was led further, you will understand.'

'Who should, if not I? You wanted what I chose for myself. How can I say I am surprised?'

'You might say other things. I am grateful for your forbearance.'

'I have too much restored to me, to dwell on what I may have lost. And somehow I feel it is not much, and will soon be mine.'

Ridley took a step aside and stood with his eyes averted, while the husband and wife approached their children.

'I find that I miss nothing,' said Fulbert. 'If life would have gone on after my death, that will happen to us all. And if it went on too soon and too far for my choice, I was not there to choose.'

Sir Jesse touched the ground with his stick, and Paul, who was standing absorbed in the scene, obeyed the summons. The resulting movement revealed Faith, standing just inside the room, with her hands held apart from her sides, and her eyes wide and unwinking, as though to avoid dwelling on the intimate scene.

'I forgot Faith was with us,' said Hope, 'but it seems she did the same.'

'Faith looks as if she were at church,' said Venice, in a clearer voice that she intended.

'I suppose we do all feel rather like that,' said Faith, in a low, quick tone.

'No doubt we ought to wish we were not here,' said Hope.

'I wish we were not,' said Faith, with a further withdrawal towards the door.

'I see why you stayed in the hall, dear. But why did you change your mind?'

'It is not much good for one of us to adopt a measure when the others do not follow it.'

'Where did Faith get the impression that her family follow her lead?' said Daniel.

Ridley turned from his place, and with a step that suggested that eyes were on him, walked to the window and stood with his back to the room.

'Ridley's eyes are resting unseeingly on the familiar landscape,' said Graham, his voice betraying that this was not the whole of his thought.

'I am glad he has got out of his place in the middle of the floor,' said Daniel. 'It was hardly his best at the moment.'

'You make me feel he is in the pillory, and that you would like to throw rotten eggs at him,' said Hope.

'How did people come by their supplies of eggs in that state?' said Isabel. 'Did they carry a stock of them, as if they were snuff or tobacco?'

'Perhaps they were on sale near the pillory,' said Daniel, 'as buns and nuts are at the Zoo, so that people could be helped to their natural dealings with captive creatures.'

Faith looked at the laughing group with steady eyes.

'Faith thinks we ought to be in low spirits,' said Isabel. 'I am sure I don't know why.'

'I know you are seriously thankful in your hearts,' said Faith.

Regan watched her son's reunion with his family, without jealousy, emotion or desire. She would have asked what she had.

Fulbert saw Ridley's solitary figure and went towards him.

'Well, Ridley, let us take our next steps over this strange gulf between us. I have much to thank you for, and I trust you do not resent my rising from the dead. I would have done it at a better moment, if I could. I did try to rise a day or two earlier, but fate was against me. And it is a good thing it was not a day or two later. I don't understand how my letter miscarried. It was an unfortunate lapse, when they occur so seldom. I will have inquiries made. You had the two letters some months ago, and then no other?'

'Fulbert,' said Ridley, lifting his eyes, 'I have had no letter from you or concerning you, save those two you name. I dealt with them as you directed. And so would I have dealt with this one, had it reached me.'

'I wished to spare my family a shock. And I wrote instead of cabling, to save them the weeks of waiting. I may have been right or wrong, but I have reached my home, and I cannot regret the manner of my coming.'

'Fulbert,' said Ridley, looking round with an emotional expression, 'I could not wish you more than this.'

'You are wise not to tell me your real feelings. And I will never ask you for them.'

'You spoke of the gulf between us,' said Ridley, in a painful manner. 'If you will come to meet me over it, I will do my part. More I cannot do.'

'Do let us gloss over this moment,' said Graham, as if he could not suppress the words. 'It will become too much.'

'Father and Ridley might have had their encounter without arranging themselves as the cynosure of every eye,' said Daniel.

'Well, nothing need be explained to us later,' said Isabel. 'And I trust nothing will be.'

'Well, you have been present at a scene that would be unique in anyone's life,' said Fulbert, looking round on his children. 'You will live to be glad you have witnessed it. You will carry the memory to your graves. And you will be the wiser. Nothing could have thrown more light on human nature.'

'I call that almost a personal remark,' said Hope.

Graham looked again at Ridley, whose eyes were on the ground. Honor came up to Gavin.

'Shall we say our "Nunc dimittis"?' she said, with a gleam in her eyes.

Gavin met the look in silence.

'I mean, shall we find a chance of going upstairs?'

'Don't you want to stay with Father?'

'I don't mind, as long as he is here. I want to enjoy my ordinary life, feeling he has come back.'

Gavin gave the matter some thought.

'We should only be sent for,' he said.

'Now let me do something more for you all, than work on your feelings,' said Fulbert, who had been unfastening a package. 'I have not come home for that. Let me show you these photographs of the places I saw, and should have seen, if I had been a sound man instead of a sick one. Now put yourselves so that you can see.'

He settled himself in an armchair. Luce leaned over the back. Isabel and Venice sat on the arms, and Honor on her father's knee. Daniel and Graham stood at the sides, and James and Gavin knelt on the floor in front. Nevill took his stand at a distance, with his eyes on the photographs. Ridley slowly advanced and stood within sight of them, as if he would take a natural part. Eleanor kept her gaze on the group of her husband and children. Regan and Sir Jesse watched it with scarcely a movement of their eyes. Faith stood as if nothing mattered, as long as she did not occupy any space round Fulbert.

'Here is the house where I lived,' said Fulbert. 'There is the window of the room where I lay. For months I saw nothing except through that square of glass.'

Nevill approached and placed his finger on the point.

'It is where Father was,' he said.

'The glass is not square,' said Gavin.

'It is oblong,' said Honor.

'Father painted the picture,' said Nevill.

'It is a photograph,' said James.

'It is a picture of a house,' said Nevill, who knew only photographs of people.

'Couldn't you even speak?' said Honor to her father.

'Not so that people knew what I meant.'

'Then they couldn't do what you wanted?'

'That was the worst, my little woman. You would have found it out, wouldn't you?'

'He would too,' said Nevill.

'She couldn't have, if she didn't know what you said,' said Gavin.

'Ah, the eyes of love can divine a good deal,' said Fulbert.

'Then didn't the people who were with you – didn't they like you very much?' said James, in a high, hardly articulate tone.

'Not as much as my own girls,' said Fulbert, putting Isabel's arm about his neck, and a moment later doing the same with Venice's.

'Not as much as him either,' said Nevill.

'The voyage must have done a good deal for you, Father,' said Luce. 'You are thinner and a little older, but you are yourself.'

'If I were not, you would not see me. I would not have offered you a ghost or a scarecrow for a father.'

'If Honor couldn't see you until you were well, she couldn't have done what you wanted,' said Gavin.

Fulbert lifted Honor's hand to his cheek.

'I wish Father would arrange some caresses for himself from me,' said Graham. 'He lets me seem so coldhearted.'

'My Isabel can't look at her father enough,' said Fulbert.

'He looks at Father too,' said Nevill. 'He *likes* to look at him.'

'Now you may have these photographs for yourselves,' said Fulbert. 'Would you like to divide them or share them?'

'Share them,' said James, at once.

'That is always a good way.'

'I should like that one with you in it, Father,' said Isabel.

Fulbert withdrew it and put it into her hand.

'Mother gave me a photograph of you on the day you went away,' said Venice.

'Well, here is another on the day I come back.'

'You gave me one of yourself on that day,' said Honor, bringing about a similar result.

James's eyes rested on the photographs in some doubt of the fate of his suggestion.

'He would like a little picture,' said Nevill.

'Come and sit on my knee like Honor, and I will show them to you,' said Fulbert.

Nevill moved forward and started back, gazed at his father, and after a moment ran to Ridley and climbed on his knee, as though he were the person interchangeable with Fulbert.

'Now I must see what I can find in my pockets,' said Ridley, holding to his line of playing a normal part. 'Here is a purse and a notebook and a cigar case, and a gold pencil case with lead in it.'

Nevill looked from the objects to Ridley's face.

'It is better than a picture, isn't it?'

'Is the pencil real gold?' said Gavin. 'Did somebody give it to you?'

'Yes, it was a present,' said Ridley, not mentioning that the giver was Eleanor. 'You can make it longer if you pull it.'

'It moves,' said Nevill, in a slightly uneasy tone, putting his hand towards it and drawing it away.

'Pull it and see how long it is,' said Ridley.

'He will pull it,' said Nevill, looking round before gingerly doing so, and breaking into nervous laughter as it yielded to his touch.

'There is a loose leaf in the notebook,' said Gavin. 'I can read grown-up writing now; I can read it as well as Honor; I even like reading it. What is the matter? I can't hurt a piece of paper. It doesn't belong to the book.'

Ridley had started and grasped at the paper, but as Gavin moved away, he changed his manner and smilingly held out his hand.

'I must ask for my property,' he said.

'Gavin, give it back at once,' said Luce. 'We never read papers belonging to other people.'

'It is only a list like Mother takes into the town. It isn't even a long one.'

'It is a memorandum,' said Honor.

'And as such, it fills a place in my life,' said Ridley, still with hand extended.

'I shan't make any mistakes,' said Gavin. 'It is sometimes two or three words and sometimes more. What is the matter? You hurt me with your great hand.'

'The moment has come for me to claim what is my own,' said Ridley, in a tone that addressed the company.

There was a stir and murmur of protest, and eyes were turned to the man and the child.

' "Arrange licence. Take house. Train and hotel",' read Gavin. 'It is quite easy. There are only a few more lines. Each one is called an item. The word is printed on the page. I shan't keep it a minute. Let me just read to the end.' He eluded Ridley's grasp and slipped into a space where he could not follow. ' "Fulbert at Crown Inn from tenth to fifteenth. Keep paper as letter destroyed. Write from abroad, as if it were delayed and forwarded. Read and send lease." Leave me alone. What harm can I do to a loose page?'

Ridley was leaning over the desk, his hand clutching the air above the paper. There was a silence that became a hush and then a stir. Fulbert rose and came towards Ridley and stood waiting for him to turn. Eleanor approached the group, and finding herself between the two men, moved nearer to her husband. Regan rustled forward, simply and fiercely accusing. Sir Jesse stood with his eyes shooting from under his brows, but so far reserving his word. Luce stood with a simply startled face. Faith watched from her place, her gaze fastened on her brother. Hope and Paul remained in their seats, now and then meeting each other's eyes. Daniel came and stood by his parents, Graham and Isabel looked at Ridley, as if they could not hold themselves from following his experience. The children watched in different stages of comprehension, Gavin awaiting the reproach that was his due.

'What is it?' he whispered to Honor.

'Nothing to do with you. It is not you who have done anything.'

'Gavin didn't mean to do it,' said Nevill to his mother, feeling this to be an unlikely view.

'So, Ridley,' said Fulbert, speaking with his head lifted, and his eyes almost covered by their lids, 'I have had this kind of friend.'

Ridley appeared to be preoccupied by the notebook and some loosened pages.

'I didn't tear the book,' said Gavin.

'If you will pardon me, you did,' said Ridley, smiling at him in an absent manner.

'Be quiet, and you will be forgotten,' said Honor, to her brother.

'So my letter arrived to time,' said Fulbert, not changing his attitude.

Ridley kept his eyes on the book, carefully replacing the leaves.

'The notebook is useful,' said Regan. 'And not for the first time. What would have happened when my son came home? His wife would have been his own.'

'In name,' said Ridley, in a gentle tone, his fingers still employed, and his eyes on them. 'But we should have remained together. Your son would have had ground for any step he chose. Eleanor would have been happier in her own home with me. This house is no home to her. Why should I not think of her and myself?' He seemed to keep his voice to its even note by an effort, as if he would not work himself up for his hearers. 'Why should I only think of a man, whose sole thought of me was to put me to his service? Why should I serve him? Why did he think that I should? Why is he so much better than I?'

Sir Jesse thrust himself between Ridley and Regan, his hands falling at his sides, as if his emotions took all his powers.

'You may cease to talk to my wife. Why should she hear and answer you? You may be silent in my house. And as you are the son of my friend, you may leave it at your own will. I will not speak to you of my son; I could not do so.'

Ridley turned as if to do Sir Jesse's bidding, but as he passed him, paused and opened the notebook and drew something else from the back. He held it under Sir Jesse's eyes, and then moved on and held it under Regan's.

'You are right that the book is useful. It proves to be so once again. It has served several of my purposes.'

Sir Jesse was not in time to find his glasses. Regan had hers in her hand and looked at the photograph. She looked also at Ridley's hand, saw that its grasp was firm, threw one glance at her husband and returned to the hearth.

Ridley moved on and held the photograph under the eyes of Fulbert, his wife and his three eldest children. Hope left her place and came and looked at it; Paul followed her example; Isabel summoned her courage and did the same. Sir Jesse, who by now had guessed its character, came up and confirmed his suspicion and moved away. Regan kept her eyes down and wore an inscrutable expression. Faith glanced at her parents and turned aside, as if she would not yield to curiosity.

The photograph was of a man and a woman, sitting in a lover-like attitude, with their arms entwined: Sir Jesse and the mother of the Marlowes.

Ridley's voice was heard again.

'You see I am not the only man who can go astray. I found that photograph amongst some business papers. It was taken years ago in South America, and it tells us what happened there. I took it with the intention of destroying it, but you set me another example. I will show that I am not the only person with the temptations of a man, and not the only one who can yield to them.'

'Why did you not fulfil your intention?' said Regan from the hearth.

Luce beckoned to Isabel and Venice and James, and led them to the door, bending to say a word to Regan.

'Grandma, some of us are too young to understand. And some of us are of an age when we must understand. These three are in between.'

Regan nodded and smiled, her face almost placid.

The three children left the room, Isabel at once startled and satisfied, James too puzzled even to be curious, Venice baffled and tormented, but encouraged by the promise in her sister's eyes.

'If you judge me, so do I judge you,' said Ridley to Sir Jesse. 'And I say you are worse than I.'

He turned and went with bent head to the door, and seemed to thrust his way through it, as though it offered some tangible resistance. As he moved his hands the photograph fell; he groped for it, and Gavin, still angry and watchful, darted on it and surrendered it to Fulbert. Faith watched her brother go, and then moved slowly and as if hardly of her own will to Daniel and Graham, and revealed the subject of her words by a sudden glance at Sir Jesse. Fulbert returned to his children and the photographs scattered on the floor.

'Well, which picture would you like?' he said, resuming his seat and bending towards Nevill.

Nevill gathered up the photographs and poured them over Fulbert's knees.

'They are all Father's,' he said.

'He may see a photograph as a sinister object,' said Graham.

'I didn't tear the paper,' said Gavin.

'We know you did not, my boy,' said Eleanor.

'Gavin took great care,' said Nevill.

'I feel grateful to Gavin,' said Daniel. 'He has ended the necessity of feeling pity for Ridley.'

'I don't know, Daniel,' said Luce. 'Is our pity any less? Of course we have other feelings.'

'Which picture do you like best?' said Fulbert, to Nevill.

'He will have that one Mr Ridley had.'

'Father has it in his pocket,' said Gavin.

'Perhaps he has a pencil too,' said Nevill.

'I will find you one tomorrow,' said Fulbert.

'Grandpa spoke in a loud voice,' said Nevill, 'loud and angry. Mr Ridley did too.'

Sir Jesse sank into a chair at the sound of his name, as if it gave him some sort of release, and sat with his head and shoulders bent, with a suggestion that he was a broken man.

'Who will live in the new house?' said Gavin. 'Now that Mother is not going to marry Mr Ridley.'

'Mother will marry him,' said Nevill, 'and have a nice house and not this one.'

'Other people will live in it,' said Honor.

'Not other people,' said Nevill.' Mr Ridley wouldn't let them.'

'Perhaps he will live in it alone.'

'No, not alone. He would be very angry.'

'Which do you like best, Mr Ridley or Father?' said Gavin suddenly to Eleanor, seeking to remedy his own situation by bringing forward hers.

'Father is my husband,' said Eleanor, without hesitation, 'and we have always loved each other, and we always shall. But Ridley was good to me when I thought Father could not return, and I shall always be grateful to him. Some day you will understand.'

'I understand now,' said Honor. 'He kept it a secret about Father's coming back, so that he could marry you before people knew. He yielded to temptation.'

'Now I think you may run away,' said Eleanor, stroking her hair.

'What did Mr Ridley do?' said Gavin, in a low tone to his sister.

'I will tell you when we are upstairs.'

'Now you may run away,' said Eleanor again. 'You will always feel kindly to him.'

'I haven't said I shall,' said Gavin.

'I have no antipathy to him,' said Honor.

'Now I said you could run away,' said Eleanor. 'You may kiss Father before you go.'

'He will kiss Mother too,' said Nevill, coming up to her. 'And Mr Ridley come back soon, and never go away again.'

'Now I said you could run away.'

'Do you think you were right, dear?' said Hope.

'Tell Hatton and Mullet that I will come up later and see them,' said Fulbert, as he parted from his children.

'He will tell them,' said Nevill, and ran before the others from the room.

'I think I ought to go home, Mother,' said Faith. 'I have a feeling that someone should be with Ridley.'

'I am glad you take the noble course, dear. It improves our family average. And it seems to need it.'

Faith went with a grave face towards the door. Sir Jesse rose and without looking at anyone did the same, as if he found it easier to follow a lead. Regan got up a minute later, and putting her knitting easily together, smiled on the company and followed. Paul came from the back of the room, as if released from some bondage.

'Well, I am going to take my wife away,' said Fulbert. 'I have a leaning towards my own armchair. It is many months since I have sat in it. And if I leave her, other people form designs upon her. I have been happy in having my friends to welcome me. And I wish you joy of your gossip; it should be a good one.'

'It should be wonderful,' said Hope, coming quickly to the centre of the group. 'And as we all have a relation disgraced, it will not be spoiled by personal embarrassment. I have not dared to dwell on our own family dishonour.'

'Perhaps we never shall,' said Paul. 'Then we shall be saved a great deal. Poor boy! Poor boy!'

'The exposure of two people upon one occasion must be very rare,' said Daniel.

'We so seldom get any exposure at all,' said Paul.

'It is better for it all to happen together,' said Graham. 'Better for the exposed people, I mean.'

'They are saved from that sense of loneliness,' said Hope. 'Men's lives are evidently what they are supposed to be. And some have the misfortune to be found out. It is all true.'

'People should keep their darker times to themselves,' said Daniel.

'They are certainly not well advised to be photographed at one of them,' said Paul.

'Would it be better not to talk about it?' said Faith.

'Nothing could be so bad,' said Hope. 'And it is because you think so that you have not gone to Ridley.'

'I thought we should all be going soon, Mother.'

'No doubt he has taken the late train to London,' said Paul.

Faith turned grave eyes on her father, in reference to his silence on this matter.

'I wonder if he has anyone to welcome him there,' said Hope.

'Grandpa was rather mature when he sowed his wild oats,' said Daniel.

'They don't seem so very wild,' said Graham. 'People must be fairly established, when they are in a position to support two families.'

'Poor Grandpa!' said Luce. 'I daresay he was very lonely out there. Not that I want to make excuses for him.'

'There is none for the various foolishness he has shown,' said Paul. 'It comes of a life without criticism.'

'How did he manage about leaving the woman, when he returned to England?' said Graham.

'It is no good to find out about it, Graham,' said Daniel. 'You will never go as far as your grandfather.'

'He told her the truth about his life,' said Paul. 'And he lived with her again, when he went out a second time. She died when Susan was born.'

'And I pitied you for having to sit by him!' said Hope. 'To think of the freemasonry among men!'

'I suppose she was not equal to him,' said Faith.

'I daresay not, to our ideas,' said her father. 'Social and other differences would count less out there.'

'And when he heard of her death, he sent for the three children,' said Faith. 'I am glad he did not shirk his responsibilities.'

'Are they to know who their father is?' said Graham.

'No, it is to be always kept from them,' said Paul. 'He feels it is better for them and for him. I am quoting his words.'

'He must be afraid of its leaking out, now it is not his own secret,' said Graham.

'It is to be the secret of us all.'

'Well, that is the least aggravating kind of secret,' said Hope.

'Poor Grandma!' said Luce, in a soft tone.

'Yes, poor Lady Sullivan!' said Faith. 'She is the really tragic figure. I think she showed a great heroism, the greater that it was quiet.'

'I think heroism is only mentioned when it is that,' said Hope.

'She has known for years,' said Paul. 'She saw Sir Jesse's interest in the young people, and saw a likeness to him, and guessed the truth.'

'To think she has carried the burden for all this time!' said Faith, slowly shaking her head.

'It is Grandpa's affair,' said Daniel, 'or it should have been.'

'Did she tell you, Paul?' said Hope.

'She said a word to him.'

'Did he mind?' said Graham.

'Well, I think he had a shock.'

'He can hardly expect not to suffer at all,' said Faith.

'It seems like Grandpa to sin for years and suffer for a moment,' said Graham, as though he were glad if this were the case.

'It is good that there is no longer that between them,' said Faith. 'And I daresay Lady Sullivan knows men.'

'I did not know you did, dear,' said Hope.

'All women must in a way, Mother.'

'Well, I don't see how, in some cases, dear.'

'There would not be definite ways, Mother.'

'Oh, well, perhaps we think the same. Now can we dwell on Sir Jesse's lapse, and hardly mention Ridley's?'

'That is what we will do, if you please,' said Paul. 'But I should not have thought the boy would be so bold.'

'I have been feeling an unwilling respect for him,' said Hope. 'And as in me respect is generally that, perhaps the rest of you feel a proper one.'

'I cannot do that,' said Faith, in a quiet tone. 'But of course I have other feelings.'

'I can't help thinking of Grandma's tragedy,' said Luce. 'It has not come today, but there must have been a day when it did come.'

'There must,' said Faith.

'When the expedition involved what it did, no wonder Grandpa thought us too young for it,' said Daniel.

'Did Father find any traces of what had happened?' said Graham.

'He did not say,' said Paul.

'Perhaps Grandpa had prepared him.'

'Does the freemasonary extend to father and son?' said Hope.

'I suppose a long period away from home does mean all kinds of things for a man,' said Faith.

'Ridley has done well enough in his own village,' said Paul. 'I hope he will not go further outside. For he will now remain away.'

'Yes, I suppose he will, Father,' said Faith.

'Is there any likeness in the Marlowes to Grandpa?' said Luce. 'And is their real name Marlowe?'

'Yes, it was their mother's name,' said Paul.

'Of course, illegitimate children are called by their mother's name,' said Faith. 'I have always seen likenesses in them, but I have never been able to place them.'

'I have always thought the resemblance was to each other,' said Graham, 'and I think it chiefly is.'

'The likeness to your grandfather would not strike people when no one looked for it,' said Paul. 'If the relationship had been known, there would have been no need to fancy it.'

'The Marlowes are our uncle and aunts by half blood,' said Luce, in her musing tone.

'You had better forget it,' said Paul. 'If things are in our minds, they come to our lips.'

'This thing does seem to,' said Hope.

'Now how are we to face Grandpa?' said Luce.

'Yes, that is how it will be,' said Daniel, 'when surely it should be the other way round.'

'Poor Grandpa!' said Luce.

'I do admire you all,' said Hope. 'You have none of the severity of youth. I should hardly have expected Faith to be so tolerant; I might not even have approved of it. I think people must be better with each generation.'

'I can hardly be accused of youth, Mother,' said Faith.

'And poor Grandma!' said Luce, as if she could not in honesty give up this idea.

'Yes, it is Sir Jesse's career of deceit that is hard to forgive,' said Faith. 'That long course of deception of his wife. It goes against the grain.'

'But you do forgive it, dear,' said Hope.

'He meant to die with that between them, Mother.'

'It is there now,' said Graham. 'That is what he did not mean. He was just keeping his own counsel. He has never meant to die at all.'

'He will never get over my being Ridley's father,' said Paul. 'It may be a release for me in a way.'

'And how about his own varied fatherhood?' said Daniel.

'I have already recovered from it. I am not the man he is.'

'Yes, I do forgive it,' said Faith, in a quick, low tone that rose as she continued. 'Poor Eleanor Sullivan is in a sad position.'

'It is greatly improved,' said Daniel. 'She prefers Father to Ridley.'

'Well, in a position of peculiar difficulty.'

'The worst is already past.'

'It was a hard homecoming for your father.'

'It was a sound instinct that led him to prepare us,' said Luce, smiling.

'He was fortunate, considering he failed to do so,' said Graham. 'He did not find his very name forgotten, or anything like that. And he seemed to be a little surprised.'

'Why do we joke about it?' said Luce.

'I have not done so,' said Faith, rising from her chair. 'Now it is not a day for lingering.'

'My heart fails before the prospect of our first family gathering,' said Graham. 'To think that Grandpa and Grandma and Mother must all be there!'

'And this on the day when Father is restored to us!' said Luce. 'This is the thing I do not incline to forgive Grandpa.'

'It must be difficult for you,' said Faith, as if there were no question of the actual forgiveness.

'It is fortunate that Father's heart is stout enough for it all,' said Daniel.

CHAPTER TWELVE

'FATHER has come home!' said Honor, bounding into the schoolroom. 'He was ill and unconscious, but he was never dead. Mother can't marry Mr Ridley, and things will be like they used to be.'

'I am so thankful for you, dear,' said Miss Pilbeam, stooping to kiss her. 'I heard last night and I rejoiced from my heart.'

Honor drew back with a look of consternation, and Gavin who was behind her, came to a sudden pause.

'We should have had a holiday, if Mother had thought of it,' resumed Honor, in an almost more than ordinary tone. 'But she said, as you would have the trouble of coming, we were to have lessons.'

'I think you would please your father by doing your very best.'

'I don't think he minds,' said Honor, turning round on one foot.

'Don't you wish your mother could come back?' said Gavin, with a simple air of superiority.

'I do indeed,' said Miss Pilbeam.

'I don't suppose she ever can, because she died in the house, didn't she?'

'No, I know she cannot.'

'But I daresay you don't mind her being dead as much as you did at first,' said Gavin, revealing his own experience of the effect of time.

'I mind quite as much. But I have had to get used to it.'

'I call that not minding so much,' said Honor, still turning round.

'You went on minding about your father.'

'I minded less; I had to. Everyone does. And other people get tired of your minding. Even Mother did. But if he really died now, I should mind more.'

'And you have not worn black since we knew you,' said Gavin to Miss Pilbeam.

'We do not stay in black for ever.'

'We do for a year, unless there is something to prevent it,' said Honor. 'We went out because Mother was going to marry again. The children can't look as if they still minded, when the mother has proved that she doesn't.'

'I don't think you quite understand your mother. She had to make the best of her life as it was.'

'If you really still minded, you wouldn't think there was any best.'

'You wouldn't think your father minded, if he was going to marry someone else,' said Gavin.

'I hope I should try to understand it. Indeed I do try to,' said Miss Pilbeam, in a lighter tone.

'Is he going to marry someone else?' said Honor.

'Yes, he told me last night,' said Miss Pilbeam, with an open, easy smile.

'It is funny that your father decided to marry someone else on the day when our mother knew she couldn't.'

Miss Pilbeam did not dwell upon the coincidence, though it was to be explained on the ground that her father had found the news an opening for himself.

'Does it make you hate your father?' said Gavin.

'No, not at all. You did not hate your mother, did you?'

'Well, she went down in my estimation,' said Honor.

'You would not have wished her to be lonely.'

'I should have thought it couldn't be helped.'

'The new woman will be your stepmother,' said Gavin, with a threat in his tone.

'Yes, she will. But she is an old friend.'

'Perhaps your father always wanted to marry her, even when your mother was alive,' said Honor.

'No, I am sure he did not.'

'Do people generally marry someone else, when their own wife or husband is dead?' said Gavin.

'No, only sometimes. I think men do it oftener than women.'

'Can they go on doing it as often as they like?'

'Yes, if they continue to lose their partners,' said Miss Pilbeam, with a touch of facetiousness.

Nevill came into the room in an absent manner, his eyes on a ball of string in his hands.

'Why, what a muddled ball!' said Miss Pilbeam.

'It is in a tangle,' said Nevill, with quiet resignation.

'I will soon put it straight for you.'

'Mullet said, do it himself,' said Nevill, with a sudden burst of tears.

'Oh, I think Mullet must have been busy.'

'Mullet was busy,' said Nevill, in a cheered, relieved tone. 'Poor

267

Mullet was very busy. She wouldn't say it another time.'

'Miss Pilbeam's father is going to be married,' said Honor.

'Not to Mr Ridley,' said Nevill, instantly.

'Of course not. A man can't marry another man.'

'He can't have Mr Ridley's house.'

'He doesn't want it. He has a house of his own. I suppose he will still live there.

'Yes, he will,' said Nevill. 'That is a nice house too.'

'You don't know anything about it.'

'Miss Pilbeam likes it,' said Nevill.

'Do you like it?' said Gavin, to Miss Pilbeam. 'I don't think it is at all nice.'

'I have not thought how it appears to other people. It has always been my home.'

'Perhaps your stepmother will turn you out,' said Gavin.

'No, I don't think she will do that,' said Miss Pilbeam, with a smile.

'You would laugh on the other side of your face, if she did.'

'Miss Pilbeam would live here with Hatton and Mullet,' said Nevill.

Honor and Gavin looked at each other, and burst into laughter at this estimation of Miss Pilbeam's place.

Miss Pilbeam looked towards the window.

'I am "he"; you are "she"; Miss Pilbeam is "it",' said Gavin, to his sister, seeming to receive an impetus from Nevill's words.

Miss Pilbeam turned sharply towards him.

'I suppose your father will like your stepmother better than you,' said Honor, quickly.

'He will have a different feeling for us.'

'No, he will like Miss Pilbeam best,' said Nevill.

'I see you are determined to waste your time this morning.'

'Well, it is natural,' said Honor.

'Yes, I think it is. Perhaps I had better read to you.'

Nevill at once ran to a book that lay on the sofa, brought it to Miss Pilbeam, and stood waiting to be lifted to her knee.

'We don't want that book,' said Honor.

Nevill put it on Miss Pilbeam's lap, turned the leaves until he came to his place, and began to read aloud to himself.

'No, no, that is not the page,' she said, putting her hand over it. 'You are saying it by heart.'

Nevill turned the pages again, reached one that he actually recognized, and resumed his recitation.

'No, you are not doing it properly. I will read a chapter of Robinson Crusoe. We are coming to the part where he sees the footprint on the ground.'

Nevill carried his book to the sofa and continued to read, resorting to improvization when his memory failed.

'Now this is an exciting part,' said Miss Pilbeam.

'Sometimes you miss things out,' said Honor. 'I know, because I read the book to myself.'

'It would be better not to read the book I am reading to you.'

'I like reading things a lot of times.'

'Well, this book is certainly worth it.'

'Then why did you tell her not to?' said Gavin.

'I thought it might make my reading dull for her. But nothing could make Robinson Crusoe dull, could it?'

'I think something makes it dull sometimes,' said Gavin, in such a light tone that Miss Pilbeam missed his meaning as he half intended.

Miss Pilbeam began to read, and Nevill raised his voice to overcome the sound, and remained absorbed in the results of his imagination. Neither Honor nor Gavin appeared to be conscious of his presence.

When things had continued for some time, Eleanor and Fulbert entered.

'Well, Miss Pilbeam,' said the latter, 'I have come to give you proof of what you have heard. We don't want you in danger of thinking a ghost has sprung on you.'

'I am rejoiced to see the proof, Mr Sullivan,' said Miss Pilbeam, as she shook hands.

'Show Father what you are doing,' said Eleanor, to the children.

'They are hardly in a state to apply themselves. I am just reading aloud. That will steady their nerves.'

'Poor little things! They will be more themselves tomorrow. And what is Nevill doing?'

Nevill just glanced at his mother and maintained his flow of words, drawing his finger down the page with an effect of keeping his place.

'Are you reading, dear?'

'Yes, him and Miss Pilbeam. Honor and Gavin aren't.'

'What is the book about?'

'Don't talk to him while he reads,' said Nevill, and resumed the pursuit.

'It is a very good imitation,' said Fulbert.

His son gave him a look, and turned the page as his finger reached the bottom of it.

Hatton entered the room, and he looked at her and hesitated, and then took the open book in both his hands and came to her side.

'It is time for your rest,' she said.

'He will read in bed,' said Nevill.

'No, you must go to sleep in bed,' said Eleanor, at once.

'He will read first,' said her son.

'He is still a little shy of me,' said Fulbert.

'Come and say good-bye to Father and me,' said Eleanor.

Nevill approached her, keeping his eyes from Fulbert.

'Mr Ridley will come back soon. Not stay away a long time like Father. And then Mother will have a nice house.'

'He tried to comfort me after you had gone. He has got into the habit of saying all the comforting things he can think of,' said Eleanor, hardly giving enough attention to her words.

'Miss Pilbeam's father is really going to marry again,' said Gavin.

Eleanor turned inquiring eyes on Miss Pilbeam.

'Yes, I heard the news last night,' said the latter, in a conversational, interested tone. 'And I shall not have my father so much on my mind. I can look forward to a time when I can think more of myself. I have not been able to be quite selfish enough in the last year.'

'A healthy resolve, Miss Pilbeam. See that you hold to it,' said Fulbert.

'Miss Pilbeam's stepmother won't turn her out,' said Gavin.

'Of course she will not,' said Eleanor. 'Why should she?'

'Well, it would hide the fact that she was not the father's first wife,' said Honor, with a slight spacing of the words. 'I wouldn't marry a man who had had a wife before me. If I had been Mr Ridley, I shouldn't have liked to marry you.'

'But Mr Ridley will marry her,' said Nevill, in a reassuring tone to his mother.

'I am the man married to Mother,' said Fulbert.

'No, Father didn't marry her. He didn't come back for a long time. But Mother will come and see poor Father.'

'Mr Ridley is not coming here any more.'

'No, because he has a house. This one is Grandma's.'

'Mother doesn't want the house now,' said Fulbert.

'Father can live in it too,' said Nevill, struck by a solution of all the human problems.

'Mother and I are both staying here.'

'Yes, until tomorrow.'

'No, we are staying here for always.'

Nevill met his eyes.

'Yes, dear Father can stay here,' he said, and ran after Hatton.

'Nevill wants to get rid of me,' said Eleanor, her tone showing that she did not believe her words.

'He doesn't know what the word, marry, means,' said Honor.

'I hope he will know some day,' said Fulbert, putting his arm in his wife's.

Honor looked after them, as they left the room.

'What is it like to have a father and no mother?' she said to Miss Pilbeam. 'But you liked your mother better than your father, didn't you?'

'I think perhaps I did.'

'You would think so now, because your father is marrying someone else,' said Gavin. 'That does make people think they don't like the person so well.'

'Well, it doesn't argue any great depth of nature,' said Honor.

'We cannot lay down rules in these matters,' said Miss Pilbeam.

Gavin looked at his sister.

'Do you like Father as much as you thought you did, when you believed he was dead?' he said in a natural tone.

Honor hesitated, or rather paused.

'Well, I don't think so much of him; I thought he was a more remarkable man. But I am quite reconciled to his being of common clay. I think that is better for those in authority over us.'

'Would you mind as much, if he died now?'

'I shouldn't think it was as great a loss. But I should mind more. I couldn't ever bear it again.'

'Would you die?' said Gavin, in a grave tone.

'If that is what people do, when they can't bear the things that have happened.'

'Come, don't forget you are children,' said Miss Pilbeam, who believed that his conversation had been unchildlike.

'Our experience has gone beyond our age,' said Honor, who shared the belief.

'Something has,' said Miss Pilbeam, smiling.

'Well, go on reading,' said Gavin in a rough tone.

'That is not the way to ask.'

'I am not asking; I am telling you to go on.'

'And something has not,' said Miss Pilbeam, deciding to continue to smile and resuming the book.

Eleanor and her husband went on to the schoolroom.

'Well, Miss Mitford, I have come to see you,' said Fulbert, 'and to give you proof that I am flesh and blood like yourself.'

Miss Mitford rose and shook hands.

'It is kind of you to say so,' she said.

Fulbert laughed though his tone had hardly been without the suggestion.

'The situation puts you at a loss, does it?' he said observing or rather assuming that this was the case, and accordingly regarding her with eyes of enjoyment.

'Well, it is quite outside my experience.'

'An experience need not be so narrow, that it does not include it,' said Fulbert, giving encouragement, where it might be needed. 'Yours has taken place within four walls, but some of the deepest has done that.'

'Mine has not been of that kind,' said Miss Mitford.

'Well, well, some of us must deal with the smaller things of life.'

'Education is not among those,' said Eleanor.

'Indeed it is not. These youngsters owe you a great deal, Miss Mitford.'

'I am sure they realize it. Don't you, James?' said Eleanor, appealing to her son from force of habit, as his debt was less than his sisters'.

'Yes.'

'Why are you not at school, my boy?'

James felt that all the difficult moments of his life culminated in this one. He had accepted his father's return to family life as too solemn an occasion for the personal interest of his own education to have a place, and had remained at home in a grave and quiet spirit, and was reading a book to which these terms would apply.

'It is Father's first day at home,' he said, in a low, uncertain voice, that awaited his parents' interpretation.

'But not James's,' said Fulbert, in an amused, rallying tone, that gave his son his answer.

'And how are the others spending their time?' said Eleanor. 'I see that lessons are not in progress.'

'I am doing nothing,' said Isabel, at once.

'Is that the way to make the most of your holiday?' said her mother, her last word showing James the extent of his misapprehension.

'I daresay it is,' said Fulbert, resting his eyes on his daughter. 'People must relax when they have been wrought up too far.'

'Well, what is Venice doing?' said his wife.

Venice revealed a piece of embroidery, or rather took no steps to hide it.

'You need not be ashamed of it, my dear. I am not such an advocate of doing nothing. Let me see it.'

Venice laid it out, appearing hardly to see it herself.

'Sewing,' said her father. 'Another way of resting.'

Venice's face cleared, and she looked at her mother for her opinion.

'You are improving very much. I wish Isabel would learn to do a little needlework. As Father says, it would do her good.'

'Did I say so?' said Fulbert. 'Well, if it would, I hope she will take to it. And how is James passing his time?'

James handed his book to his mother with a smile, feeling a reluctance to show it to the parent responsible for it.

'That is a very nice book for today. I think James is developing, Fulbert.'

'This continual process in James should take him far,' said Isabel.

'I won't put him through his paces this morning,' said Fulbert, looking at his son with his old, quizzical air.

'The world is a different place to all of them,' said Eleanor.

'And to me it is the same place, and I would ask no more. Well, good-bye, Miss Mitford. It is good of you to let us intrude on your province.'

'Now you will settle down to a life where you have nothing to wish for,' said Eleanor, addressing her children at the door. 'That is a pleasant thought for your mother and for you.'

There was silence after she had gone.

'Nothing that could conceivably be realized,' said Isabel.

Her sister looked at her, and for a moment they held each other's eyes; then they suddenly rose and staggered to a distant sofa and fell on it in a fit of mirth.

James glanced up from his book, for once completely at a loss. Miss Mitford made a survey of her pupils and looked down with curiosity essentially satisfied. The two girls leant towards each other and spoke in tones audible to no one else.

'Our imagination ran away,' said Isabel. 'It is so rarely put to the proof. People have never lost what they think they have. And if they recover it, the moment comes.'

'Do you mind much?' whispered Venice.

'Not now the shock is over. In a way it is a relief. I can be at ease with everyone in the house. There is no one superior to me.'

'I am not like you,' said Venice.

'I can always protect you,' said Isabel.

'Mother will always be here as well as Father,' said James, closing his book.

'It is a small price to pay for Father's coming back,' said Isabel, causing Miss Mitford to raise her eyes. 'And she will be a great deal with him.'

'She will at first,' said James, and took up another book, as if he could leave the future.

'We can't have Father without his wife. And Mother has nothing contemptible about her.'

'You talk like Honor,' said James, in an absent tone.

'She and I are said to be alike.'

'I don't think you are,' said Venice.

'No one is really like anyone else.'

'That is true,' said Miss Mitford. 'We are struck by a little likeness because it is imposed on so much difference.'

'Venice is not like anyone. She is almost a beauty,' said Isabel, as if this precluded resemblance.

Venice fixed her eyes in front of her, while a great pleasure welled up within her, and James looked almost troubled by such an idea in connection with anyone so intimate.

Eleanor returned to the room.

'Father is worried about you, Isabel. Are you really exhausted?'

'No, only feeling a slight reaction, Mother.'

'That is my good girl,' said Eleanor, with surprised approval. 'I heard all that laughing, and I did not think it sounded much like exhaustion.'

'It was a schoolroom joke, Mother.'

'I expect you have all sorts of nonsense among yourselves,' said Eleanor, little thinking how much more worth her while such jests might be, than those she pursued downstairs.

'Is Venice really a beauty?' said James.

'Who has been saying she is?' said Eleanor, giving a deprecating look at Venice and suspecting Fulbert of the indiscretion.

'Isabel,' said James.

'Oh, Isabel,' said Eleanor, as if this testimony hardly counted. 'Why, what a flattering sister to have! What has Venice to say about her in return?'

'She often says she is clever,' said James. 'A lot of people do.'

'Well, so she is,' said Eleanor, thinking more easily of tribute along this line. 'And what of James? Are people going to say the same thing about him?'

James was taken aback by this result of his generosity, though he should have been learning that most things gave rise to it.

275

'Yes,' he said, in a light tone.

'And what grounds are they going to have for saying it?'

James could not refer to his choice of books for an occasion, as it had already been forgotten; or to the poems which to himself were proof of it, as he had revealed them to no one, and was postponing publication until his maturity; and merely made uneasy movements.

'Well, we won't talk about it on Father's first day,' said Eleanor, allowing that it was an awkward subject.

James returned to the book he had been reading when his parents entered.

'I should not read while your mother is in the room, my boy.'

James kept his eyes on the page until he seemed to reach a climax, put in his marker and smiled at his mother, while he put out his hand to the other book, whose appearance might need explanation.

'You were just reading to a place where you could stop.'

'Yes.'

'And now you are going to have a change,' said Eleanor, with a condoning smile and a sense of relief, as solemn spirits on seriously joyful occasions affected her as they did most people. 'And now I hear Father calling me. I must remember who has the right to my time. I may not be able to visit you again today.'

She descended to the hall and came upon Fulbert and Luce engaged in talk. Her daughter turned to meet her.

'Mother, the Cambridge results are out. They really came some days ago, but they have only transpired today. Daniel has a first, and Graham a low third. It is what they expected, so do not let us make a disturbance.'

'Was anyone showing any tendency to do so, my dear?'

Fulbert jerked his thumb towards the door of the library with an air of giving an answer.

Sir Jesse emerged and walked in to luncheon, looking at no one. His grandsons followed him and paused to join their parents.

'Well done, my boy,' said Fulbert, bringing his hand down on

Daniel's shoulder. 'Some people belittle this kind of success, but I am not one of them. This is a happy chance on my first day with you all.'

'We were keeping the news for an opportune moment,' said Daniel, not mentioning that they had postponed it until after their mother's marriage. 'And then we forgot it in the excitement of your return. It was in the *Times* on Tuesday, and Grandpa scanned the lists this morning and found our place. Somehow it seems an odd thing for him to do.'

'There is no limit to what he is capable of,' said Graham. 'But I suppose not even he will think it a moment for dwelling on people's weaker sides.'

'Have you already forgotten that some things are not to be mentioned?' said Eleanor.

'I will remind myself of it, Mother. I am all for following the course.'

'You shall have my support, my boy,' said Fulbert, 'I have not come back to expect great things of you. I have done little myself but survive. I ask nothing but your welcome.'

'He has it,' said Graham, in a fervent undertone.

'You could not make an effort for your mother, Graham?' said Eleanor.

'Graham, some day you may tell people what was the bitterest moment of your life,' said Daniel.

Fulbert signed towards the dining-room.

'Is it wise to keep the old man waiting for his luncheon?'

Luce tiptoed to the room and back again, with a smile spreading over her face.

'We have not done so, Father.'

'We may as well go and catch him up,' said Fulbert, walking through the open door.

Sir Jesse gave no sign while his family took their seats, but presently turned to Graham.

'I mentioned to you that I saw those lists in the *Times*. I asked you if I was to believe the evidence of my eyes. You did not answer my question.'

'Well, I wish you would not do so, Grandpa.'

'Am I to gather there is some mistake?'

'Things in the *Times* tend to be true. And the same must be said of the testimony of people's senses.'

'Are you speaking to me?'

'I am answering you, Grandpa.'

'Would you prefer to be apprenticed to a shoemaker or a shoe-black?'

'The first; I should say there is no comparison. The work would be more skilled and more remunerative.'

'Good reasons, my boy,' said Fulbert, under his breath.

'Why are unsuccessful sons supposed to apply themselves to callings connected with shoes?' said Daniel.

'No wonder good boots seem so very good,' said Graham. 'A great deal of good blood must be behind the making of them.'

'If you cannot apply your sharpness to your work, I want none of it,' said Sir Jesse.

'Miss Mitford was so pleased about your place, Daniel,' said Luce. 'She also saw the lists in the *Times*.'

'The *Times*?' said Sir Jesse, Regan and Eleanor at once.

'Not the family copy,' said Luce, laughing. 'She has her own.'

'How like her!' said Regan, her tone almost giving way under her feeling.

'Why, Grandma, she may want to know the news of the day.'

'And no doubt does what she wants,' said Regan, in the same tone.

'You appear to be eating your luncheon, Graham,' said Sir Jesse, seeming to view ordinary proceeding in his grandson, as his wife did in the governess. 'What are your ideas about your ultimate provision?'

'If only Graham could be cured, what problems it would solve!' said Daniel.

'You have never needed to have any on the subject yourself, Grandpa,' said Graham.

'You need not compare yourself with me. I have done many other things.'

'Yes, I know you have,' said Graham, drawing his mother's eyes.

'Do you feel no gratitude to me for your home and your education?'

'You make me pay too heavy a price for them.'

'I hope that sort of payment will stand you in stead with other people.'

The three children ran into the room in outdoor clothes.

'They have just come in to see us,' said Eleanor. 'I thought they would be too much for their father today. He is not strong yet.'

'Come and have a piece of my chicken,' said Fulbert, to his youngest son.

Nevill came up and waited while a spoon was supplied, not standing very close or looking at the process.

'Did you like it?' said his father.

'No, it burnt his tongue,' said Nevill, and turned away.

'How shall I pay for my future portions of chicken?' said Graham.

'I should be glad to know,' said Sir Jesse.

'Why can't Graham just be a man like Grandpa and Father?' said Gavin, who had grasped the nature of the conversation.

'He has no money,' said Eleanor. 'You will all have to earn your living.'

'Shall we? I thought it was only James.'

'No, of course not. You are all in the same position.'

'Then I shall be a traveller.'

'You would not earn much like that.'

'If I confronted great dangers, I should.'

'Who would pay you for doing it? It would not be much good to other people.'

'There are societies who pay,' said Honor. 'People like things to be discovered.'

'Graham's occupation is the immediate point,' said Sir Jesse.

'I thought you had arranged it, sir,' said Graham.

'He will call Grandpa, sir,' said Nevill, in an admiring tone.

'Shall we say a word about Daniel?' said Fulbert. 'We may as well dwell upon our success.'

'He knows how glad and proud he has made us,' said Eleanor. 'We do not need to talk about it.'

'I also have grasped the general feeling,' said Graham.

'I suppose Graham will be a tutor,' said Sir Jesse, in a tone that did not exalt this calling.

'I should be the first of Miss Mitford's pupils to follow in her steps.'

'Why isn't it nice to be a tutor?' said Honor. 'Royal people have tutors, and their names are put in the papers.'

'So are the ladies-in-waiting,' said Sir Jesse.

'Grandpa spoke to Honor,' said Nevill, impressed by this equal answer.

'Does Hatton also have the *Times*?' said Fulbert.

'Hatton has it all,' said Nevill.

'What are you going to be when you grow up?' said Fulbert, catching his son and lifting him to his knee.

'He will be a king,' said Nevill, reconciling himself to his situation.

'Then you will be above your father.'

'Yes, Father is only a man.'

'Why do you want to look down on us all?'

'He will take care of you. And he will take care of Hatton and Mullet too.'

'And what will Hatton be?'

'She will be a lady when he marries her.'

'But then she will be a queen.'

'No, he will. There is only one. Hatton likes it to be him.'

'What will the rest of us be?'

'All stand round him and wear long clothes. Not a king, but very nice.'

'And what will you wear?'

'A crown.'

'He has seen a picture,' said Luce.

'He will sit on a throne,' said Nevill, raising his arms, 'And a man will kneel down on a cushion with his gold stick.'

'I am going to leave the table before that office is suggested for me,' said Graham, to his brother. 'It seems to have points in common with that of a shoeblack. You can come with me to cover my retreat.'

'Where are you going?' said Daniel, when they gained the hall.

'To visit the Marlowes. That is a thing that Grandpa would dislike. You can come and scan their faces for signs of their parentage. That is what you want to do. I am glad I am not so nearly related to Grandpa.'

'We must keep a stern hold on our tongues.'

'Oh, I will keep Grandpa's guilty secrets,' said Graham, relapsing into his usual manner. 'And in future I will commit errors base enough to be hushed up.'

'He feels you have caused him to waste his substance. And I see there have been drains upon it. A second family is not exactly an economy.'

'He has rendered it as much of one as possible,' said Graham, looking at the cottage. 'Why did he establish the fruits of his sin at his gates?'

'Because he could do it most cheaply there,' said Daniel, hardly realizing that he spoke the simple truth.

Priscilla came at once to meet them.

'Well, there ought to be a bond between us. We all thought we were fatherless, and we all find we are not.'

'So the truth has escaped,' said Daniel, 'and with its accustomed dispatch.'

'And we find that our feelings do not go beyond speech. And we are glad of that. The speech will be a relief. We are looking forward to it.'

'Mother and Sir Jesse decided to set conventions at nought,' said Susan.

'And there is one law for the man and another for the woman,' said Priscilla. 'That makes it braver of Mother. And she has to be coupled with Sir Jesse. And that does seem a credit to her.'

'How has it got out?' said Daniel.

'Hope thinks Ridley spread it abroad,' said Susan. 'Out of revenge on your family.'

'Revenge for what?' said Graham. 'For patience and hospitality and welcome of him in our father's place? If a word was wrung from us, when his full plan emerged, it is surely to be understood.'

'He is angry at having fallen from his pedestal.'

'So Grandpa is to do the same. Well, he will not do so,' said Daniel. 'No one can speak of the truth to him, and he will die in ignorance that anyone knows. He has already forgotten that we do.'

'So you know the whole,' said Graham, to Priscilla.

'We hope we do. We have done our best. The full story may never come to us. But the bare facts are enough. We are quite satisfied.'

'It should go no further,' said Susan. 'In our case it hardly can. But James goes to school.'

'James does not know,' said Daniel.

'No doubt the boys at the school do. And James will give his own evidence. And soon know himself.'

'He cannot bring his friends home. We escape that risk,' said Graham, leaning back. 'He might be put to have tea in the nursery, or have to obey the governess, or be asked how his lessons were progressing.'

'Anything might happen,' said Daniel; 'anything would; anything did, when we were young.'

'I wish Ridley's crime had not a tragic side,' said Graham.

'It does spoil one's full enjoyment of it,' said Priscilla. 'But people's reasons for crimes always make one want to cry. Think of Sir Jesse, lonely in a far land and needing Mother. And think of Mother, prepared to face anything for Sir Jesse's sake. Between ourselves, it does seem rather odd of Mother.'

'Think of Ridley,' began Graham, and broke off.

'I am glad Sir Jesse need never know that we know,' said Lester. 'It would make it awkward for Priscilla to show him our accounts. It would seem too businesslike a relation.'

'Surely you do not owe him your confidence to that extent?' said Daniel.

'We owe him everything, even life,' said Priscilla. 'And we might have known that it is only owing people that, that leads to owing them other things.'

'It is a good thing he is the father of all three of us,' said Susan. 'It would be a poor exchange to gain Sir Jesse and lose each other.'

Lester raised his eyes.

'Have you ever suspected the truth?' said Daniel.

'We shall think we have, unless we check ourselves in time,' said Susan. 'I have thought of it, but it seemed that Sir Jesse had not enough feeling for us.'

'I have no excuse to make; it simply never occurred to me,' said Priscilla. 'That is what my woman's instinct has done. I hope it means that I am a masculine type. And I believe Sir Jesse has sometimes looked at me with a parent's eye. I have had every chance.'

'It seems almost too obvious a solution,' said Susan. 'And a good many things did point the other way. Sir Jesse's lack of affection, his putting us so near his house, his not disclaiming interest in us. But no doubt he knew they did.'

'Did Hope tell you?' said Daniel.

'She said nothing until she found we knew,' said Susan. 'No one told us in words, but something in the air was too much.'

'Hope knows where to draw the line,' said Lester.

'I had no idea of that,' said Priscilla. 'I was quite self-reproachful when I knew.'

'It is a great thing to feel we have a claim on Sir Jesse,' Lester said in a grave tone.

'No legal claim after you are fourteen,' said Daniel.

'Well, people are always children to their parents,' said Priscilla. 'And it does not seem that Sir Jesse has a great regard for rules.'

'When our origin is what it is, why is not Luce allowed to visit us?' said Susan.

'That is the reason,' said Daniel. 'It is the blood relationship. Lester might fall in love with his niece. So might you with your nephews, but Grandpa would think that was unlikely.'

'The difference in age would be supposed to prevent it,' said Susan.

'Something has done so,' said Graham.

'I wonder Sir Jesse never thought we might suspect the truth,' said Susan.

'I think he had almost forgotten it himself,' said Priscilla, 'until the loss of his son reminded him, and he saw himself as childless except for us. I see it all now. Of course people always say that, but why shouldn't they, when it is true? What is the good of their having the help, if they don't take advantage of it?'

'I wonder if he had a family anywhere else,' said Lester, as if struck by a new idea.

'He has only lived in two places,' said Daniel, 'and he was provided for in both of those.'

'I should have liked to be there when the truth came out,' said Susan.

'You little know,' said Graham.

'I am not afraid of saying that I feel with Susan,' said Priscilla. 'Women may be tough, but falsehood does not make it any better. I wish we had been present, and I almost feel we had a right to be.'

'Did you ever suspect, Lester?' said Graham.

'I cannot claim that I did,' said Lester, with a laugh. 'I once hinted to Sir Jesse that we should like a photograph of our father, and that disposes of the question. But on that day when he paid us a visit to talk of his son, I knew.'

'Why did you not tell us?' said his sisters at once, neither of them throwing doubt on his word.

'I thought it might be disturbing for you to know.'

'It is disquieting news,' said Priscilla, 'but I am glad we have such a respectable father. Sir Jesse will still be esteemed.'

'Ridley will have to live in exile, and Grandpa will remain the head of the village,' said Daniel. 'And I feel it is right.'

'If it were not for the art of photography, Grandpa would still be held a perfect man,' said Graham, in a tone of sympathy with his grandfather.

'Mankind is known to use his inventions for his own destruction,' said Priscilla.

'Suppose there should be a great deal of talk about it,' said Lester.

'Only Ridley would want that,' said Daniel. 'And he can hardly cast the first stone.'

'Grandpa can take that initiative,' said Graham. 'I can bear witness to it.'

'No doubt many people have guessed,' said Susan. 'Now that the truth is out, the position will hardly be different.'

'It is a good thing Grandpa is a man who can carry off anything,' said Daniel.

'I always wanted to meet a person like that,' said Priscilla. 'And now I am the daughter of one. I hope we have inherited the quality. It should be useful to us.'

'Perhaps it has always been so,' said Lester.

'People will have a tinge of respect for us for our descent,' said Priscilla. 'And we shall share the feeling.'

'You cannot bring your lips to utter the word, Father,' said Daniel.

'No, no,' said Lester, almost before the words were out, 'there is no need for that.'

'Here are a note and a book from Hope,' said Priscilla, as a parcel was brought to her. 'She left them herself. I can see her going down the road. I wonder if she has any more news for us.'

DEAR PRISCILLA,

I meant to come in, but I caught sight of your guests, and I could not be the only person among so many, not related to Sir Jesse. I still hope it will be found out that I am, but meanwhile I just offer my love and congratulations.

HOPE CRANMER.

'Someone else is approaching,' said Susan. 'That is why Hope did not wait. She wanted to meet Sir Jesse. He is going to that lane where he walks by himself, and he seems not to see her. Someone get in front of the window. He will be passing in a moment.'

'It seems odd that he should be following his usual course,' said Priscilla. 'But no revelation has come to him. To think what pictures of the past must be crowding through his mind! Perhaps they have always done so, and that explains his absent ways. But I daresay we are judging by our own minds.'

She moved to the window and stood with her figure shadowing the room, and Sir Jesse gave her a glance as he passed, and raised his hat and walked on.

MORE ABOUT PENGUINS, PELICANS
AND PUFFINS

For further information about books available from Penguins please write to Dept EP, Penguin Books Ltd, Harmondsworth, Middlesex UB7 0DA.

In the U.S.A.: For a complete list of books available from Penguins in the United States write to Dept DG, Penguin Books, 299 Murray Hill Parkway, East Rutherford, New Jersey 07073.

In Canada: For a complete list of books available from Penguins in Canada write to Penguin Books Canada Ltd, 2801 John Street, Markham, Ontario L3R 1B4.

In Australia: For a complete list of books available from Penguins in Australia write to the Marketing Department, Penguin Books Australia Ltd, P.O. Box 257, Ringwood, Victoria 3134.

In New Zealand: For a complete list of books available from Penguins in New Zealand write to the Marketing Department, Penguin Books (N.Z.) Ltd, P.O. Box 4019, Auckland 10.

In India: For a complete list of books available from Penguins in India write to Penguin Overseas Ltd, 706 Eros Apartments, 56 Nehru Place, New Delhi 110019.